P

"Courtland '...'
most lethal fo...
hope the Gray Man survives to fight another day."
—*Publishers Weekly*

"Political intrigue at its finest . . . *Dead Eye* twists and turns with each new revelation as Mark Greaney takes the reader on one heck of a wild ride!"　　　—Fresh Fiction

"*Dead Eye* . . . happens to be Greaney's best effort to date, worth sweeping aside whatever duties you have to steal several hours of your time and attention as it raises your pulse and blood pressure from first page to last."

—Bookreporter.com

"The Gray Man is back in this fine fourth addition to Greaney's popular series . . . Gripping, nonstop action."
—RT Book Reviews

PRAISE FOR MARK GREANEY AND THE GRAY MAN NOVELS

"Fast-paced [and] tightly written . . . A great ride."
—Larry Bond, *New York Times* bestselling author of *Red Dragon Rising*

"The story is so propulsive, the murders so explosive, that flipping the pages feels like playing the ultimate video game."
—*The New York Times*

"Hard, fast, and unflinching."
—Lee Child, #1 *New York Times* bestselling author of *Make Me*

continued . . .

"Greaney is a master among the top thriller writers in the world." —Ben Coes, *New York Times* bestselling author of *First Strike*

"Fine characterization, witty dialogue, breathtaking chase and battle scenes, and as many unforeseen twists and turns as your favorite Robert Ludlum or Vince Flynn novel—combined." —Keith Thomson, *New York Times* bestselling author of *Twice a Spy*

"Punches with bone-busting power . . . Flesh-and-blood priceless." —Stephen Templin, *New York Times* bestselling author of *Trident's First Gleaming*

"For readers looking for a thriller where the action comes fast and furious, this is the ticket." —*Chicago Sun-Times*

"Takes the best of Clancy and Ludlum and mixes them into a fantastic story with an unforgettable character." —James O. Born, author of *Burn Zone*

DEAD EYE

MARK GREANEY

BERKLEY
New York

BERKLEY

An imprint of Penguin Random House LLC
375 Hudson Street, New York, New York 10014

Copyright © 2013 by Mark Strode Greaney
Excerpt from *Back Blast* copyright © 2016 by Mark Strode Greaney
Penguin Random House supports copyright. Copyright fuels creativity, encourages
diverse voices, promotes free speech, and creates a vibrant culture. Thank you for buying
an authorized edition of this book and for complying with copyright laws by not
reproducing, scanning, or distributing any part of it in any form without permission.
You are supporting writers and allowing Penguin Random House to continue to
publish books for every reader.

BERKLEY is a registered trademark and the B colophon
is a trademark of Penguin Random House LLC.

ISBN: 9780399586675

Berkley trade paperback edition / December 2013
Berkley premium edition / August 2018

Printed in the United States of America
5   7   9   10   8   6   4

Cover photographs: Man by Ilona Wellman / Arcangel; snow by railway fx / Shutterstock;
dark alley by peeterv / Getty Images
Book design by Laura K. Corless

For my awesome nephew,
Kyle Edward Greaney

ACKNOWLEDGMENTS

I would like to thank Nick Ciubotariu, Christopher Clarke, Nichole Geer Roberts, J. T. Patten, Hooligan 003, James Yeager and his team at Tactical Response, Jeff Belanger, Dalton Fury, Keith Thomson, Igor Veksler, Michael Hagan, Chris Owens, Devon Gilliland, Devin Greaney, the Tulsa Greaneys, Dan and Judy Lesley, Jennifer Dalsky, John and Wanda Anderson, Captain Michael Hill, United States Army, the Echols family, the Leslies, Amanda Ng and Caitlin Mulrooney-Lyski at Penguin, Stephanie Hoover at Trident, Jon Cassir at CAA, Mystery Mike Bursaw, and George Easter.

Special thanks to Scott Miller at Trident Media Group and Tom Colgan at Penguin.

But the bravest are surely those who have the clearest vision of what is before them, glory and danger alike, and yet notwithstanding, go out to meet it.

THUCYDIDES

PROLOGUE

Leland Babbitt shot through the doors of the Hay-Adams Hotel and ran down the steps to the street like he had someplace to be.

The White House was just across Lafayette Square, awash in lights and radiant in the cold rainy evening, but Babbitt ignored the view, looked to his right, and began racing toward the limo waiting for him there.

The chauffeur hadn't been expecting his passenger for another hour and a half, but he was a pro; he quickly extracted himself from the warm Town Car and opened the back door. He noticed that the man seemed to have forgotten his overcoat in his haste—to say nothing of his wife.

The thickly built passenger folded quickly into the limo; the driver climbed back behind the wheel and looked into the rearview mirror for instructions.

In a voice commanding yet hurried, Babbitt said, "Sixteen twenty-six Crescent Place. Break every law you need to break, but get me there now!"

The chauffeur didn't know his passenger; he'd only been hired for the night to ferry Mr. Babbitt and his wife from their home in Chevy Chase to a black-tie gala here at the Hay-Adams, and then back home again. But the driver knew this town. He'd been shuffling VIPs around D.C. for a quarter century; this wasn't the first time some suit had told him to blow through the lights to get to a destination on the double.

He started the engine. "You got a badge?" he asked, still making eye contact with the man in the backseat via the rearview mirror.

"Play like I said yes."

The chauffeur's eyebrows rose now. He'd danced this dance before. "National security?" he asked.

"You bet your ass."

With a shrug the driver said, "That'll work," and he shoved the transmission into gear and squealed the tires. Behind him, his passenger lifted his cell phone to his ear.

"En route."

———————

The chauffeur couldn't imagine what was so important on Crescent Place, a two-lane road of majestic Georgians and neo-Colonials, and he was certain he would never know. This was D.C., after all. Shit went down behind the gates of tony residences all over the city that was far above the driver's pay grade.

His job began at the front door of one building, and

it ended at the front door of another, and whatever went on inside was not his problem.

Babbitt had his phone clutched to his ear now, and even at speed the driver could hear the man's voice clearly over the engine of the whisper-quiet Lincoln—short, soft blasts of interrogatives and shorter bleats that sounded like commands. The man behind the wheel did his best to tune the words out, standard operating procedure for a limo driver in Washington. Twenty-five years hauling dips, pols, spooks, K Street douchebags, and foreign dignitaries around the nation's capital had taught the driver discretion, to ignore his passenger's voice unless he himself was being addressed.

He could have listened in; surely the fate of nations had been decided in the backseat of his limo more than once in his career.

But the driver, quite frankly, didn't give a damn.

And tonight, even if he had tried to pick up any of his passenger's side of the conversation, he would have heard only generic phrases, cryptic-speak, and alphanumeric references. The man in back had himself spent a lot of time in limos, and he had his own standard operating procedure when being chauffeured around—if he did not know good and well that the guy behind the wheel had Top Secret/Sensitive Compartmented Information clearance with a full-scope polygraph and codeword access to the relevant program, then it was cryptic-speak or nothing at all.

Leland Babbitt had been in this game too damn long to rely on the professional discretion of a fucking limo driver.

ONE

The Lincoln squealed through a hard left turn, drifting in the slick intersection awash in the glow of headlights from angry oncoming traffic. It raced up Crescent Place and then past a small, unlit sign that read TOWNSEND GOVERNMENT SERVICES. After squeezing through electronically-operated iron gates still in the process of opening, it rolled up a winding driveway lined with bare cherry trees to a huge peach-hued brick mansion bathed in floodlights. Lee Babbitt climbed out of the Lincoln without a word to the driver and ran through the cold rain up the stone steps of the residence, passing through a door held open by a lean man in a sport coat.

In the round marble foyer of the building, two more young men with military haircuts and civilian clothing stood with Heckler & Koch automatic weapons hanging from slings over their shoulders. Before anyone spoke, a man in his late thirties, some decade younger than Babbitt, came rushing up a long hallway that led to the rear of the building. He wore a cardigan sweater and corduroy slacks, and an assortment of card keys and laminated badges bounced on his chest from a chain around his neck.

Babbitt met the younger man in the middle of the foyer, and his voice echoed off marble. "It's happening?"

"It's happening," the man in the cardigan confirmed.

"The assault is underway?"

"Infiltrating to target as we speak."

"One man? *One man* is going to hit that fucking fortress?"

"Yes, sir."

"And it's him? It's our boy?"

Jeff Parks took his boss by the arm and quickly ushered him back up the hall. "We think so."

"You'll have to do better than that," Babbitt said. While he walked, he unfastened his bow tie and opened the top button on his shirt, freeing his thick neck. "There is more than one motherfucker out there who wants to stick a knife into the neck of Gregor Sidorenko."

The long hallway was trimmed in stained cherry, and the tastefully lit walls were adorned with fine art of the American West. There were Russell watercolors of cowboys on a cattle drive, regal George Catlin portraits of Native Americans, and a pair of Frederick Remington desertscapes worth hundreds of thousands of dollars, as well as a Remington bronzed buffalo statue on a side table lit by antler lamps.

As they rushed up the corridor, Babbitt pulled off his damp jacket and slung it over his arm. He asked, "How did we pick him up?"

"One of the UAVs was up on a calibration flight. No one expected activity tonight. It's Saturday; a party was in full swing at the target location until about an hour ago, which put three times the number of personnel on scene as normal. Plus, the weather's shit and the next illumination cycle isn't for two days."

"Right."

"The ScanEagle pilot spotted movement a half mile off the coast. We tracked the signature for less than a minute before determining we were most likely looking at a singleton attack on Sid's property."

"Speedboat?"

"Negative."

"Scuba? That water must be less than forty deg—"

"He's not swimming."

"Then how—"

Parks stopped at a door and looked up to his boss with a grin. "You need to see this shit for yourself."

Parks scanned a card from his chain through a reader next to a heavy oaken door, then opened the door to reveal a staircase. He followed his boss down, the older man's patent leather shoes echoing in the stairwell. At the base of the stairs was another corridor; this one went back in the opposite direction, and it was, in contrast to the hallway above, narrow, dimly lit, and utilitarian, though its walls were also adorned.

As the two men hurried up the hall they passed several lighted shadow boxes of differing size. Inside the first ones were tintypes and wet-plate prints of severe, bearded men in black coats and top hats, hefting shotguns and standing alongside caskets propped up, dead men inside pine boxes looking back at the photographer with eyes covered with coins. With these photos were mounted artifacts of the Old West—faded telegrams, single-action revolvers, stirrups and handcuffs, even a man's dress shirt, torn and stained with old black blood.

Babbitt and Parks ignored the shadow boxes as they walked. They'd passed them countless times. "So we have no assets in place?" Babbitt asked.

"I established comms with Trestle Actual, told him he had twenty mikes to assemble his boys and kit up. They are thirty miles away in St. Pete on R & R, but no worries. The UAV will track the target through the exfil. We've found him." A satisfied smile. "We'll get him."

A display containing a costume beard and wads of deutschmarks taken from a captured Serbian war criminal was on their left now, and, on their right, a photograph of two men with wide smiles and thumbs up, their eyes obscured with superimposed black bands, standing next to a bleary-eyed and shackled Manuel Noriega in the back of a cargo aircraft.

A gold automatic pistol taken from one of Saddam's palaces was mounted in a case near the end of the hallway, and a row of photos of more men and even a few women, their eyes again blacked out, standing around men with bagged heads and shackles.

The hallway displayed the secret history of this organization, a force of outlaw hunters that reached back one hundred fifty years, and although neither of the two men hurrying up the corridor were thinking of it now, they fully expected to commission a new memorial very soon to commemorate the successful resolution of their current hunt.

At the end of the hall was a well-lit alcove, and here another man with a military haircut stood at parade rest next to a small desk. An HK submachine gun hung from a sling over his shoulder, and to his right, a heavy steel door was flush with the wall.

A small sign on the door read SIGNAL ROOM—BIOMETRIC ACCESS ONLY.

The guard at the door said, "Evening, Mr. Babbitt. Sweet tux."

Lee Babbitt placed his hand on a small screen on the wall next to the door. As he waited there for the biometric finger reader to confirm his identity, he acknowledged the man. "Al."

"Just say the word and we're wheels up."

Babbitt shrugged as he waited impatiently. "Trestle's turn at bat, Al. Jumper's on deck. You guys will get a shot next time."

A muffled click came from inside the door, and Al reached for the handle, pulling it open and allowing Babbitt and Parks to pass through.

As the two men entered, the guard outside shut the door behind them and the heavy lock reengaged.

This room was lit only by computer monitors and video screens; the opposite wall was half-filled with a ten-foot-wide and seven-foot-high plasma display, and small glass-walled offices ran off the left and right of the main area. A young woman in jeans and a Georgetown sweatshirt appeared in the dim glow and handed Babbitt and Parks wireless headsets, which they both donned. The room was mostly quiet, though alive with movement on every display. Men and women, some dozen in all, sat at their desks, attached by headset umbilical cords to communications equipment and computers.

Babbitt was still positioning his earpiece and pulling the microphone into place over his lips as he asked, "Time to target?"

A female voice came through his headset. "Feet dry in ten seconds. He'll be on the X in under five mikes."

Babbitt stared at the center screen. An infrared image was projected in the middle, and it was surrounded by digital readouts. Altitude, temperature, barometric pressure, compass heading, and wind speed.

He leaned closer, squinting at the image being tracked by the camera.

The female voice followed up her last transmission. "Feet dry. Oh three five six local time."

The cold sea had sharpened the relief of the target when it traveled over water, but now, over land, the image was less clear. A sensor operator flipped a button and the infrared signature reversed. Now the white-hot moving object became black-hot, the earth below turned lighter hues of gray, and the new picture clearly identified the target as a man under a small delta wing, with an engine pouring heat into the cold air behind it.

"What the hell am I looking at?" Babbitt asked the room, a tinge of marvel in his voice.

Next to him, Parks answered, "He's *flying*, Lee. It's a one-man air raid."

"Flying *what*?" Babbitt muttered, and he stepped closer to the screen. "That's not an airplane. Not a helo, either."

"No sir, it is not," Parks confirmed with a smile.

TWO

Four thousand four hundred fifty-two miles east of Washington, D.C., a small craft buzzed six hundred feet above snow-covered treetops, its thin fluttering wings reaching wide for lift in the unstable air and its sharp nose pointing toward its next waypoint, just under a kilometer away.

St. Petersburg glowed gray in the east, its waterfront lights barely penetrating the snow and the darkness. To the west was nothing but black. The Gulf of Finland. Open water all the way to Helsinki, nearly two hundred miles distant.

And directly ahead, a few pinpricks of light. The hamlet of Ushkovo was not much, just a dozen homes and buildings and a railroad station, but it was surrounded by the Lintula Larch Forest, so the lights on there at four A.M. made an easily identifiable waypoint for the man flying through the black sky.

The aircraft was a microlight trike, a hang glider with a tiny fiberglass open cockpit below for the pilot and a propeller behind to give powered flight. Courtland Gentry flew with his gloved hands on the control bar. His eyes darted between the lights ahead and a small tablet computer Velcroed to his thigh. The tablet kept him informed of his altitude, his speed, and his position by way of a GPS fix over a tiny moving map display.

He also had an anemometer attached to the center console, and this told him his wind speed every five seconds. It varied by as much as ten knots from one reading to the next as the coastal breeze buffeted the delta wing, however, so it wasn't providing him much in the way of actionable intelligence.

Court wore NODs, a night observation device, but the monocle was high on his forehead now, stowed up in a way that made Court look like a unicorn. The night vision technology was better than nothing, but this unit was old and simple and the device only allowed him a forty-degree field of view. This narrow field, and a lens no doubt wet with the blowing snowfall, made the NODs ineffective at this altitude, but he knew he would be forced to use it as he neared his target.

Court passed just west of Ushkovo, his buzzing engine just out of earshot of the sleeping villagers, then banked twenty degrees east to his new heading, deeper in the Lintula Larch Forest. He added power and pushed the bar forward slightly, and his microlight began to climb higher into the snowy air.

Ahead in the distance a new pinprick of light grew into a thumbnail of light as he closed on it. It was the town of Rochino, and just east of that a palatial mansion rose from the trees, four stories high and surrounded by outbuildings and other structures.

This was the target, the objective waypoint.

The X.

As he neared Rochino, Court reluctantly unfastened a wool blanket he'd lashed over his legs and he tossed it over the side, letting it fall away to the forest below.

Now he ran his hands over his body and in the cockpit around him, putting his hands on each piece of his critical gear, methodically making one last check that everything was both secure and positioned for easy access.

Over a black cotton fleece and black cotton pants that would have been no real protection from the cold without the wool base layers under them, Gentry had only a few pounds of equipment strapped to his body. It was not much gear, but Court had cut kit for mobility and ease of access, and he'd cut weight for speed.

He'd spent months preparing for tonight, and his load out reflected this. He wore a Glock 19 nine-millimeter pistol in a thigh rig with an attached silencer that reached all the way to his knee on the outside of his right leg.

On his lower back was a nylon pack that held two cables, each one attached to a climbing harness under his clothes, and they were both spooled around electric spring retractors. One of the cables was quarter-inch climbing rope; the other was a thicker bungee cord. Collapsible remote activated grappling hooks were attached to the end of each cord, with the rubber-tipped noses of the titanium hooks protruding from the nylon bag for quick access.

On his belt he'd strapped the controls for the retractors and the hooks, a cell phone–sized panel consisting of
four small three-position levers.

Also adorning his utility belt was a multi-tool in a
pouch and two black-bladed combat knives in quick-access
sheaths.

He wore a small backpack stuffed with clothing and a
medical kit, and on his black, low-profile chest rig, magazines for his nine-millimeter were fastened in Velcro
pouches, as well as a 26.5-millimeter single-shot flare gun
that looked like a snub-nosed revolver with a fat barrel. It
was loaded with a smoke grenade, and several more ballistic smokes adorned his chest rig, held in place with
Velcro straps.

On his right ankle Court wore a Glock 26, a subcom-
pact nine-millimeter pistol. He was hoping he wouldn't
have to go for the 26 since it was not suppressed, but
Court had been around long enough to know to be prepared.

Back when he was with the CIA, his principal trainer's
name was Maurice, and Maurice used to preach prepared-
ness versus luck with a mantra, often shouted into Gentry's
ear when he'd left something to chance. "Hope in one
hand and shit in the other. See which one fills up first!"

That visual never left Court when hoping for the best,
or when preparing for the worst.

Court shivered in the cold; he missed that blanket
already, but he ignored the discomfort, checked his altitude, and pushed the control bar forward again for more
lift.

With a jaw fixed in determination he looked to his

target in the distance, reached to his center console, and added full power to the engine.

———————

At Townsend House in D.C., the fourteen men and women in the signal room watched an infrared black-hot heat signature float over a hazy white forest on the other side of the world. After a command from a surveillance technician over the commo link to the drone pilot, a laser reached out from the UAV. It touched the moving craft like an invisible finger and then reported the speed and altitude back to the sensor operator.

A disembodied male voice spoke through the headsets. "He's in the climb and accelerating."

Babbitt was still trying to get his head around the event unfolding in front of him. "How does he expect to make it to the target area without the Russians hearing that thing?" he asked.

A young man answered from his desk near the front of the room. "We assume he will cut power for stealth. The wind is inland from the water, at his back. Even with the weight of the engine and the cockpit, that microlight's glide ratio is good. If he climbs to a thousand feet or so, he can sail a good two or three klicks while totally silent."

"And *then* what? He just lands on the lawn?" That seemed, to Babbitt, like a terrible idea. Even though the first rays of morning light would not appear over northwestern Russia for another four hours, everyone in the basement signal room knew Sidorenko's property was crawling with gunmen.

A female voice said, "We think he will try to land on

the north side of the property—*crash-land* is probably the better term. There is less security there, but still, he's going to have to pull a few tricks out of his sleeve to make this happen."

Babbitt did not avert his eyes from the screen. He said, "He's thought this through. He knows what he's doing. If he's got a way in, he's got a way out." The prospect of losing this opportunity to get his man was almost too much to contemplate. "The UAV team on site. How close are they?"

Jeff Parks was still at his boss's side. "They are in Rochino. Two klicks from the X."

Lee called out to the room in a voice unnecessarily loud, considering he was wearing a head mic. "Who's in contact with the UAV team in Rochino?"

"I am, sir," said a middle-aged African American woman. She stood at her workstation to Babbitt's right, the coiled wire of her headset hanging from the side of her head down to her commo box.

"I want their second drone in the air and loitering on station. Bring the other ScanEagle down and refuel it. We can't lose him when this is over."

"On it, sir."

Parks said, "Lee, there are fifty armed men around that dacha. We have to allow for the possibility that this will end, tonight, right inside those walls."

Babbitt chuffed. "If Sid's boys kill him, we don't get paid. Tonight I'm rooting for Court Gentry."

————

Court looked at the moving map on his thigh one last time, then pulled the tablet off his leg and tossed it over

the side of the microlight. He then reached down between his knees to the tiny console and flipped a switch,
killing power to the engine behind him. The propeller
slowed, then stopped; all engine noise ceased and, other
than a soft flapping of the wind over the fabric of the
delta wing, Gentry was enveloped by the silence and
stillness and darkness of the night.

The sensation was startling. He soared quietly through
the air, riding a powerful and comforting tailwind eight
hundred fifty feet above the treetops, his target dead
ahead at twelve o'clock. He flipped down his NODs and
the green haze from his image-intensifying equipment,
diffused by the wet lens, added to this surreal experience.

He descended slowly, sailing silently toward his objective waypoint, a spot just above the tiled roof of the massive dacha in the center of the target location.

He'd be involved in furious activity in moments, but for
now there was little to do but hold the control bar steady
and clear his mind to prepare himself for the unknowns of
the impending op.

And, Court admitted to himself, there were a hell of
a lot of unknowns.

He was not here by choice, although he was under
contract. The man in the dacha at his target location,
Gregor Sidorenko, was the head of a large and dangerous
Bratva, or brotherhood of Russian mafia, and Sidorenko
had spent the past year chasing Court, quite literally, to
the ends of the earth, sparing no expense in the hunt.

Sid operated in a state of rage and fear and obsessive
compulsion. Sid knew that if he did not kill Gentry, then

surely Gentry would kill him. Gentry realized this; he knew Sid would never stop throwing men and money at the task, so Court knew he could not keep running.

He had to attack into this threat.

To this end Court made contact with a competitor of Sidorenko, the leader of a Moscow-based *Bratva*, and the two men negotiated a contract price. The Muscovite mobster used his extensive organization to help Gentry with equipment and intelligence, and this, along with training Gentry underwent near Moscow, had all coalesced into this evening's operation.

Court didn't like partnering with the Muscovite and his shitty gang any more than he liked taking on Sidorenko and *his* shitty gang, but he knew he had no choice.

Court had to take out Sid, and in so doing reduce the incredible number of threats against him by a grand total of one.

It wasn't much, but it was something.

Court flipped the NODs back up for a moment and made a slight course correction. He reached down and unfastened his seat belt, then grabbed the metal hook at the end of a bungee cord attached to the fiberglass cockpit of the vehicle. This he hooked into a hole drilled into the right side of the control bar. He pulled a slightly less taut cord on the left side of the cockpit, and this he hooked on the left side of the bar. A third bungee connected the center of the bar and the front of the cockpit.

He let go of the control bar, and the microlight continued to fly, steady in its descent, its fluttering wings held in place with the bungee cables. Each end of the control bar had a long cord tied around it and stored in a bag, and Court removed the cords and tossed one over each side of the cockpit.

Stowed under his knees on the floor of the cockpit was a small vinyl gym bag. He retrieved it, opened it up, and pulled out a banded string of fireworks, sixty in all. There were several different sizes, shapes, and functions. Glowing rockets; super loud, flashless boomers; and multistage aerial shells. Like Christmas lights, each of the fireworks was attached with a wick to a long fuse, and the fuse terminated in a small black metal box, inside which was housed a wireless igniter. Court quickly pulled the band from the collection, then let the fourteen-foot-long snake of small explosives drop over the side of the craft, whipping through the darkness to the forest below.

Quickly now Court unhooked a rope ladder attached to the left side of the aircraft, then gingerly turned, kicked his legs out and over, and found the first rung of the ladder with his foot.

The wings did not like the jarring movement; the craft banked left, then back to the right when Court leaned back over the cockpit to right the turn. Gentry worried he'd given up more altitude in the past few seconds than he had to lose, but the tailwind kept him steady enough, and he knew there was little he could do now but hope for the best.

With one last glance to check the stability of the control bar, he disappeared over the side, descending into the darkness over the treetops, sailing forward at just over twenty-five miles an hour. As he descended he reached out and found the control bar cords, giving him basic ability to steer the delta wing while under the cockpit.

———————

Lee Babbitt watched the ten-foot plasma display while he barked instructions into his headset. "I want that UAV down closer. No thermal, no infrared. We need visual confirmation of the target. He isn't Sid's only enemy. If this turns out to be some other asshole who—"

Babbitt stopped talking as the black-hot figure moved off the side of the small vehicle but did not fall; instead he hung there, below the cockpit, and then he lowered into thin air.

Fourteen men and women gasped into their live mics. This was clearly not some other asshole.

"Never mind," Lee Babbitt said. "That's Gentry."

Babbitt felt the hair stand on the back of his neck. It had been a long wait, tens of thousands of man-hours of prep and hold, but there was money in the budget for the hunt, and there were incentive bonuses and cost-plus billing and hazard pay bumps that kept his employees on task and his drones in the air.

And a wide-open spigot of black fund dollars from the CIA made this all possible.

The ScanEagle's sensor operator switched from the thermal camera to the night vision camera, and he zoomed in on the man below the cockpit, revealing a rope ladder some seventy-five feet long.

Gentry descended, hand over hand, quickly and adroitly climbing down the ladder.

"Who the hell is flying the microlight?" someone asked.

"No one," said Parks. "He's stabilized the wings, trimmed them to maintain a straight descent, probably by tying the control bar in position. He's trusting that it will stay on its glide path till he lands."

"Bet he's going for the roof," someone said into his mic. And then he added, softly, "Jee-sus, this guy is brazen."

Lee Babbitt pulled off his headset and grabbed Parks by the arm, drawing him closer. With his eyes still on the screen, Babbitt spoke quickly, "Deploy the assets. Trestle to the target location. Alert Jumper Actual in Berlin and tell him to get his team on standby, ready to react to intel from the UAV. I want everyone on the move and prepared to tail Court off the X to his safe house, or wherever the hell he's going, before the last shell casing hits the floor at Sid's place."

"Roger that." Parks then asked, "What about the singleton?"

Babbitt turned away from the screen for the first time since entering the signal room. He blew out a long sigh. "He called it, didn't he? Gentry is doing just exactly what the singleton said he'd do."

"Yes, sir."

Babbitt thought for a moment. With a quick nod he said, "Okay. Establish comms with Dead Eye. Have him drop his current op. I want him wheels up within the hour."

Parks left his boss's side and headed to a glass-enclosed office off the signal room's main floor.

Babbitt stayed where he was; he watched the image of the man below the microlight again. Gentry was now less than eighty feet above the ground, just a few moments from crossing over the outer wall of Sid's dacha.

Babbitt reached behind him and, without taking his eyes from the screen, pulled a rolling chair away from a desk.

He sat down. "Ladies and gentlemen, there is nothing left for us to do but to sit back and observe a master at work. It's not every day you get to watch the Gray Man kill in real time."

THREE

Court hung halfway between the cockpit of the micro-light, thirty-five feet above, and the bottom rung of the rope ladder, thirty-five feet below. A few weeks earlier, in a manner he tried to pass off as idle conversation, he'd asked his Russian glider instructor if someone could hang suspended from a microlight in flight, and the young man had looked at the American like he was insane. He explained that it could be done, in theory, if the wings were stabilized and the center of gravity of the suspended person was directly below the vehicle, but a craft the size Gentry was using could not handle the weight of two people and, needless to say, no one would be foolish enough to try such a stunt below the microlight with no one at the controls. Court laughed off his stupid question, nodded politely, and then went back to his room to fashion the hooks and straps to act as his copilot, and a rope ladder carriage that could pull from both sides of the cockpit equally.

Several times when flying alone over snow-covered fields south of Moscow, Gentry had sat in the microlight with his hands in his lap, the hooks and straps doing the flying. He'd also practiced power-off landings, piloting the craft back to earth without using the engine, usually placing his wheels within a few yards of his target touch-down point, although a few times he tumbled into the snow after coming down too fast and hitting too hard.

Now Gentry flew through the night above the southern wall of the compound, more or less on course, though he was coming in a little lower than he'd planned. He looked down at the property below and saw several out-buildings south of the main house, and near them two fire pits, around which several men sat, still awake at four A.M. Simple tents were erected here and there, and on the muddy drive and snow-covered lawn, snowmobiles sat parked haphazardly, some with their headlights on and illuminating the southern portion of the compound. Trucks were parked near a tin-roofed barn, and two men with flashlights walked between them.

And Court Gentry sailed above them all. He knew he was silent, and there was no way anyone below would see him without night vision optics and a reason to be looking up in the sky, but he could not help but wish he had a free hand with which to draw his pistol.

There were a lot of guys down there in the open air, which meant there would probably be even more guys inside the warm buildings.

But Court knew this going in. Gregor Sidorenko was

no typical mobster. While he himself was urbane and mega rich, his personal security needs were handled by a rough crew of young Russian skinheads, all well armed, if not particularly well trained. Sid was their patron, and in return for his patronage they lived on and around his various properties, committed low-skill crime on his behalf, and kept gangsters and competing *Bratva*s off his territory.

Court's intelligence reports suggested there would be more than forty goons on the property tonight, since most every Saturday they all came to the compound to drink and to party and to engage in their favorite pastime—bare-knuckled brawling, beating one another to a bloody pulp and then falling over piss-drunk.

Though Court would much rather pit himself against the normal guard force of twenty or so, he knew that many of those on the premises tonight would be shitfaced or passed out completely, and the large number of armed warm bodies would lead to a groupthink around the compound that no one in their right mind would come after Sid this evening.

As Court hung on, flying through the sky toward the roof, he allowed for the possibility that anyone who thought this might well be correct.

He was not in his right mind.

But now all his attention was focused on his immediate objective. The roof was steeply angled and just darker than the snow-covered forest beyond, and in the center of the mansion, a round clear dome bulged out like a blister. Court had seen the dome on overhead photos; it was an odd architectural feature for a forest dacha in Russia, even one as monstrous as this.

Court scanned the length of the roof as he neared, looking for stationary guards or lookouts positioned there, but he saw no one.

When he was less than fifty yards from contact, he realized he was veering to the left and dropping too low. He knew that by descending the ladder he would lower the center of gravity under the wings and cause the craft to lose altitude, and he'd allotted for this, but it seemed now he'd underestimated just how much effect hanging below the cockpit had on his flight path. As he watched the building rush up closer, he realized he now ran the risk of passing wide to the left, missing the roof altogether and tumbling to a landing on the lawn surrounded by drunk and armed goons or—and this could conceivably be worse—slamming into the flat wall of the mansion below the roof. If that happened, he knew the Russians would wake up in the morning to find a battered and frozen dead man on the ground next to the wall, surrounded by bloodred snow. He would be ID'd as Sid's nemesis, the microlight would be discovered, and everyone would have a good laugh about the world's greatest assassin dying while executing the world's most asinine plan.

But Court wasn't going to let that happen. He race-climbed the ladder, putting himself back in line with the lower portion of the ceramic-tiled roof. At the same time he pulled on the right toggle cord of the delta wing, wrenching the microlight back to the correct flight path.

He made it just in time. Eight feet from impact he let go of the ladder and made a controlled collision with the snow-covered ceramic tiles on the southwest corner of the building. He ran up the pitched roof several feet to slow himself, hands and feet scampering up to bleed off energy, and then he dropped down, his gloved hands and his soft padded kneepads absorbing most of the shock and the noise, and he found purchase with the rubber soles of his shoes.

The rope ladder dragged across the snow on the roof, but silently, sliding behind the empty microlight, which missed the apex of the building by no more than twenty feet. Court steadied himself as he looked up and saw the rear of the vehicle in his NODs as it disappeared over the dome, sailing on toward the dense forest on the other side of the compound's northern wall.

The aircraft was lower than he'd envisioned, much lower. He could only hope now that it made it over the northern wall, and he hoped when it crashed there in the impenetrable forest it wouldn't make too much noise.

Court turned back around to face the property, and he scanned the grounds four stories below with his NODs, seeing all the men on the ground either stationary or moving idly in the distance.

There were no shouts of alarm, no cracks of gunfire, and no movement that seemed out of place.

Court took off his backpack, unzipped an outer pocket, and removed a second, smaller, snaking fuse full of fireworks, also attached to a wireless igniter. This string was a battery of Yanisars, a dozen four-inch cardboard tubes filled with a lift charge of black powder under a paper shell filled with more powder designed to create a bright flash and a loud report. He took off the rubber band, uncoiled the strand, and threw it over the south side of the mansion. It fell the four stories, landing in the snow.

He re-donned his pack and moved up the roof, heading to an attic window jutting out of the ceramic tiles. He knelt down; there was no alarm system he could see. The lock was ancient and would be a cinch to defeat, had Gentry's hands not been so damn cold.

But he shook his fingers to warm them and got the window open in under a minute, then slipped into the attic, shut the window behind him, and drew his suppressed Glock 19 pistol. He flipped up his wet NODs and actuated a red light under the barrel of his gun; with this he searched the expansive but cluttered space for motion detectors. Instead he saw rat droppings in the dusty corners of the room, and he knew the attic was accustomed to unwanted guests that would render motion detectors useless.

He kept his silenced Glock out in front of him as he made his way forward through the attic toward a door ahead.

He'd done it. Ingress to target complete. Court was in.

———————

Lev and Yevgeny were cold, but not as cold as they would have been without all the vodka in their bloodstream. Tonight's festivities were long over; most of the security forces in the compound were in tents or the dacha's barracks, a long, coal-furnace-heated shack just north of the barn. Inside, two dozen skinheaded neo-Nazis slept, most of them facedown on bunks or on the floor with puke-stained olive drab winter gear, many with unattended cuts and bruises from the evening's fights, and all of them passed out from the marathon session of drinking that had taken place for much of the past ten hours.

But Lev and Yevgeny were among the twelve men forced to work the night detail, and though they had consumed nearly as much vodka and beer as the rest of the toughs around the property, they still had a job to do. They were off on the second of three half-hour patrols of the forest tracks and dirt roads just north of the property.

Both men were armed with AK-47s, radios, and thermoses of vodka-laced tea. They shuffled through wet snow, their flashlights swinging low, not really looking for anything, just killing time until they could return to the north guard shack and warm themselves at the stove.

Both men were just twenty-one years old, and they had been working with the Sidorenko organization since they were adolescents, manning mobile phones in St. Petersburg to report police presence in the red-light district. They pledged no allegiance to the effeminate millionaire in the dacha they guarded. No, they were fascists and Sid would hardly be the one to rule their ideal Russia. But Sid was a means to an end for them; he provided them safety and security and enough money to pay for their basic needs, and in return they spent a few nights a week guarding his property when he was here west of the city.

A single frozen mud road led through the forest from the compound gate to the north, and it ran straight for almost a kilometer before coming to a T. Lev and Yevgeny walked the length of the road, occasionally shining their flashlights into the thick larch that ran on either side. They expected no trouble but if trouble came, both young men were drunk enough and replete with enough testosterone to know unequivocally that they could handle it.

They stopped for a moment so Lev could piss; he

shifted his rifle to his shoulder and opened his coat and pants right there in the road while Yevgeny took a sip from his thermos.

From the dark above them came a quick movement, sending both men diving headlong into the snow. Something large shot past just feet from their heads, and then a dark form was silhouetted against the white bark of the larch trunks for an instant before it slammed into the trees, cracking and popping branches before a last thud of impact with the ground.

The two young Russians scrambled to their feet and ran toward the noise. Yevgeny chambered a round in his Kalashnikov and Lev shined his flashlight on the big dark mass in the snow.

It was a hang glider, its frame twisted, its dark blue wings torn to shreds by the broken larch. A propeller jutted from the broken tree limbs.

"What the fuck?" Lev muttered, his flashlight scanning all around the forest, searching for a hint as to where the hell this thing came from.

Yevgeny did not answer Lev's question, because he did not know what the fuck. But he did know what to do. He reached for the radio inside his coat. "North patrol to north shack! Something's going on out here!"

———

Court moved up a quiet fourth-floor hallway with his pistol leveled in front of him. He'd wiped moisture from the lens of his night vision monocle, and through it he had a narrow, dim, green view of the way ahead over the top of his long silencer, and he saw no threats.

The intel he had been provided by the Moscow *Bratva* had not given him a clear picture of the inside of the mansion, so Court was doing much of this by feel. Court had been inside another of Sid's St. Petersburg properties, and there Sid kept an office and bedroom on the top floor, no doubt because he felt he was safer up here. Court decided he would clear the top floor first, imagining Sid's paranoia would force him to keep the same setup for all of his properties.

The dark hallway ended at a balcony that overlooked a wide circular atrium. He peered over the railing and, four stories down, he saw a low fountain in the center of a courtyardlike space, along with a few tables and chairs nestled between potted plants and trees.

Above him, over the center of the atrium, the glass-domed roof, some thirty feet across, was rimmed with ornate iron support beams, from which lights hung. The lights were off now, and only a faint glow of the moonless night through the glass hazed his night vision monocle.

Scanning the open balconies on the floor below him, he saw two guards one floor down on the other side of the atrium. They sat in chairs by an open staircase. Court thought it likely there would be more men directly under him.

Gentry had no plan to return to this part of the house, but he took a quick mental picture of the area. If he needed a fallback option, he might well find himself here again, and with no time to get a proper look at the layout.

This done, he left the balcony and began heading up a hallway that shot off to his right. It was dark here; there were electric lighting sconces along the corridor, but they were turned off for the night. Upon making a turn in the hall, however, he saw a single sconce shining brightly outside a heavy wooden door at the far end of the passage. The rug that ran all the way down to the end of the hall was more ornate than the bare floor of the hall he had just left, and there was an unmistakable scent of wood smoke and incense in the air.

Court got the impression he was nearing his target.

He'd made it only a few feet up the hall when a door on his right opened. The muzzle of his pistol swiveled toward the movement, and his finger left his trigger guard and took up the scant slack of the Glock's trigger safety. At first he saw no one in the doorway, but he lowered his aim and centered his pistol on a small boy, no more than six or seven years old. The boy looked at him with sleepy, unfixed eyes. Behind the boy Gentry saw a child's bedroom.

There was little light in the hall and no light in the bedroom, and Court doubted the boy could see the gun or even identify the man standing in the hall five feet in front of him.

Court knew who the boy belonged to. His intel indicated that Sidorenko, a bachelor, had family who lived with him: two male cousins who were part of his organization and a sister, and his sister had several children. Court braced himself to encounter kids here in the mansion, but he hoped that hitting in the dead of night would help keep them from straying downrange of his gun barrel.

No such luck.

"I can't sleep." The boy said it in Russian, but Court understood.

Court lowered his pistol and hid it behind his leg, but his long night vision optic protruded from between his eyes. The boy noticed it and peered closer.

"Back inside," Court replied in Russian. "Lock the door."

"Who are you?"

"Back inside," Court repeated.

"Are you a monster?" the boy asked.

Court knelt down, his NOD's monocle inches from the boy's face. "Yes, I am. I *am* a monster. Run. Back inside. Get under your bed and hide until your mother comes for you."

The boy's eyes widened in fear. He stepped back in the room and shut the door.

Court stood back up and began moving quickly up the hall toward the light by the heavy door.

FOUR

One thousand ninety-one miles south of St. Petersburg, the Lipscani neighborhood of Bucharest, Romania, had quieted down much in the past hour. For most of this Saturday evening the district had been full of young party-goers, as many of the city's best clubs were located in this warren of winding streets and back alleys. But it was four A.M. now, and the late hour along with an icy wind had driven everyone indoors, either to the dance floors at Kulturhaus or Terminus or Club A, or back to flats and hotels around Romania's capital.

On the fifth-floor rooftop of an office building directly on the opposite side of the Dambovita River from Lipscani, a man lay prone behind a Knight's Armament SR-25 sniper rifle. He peered through his weapon's optics, centering his crosshairs on the back of a man's head, just visible through sheer silk curtains, two hundred twenty meters away.

The sniper's nine-power scope showed him everything he needed to see. In a fifth-floor luxury apartment on Splaiul Independentei, the heavyset man, well into his sixties, stood in his bedroom in his underwear and socks, slowly and ceremoniously undressing a much younger woman, a girl, really, who stood obediently in front of the bed, her eyes fixed to a point somewhere out the window.

The sniper's target was supposed to be alone, but either the target or his security detail had ordered a teen-aged prostitute, and she was throwing a wrench into the sniper's plan.

This was not optimal, the man behind the SR-25 concluded.

The girl would see the muzzle flash, and the girl would point to the rooftop upon which the sniper had set up his hide, and the target's security would run to the window, scanning for the sniper, and then they would rush down to the streets, cutting off the sniper's escape.

They would call the police, as well, and roadblocks would be set up and patrol cars would start pulling over anyone driving around at four in the morning.

The sniper wanted to wait until the girl turned away, but his target was taking his sweet time, and the sniper knew that at any moment, the man's bodyguards in the next room might come to the window there and gaze out, putting even more eyes on his position.

No, this hit was not optimal. Not optimal at all.

But it was doable.

The sniper decided to proceed. He would send a round into the back of his target's head.

And then he would shoot the hooker.

Quickly the sniper scanned the bedroom, determining where the girl would go after her john's brains blew all over her naked body. Most likely, he decided, she would just stand there in shock, giving the sniper plenty of time to line up a second 220-meter shot with his semiautomatic rifle. He'd need no more than a second for this, and he expected the girl would not process the danger in so little time.

But if she did drop to the ground, or move left or right, the sniper saw that she had no cover that would protect her from a .556 copper-jacketed bullet.

The girl was not his target, but killing the girl was necessary for a smooth egress from the target area, so he gave it no more thought.

Satisfied that he had prepared for any eventuality, the sniper recentered the crosshairs on the back of the man's head, thumbed the safety off his rifle, then placed his finger on the trigger. He slowed his breathing, even exerted control over the beating of his heart by consciously relaxing his blood pressure.

A beep in his left ear caused the sniper to blow out the air in his lungs in a soft sigh. He allowed himself a moment to regain his normal breath; his fingertip left the trigger and rested on the trigger guard, and his left hand moved out from under the weapon. He touched the button on his Bluetooth earpiece.

Softly he said, "Go."

"This is Metronome."

"Bad timing," the sniper muttered. And then, "Say iden, Metronome."

"Two, seven, seven, four, nine, two, four, three, eight."

"Iden confirmed. This is Dead Eye."

"Say iden, Dead Eye."

"Four, eight, one, oh, six, oh, five, two, oh."

After a quick pause on the other end, the man on the roof heard, "Good evening, Whitlock."

"It might be evening where you are, Parks, but it's four A.M. here."

There was no response to this. Instead Parks said, "Execute immediate stand down. We need to get you moving to the airport."

The man prone on the rooftop kept his eye in the glass a moment more; he watched the man kneel down and begin pulling off the girl's panties. But the sniper did not continue to watch. Why should he? His mission was over. He rolled away from the gun, crawled back a few feet, and dragged the weapon back to him by the butt stock. He closed the bipod, unloaded the rifle, and began dismantling it. While he did this, executed with efficiency gained from many years of practice, he said, "Only one reason you would pull me right now."

As a confirmation Parks said, "The primary target has been located."

The sniper smiled, but his smile did not carry over into the tenor of his voice. He kept it clipped and professional. "At Sid's palace in Rochino."

"Affirmative." A pause. "You were right, Whitlock."

Whitlock continued breaking down his weapon as he said, "Of course I was right. You have real-time viz?"

"He is inside the main house now. We'll have eyes on via the ScanEagle when he comes out."

"Understood. Is the audio equipment picking up anything?"

"Quiet as a tomb."

The sniper was pleased for many reasons. He opened a black Pelican case and placed the disassembled rifle in it. He kept his voice soft, though he was alone on the rooftop and the offices below him were vacant. "Expect that to change. He won't get out of there without it going loud."

Parks said, "We are moving you to St. Petersburg this morning. Get to the airport; we'll have the plane prepped and ready by the time you arrive."

Quickly Dead Eye entered the stairwell and began descending swiftly and silently in the dark, a penlight in his left hand leading the way forward and his Pelican case in his right. "Why would I go to St. Petersburg? *Gentry* isn't going to St. Petersburg."

"Probably not, but we need to get you into the area. St. Petersburg is closest. We can update the flight plan while you are in the air if we track him somewhere else."

"Is Jumper on alert?"

"Negative. Trestle is the alert team. They are in St. Pete. Heading to the X now. Jumper will come up from Berlin, if necessary, to back them up."

"Bad idea, Parks. Both strike teams need to stay out of sight until Gentry goes to ground after the operation. Keep the ScanEagle overhead and lead me into his path; I will surveil and then set up the strikers once I'm on station."

Parks replied dismissively. "I will pass on your thoughts to Babbitt. For now, Russ, just get moving. Graveside out."

Russell "Dead Eye" Whitlock tapped his earpiece and

continued down the stairs. He was disappointed about his mission tonight. He'd been working on this Bucharest op for weeks. In theory he could have gone ahead, shot the target and then shot the girl, and in so doing achieve his objective here in Romania, but this would have slowed his ability to get out of town quickly and cleanly, and that was paramount.

Court Gentry was one hundred times more important than this Muslim Brotherhood terrorist. Moreover, someone else from Townsend Government Services would show up here, in a few days or in a few weeks, to finish the job.

It did not matter to Dead Eye. He was a prideful man, but in his eyes, he'd long since outgrown ops like tonight. To him there was no real challenge in this hit, which meant there was no real pride in this hit. A two-hundred-twenty-meter shot through window glass into the heads of an unsuspecting tango and his teenaged hooker.

So fucking what?

Dead Eye was out for big game.

Hard targets.

And very soon it would be time to go after the hardest target on earth.

On the ground floor of the darkened office building he passed a security guard sprawled on the floor, arms and legs askew, his eyes wide open in death. Dead Eye shined his penlight over the body quickly as he headed for the exit and saw the rich bruising around the neck, a single band of color from a garrote's bite.

Dead Eye regarded the wound as he passed, acknowledging a job well done. The guard never saw him coming.

But as he reached the lobby door, he allowed himself no more time to think of tonight's action. There was much work to do in the days ahead, and he needed to focus all his attention on his new mission.

Back on the street now, Russ Whitlock climbed into his BMW after tossing his Pelican case in the trunk. He drove off through the cool, dry morning, heading toward Borg El Arab airport. There would be a Townsend jet there ready to take him to St. Petersburg.

But Dead Eye would not be boarding the airplane. He would, instead, take a domestic flight to Berlin, and from there he'd catch a second plane heading north. Lee Babbitt and Jeff Parks and the other Townsend suits would be pissed, but Dead Eye did not give a damn.

Russ Whitlock, like his primary target, Court Gentry, was a singleton asset, and singletons did things their way.

FIVE

Gregor Ivanovic Sidorenko sat at his desk, hard at work, even now at four in the morning. He was a night owl, partly due to natural tendencies and partly due to the large quantities of barbiturates he took for his various physical maladies, all of which—both the maladies and the pills to combat them—affected his mood and sleep patterns. He often did not go to bed until after breakfast, and then he remained there through most of the daylight hours.

Behind his back, the young skinheads who worked for him called him *vampir*, "vampire," a moniker that also took into account his pasty white skin and sunken dark eyes.

Sid's office here at his Rochino palace was a large open room with wooden flooring and high ceilings of smooth plaster. The bare floor looked like it would be more suitable for dance parties than mob business. It was half the size of a basketball court and had the acoustics to match, but Sid liked the regal feel of large open spaces. The echoes of the room were only partially muted by bloodred curtains on the wall to his right, and a large crackling fireplace on his left kept his end of the room not warm, but bearable.

Sid's massive desk was centered at the back wall, facing the door to the hallway across the room. Another door was behind him, and this led to his sleeping chambers.

A large incense burner was perched on the desk near his laptop computer. These items, along with a telephone and a cup of tea, sat amid reams of paper, and Sid read through page after page of the document pile with only the light of the fireplace and the ambient glow of his laptop.

A portrait of Joseph Stalin hung from the wall behind his desk; the dark eyes of Uncle Joe seemed to look over Sid's shoulder while he worked.

And Sid had been working since early evening. Though his home had been the site of a party tonight, Sid had not even gone downstairs; instead he took his meal here at his desk. The skinheads—he didn't call them that, he called them "his boys"—threw their wild celebrations on the first floor and outside in the snow; they brought girls and booze and often a little coke, and they had a hell of a time, but Sid did not partake. He wasn't like them, and they weren't like him.

That was not to say he was bothered by the festivities.

Much to the contrary, his boys could party at his place every night as far as he was concerned. He liked the fact that some fifty or sixty feared and loathed men, all of whom worked for him in one form or another, were here on the grounds. It made him feel safe, up on the fourth floor with only his extended family, his sister and her kids, and his cousins living up here with him. They avoided the freak show on the weekends as well, staying up here away from the skinheads.

Despite the slight inconvenience, Sid knew that no one would dare attack him with a small army of soldiers at the ready—well, sort of ready—to respond to any threat.

Sidorenko enjoyed spending his time at his desk counting his money. He had entered the underworld originally as an accountant for a large crime boss in the early nineties before taking over the reins of his own *Bratva* a few years later, and he still spent his days, or more precisely his nights, looking over the meticulously maintained ledgers of his various enterprises.

He slurped a sip of his sugary-sweet tea, and then, with a reed-thin finger, he scanned down a printout ledger showing receipts from his prostitution and human trafficking concerns in the Czech Republic.

The phone on his desk rang and he answered it, not surprised at all to receive a call at four in the morning, as he had employees all over the world who knew Sidorenko could be reached throughout the night St. Petersburg time.

"What?" Sid asked distractedly, the index finger of his right hand still skimming a balance sheet stacked on hundreds of others.

"Sir. Ivan at the north gate."

Sid's finger stopped moving and his eyes narrowed with concern.

"What's wrong?"

"Probably nothing, sir. I almost did not call. But it is strange."

"Well *talk*, damn you!" Sid shouted as he stood from his chair. He was a paranoid man, and it was a short trip for him to switch from comfortable relaxation to shaking terror. He was well on his way from the former to the latter; only his security man's indecision kept him from bolting the door and reaching for his shotgun.

"Uh . . . A hang glider just crashed in the forest about twenty-five meters from the north wall. No one is with it."

Sid cocked his head, his birdlike features pinched tighter in confusion.

"A hang glider?"

Ivan said, "We have two men searching the larch to see if a body—"

"It's him!" Sid interrupted, his voice tight with tension. "It's Gray. He's here. Get everyone to the house! Send men to my office. A *lot* of men. Everyone else will search this building. You have to find him before he comes upstairs!"

"Sir, he did not pass the gate. I would have seen him. He must still be out—"

"Listen to me! He's in the—"

Sid stopped speaking when he heard it: the slow creaking of old hinges, the sound of the heavy door to the hallway opening. He could not see the door across the room, as the light from the fireplace did not reach more than fifteen feet past the front of his desk. Normally when the door opened he knew it instantly, as there was a light in the hallway, and a long shaft of light across the cold hardwood floor accompanied the creaking hinges.

But not now. Clearly the hall light had been disabled.

Panic washed over his body; his knees weakened. He fought a wave of nausea and then croaked softly into the phone, "Hurry." He placed the handset back in the cradle with a trembling hand and sat back down.

Sidorenko had thought of this moment for a long time. It was at the center of his every nightmare, true, but he had also taken the time when awake to put his mind to the situation. If, somehow, all his defensive measures came to nothing and it was down to Court and him, alone in a room somewhere, he had a plan.

Sid's right hand wrapped around the cold grip of a double-barreled shotgun attached to a swivel hanger on the underside of the desk. He rotated the weapon's business end to the left, toward the doorway, but he could see nothing past the firelight's glow around his desk.

He heard no footsteps, but he knew the Gray Man was out there, approaching in the impenetrable darkness.

———

When Court entered the big dark room he saw the man standing at the desk at the far end in front of the Stalin portrait, illuminated by the light of the big fireplace. The man hung up a telephone and sat down slowly, clearly aware now that he was not alone.

The man looked like Sidorenko, but the distance and a long shadow cast by a chair in front of the fireplace made positive identification impossible.

Court shifted swiftly to his left and then began approaching up the wall along the curtains on Sid's right, moving through black shadow on the opposite wall from the fireplace.

He saw the man peer into the dim in front of him, his right hand slipping casually under the desk.

———————

Below the desk Gregor Sidorenko's swivel-mounted shotgun scanned slowly to the left and to the right, searching for a target, belying the calm appearance he attempted to portray with his upper body. His face affected an air of nonchalance; he even smiled a little as he looked into the darkness before him.

And while his eyes searched for a target his mind raced. *Sixty seconds*, he told himself. Surely the men positioned on the second-floor landing had already heard from the north guard shack and were on their way, and it should not take them more than a minute from receiving the alarm before they came bursting through the door.

Sid knew he needed to find Court downrange of his shotgun and put two barrels of lead into him, or else keep him busy for just a minute more.

The Russian relaxed a little. He could do this. He knew he could.

With a wider smile now he spoke to the darkness. "I knew you would come. It was inevitable." A nervous chuckle. "I have been anxiously awaiting this moment. That might surprise you, but just listen. You will be glad to know that an opportunity has arisen, something I am certain you will find impossible to—"

A figure in black, a face obscured with a ski mask,

moved into the glow of the crackling firelight by the curtains, far to Sid's right in front of the desk. The figure held a suppressed pistol at the end of an outstretched arm; the long silencer was pointed directly at Sidorenko's face. A tubular night vision device protruded from the figure's forehead.

Though Sid could not see the man's face, there was no question that this was Court Gentry. Sid was surprised by how silently the American had approached. Court was not three meters from him now. It would be impossible to miss with the shotgun; he just had to swivel the weapon all the way to the right and wait for the man to move a foot or two closer to place himself in the line of fire. Sid made no sudden move; he squeezed the grip tighter and slowly rotated the gun to the right while he spoke.

Sid said, "There is a mission only you could possibly achieve. By your actions tonight I am even more certain that you are the right man for the—"

Gentry shot Gregor Sidorenko through the forehead. Blood sprayed across the portrait of Stalin behind him as his head snapped back. He spun away, tumbled out of his chair behind his desk, and came to rest faceup, eyes wide open, dead on the cool wooden floor.

Court hadn't come all this way to listen to Sid talk.

SIX

The Gray Man stepped past the desk and fired a second round into the Russian mob boss; the body jerked and blood sprayed, twinkling in the firelight. And then Court turned away, holstering his pistol and moving to the long row of curtains. He yanked them down with a single pull to gain access to the window.

But there was no window. The curtains had covered a massive brick wall.

Sid had been so scared of Gentry he'd had the windows removed, bricking himself away from the dangers of the outside world.

Court ran back around the desk, vaulted Sid's body and the pool of blood growing on the floor, and ducked into the bedroom.

There were no windows here, either.

Oh shit.

In an instant, Court's escape plan evaporated. He had planned to break or blow the glass of the first window he found after killing Sid, and then just rappel or bungee down the side of the building, bypassing all the security inside the mansion's walls.

But Gentry had not allowed for the possibility that there would be no windows.

Hope in one hand, shit in the other.

There was only one way out. He turned and faced the hallway door just as the sounds of shouting men came from up the hall.

At the same time, sirens began to wail around the property.

Court sprinted for the door, reloading his pistol with a fresh magazine from his chest rig as he advanced on the danger.

———————

"It's getting lively." Jeff Parks had finished his call to Dead Eye and returned to watch the monitor. Now he stood at the back wall, just behind the seated Leland Babbitt. Together they watched the main display along with the rest of the signal room. Tiny white spots moved in ones and twos toward the main building, no real coordination evident, but all the figures were obviously responding to orders.

Parks gave his reading of the events. "The guys who found the microlight called it in, and now the compound is on full alert."

A woman near the front of the room had been listening to the audio feeds from the bugs set up outside the walls of the dacha. She turned away from her desk with her hand to her earpiece and spoke into her microphone. "Sirens sounding at the target location."

Someone else said, "It's going loud."

Parks muttered to himself now, although his mic picked up the concern in his voice. "C'mon, Court, old buddy. I sure as shit hope you have an exfil planned that's cleaner than your infil."

Babbitt sat next to him, his tuxedo straining against his corpulent frame. With absolute confidence he said, "He's got a plan."

Court did *not*, in fact, have a plan.

He ran headlong up the narrow corridor toward what sounded like a half-dozen men, just on the other side of the corner not fifty feet ahead. Bouncing flashlight beams pulsed around the turn, the throw of the lights narrowing as the men drew closer. Court was hoping to improvise, to find some way to avoid contact with that number of enemy, but as he closed on them, and they on him, he realized his chances for something other than a six-on-one gunfight in a narrow hallway were rapidly diminishing.

Court sprinted, his night vision lens providing him a narrow monochromatic view. He held his weapon steady and his eyes scanned past the front sight, ready to engage the first armed man he saw.

A door opened twenty feet ahead on his right, opposite the door the child had appeared from a few minutes earlier. A man stepped out, facing in the direction of the noise of the men around the corner.

Gentry closed on the man, his Glock at the ready, and he scanned the man's hands. The right hand was empty, but the left hand swung out with a silver automatic pistol clutched in it.

Court pressed the palm of his left hand into the back of his Glock's side, and it fired once at the target in front of him. His left hand kept his suppressed pistol from cycling, and this held the spent shell casing in the weapon. It also lessened the noise made by firing the gun.

The man pitched forward into the hall, tumbling onto the carpet with a muted thud.

Court leapt over the fallen man and through the doorway, then grabbed the legs of the dead body, and pulled it back inside. He reached out into the hall, scooped up the silver pistol, and retreated back into the room just as the crew of skinheads made the turn.

He shut the door not one full second before their flashlights trained on it, and they rushed past seconds later, hurrying to surround their benefactor in his office.

There were no lights on in this bedroom, but through his monocle Gentry scanned the empty space. The dead man was a cousin of Sidorenko and a lieutenant in his organization, but Court neither knew nor cared. He was looking for a window, and he found two. He ran to them, pulled back the heavy curtains, and saw thick iron bars.

"Fucking Sid," Court muttered under his breath.

He cleared the spent shell casing from his pistol and reholstered it, then reached into the cargo pocket of his pants, pulled out a mobile phone, and lit up the screen. With the touch of a three-button code, made difficult by a slight tremor in his hand brought on by adrenaline, he sent a wireless message to the detonators of both strands of fireworks.

Within ten seconds cracks and booms began in the forest more than one hundred yards beyond the southern gate of the compound. He knew in forty-five seconds the igniter would initiate in the second strand, and mortars would fire all over the southern side of the building.

He headed back to the door, cracked it open, then launched himself once again into the hallway, turned the corner and ran toward the atrium. He saw no one ahead, so he holstered his pistol and pulled the small flare gun from a Velcro pouch on his chest harness. It was loaded with a single smoke grenade, and he raised the device and fired a cartridge with a loud pop. The smoke grenade arced up the long passage, flew over the balcony, and dropped into the atrium, four stories below. Before the first grenade hit the ground and began extruding its thick red billowing cloud, Court had slammed a second ballistic smoke into the gun and snapped it closed, and he fired again. Another champagne-cork pop echoed in the darkened hallway. He loaded a third smoke as he began running up the hall as fast as he could. He fired the third grenade, and he let the flare gun fall to the hallway carpet as he pulled his suppressed Glock once again.

Two men appeared at the balcony in front of him now; they were backlit with the dim glow from the glass dome roof of the atrium, and Court saw them easily in his night vision monocle, saw the rifles in their hands, saw them running in his direction.

Court, dressed in black and sprinting up a dark hallway, was invisible to the men. All they saw before them were a pair of bright orange flashes before both of their worlds went dark.

With less than fifty feet to the balcony Court reholstered his sidearm, then reached behind him and pulled a grappling hook from his hip bag. The spring-loaded spool spun as he drew out a length of bungee cord attached to it, looping it in his hand as it came out. As he ran he swung the hook in a forward motion, playing out longer lengths of the bungee with each whipping revolution.

Gentry heard shouting in the atrium, many men calling out to one another in confusion, fury, and resolve. They would see the red smoke, black in the dim light, and they would not know what it meant, but any men on the higher floors would have heard the pops of the grenade launcher or the supersonic cracks of the suppressed Glock, and they would know danger was seconds away.

They would be waiting for him, Court knew, and he could not prevent that. The only way he could help himself now was to do the unexpected, and to move as quickly as possible out of their line of fire.

Ten feet from the balcony he swung the grappling hook overhand, then let it go and dropped the loops. The weighted hook sailed away from him, drawing the springy black cord behind it.

With a loud metallic clang it hit the iron beam that ran the length of the dome over the atrium, then swung around over the top of the bar, where its claw grabbed the bungee.

Outside the building, to the rear of Court's position, a series of low thuds began as the twelve Yanisars attached to the fuse ignited by the wireless signal began launching, skipping across the ground before booms as loud as shotgun blasts shook windowpanes, set off car alarms, and echoed off the walls of the property.

During this distraction Gentry shot out of the fourth-floor hallway and, vaulting high with a single bound, pushed off on the top of the balcony railing with his leading foot, then leapt off the balcony face-first, arms out wide with his pistol in his right hand, his body arcing over the atrium below.

SEVEN

Gravity took him and he fell through the darkness, past the third-floor mezzanine, past armed men racing up the open staircase, past more men storming down the hallways on the second floor.

And into the thick red smoke.

The bungee had been set for a leap out a fourth-floor window; it was thirty feet long and would extend to exactly forty feet, which would leave him a short drop to the ground at full extension if he'd attached the hook to a fixture in a room on the fourth floor.

But throwing the hook over the bars below the dome meant he'd have a good ten-to-fifteen-foot drop at maximum extension.

There were eight men who conceivably could have gotten a shot off at Gentry as he fell past them, but no one fired. The darkness, the confusion, the early hour, and the brains addled by drink, along with the concern about firing and missing the target but hitting a colleague on the far balcony, put just enough hesitation into the trigger fingers of the men, causing them all to miss their tiny window of opportunity as the masked man dropped like a stone past their positions.

Court felt the gripping in his harness even before he disappeared into the smoke; the bungee pulled taut and he went from an eighty-mile-an-hour fall to a dead stop in less than twenty feet, wrenching the straps under his clothing at his inner thigh and across his chest. His night vision monocle fell off his head, and he felt gear straining from the weight of gravity in pouches and packs around his body.

At full extension he reached to his left hip to flip the wireless grappling disconnect lever on the control panel. A simple flip of an inch-long switch would send a wireless signal up to the grappling hook, causing its claws to pop open like an umbrella blowing up in high winds. This would release the hook and cause Court to drop to the floor below him.

He'd pulled this off in training dozens of times; the technology was solid and straightforward.

But this time it went wrong. The control panel had popped off his belt at some point in the action and it swung freely now from a nylon strap, knocking against webbing and pistol magazines on his chest. He had less than a second to find it, flip the lever, and free himself, not nearly enough time to root it out of all the gear on his harness.

Court had braced himself for a ten-foot free fall to the

floor, but instead the bungee held tight, and he shot back upward like a marble in a slingshot, launching out of the protection of the dark smoke and back up into the dim atrium.

The four men on the first floor were obstructed by the smoke, and they had no time to react. Gentry shot past them, just a few feet away, and as he passed he swung his body around to try to get his gun pointed in their direction.

But neither Gentry nor the skinheads got a shot off in the half second between his emergence from the red smoke and his disappearance above them.

Now Court's climb rate increased; he passed the second-floor balcony, propelled by his long fall and the spring of the bungee cord. There were two men here; both had their AKs sticking over the railing in his direction.

As Court rocketed upward he grabbed at the barrel of one rifle and knocked it away, then shot the other man once in the body armor on his chest. A second shot at the still-standing skinhead slammed into the man's radio on his shoulder. The round penetrated just an inch or so through the Russian's skin, cracking his collarbone and sending him back to the floor, more from the panic of being shot than any real momentum from the bullet.

Four men stood on the third-floor balcony, leaning over just as Court reached eye level. The shock in the Russians' faces told Court he had the advantage. He opened fire, dumping round after round from the suppressed pistol at the men there, shooting two of the four dead and sending the other two diving for cover.

Court's momentum had ceased at the third floor, and he hung in midair a moment before he began falling again. His pistol was empty now, so as he dropped, preparing himself to sail past the vertical gauntlet of guns once more, he let go of his Glock 19 and reached down to his right ankle.

On the second-floor balcony a group of gunmen ran out of the hallway directly in front of him. They saw their target dropping past them, not more than twenty feet away. One man fired a burst in Court's direction as he fell by them, and the rest ran up to the balcony railing, readying to dump rounds on him from above.

Court was back in the smoke again, and he'd yanked his backup gun free of its ankle holster with his right hand and, with his left, he took hold of the stretching bungee cord that was attached to his lower back and pulled himself around to face it.

He had one chance to get this right. There was no way in hell he could spring back up again, now in the sights of a dozen rifles, without being torn to bloody shreds by AK rounds. As he bottomed out, his harness squeezed him tight again and pressed air from his lungs. At ten feet above the atrium floor he jammed the muzzle of the compact Glock 26 into the taut cord, one foot away from his body, and fired.

The rope snapped in two; Court dropped like a stone, breaking his fall with his arms and legs, but still he slammed into the ground next to the fountain on his right side.

The wind was knocked from his lungs, but he knew he could not stay there. Instead he began rolling; he'd dropped the Glock on impact, but he felt for it and grabbed it up, kept rolling, still not breathing, and he banged into tables and chairs, knocking them out of the way as he crawled forward and then scrambled to his feet. He could not see the way ahead in the thick red smoke but he moved anyway, still struggling to catch a breath.

Above him he heard the rattling gunfire, and all around him he heard cracking strikes of the 7.62-millimeter rounds.

He ran out of the smoke choking the atrium floor and into a large banquet room that ran off the north side, hoping like hell he could either find an exit or make one.

———————

"That one! *There!* Where is he going?"

Jeff Parks ran to the screen in the front of the signal room, and he used the tip of a ballpoint pen to point to a single white-hot heat signature that exited a side entrance on the north side of the massive dacha. The lone figure passed two men rushing toward the entrance, and they did not break stride.

"He walked right by them!" someone shouted.

Parks said, "That's him. He must have clothing that matches what the goons on the ground there are wearing."

The figure continued walking. All around the signal room, commands were given to the drone pilots to tighten up on the figure, to the audio techs to focus mics hidden in the forest on the north side, to those in contact with Trestle Actual to let him and his unit know that it appeared the Gray Man was hoofing it off the X in some sort of disguise.

On the screen figures poured out of the building now, mostly through the main door on the south side but some on the west and north. Men ran in one direction and then another; the audio picked up cracks and booms and shouts and barking dogs and then the sounds of gas engines firing up, but soon the *tap-tap-tap-tap* of cyclic Kalashnikov fire piped through the tiny surveillance mics. Someone was blasting his AK on the south side of the building, apparently at nothing in the darkness.

One of the signal room techs counted twenty-four pax moving about the property and announced it through the commo net. But the one lone heat signature walked on, first between a metal shed and an uneven row of snowmobiles, and then straight toward the north gate, where three men stood at the wall next to the guard shack, facing in his direction.

"Tell the UAV operator I want it as tight as he can make it," Babbitt demanded. "Don't worry about image quality; I want to see this up close."

A moment later the camera zoomed in on the lone man approaching the guard shack along the wall at the north gate. For the first time signal room personnel could make out folds in clothing, could see a hood over the man's head, and they could also see that his hands were empty.

A female voice muttered into her mic, "He's gonna try to talk his way through—"

A male voice with a southern drawl spoke over her. "He ain't *talkin'* his way through shit."

The room fell silent as the figure closed to within ten feet of the armed men at the gate. He did not stop, just kept moving toward them. The three guards had been holding their guns at the low ready, but something must have alarmed them because all three raised their weapons at once and backed up; one bumped against the wall. The approaching man moved the last ten feet in the blink of an eye, knocked the first AK to the side, and drove his arm up; it looked like his open hand connected with the first guard's throat, but it was hard to tell. The Russian left the ground, kicked back, and fell into the second guard; two rifles were on the ground and Gentry—of course this was Gentry—leapt forward, pushed off the stone wall with his right leg to give himself more lift, and launched himself on the third man. He got inside the guard's weapon just as he fired, a flash of light from the barrel and a thump of noise through the surveillance microphone in the forest to the north. But the round missed; the Gray Man had the guard in a violent embrace and they spun in the snow, the AK twirling through the air. The guard flailed, but the Gray Man got his arms around the man's head, turned him around, and shoved him violently, face-first, into the wall.

The second man leapt upon the Gray Man from behind, but a right elbow knocked him off balance, and then a high roundhouse kick to the face crumpled the man in the snow in a heap.

"My God!" someone yelled.

All three guards were down now. Motionless. The Gray Man had landed on his back after his roundhouse kick, but he sprang to his feet, pulling a Kalashnikov up with him from the snow as he stood.

He seemed to look up, back at the activity near the house, and then he turned away, slinging the rifle on his back and heading out through the gates.

Babbitt, Parks, and the others in the Townsend signal room watched the glowing silhouette cross a road and enter the forest; his signature was intermittent now as he passed under the trees, but within seconds it was clear that he was moving faster.

Much faster.

The UAV tightened up on the movement; arms and legs pumping from the body were evident at this magnification.

"He's running."

Lee Babbitt walked forward to the front of the room and stood in front of the plasma screen facing his surveillance personnel. "And just like that, ladies and gentlemen, he is clear of his target. Sidorenko is dead; we won't need to wait to hear that from official sources."

There were claps of amazement in the room. This team had been tracking Gentry for months with no joy, and now they had a fix on his position.

———

Court had lost his night vision monocle during his jump in the atrium, and there was little illumination here under the snow-covered larch branches to guide him, but the low light and dense canopy was more help than hindrance.

While still in the building he'd pulled the top article of clothing from his backpack, a thin camouflaged pullover. He'd ripped off his ski mask and donned the green and black garment, and out here in the dark he looked much like everyone else running around in the snow. He made it past the guard shack and out through the front gate just as the frantic men came outside, looking desperately for the assassin.

At that point the men with radios shouted and screamed into them, and the men without radios shouted and screamed even louder, and the hunt for the killer in their

midst turned into a shambles and young men full on testosterone, booze, and coke ran all over the property pointing guns at one another in the dark.

The chase did lead out past the walls, finally, but most
of the goons headed out to the south, following the noise
and lights from the fireworks there, and several men
opened fire on parked trucks, the silhouette of a garbage
can, and even a patrol of two men in the forest that had
become separated from the rest of the group. By then
Court had taken out the three guards at the north gate
and entered the forest. Once under cover of the trees he
reached under his camo pullover, pulled out a white nylon
hooded windbreaker, and zipped that over his other layers.

After this he knew his only job was to move and to
keep moving. He wanted to put space between himself
and the dacha, and he needed the heat generated by the
activity to keep him alive.

Sid's skinheads had dogs, but they were untrained, and
Court wore a silver-lined base layer that shielded 90 percent of his body's natural odors, cloaking him to a scent
tracker. He pulled a freezer bag from his backpack and out
of it he took six hunks of raw, putrefying bear meat, and as
he ran he flung the steaks in all directions. The dogs would
focus on the meat, not for long, but hopefully it would
screw with their hunt long enough to get him some distance off the X, and render what little bit of his smell did
emanate from him faint and untraceable.

Gentry met his extraction an hour before dawn, after
nearly three hours of trudging, running, tripping, and fall-

ing in the snow. He'd heard vehicles on the road and he'd heard the shouts of men and he'd heard the barking of dogs, but the only direct threat to him had been frostbite. He'd kept moving, kept his body temperature up, and he knew he'd thaw out once he got to where he was going.

The truck that came to pick him up was driven by a local who'd been hired by the Moscow *Bratva*. The man only knew that his job entailed collecting an individual in the forest just before nine A.M., when the skies were still pitch-black, and then driving him twenty kilometers to an inlet where a speedboat would be waiting. This part of Gentry's exfil went off without a hitch. There were no words between the two men; the driver had, on his own initiative, brought Court a thermos of tea. Court held it in his hands to warm them, and he held it to his face so that the heat would thaw his nose, but he did not drink even a sip.

Court appreciated the gesture, but he didn't know this bastard. For all he knew the tea was pure poison.

Gentry was not the trusting type.

As the sun grayed the low clouds over the Gulf of Finland, Gentry found himself on his extraction boat. The term *speedboat* didn't really fit. It was a fourteen-foot tender with an underpowered engine and a captain who looked like he might have been all of seventeen years old. But they cut through the glassy water of the gulf easily enough, and shortly before noon he was brought alongside the *Helsinki Polaris*, a Russian-flagged dry-store cargo hauler on its way to Finland.

As he left the tender the captain reached under a seat and handed Gentry a backpack and a small knapsack. Court took them without a word. The backpack was his;

he'd packed it himself in Moscow, filling it with things he would need to go on the run after the Sidorenko operation. A new pistol, a trauma kit, clothes, and a few other odds and ends. And the knapsack contained two hundred fifty thousand euros in bundles of one hundred euro notes. This was operating money he'd been promised for his getaway, and he imagined he would need much or all of it to adequately disappear.

By noon he stood in his small quarters in the rear of the ship; he'd consolidated the money into the backpack and the pockets of his heavy coat and now he stood naked in front of a grimy mirror, examining his bruises and scrapes from the activity of the morning. He was beat-up to be sure, but in better condition than he expected to find himself at the end of this ride. More importantly, he'd done it. He'd ended Sid Sidorenko and removed the most passionate and headstrong of those hunting him. It was a good day's work, and now he was looking forward to melting away for a while, living off grid and biding his time until he figured out where he would go from here.

————

The Townsend Government Services ScanEagle drone had remained overhead throughout Gentry's extraction. Babbitt decided to stand down his strike team within minutes of Gentry's entering the forest. Sid had too many goons out and about; the eight members of Trestle could have handled themselves against any three dozen Russian skinheads, but their objective was to kill Gentry, and Gentry was safely under surveillance. Trestle could easily wait for him to get clear of the Russians and then hit him later when he was alone.

The ScanEagle tracked its target to the truck, and then the first UAV switched out with a second, which followed the truck to the fourteen-foot boat and remained high overhead as the tender came along a ship sailing west in the Gulf of Finland. The camera onboard the drone picked up the name of the ship—*Helsinki Polaris*. The Townsend investigators ran the name of the boat through Vesseltracker, a database of the world's ships, and this showed the *Helsinki Polaris*'s details and scheduled course, and from this they learned the ship was an 1,800-ton dry-goods cargo hauler and though Helsinki was its home port, it was Russian owned and Antigua and Barbuda flagged. It was on its way to deliver a shipment to Finland and would be calling in Mariehamn at eight A.M. the following morning.

"We've got him," Babbitt said to Parks when everything was confirmed. "We'll take him right there on the ship. Alert Trestle, let him know they will be doing an underway."

"Yes, sir. We have the fast boats and all the equipment necessary for a marine assault in the port of St. Petersburg. We'll fly them to Helsinki and get ahead of the *Polaris*."

"Good."

Parks asked, "What about Dead Eye? Should I stand him down?"

"Negative. Have him proceed to Mariehamn. I want him waiting at the port in case something goes wrong."

The phone on Jeff Parks's hip rang; he put it on

speaker and took the call from one of his signal room's communications staff.

"Go for Jeff."

"Jeff, the pilot of the Beechcraft assigned to Dead Eye just called. The asset's a no-show. He was supposed to be at the airport two hours ago. The pilot wants to know how long he should wait for him."

Parks turned to Babbitt, who was already looking up at the ceiling in a show of frustration.

"I hate singletons," Babbitt groaned. "Call him. He won't answer, but do it anyway. I want everyone in the signal room to keep pushing data about the operation to Dead Eye's phone. Even if he won't talk to us, I want him to know what's happening with the hunt."

"And then?" asked Parks.

"And then we wait for Dead Eye to turn up in the AO. He wants Gentry as bad as we do. He'll be there. He just won't follow our game plan."

Parks shook his head as he disconnected the call. "Prick."

Babbitt said, "Part of managing individualists like Whitlock is knowing when to back off. Let him think he's the brains of this operation; I don't give a shit. The only thing I care about is getting a picture of Court Gentry's ugly mug in a pine box when this is all said and done."

EIGHT

The woman was pretty, although she looked a little sad. She sat there, alone, deep in the shadows of a potted orange tree at a table in the outdoor café, ignoring the patrons sitting in the sun as all but a few of the men there ignored her. Her face was half-hidden behind her huge designer sunglasses, and her head hung over the demitasse of espresso nested in her hands on the bistro table. Occasionally she appeared to gaze out across the street in front of her, past four lanes of moderate traffic and toward an alley that ran behind a four-story apartment building and a parking garage.

It was a perfect December afternoon in Faro, Portugal, with sunny skies and temperatures in the midfifties. And although this was certainly not an intersection with a scenic view, nor did this urban neighborhood possess any tourist value whatsoever, the tables that poured onto the sidewalk from the café were more than half occupied, mostly by afternoon shoppers and locals from the nearby middle-class apartment building and the alley behind it.

But the woman under the orange tree just sat by herself, far away from the rest of the patrons, nursing her espresso. She flicked her midlength brown hair out of her face and glanced again to the apartment building.

A text appeared on the iPhone lying next to her purse on the table. She picked up the phone and glanced at it.

Where are you?

She tapped back a response with her thumb.

Watching TV on the sofa. Why?

She put the phone back on the table and resumed her languid gaze across the street, but seconds later she heard the screech of metal chair legs dragging across the sidewalk next to her. An attractive middle-aged man in a gray suit sat down, putting his phone on the table alongside hers. She saw the text she had just sent displayed on the screen of his phone.

He spoke softly as he settled in. "It hurts my feelings when you lie to me." His accent was thick, but his English flawless.

The woman smiled a little now, but she did not turn to look at the man. "You know me too well, Yanis."

Yanis had already bought a cup of tea from the counter inside, and he stirred sugar into it while he talked. He, unlike the woman, did not smile.

"You aren't supposed to be here," he said.

"I know."

"You did the same thing in Buenos Aires, and you did the same thing in Tangiers."

"And in Manila. But you didn't catch me in Manila." She turned to him; her smile was no longer sheepish. It had turned sexy. Coquettish. "What can I say? I like to watch."

Yanis was not as playful. "It's not the protocol. You know that. This could be dangerous."

She turned back to the building across the street. "Were you so concerned for my safety at any time during the past six weeks? I don't recall you once asking me if I was keeping a safe distance from those two bastards in that apartment over there. As a matter of fact, weren't you pressing me to get even closer?"

Yanis Alvey softened his tone. "The investigation is over, Ruth. Your role is complete. Let's get out of here and let the bad boys do their part."

"I'm not in the way. And I am not going anywhere."

Yanis sighed. He'd fought these battles with Ruth Ettinger before, and he'd always lost. He was senior to her in their organization, but she was both so damned obstinate and so damned good at her job that he let her get away with little things like this.

Yanis knew he would lose now unless he claimed victory. "All right. You can stay. I guess you deserve it." Yanis gazed up and down the street, then spoke into his phone. "Clear." He put the phone down and turned his attention back to the pretty brunette. "It feels odd executing in daylight."

"That was my suggestion. The targets stayed up all night, worked till past noon. Right now is the best time to hit them."

"I hope you are right." He cleared his throat. "You aren't armed, are you?"

"I've got Mace in my purse."

"That must be of great comfort to you." His sarcasm was clear. "I am armed, of course. If there is any trouble, stay with me."

"Thank you, Yanis." She said it like she meant it. And then, "How are they going to play it?"

Yanis sipped his tea and, over the top of the cup, he cast his eyes to the apartment building next to the parking garage. "In a moment two sedans will arrive, each carrying three men and a driver. A third van will provide a blocking force at the top of the exit to the garage. The six will go upstairs and effect the action."

Ruth nodded. "You wish you were on the team going in, don't you?"

"Of course I do." He said it without equivocation. "I enjoyed that part of my life very much. But now I am the man who sits across the street to watch instead of one of the men who swoops in to carry out justice."

"You could still do it, I'm sure," she said.

He waved the comment away. "Someone has to evaluate the surroundings to give the all clear. Plus, none of those boys get to enjoy the afternoon at a café with a beautiful woman. They are probably all jealous of me."

Ruth just smiled softly.

He looked at her a long moment. "You feel okay about this one, yes?"

"Yes. Of course I do."

"Good. I know it has been difficult for you since—"

"Shhh." She hushed him, then gestured with a subtle tip of her head toward the building across the street. Two gray cars turned into the alley and disappeared. A van pulled in behind them, turned into the mouth of the alley, and then stopped, blocking anyone trying to leave from the alley or the parking garage exit on the right.

Yanis said softly, "Fifty euros says it goes wet."

Ruth shook her head. "Sucker's bet. It *will* go wet. Somebody is about to die on the third floor of that building over there."

They sat silently for a moment; Yanis drummed his fingers on the tabletop. He was thinking about how damn much he missed it, the action going on across the street. Ruth reached out and put her hand over his hand and the drumming stopped, and then she rewrapped her thin fingers around the espresso.

Across the street a Toyota hatchback pulled out of the parking garage adjacent to the building but was blocked from leaving by the van. The Toyota honked, but the van did not move.

Ruth knew this, very likely, was the only excitement she would see of the operation across the street. It wasn't much, but she did not care.

As she'd told Yanis Alvey, she liked to watch.

———

Ruth Ettinger was thirty-seven years old, and though she had a clean and bureaucratic-sounding official title, her job description was really quite simple: She was a targeting officer for Mossad, Israeli intelligence.

Ruth ran a team of operatives on one of several task forces under Mossad's Collections Department, all given the mandate of protecting Israeli government officials from assassination and kidnapping. In actuality, virtually all of her cases involved threats against the prime minister of Israel, Ehud Kalb, the sixty-seven-year-old ex-IDF Special Forces officer who led her nation.

Ettinger had never met Kalb, had never even been in the same room as her prime minister, but she had taken it as her life's work, her one overbearing responsibility, to find those suspected of harming him, assess the credibility of the threat, and then, if that threat was determined to be real, to call in Mossad's action arm, Metsada, to finish the job.

Yanis was Metsada, in control of the operators and her link to the Operations Department, and she was his link to the Collections Department.

Together they had chased terrorists, hit men, and nut jobs all over the globe. For more than five years Ruth had been serving on this task force, first as a support officer, and then as a targeting team leader. Ruth had become the best targeter in the Collections Department at locating, tracking, and assessing threats, and Ruth damn well knew it.

And then, the previous spring, Rome happened.

An incident in Rome had turned into a debacle for her agency, but she had not been blamed; a Mossad psychologist had cleared her to return to the field just days later, and soon Ruth was back short-circuiting the nefarious schemes of her nation's enemies.

The job that had encompassed her every waking moment for the past six weeks had been the hunt for a pair of Palestinian brothers who had learned the art and science of bomb making in the territories, then detonated explosives in Afghanistan to hone their craft. As awful as this was, it was not, in and of itself, enough to garner the dogged focus of Mossad's top headhunter. But when the two brothers masked their faces and appeared on Lebanese television proclaiming themselves to be the men who would bring Israel to its knees, Ruth was given the job of looking into their bold claim to see if there was anything behind their braggadocio. She tracked them from Beirut to Ankara to Madrid and then, finally, to Faro, and here she found them amassing chemicals and timers and researching the travel plans of the Israeli prime minister. Kalb was due at an economic conference in London the following week, and the two bomb brothers had booked ferry tickets to the United Kingdom.

Ettinger and her team determined that this was, in fact, a credible threat on their PM, so they called in Yanis and his kill/capture crew from Metsada, and then Ruth and her team were ordered to stay the hell away from the target location while the hard men from Tel Aviv swooped in to end the threat.

But now Ruth sat less than a hundred yards from the action, sipping espresso in the cool shade.

She was not worried about her colleagues in Metsada. The bomb brothers had been mixing chemicals and constructing timers for the past eighteen hours and they were sound asleep, and the cameras her team had passed through the ventilation ducts in the apartment across the street confirmed that the front door to their flat was not booby-trapped. She knew the Israeli operatives would burst through the door with orders to capture the men if it was feasible to do so. But she also knew the two men in that flat had exactly one Kalashnikov rifle, and it was staged on the floor directly between their two beds, and they would both wake, both reach for it, and both fumble it.

And the Metsada officers would make the decision in a single heartbeat to shoot the two young men with their silenced pistols.

And then they would back up through the door and leave not a trace of their act behind other than the bloody bodies and a few untraceable shell casings.

Across the street the Toyota had stopped honking. One of the operatives in the blocking van climbed out and, in halting Portuguese, explained to the Toyota driver that his friend was having trouble with his van's transmission and, if the man in the Toyota could just give them a moment, they would push the vehicle out of the way. The Toyota driver complied, perhaps recognizing that the polite foreigner was doing his best to rectify the situation, and perhaps also noticing that the polite foreigner had a hard and formidable look about him, and it might be best not to piss him off.

There was a brief screech of tires now. Ruth and Yanis watched as the two carloads of Mossad operators backed out off the alley, stopping behind the Toyota. The blocking van rolled off to the west, the Toyota pulled into the street and turned to the east, and the two cars then executed perfect three-point turns in the narrow alley and followed the van to the west.

No one sitting at the outdoor café around them had any idea they were witnessing the ending of the perfectly choreographed assassination across the street.

Yanis Alvey said, "And . . . scene."

"Never gets old," Ruth said, no happiness or levity in her voice now. Yanis noticed this.

"You hate when it's over."

She corrected him. "I love when it's over. As long as we have done our jobs correctly, and there is no collateral."

Unlike Rome, Yanis thought, but did not say.

Ruth added, "What I *hate* is the day after. When I don't have anything to do."

"Dinner tonight?" Yanis asked, sounding a little more hopeful than he would have liked.

Ruth finished her espresso. "Sorry. I have to sanitize the safe house."

He nodded, careful to affect an air of nonchalance. He wasn't surprised, really. "Not a problem. I imagine you wouldn't be much company. You get incredibly disagreeable and difficult to be around when you don't have a head to hunt."

Ruth stood, then knelt back down, speaking softly into Alvey's ear. "I can only hope someone proclaims their intention to kill our prime minister in the next few days so that I can have a raison d'être."

She drifted away through the bistro tables, and Yanis reached for his wallet to pay her tab. He was not offended by her brush-off. It was part of her show, her faux tough exterior. He knew this, and he also knew what lay beneath.

She was brave and proud and smart and competent. But she was also vulnerable.

Yanis Alvey was glad for her success today in bringing down the Palestinian bomb brothers cleanly and quietly. But as she walked off he thought, not for the first time, that one more Rome just might destroy her.

NINE

At oh one hundred hours the *Helsinki Polaris* and the two tiny vessels chasing it converged in the black waters of the Baltic Sea, twenty miles due south of Helsinki.

The eight Townsend operators of Trestle Team rode in the two black Zodiac MK2s, powered by beefy but quiet motors that allowed them to cut through the cargo ship's wake and advance on the stern unnoticed but with commanding speed.

The Zodiacs had one man at the helm, while the three others on each boat held on to rope handles on the craft's inflatable rubber walls. The two small rubber boats separated behind the cargo ship, with one heading to the starboard side and the other to port. They came abreast of the *Polaris* simultaneously, and telescoping climbing poles with padded hooks at their tips were raised and hung over the railing of the main deck. Within sixty seconds the first two men were up the poles, over the railing, and lowering a rope ladder so the poles could be removed and the second and third men on each Zodiac could climb more quickly and more safely. After another minute the rope ladders were unhooked from the railing and stored on the deck, and the six men concealed themselves from anyone awake above on the bridge who decided to gaze back to stern.

Within two minutes of arriving alongside the cargo ship, the six-man boarding party was moving up the deck with their Heckler & Koch MP7s held at the high ready.

In the Adams Morgan neighborhood of Washington, D.C., the entire staff of the signal room watched the giant screen in front of them. It displayed the action via a Scan-Eagle UAV flying overhead. The drone had been deployed from the backyard of a safe house in Helsinki and operated by the same team who, only twenty hours earlier, had been working from a safe house near Gregor Sidorenko's dacha.

The direct action team searched the vessel, staying low profile, using their night vision equipment to move in the shadows and soft communications over their headsets to remain in contact with one another while moving through the cargo ship's labyrinthine passageways.

Twenty-six minutes after boarding, Trestle Actual entered the captain's cabin and knelt down over the captain's bunk. He placed his gloved hand over the silver-haired Russian's mouth and, shining a tactical flashlight in his eyes, woke the man with a hard shake.

"*G'de Americanskiy?*" *Where is the American?*

The man's eyes were wide, the pupils pinpricks in the

bright light. He tried to turn away from the beam but the hand held him firm. The light burned through his lids as he squeezed them shut.

"G'de Americanskiy?"

The gloved hand let go of the face and the captain spoke hesitantly.

"The passenger? He said he was German."

"That doesn't matter. Where is he now?"

"He disembarked."

"When?"

"Wha—what time is it?"

"It's one thirty."

"About midnight, I think."

"*How* did he leave the ship?"

"A boat came for him. It must have been prearranged. We were not told about it until it appeared. On the radio they said it had come for the passenger. He was already on the deck waiting for it."

"What kind of boat?"

"A Bayliner, I think. White. Canvas canopy." The man shook his head. "Just a regular little twenty-footer."

"What language did the man on the radio speak?"

"Russian."

"Where did it take him?"

"I . . . I don't know. Helsinki, maybe? It was the closest port. Forty kilometers from our position at the time. Must have been going to Helsinki."

Trestle Actual evaluated the captain's responses and deemed him credible. He seemed entirely too bewildered and terrified to attempt to deceive the armed men in black over him.

The lead Townsend commando looked over his shoulder and reached back a hand, and a teammate placed a syringe in it. He popped the cap of the needle with his mouth, held it there between his lips, and reclamped his hand over the captain's mouth, just as the man started to scream and thrash, the fear of what was about to happen engulfing him.

The black-clad commando jabbed the needle into the captain's neck and pressed the plunger down, and the man in the bunk went still.

It was Versed, a powerful muscle relaxer. The captain would not die, but he would be out for hours. Though his memory of what had happened the previous evening would likely be fuzzy, the aim was not to wipe away the appearance of the commandos. It was to keep the captain from raising the alarm until long after Trestle piled into their Zodiacs and left the boat.

Five minutes later the Zodiacs reappeared alongside the *Helsinki Polaris*, and the six-man boarding party descended into the two boats via the climbing poles. When everyone was back on board the Zodiacs, both craft turned to the north, leaving the cargo ship to continue on to its destination in Mariehamn.

In Washington, D.C., the signal room had been watching the drone feed of the non-event on the main monitor, but it remained Trestle Actual's duty to call Babbitt on the sat phone and fill him in once they were clear of their target.

Trestle had to all but shout over the Yamaha outboard motor that churned the water just feet behind him. "Negative contact. The target has been off the boat over an hour. Left on a white Bayliner with a canopy. Destination unknown."

"Understood," Babbitt replied. "Head back to Helsinki. We'll check radar data and determine where he went, but it might take a few hours."

"Helsinki it is. Trestle out."

TEN

Snow had fallen overnight in Tallinn, the capital of Estonia, but the morning sky was crisp and blue with only a few puffs of white. Monday road traffic was heavy; tires turned the streets to slush, and coughing exhaust pipes blackened the ice and snow on the roadside.

Thirty-four-year-old American Russell Whitlock sat on a park bench high on a hill, breathed vapor, ignored the stinging cold on his exposed cheeks, and sipped glogg, a spiced wine consumed in plentiful quantities in the Baltic during the winter.

He looked past the road below him and out to the sea beyond.

Russ had come to Tallinn not because he had been ordered here by his employer, Townsend Government Services, but rather because he'd made an educated guess. He'd arrived late the evening before; taken a cab from the train station to a three-star hotel on Toompea, the Cathedral Hill; thrown his luggage on his bed; and then immediately headed out into the light snowfall to scout a perfect location for his work the next morning.

It took him less than an hour to find this bench and then make it back to the warmth of his room, and he'd returned here at first light, equipped with food and a thermos full of glogg provided by the hotel restaurant. His spot was high on a hill along a thin band of park that ran with the northern portion of the medieval city wall that circled the Old Town and Cathedral Hill. Just behind him was the Oleviste Church and one of the city's twenty conical-roofed wall towers, built in the 1400s when Tallinn was a wealthy Hanseatic League capital.

From this hilltop position he could see the length of the Port of Tallinn below him, and this was what made the location perfect for his needs.

His backpack sat next to him on the bench. In his lap lay a powerful pair of 20 × 80 Steiner binoculars. He also wore a Canon camera around his neck, just another tourist shooting pictures of the town and the ships in port below him from his high vantage point. He wore a black down coat that he'd purchased in Berlin the day before, and this kept him warm, though the sips of hot spiced wine certainly didn't hurt in this regard.

A car ferry the size of a small shopping mall was in its berth by the terminal at the mouth of the port, and farther along to the east, dozens of smaller boats were docked. Most large cargo ships were moored offshore in the Bay of Tallinn, but more than a dozen midsized cargo ships were closer to land, their tenders occasionally offloading men and goods.

There was also a constant influx of even smaller water-craft, tiny fishing vessels returning with the morning's catch.

He lifted his Steiner binoculars to his eyes and checked out to sea, monitoring the small vessels as they came in, and then he shifted them back to a spot a half mile below his position. At the mouth of the port near the massive Tallink Ferry terminal was a choke point that anyone who had disembarked from a vessel in the port would need to pass on the way into town, and this was the main focus of Whitlock's attention. Most people leaving the docks did so in groups, clusters of three to ten men, heav-ily bundled in coats and hats to protect them from the cold sea air. They would then head to buses or cars and trucks in one of the parking lots in the area.

Russ ignored these groups; he was on the lookout for a loner.

Although he had not checked in with his masters at Townsend House in well over a day, he was reading the secure messages about the target and the status of the hunt for him that they sent to his mobile. From this data he knew the *Helsinki Polaris* had been a dry hole, and this had not surprised him in the least. Russ did not think for a moment that Court would sit on that boat and wait to get sold out by the Russian mob or tracked by boarding parties sent to conduct underway assaults on all ships in the Gulf of Finland near the Sidorenko hit.

Court was too smart for that, and Russell Whitlock

gave him full credit for being so. Court would have arranged a third party to collect him from the boat, someone not aligned with the Russians and not aware of any part of Gentry's mission in Rochino.

That was what Whitlock would have done, so, he decided, that was what Gentry would do.

Russ took a short break to finish his glogg and eat a few bites of an egg sandwich he'd made himself from the offerings at the breakfast buffet in the hotel, and then he brought the binos back to his eyes. He waited for the vapor in the air around his mouth to clear, and then he noticed a small white craft pulling up to a pier midway between the western and eastern sides of the port. He thought it possible he was looking at a twenty-foot Bayliner runabout, though there was no canvas top visible. He knew his target might have had the top removed during the journey to Tallinn, and almost immediately he saw a lone man stepping onto the dock without glancing back to the captain. He had with him only a single black backpack, and he slung this over his shoulder and trudged purposefully up the dock toward the exit of the port. Whitlock followed him for several yards with his twenty-power lenses, then checked the area quickly for other possibles before returning his attention to the only solo traveler in sight.

The individual left the port, walked past the taxis waiting for fares, passed the bus stop, and then turned to the southwest. He was moving in Whitlock's general direction now, walking up a snow-covered sidewalk along a busy road leading toward Old Town Tallinn.

Whitlock continued tracking him through his binoculars. With the magnification of the Steiners the individual appeared to be only fifteen yards away from Whitlock's position, but Russ still could not identify his target. The man wore the hood up on his black coat and a wool scarf over his nose and mouth, and this made a positive ID impossible, irrespective of the distance.

But Russ had a feeling. "That you, Court?" he asked aloud.

Russ put the rubber lens covers back on his binoculars, then slid them and his Canon camera into his backpack along with his thermos. He slung his pack over his back and began heading toward the entrance to the Old Town, more hopeful than confident that he had found his man.

———————

The confidence came fifteen minutes later. Whitlock had positioned himself at a table on the second floor of a small restaurant near the Viru Gates, the main entrance through the walls of the Old Town. Below him he watched the man from the port moving up the cobblestone street. The man's face was still obscured by the scarf and the hood of his black coat, but Whitlock could judge height and build, and it matched what he knew about his target. He lifted his Steiners and locked them on the face of the individual. At this distance the eyes filled the lenses, and Whitlock felt his heart rate increase; it seemed as if the two men were standing only inches apart.

The eyes of the man were intense, searching.

Whitlock was certain. Those were the eyes of the Gray Man.

Russ had spent hours staring into those eyes. Lee

Babbitt had sent him every photo the CIA had of the man. They were all old; most showed him wearing some sort of disguise, for either a passport picture or a visa application, but Court could not change his hard and piercing eyes.

Russell Whitlock turned away from the window, his heart pounding with excitement.

"I've got you. I've *fucking* got you." He left the table before the waitress arrived to take his order, descended the restaurant's staircase, and headed back outside into the cold.

———————

The target moved through the crowd with his head down. In the space of a two-minute tail, Russ watched Gentry raise and lower the hood of his coat, then put a black watch cap over his brown hair and take it off again. All these changes, each one done with supreme nonchalance, made tailing him from a distance nearly impossible.

Gentry entered the Town Hall Square, the center of activity in the medieval portion of the city. A winter market was under way, and dozens of morning shoppers strolled through wooden kiosks set up to sell food and drink and handicrafts. The smell of grilled sausage, hot chocolate, and glogg was in the air, but Whitlock watched Gentry pass it all by, ignoring the happy sights and sounds and smells of the holidays, as he stayed rooted to his mission.

His mission to stay alive.

He stopped suddenly, crossed the street toward a bakery, and looked in the window glass.

Whitlock turned his head down to the cobblestones in front of his shoes and kept walking until he turned the corner, leaving his target behind.

He picked him up again a minute later, just by chance really, in the winding and narrow Old Town streets. As Russ tried to move on a street parallel to Gentry, he found himself folding in fifty feet behind him. Court crossed the street again, just ahead of an SUV that rumbled slowly on the icy cobblestones, and he began climbing steps through a medieval archway, leading up the Cathedral Hill.

Whitlock watched Gentry disappear up the snowy stone staircase, and he did not follow. His quarry was highly skilled, and he was conducting an SDR, a surveillance detection run. He would begin a complicated ballet of subterfuge, ducking into shops, leaving through random exits, turning in different directions and generally making himself impossible to follow without his tail losing him or revealing himself. Dead Eye could stick behind a lot of seasoned pros as they carried out SDRs and remain invisible doing so. But not Court. Russ knew the only way to keep the Gray Man in sight was to get close to him and stick like glue, and if Russ did that, the Gray Man would immediately light on to the fact he was being followed.

And that would be that.

So Russ let him go. He returned to the Town Hall Square and purchased a cup of glogg from a kiosk, and he sipped it slowly while he stood, watching the shoppers move from stand to stand. Women pushed prams or pulled their children along behind them on sleds; men stood in small groups talking or walked hand in hand with their wives. He pulled a folded map out of his coat pocket and began studying it, orienting himself and determining where he'd last seen Court, walking up the steps. Russ decided he would pick out a high-probability choke point and head there to wait for his target to pass.

His phone chirped in his ear, just as it had every three or four hours during the past day. He had ignored all incoming calls since Bucharest, but he was ready to talk now. He tapped the receiver, opening the call and connecting it through his Bluetooth device.

"Go."

"This is Graveside." Lee Babbitt's code name was Graveside, and Whitlock recognized Babbitt's voice over the satellite connection, but there was a protocol to follow nonetheless.

"Say iden," Whitlock said while still looking over the map in his gloved hand and sipping his hot wine.

"Iden key eight, two, four, four, niner, seven, two, niner, three."

"Iden confirmed. This is Dead Eye. Iden four, eight, one, oh, six, oh, five, two, oh."

"Identity confirmed. Hello, Russell." Babbitt's voice was taciturn, but Whitlock imagined his employer must be furious with him for going off on his own script over the past thirty hours.

"Hi, Lee."

Babbitt was all business. "I trust you got the data we pushed about the underway assault last night?"

"Dry hole." Russ said it flatly.

"Yes, but I think we're back on track. My analysts went through several hours of sat feeds. They picked up a vessel fitting the description of the one described by the *Polaris*'s captain. It docked in Tallinn, Estonia, forty minutes ago. I need you to head to Tallinn and we'll update you as soon as we can get more intel to pinpoint the target."

Whitlock sipped his glogg and began walking, still studying the map in his hand. He headed out of the square and toward Castle Hill, his boots crunching the snow. "A step ahead of you, boss. I'm on scene."

There was a pause on Babbitt's end. Finally, he replied, "You are in Tallinn?"

"Affirmative."

"What are you doing?"

"I am conducting surveillance on the target."

Whitlock knew that would take a moment to sink in. He took another sip of his glogg and walked.

"You have eyes on Gentry?"

"I tracked him from the port. He's conducting an SDR at present, which I expect to continue well into the afternoon. I've pulled back from him, but I'm not far behind."

There was another pause that lasted precisely as long as Whitlock expected. He imagined what would be running through Babbitt's mind. Excitement tempered with no small measure of confusion and even suspicion, but Babbitt was an exec, which meant, to Whitlock, that more than anything Babbitt's brain would be focusing on concocting a way to show that he remained in control of a situation he clearly did not understand.

On cue the man in Washington asked, "How did you know he would go to Estonia?"

Whitlock took another sip of the mulled wine. He luxuriated in the flavor, just as he savored the explanation of his accomplishment. "I solved the equation."

"The equation?"

"Yes. I determined what his best course of action would be, taking into account all of his training. I decided he wasn't going to sit on that boat for two days for reasons of PERSEC. I knew he'd get off somehow, and I figured he'd do it as soon as it got dark, which meant he'd be closest to Tallinn to the south or Helsinki to the north. He could have gone either direction, but I leaned toward Tallinn. He doesn't speak Estonian, but he knows Russian, and you can get by in Estonia in Russian. Less easily so in Finland." Whitlock added, "And I knew he wasn't going back to Russia; that was a given."

Babbitt asked, "What's keeping him from leaving Tallinn immediately?"

"He will like it here. He'll see the crowds, the tourists, the negligible police presence, the abundance of little places to sleep and eat, the plentiful transport options out of town via rail, road, and sea, and he'll park his ass right here for a couple of days. That's what I'd do, so that's what he'll do."

Whitlock polished off the rest of his hot glogg with a long gulp and crushed the cup in his gloved hand, throwing it in a can on the street corner. He arrived at a staircase that would take him up the hill through a pedestrian tunnel, and he began ascending.

Babbitt said, "I'll have Trestle moved into the area. They can fly over from Helsinki and be there before Jumper can move up from Berlin."

Whitlock said, "Do what you have to do, but keep them far back out of the way until I call them to the target. Gray Man will find a place to stay tonight, and I'll find it. There is no reason to bring Trestle and his boys in too close. I've got everything under control."

"Very well."

"Of course," Russ added, "if you like, I can just go ahead and take care of this. No sense in spinning everyone up. I'll do it myself."

Babbitt responded in a stern voice. "You are *not* to take him down on your own. The word from the Russians is Gentry killed eight men at Sid's house. Wounded several more. As impressive as that is, there were fifty-some-odd armed personnel on the property."

Russ sighed and made sure Babbitt heard it through the satellite connection. "I understand. I'll just keep tabs on the target and provide the strike team whatever support they require. Trestle will do the deed."

"Good." And then, "If you are waiting for me to say I am impressed with your ability to discern his every move, I am."

"Gentry is easy for me to read. He and I are one and the same."

Lee seemed confused by the remark, and he had no direct response. Instead he said, "I'll put you in touch with Trestle Actual when he gets to Tallinn."

"Roger that."

Now Babbitt's tone turned fatherly. "Obviously your handlers here would like a little more communication from you, but I'm not going to read you the riot act. I know you are accustomed to a certain amount of operational flexibility, and I can respect that."

"But?"

"But the one thing I will not be flexible with is the

takedown. That *will* be done by the direct action team. I want you out of the way when the time comes."

"Message received. I'll help Trestle get into position, and then I'll get out of the way."

Babbitt let Dead Eye's compliant comment hang for a moment. Finally he said, "Very well. Graveside out."

ELEVEN

Court walked the streets of Tallinn for hours, then spent another hour shopping for a hotel that suited a laundry list of needs. The one he settled on was a three-story stone building on Kooli Street built into a long row of buildings, all running along the fifteenth-century city wall that partially circled the Old Town. Court's tiny room was cold and damp due to the fact that it shared a stone wall with the town's ancient battlements. The room did not, however, have much else going for it. Just a bed on a low platform off the floor, a tiny desk, a toilet, and a small window that looked through the stone wall and out to a park to the north.

But the room was perfect for him; it was at the end of a hall full of creaky floorboards, and he knew if he was attacked, he would hear anyone approaching, and he could quickly get out the window and descend to the ground, using the rope he'd already tied to the leg of his twin bed and stashed under it.

He took a long hot shower down the hall, soaking his bruises and sore joints picked up from slamming his body around Sidorenko's property. After he redressed himself and put his boots back on, he packed his backpack up with all his belongings and secured his heavy coat between the straps. When Court was operational, his training taught him to sleep with his clothes on and keep everything he owned ready to snatch and run if he had to bug out at a moment's notice. And since Court was virtually always operational, he had been living this way for years.

He sat at the little desk in the room and ate a can of beans and a tin of salmon he'd bought at a market during his SDR, washing it down with a large bottle of A. Le Coq, the local beer. He would have preferred heading out to a little bar for a drink and a hot meal, but he liked to take a day or two in a new place before venturing out. This first night he would remain in his room, listening to the sounds of the hotel, getting a feel for the normal action around him.

He sat on the bed and turned the TV on to CNN. There was no news about the action near St. Petersburg, but that was no surprise. Mob shootouts in Russia only received international coverage if there was gripping video to play along with the reportage, and although Gentry assumed there were CCTV cameras all over Sid's place, he was equally certain that whoever was running Sid's *Bratva* now would have no interest in releasing that video to the public.

Court flipped through the channels as he lay in bed. He hoped to relax now; this was his first real downtime in weeks.

It felt good to get the Russian mafia off his ass; it let him concentrate on the main threat to him. The United States of America. For five years Court had been on the run from the CIA after a shoot-on-sight order was placed on him by his Langley masters. He did not know why they wanted him dead; he only knew they had sent wave after wave of men after him, and he did not expect that to change any time soon.

The CIA's manhunt for him had kept him out of the USA for the past half decade, living off the net, in the third world mostly, taking contracts for hire to fund his run. He'd worked for a string of handlers and benefactors over the years, from a venerable British spymaster who'd double-crossed him, to Sid, the Russian mobster whom Court had double-crossed and now killed. He'd also double-crossed a Mexican drug cartel boss along the way.

Court had developed a habit of subverting the goals of the men who paid him in order to achieve a greater good.

Gentry didn't feel bad about fucking over his employer when his employer was scum of the earth. But achieving these little victories had never been his ultimate goal. Court wanted, more than anything else in this world, to return to the USA. To be free of the CIA's shoot-on-sight sanction.

But for now he was a man without a country, an expatriate assassin for hire.

He flipped channels on the television in the dark, found a French comedy, and despite the persistent worries hanging heavily over him, he started to laugh at the absurdity of the story.

Outside gentle snowflakes began drifting in the breeze, and two floors below him, another solitary traveler entered the tiny lobby of the hotel.

———————

It took hours of hunting, but Russ Whitlock hit pay dirt on his fourth try.

At one hotel he had trouble getting information about the other guests, so he went ahead and rented a room, then learned from the innkeeper that he was the first new guest of the day. He went up to his room, unmade the bed, and then immediately slipped away out the back. At the second location he learned the only other guests were a group of Asians in town for a boat show, so he politely demurred at the nightly rate, making his apologies and leaving before the woman behind the counter could offer a negotiated price.

A third location also turned into a dry hole.

It was dark by the time he found the fourth hotel that had everything he would look for if he were the man on the run after an op. It was in the Old Town, the touristy part of the city, which meant a steady influx of foreigners and strangers, but it was small and out of the way at the northern tip of the quarter, which meant it was quiet enough at night, and anyone entering the building might be noticed.

The windows in front overlooked an open parking lot that was surrounded on three sides by other buildings, making a small square open space in front of the hotel that amplified the echoes of approaching vehicles and shouted voices.

He walked around back to find a park, and here he saw that the wood-and-stone building was built along the wall that had surrounded this part of the town for six centuries. A large circular stone tower, peaked with a conical wooden roof, was attached to it, and there were windows in the stone wall that must have led to the hotel rooms in the back of the building.

Yeah, Russ thought. *This looks right.*

He entered the lobby, asked the girl behind the desk for a room, and then looked down at the ledger.

Someone had taken room 301 just an hour earlier. Russ saw the signature, just a scratch of a pen on a line. He did not expect it to say *Court Gentry* and it did not, but the timing was right. He was sure it was his man.

The girl wanted to put him on the third floor as well, but he told her he had hurt his knee falling on the ice and asked if she had anything lower. She complied with a sympathetic smile, giving him room 201, directly below his target.

He paid in euros for three nights; she asked to see his passport and he slipped it out confidently. Russ knew his paperwork was solid, thanks to the document people at Townsend. Their special relationship with the CIA allowed Townsend personnel to operate with credentials that came directly from a program the Agency operated with the Department of State.

Whitlock, unlike Gentry, could go wherever he wanted in the world, and he knew his credos would hold up to scrutiny.

After heading upstairs and dropping his backpack, he walked around the hotel for several minutes more to take a mental picture of the layout of the building. He then zipped up his coat and returned outside into the cold air. Snow fell steadily now, blowing in the breeze under an overcast sky. He entered the neighboring buildings, still creating a mental map of his surroundings. Then he moved around back to the park that ran along the city wall and determined which window corresponded to Gentry's room. Once finished with his recon, he headed back to the town square for dinner.

He called in to Townsend, reported that he had located the target, and asked to be put in touch with the leader of the strike team as soon as he arrived.

Just south of Old Town he enjoyed a meal of elk stew and a bottle of red wine; he ate and drank slowly, sitting alone in a dark corner of the restaurant. While he dined he used his smart phone to study the greater neighborhood around his new hotel, adding a bird's-eye-view perspective to the area he had seen with his eyes. When he had completed this task, he pulled up a map of the country and traced several routes along train lines and highways that would get him out of town quickly and easily.

A call came through his headset when he was almost finished with his meal.

"Go," he said, speaking softly.

"Trestle Actual here."

"Say iden," Russ instructed, and then he picked his last bite of soda bread off his plate, dipping it in the elk stew before popping it in his mouth.

"Iden key, niner, three, three, oh, eight, seven, two, five, niner."

"Confirmed. Dead Eye here. Iden number four, eight, one, oh, six, oh, five, two, oh."

"I'm at the airport. Will be in the AO in an hour. Have you located the target?"

"Of course I have."

"All right. We can meet at twenty-two hundred."

Russ pulled his paper map of the city from his pocket and looked it over for a few seconds. "Open your map. You'll need to write this down."

TWELVE

Whitlock walked alone with his hands in his pockets and his head down, making his way through a steady snow shower across Freedom Square, a large plaza illuminated by the floodlights of St. John's Church. Light traffic rumbled by on the streets, but there were few pedestrians passing through the square or walking along the sidewalks at this time of night.

He crossed the street and entered a park, left the path, and walked through the trees, trudging up a hill, his boots gripping the frozen ground below the fresh snowfall. He saw no one around save for the light traffic on Falgi Tee and a few people waiting at a bus stop at the edge of the park. He gave them a wide berth and moved deeper into the woods, finally making his way to a ring of park benches on the top of a little hill.

He stood by a bench, waiting in the cold, watching his

breath fog the air in the faint light from the street that reached this deep into the park. The sounds of millions of snowflakes hitting the ground made a noise like soft static.

Whitlock waited a few seconds to be polite, then cleared his throat. "Where are the rest of you?"

There was no answer.

With a sigh he added, "I don't have a tail. Cut the crap."

After a few more seconds a voice in the trees behind him said, "No one likes a show-off, Russ." Soon the crunching of three pairs of boots came from behind as well, just audible over the snowfall. Russ turned to face three men, all in their thirties, all wearing high-tech winter gear.

The same man who'd spoken before said, "We flew in. The rest of the team is coming over water with our equipment. They will be in the city by oh two hundred." He stuck out a hand. "How's it going, Russ?"

"Nick," Whitlock said, and he nodded to the other two.

Nick was Trestle Actual, team leader of Trestle. Russ had worked with all the strike teams involved in the Gentry operation in his year working for Townsend. To Whitlock's thinking, all the men were excellent shooters and door kickers, but he knew they could not spend any time at all in Court Gentry's area of operations without Court picking up their scent. These guys weren't low profile. They wore Oakley specs and Woolrich Elite pants and G-Shock watches and Salomon boots, efficient gear for combat ops, but too high profile for Russ's tastes. Russ knew that even though Nick and his dudes could double-tap Court's brain pan as well as anybody else on the planet, Court would see these guys coming a mile away if Russ wasn't there to set the whole op up first.

Whitlock grabbed a pen and a notepad from one of the Trestle men and then took a knee in the snow. Under the beam of a tactical flashlight he drew a quick rendition of the hotel, indicating the exits, stairwells, and Gentry's room at the end of the hall on the third floor. The diagram was passed around among the three men standing in the snow, and they looked it over.

"What about access to the roof?" Trestle Actual asked.

"I scouted the third floor and the adjacent properties. No way upstairs from the hallway at all. The attic is space that belongs to the apartment building next door, not part of the hotel."

"You're certain?"

Russ nodded. "No access above the third floor of the hotel without blasting a hole in the ceiling."

Trestle Actual made a note on his own pad.

Russ added, "One other thing. That hallway outside the target's door is creaky as hell. Old loose floorboards. Suggest you start the assault from back at the stairs, just up the hall from the target's room, because there is no way you can hit that door without him hearing you coming. Just move dynamically up the hall and take the door down."

"Understood."

Russ looked around at the snow. It was blowing around now; it had picked up even since he'd arrived in the park. "You're going to have a problem with this weather if he makes it outside."

"Roger that," said Nick. "Latest meteorological report says we'll be in a blizzard by oh three hundred. We won't get UAV support tonight. We didn't even bother to bring the team over with us from Finland."

"You want to stand down till the weather clears?"

"Negative. We can work around a little snow. I'll send four men to his room. Distribute the rest downstairs in case he tries to squirt."

Russ said, "I'll stay in the stairwell. Cut off his escape if he makes it past your team."

Trestle Actual shook his head. "Negative. Babbitt wants you off the X."

"We don't have to tell him, do we? You will have blizzard conditions outside. All Court has to do is make it out a door or window and your op is going to go tits up."

"Babbitt wants—"

Russ said, "I don't give a shit what Babbitt wants. *You* are the onsite commander. It's your call. You'll take the heat if you fail. Be flexible about this, man. Babbitt's in the rear with the gear; we do what we have to do in the field."

Nick would not relent. "I don't want you in the way." He pointed his finger in Whitlock's face. "That's fucking final."

Whitlock shrugged. "It's your call, dude. Just trying to help."

Nick added, "Relax, Dead Eye. Gentry's not going to squeeze by us. We'll lay waste to his room, put his ass down right there."

———

Lennart Meri Tallinn Airport is no bustling airport compared to the major air transit hubs of Europe, but this Tuesday morning, at three A.M., in a full-on snowstorm, there was virtually no activity in the outer hangars northeast of the end of runway 26, some half mile from the main terminal.

Virtually no activity.

One small hangar did have a few lights on, and a large portable fan heater blasted warm air across the floor. A Gulfstream 200 was parked in the center of the space, still wet from its flight over from Helsinki and its long wait on the tarmac in the customs clearance portion of the airport. Next to the G-200, a white twelve-passenger van sat parked facing the exit.

Eight men also occupied the small hangar; some sat on trunks and loaded weapons, others affixed knee and elbow pads to their bodies, and one man stood near the closed hangar doors, pacing back and forth, frustrated in his attempt to get a signal from his phone to bounce off a satellite somewhere up through the thick soup of clouds.

Their makeshift staging area was far away from security and customs, but they prepared themselves as quickly as possible, because they knew their luck could not last. Some airport rent-a-cop might get curious or some ramp agent might come looking for a place to sneak a quick nap, and their activities here would be discovered.

The team prepped with extreme efficiency; they'd been doing this sort of thing for years. Each man had his primary, the HK MP7 PDW, or personal defense weapon. It was built for close-quarters battle, as it was both more powerful than a submachine gun and less bulky than an assault rifle.

They also carried SIG Sauer nine-millimeter pistols on their hips, Peltor ComTac II radio headsets under their helmets, and light Kevlar body armor across their chests and backs. They had the option of wearing full SAPI (Small Arms Protective Insert) plates made of high-tech ceramic that would stop a rifle round, but all their intelligence had led them to believe that their target was not carrying a rifle with him. The Kevlar would stop any handgun round, so it would do for this evening's operation.

The men checked their watches, actuated the laser sights and flashlights on their guns to test them, and finished double-checking their Velcro pouches to make sure everything they needed was in place.

Trestle Actual finally got through to Townsend House, though he had to leave the hangar and stand in the snow to get a signal. It took a moment for the two-way ID check, but just like the preparation of their equipment for tonight's operation, both Trestle Actual and the recipient of his call had executed enough ID checks to make them second nature and correspondingly fast.

Lee Babbitt, code name Graveside, knew better than to ask the team leader of his strike force a lot of unnecessary questions. Babbitt knew Nick considered him to be an REMF, a rear-echelon motherfucker, and the last thing Babbitt wanted to do was give any of his front-line men the impression that he was micromanaging his shooters from four thousand miles away. So instead of asking questions, he used these quick briefs before missions to provide last-minute intel to his operators in the field. "Weather isn't going to get much better till midmorning. Might slack off a little before dawn, but the front is basically stalled right over the Baltic, so you'll just have to contend with the snow. We'll have no overhead viz on you."

Nick's gear and helmet were already covered in white from standing outside the hangar. "Understood."

"You've spoken to Dead Eye?"

"Met with him a few hours ago. He's a squirrelly motherfucker, isn't he?"

"He's a singleton," replied Babbitt, as if that explained everything.

"He's got a room one floor below the target, he can hear it when Gray Man moves around, and he'll let us know if there is any change of disposition."

"Dead Eye wanted to do the action himself."

"Yeah," said Nick. "He made that clear. I told him to sit his ass down in his room and stay the hell out of our way."

"Good." Babbitt paused a moment. Cleared his throat. "We end Gentry tonight, got it?"

"Yes, sir."

"We had hoped to do this on the ship. Not in an urban environment. Less messy that way."

"Roger that. We'll keep it contained."

Babbitt's voice took a lower, graver tone, the change noticeable even over the crackling sat phone. "Do that, but know *this*. Collateral damage, in this very special case, will be understood as a necessary evil. Mr. Gentry is a clear and present danger to the United States of America. We cannot and we will not forfeit this opportunity to eliminate him."

Nick had been briefed on this, of course. This was no kill/capture mission. This was get in, shoot the son of a bitch till he was flat on his back, shoot the son of a bitch some more, then get out. If some locals got in the way, then, Nick understood, he was to shoot his way through them to get to his target.

Nick, and the other seven men of Trestle, were all good with that.

"Got it," he replied. It was no small thing to steel oneself to shoot noncombatants, but Nick had done it before, and Nick knew Townsend Government Services had been brought into this hunt not because they were saints, but because they got shit done.

Babbitt added, "When it's over, you get pictures, that's mandatory, but you leave the body, get back to the airport, and get out of there. If the weather is below minimums, just exfiltrate overland and we'll get you extracted ASAP."

"Yes, sir."

"Good luck, Nick. Remember . . . For America."

Now there was a pause on Nick's side of the conversation. "You know . . . if you ever wanted to tell me what this prick did to earn his shoot-on-sight sanction . . . now *would* be the time."

Babbitt replied tersely, "Just do your duty. Graveside out."

Nick ended the call and stowed his sat phone. As he stepped back into the hangar, Trestle Two came up to him; he'd already put on his helmet and goggles, he was head-to-toe in black ballistic gear, and his MP7 PDW hung straight down from his chest. In his hands he carried Trestle Actual's primary weapon. "We're ready," he said, and he held out the HK.

Nick took the gun. "Good."

"I don't suppose Graveside finally came through and told you what this is all about?"

Nick shrugged now, dropping the sling over his head and positioning the PDW on his chest. "Same as ever. Management doesn't tell labor anything except the rah-rah shit. 'Do your duty, God and country, Gentry is a clear and present danger.'"

Trestle Two rolled his eyes and made a gesture like he was performing a hand job.

Nick finished adjusting his gear on his chest. Normally he would have laughed, but his game face was on now. He looked up to his second in command. "It's all good. Gentry did something to make himself an enemy of the state. We're the state. Well . . . sort of. Close enough, anyhow." He smiled now. "Let's go kill that miserable fuck."

"Yeah, let's."

The two men headed back to join the others loading into the van.

THIRTEEN

Court lay awake, listening to the wind whipping fine grainlike snow against the window of his tiny third-floor room. He glanced at his watch and saw it was nearly four A.M., and as near as he could tell from his view out the window, there was one hell of a storm raging outside.

He wanted to sleep; he'd dozed off and on for hours, but he couldn't seem to shut off his mind. He often took a few days to decompress after an action, and this was no different. The good result of the Sidorenko hit notwithstanding, he found himself stressing, reliving everything that happened.

Maybe it was the kid that was getting to him. The little boy he'd run into in the hallway of the mansion. Court had done his best to scare the living shit out of him to make sure he would go back into his room and hide. He'd probably saved the boy's life; had he been wandering the dark hallways when the shooting started he could easily imagine one of the drugged-up gun-wielding skinheads on the property spooking at the movement and shooting the boy dead.

Yes, Court acknowledged, he'd done the right thing, in the short term anyhow. But long term?

Would the boy have nightmares about his encounter with the monster who broke into his house in the dead of night and killed his uncle? Surely he would put together that a rival had sent an assassin to the house, and the assassin, while obviously talented, was no ghost. No monster.

Or was he?

Court stared out the window. *What are you, Gentry?*

Court was known by many names. His given name, of course, but almost no one referred to him by that anymore. His mom died when he was young, he hadn't spoken to his dad in years, and he'd lost his brother a few years earlier.

At the CIA he had first been known as Violator, a code name he'd been given when he was admitted into AADP, the Autonomous Asset Development Program, a school of sorts in Harvey Point, North Carolina, where lost-boy renegade-types were taken in and taught how to channel their wild side into doing dirty jobs for the United States of America.

After 9/11, Court was pulled out of solo work and folded into a tip-of-the-spear unit called Golf Sierra, jokingly referred to as the Goon Squad, an anti-terror task force in the CIA's Special Activities Division, and during those years Violator became Sierra Six, the low man in the six-member team. He spent his days on snatch-and-grab missions, rendering America's greatest enemies to black sites for interrogation, or shooting them in the head when so ordered.

And then suddenly—extraordinarily suddenly, as a matter of fact—he was no longer Sierra Six, no longer part of the team. The Goon Squad turned on him; clearly they'd been ordered to kill him.

But Sierra Six retained enough of his training as Violator to single-handedly take down his entire team, one against five. It also marked the end of his life in the USA. He left the country a day later, running to stay ahead of the hunters on his trail.

To survive on the lam from the most powerful nation on earth, Court, Violator, Sierra Six, became the Gray Man, an assassin for hire, executing private contract killings only against those he deemed worthy of capital punishment for their crimes. In five years he had eliminated terrorists, drug lords, mafia leaders, despots, and even other assassins.

His goal, through the years living abroad and off the net, had always been to win his way back to the United States. While his one attempt at reconciliation with the CIA had ended poorly, on the banks of the Red Sea with a former friend and Special Activities Division operative declaring his intent to chase him to the ends of the earth, Court had not given up hope that somehow, someday, he would be allowed back into the USA, either into the open arms of the CIA or at least with their grudging approval.

But the years were adding up, and his relationship with Langley had not improved.

And there was something else. He'd spent the last months preparing for the Sidorenko hit, putting all of his efforts into this task to the extent that he had thought of little else. Now that it was over, something had entered the forefront of his consciousness that he could no longer avoid thinking about. His relationships with nefarious personalities like Sidorenko had created so many new enemies for him to deal with, the CIA situation had become a backburner problem for him. His killing of Sid had been necessary, but now that it was done, it felt like time wasted.

There were so many others out there who wanted him dead. A French oil concern he'd worked against, and then worked for, now held a grudge because of the manner in which they had parted ways.

A Mexican cartel boss he'd worked for, then worked against, had recently placed a video on YouTube. In it, Constantino Madrigal, one of the most wanted men on earth, addressed the camera with his face all but obscured by a cowboy hat and a bandanna.

He said, "This message is to José, the gringo *pistolero*. Your amigos, the Cowboys, have some advice for you. Don't buy any green bananas."

Madrigal ended the video with a raspy laugh and a wave of his gold-plated AK-47.

The first appearance of Madrigal on camera in years made the international press, and Court had caught the video while living in his safe house in Moscow, prepping for the Sidorenko operation. Though the clip was cryptic to everyone else, Court got the message. He had called himself José in Mexico, and the reference to green bananas was clear.

In Moscow, Court triaged this problem well behind the Sidorenko situation. He was in Russia, after all, and Sid was a bigger fish to fry than a Mexican drug lord.

But now Sid was dead, and Court wondered how much trouble Madrigal, or the French energy company LaurentGroup, could still make for him.

All the bad guys out there on his ass were really cutting into his free time.

Court knew the only way around this problem, long term, was to stop making deals with these devils. He knew he had to get out of the industry, to stop working for handlers he could not trust and accepting patronage from those who had as much blood on their hands as the evil men he targeted.

Court knew he had to, somehow, cease his life as the Gray Man.

It seemed as if the thought had just come to him, but he realized after a moment of reflection he had been moving toward this line of thinking for some time.

What good had he done in the past five years? There were still evil multinationals, still despots in Africa, still thriving brotherhoods in Russia, still calamitous drug wars in Mexico.

Court got older, more beaten and battered and shell-shocked and defeated, but the world around him kept turning, unchanged and unimproved.

The only thing he'd managed to accomplish was stay alive, and if he kept up this lifestyle, he knew it was only a matter of time before he pissed away this tiny victory by getting his ass killed, dead in a jungle in Asia or a dirty back alley in Europe or a putrid ditch in South America or, just maybe, a soulless hotel room in the Baltic.

The end would be ignominious and sudden.

Don't buy any green bananas, indeed.

As he lay there on the bed, he thought back to something Maurice, his principal trainer at AADP in Harvey Point, had said to him.

"The true soldier fights not because he hates what is in front of him, but because he loves what is behind him." It was a Chesterton quote, and at the time Court was a nineteen-year-old kid, an aimless and troubled young man who just happened to be incredible with a weapon in his hand. He did not understand the quote, so Maurice explained it this way: "If you are going to fight, do it *for* something you love. Do it for your country."

In the past five years Court had been a man without a country, and, for some reason he did not really understand, he seemed to keep seeking out new things to hate.

What am I doing? he asked himself. *That* was no long-term plan. He wasn't making a difference, it had ceased to provide sufficient motivation, and Court just did not want to *fucking* do it anymore.

He made a decision then and there. He would lie low here in Tallinn for a couple of days, then push off, find a quiet place where he could do something productive other than kill, do something other than spin his wheels until the inevitable happened.

Court forced himself to focus on the snow blowing against the window, trying to put greater thoughts out of his mind and fall back asleep.

———

Whitlock sat at the desk in his little room, thinking about the man directly above him.

On the desk in front of him was a Glock 19 pistol and

two extra fifteen-round magazines. Russ was not a Glock man himself, but he had reason to carry one tonight. Next to his pistol lay his smart phone and his backpack. And next to these, an open half-liter and half-consumed bottle of A. Le Coq beer dripped a ring of sweat on the desk.

He checked the time and saw that it was four A.M. He reached into a pocket of his bag, then pulled out a small white medicine bottle. From this he fished out two pills. They were Adderall, a psychostimulant, an amphetamine. He downed the pills with a long swig of the A. Le Coq.

The Bluetooth headset in his ear chirped. He touched a finger to it.

"Go."

It was Trestle Actual, and he initiated the identity check. When this was complete he asked, "Where are you?"

"I'm in room 201. The target is still upstairs, directly above. He used the toilet at oh two hundred, then went back to bed. He hasn't moved since."

"Understood."

"You sure I can't help?"

"I'm not telling you again. You do *not* leave that room."

Whitlock sighed. "Fine. I'm packed and ready to exfil as soon as you give me the all clear."

"Good. I'll be with the breach team. We hit in five mikes. I'll notify you when it is over and safe for you to leave."

"Roger that. Good luck." Russ disconnected the call.

As soon as the conversation ended, Russ Whitlock began moving. He unzipped his backpack, and from it he pulled a tiny pinhole camera with a wireless radio attached to it. The entire device was no larger than a matchbook, and it had an adhesive puttylike backing. He stuck it on the wall by the desk to test its hold, then pulled it off again. He picked up his smart phone and opened an app on it. In seconds the screen on his phone was displaying the image from the pinhole camera. He then pocketed both devices.

Russ stood up from the desk, slipped his gun into a holster inside the waistband on the right side of his jeans, the two extra magazines into a mag carrier inside the waistband on the left, and then he put on his black coat. He slung his backpack over his shoulder, chugged the rest of the beer, then dropped the empty bottle into a pocket on the outside of the pack. Finally, he put his hand on the door latch and paused.

Russ would not be following Trestle's instructions. He would not sit quietly in his room. His upcoming course of action had been decided by Russ himself, and he was not following the orders of his company. He had concocted his plan, labored over every detail, refined and revised it as time went on.

And then he put the plan on hold, waiting for the day Townsend Government Services would lead him to the most infamous assassin on the planet.

The Gray Man.

Russ was out for the biggest game on earth, the hardest target.

With a long breath and a determined mind-set helped on by the Adderall, he opened the door and exited his room, leaving not a trace behind.

Gentry had not fallen back to sleep; he lay fully clothed and faceup, still listening to the whipping snow on the window. But his head jolted from his pillow when the sound of footsteps in the hallway outside caught his attention. The footsteps weren't tentative, but they slowed a little as they approached his door, and Court found their cadence unnatural and suspicious. His right hand shot out and wrapped around the cool plastic grip of his Glock 19 as he sat up.

The footfalls stopped. Court aimed his gun at the door, ready to open fire.

There was a knock, and Court started moving, low across the hardwood, moving close to the walls to minimize the creaking of the floorboards. As he passed the single window in the tiny room, he glanced out across the park. The snow was heavy and he couldn't see past it to the ground.

Another knock. This time it was louder, faster.

Shit. Another phrase oft uttered by his trainer Maurice popped into his head. "Nothing good ever happens at three A.M."

It was four now, but the concept was no less valid.

In German Court called out, *"Wer ist da?" Who is there?*

Russ Whitlock stood in front of the door to room 301, his hands empty and high over his head to show he posed no threat. He did not speak German, and he did not know Court Gentry's voice. He faced the door in the dimly lit hall, wondering suddenly if he had made a mistake. He thought quickly back to all the intel on Court he'd studied over the past months. *Language skill: Russian good, Spanish very good, French good, German fair.*

Yep. Court spoke German.

Russ replied in English, "Court. I am a friend. And I am alone. I need to talk to you. It is *extremely* important."

There was a pause. *"Wer ist da?"* the man on the other side of the door repeated.

Russ leaned close to the door, still keeping his hands up in case the door opened. "There is no time to fuck around, Violator. I'm on your side. You have to trust me."

After a moment he heard the lock retracting, and he saw the latch turn. The door creaked open and Russ kept his hands raised, displaying his empty palms.

The chain caught the door when it opened three inches. It was dark inside. Russ peered in, could see faint light coming from the window, and he could tell that whoever had opened the door had stepped to the side.

"Who are you?" It was English now. The voice came from behind the wall on Whitlock's right, not from behind the door.

Whitlock looked back over his shoulder quickly, then said, "Right now, I'm the guy holding your life in his hands."

From the darkness came the response. "And right now, *I'm* the guy pointing a gun at your dick."

Whitlock cocked his head, then looked down. He saw it now, the square tip of a Glock pistol, low in the dark,

held by a hand that disappeared around the side of the
doorjamb. He looked into the room farther, searching
for a mirror or some other reflective surface that Gentry
could be using to target him while keeping himself out
of the line of fire. He saw nothing, but he knew the
lights of the hallway had him well silhouetted.

He said, "My name is Russ. It looks like you and me
better make friends."

"Or you could just back the fuck up and leave."

Russ said, "You're going to find this hard to believe,
but I'm not your biggest problem."

A figure stepped into the middle of the room from
behind the wall. In his hand the gun was raised now,
level with Russ's chest. "I'm listening."

Russ found himself face-to-face with the Gray Man.
He'd thought of this moment for months. He knew his
entire future depended on the success of this conversation. "Can I come in?"

"No."

"I've got something you need to see. I'm reaching
into my right coat pocket and pulling out my cell phone.
I'll move slowly."

"Don't move at all," Court ordered, then took a step
forward, unhooked the chain from the door and opened
it, reached into Whitlock's coat, and pulled out the
phone. He took a single step back from the doorway.

"Look at the screen," Russ instructed.

Court did as instructed, keeping his gun trained on
the stranger's chest.

It was an image from a camera; it looked like the stairwell here in the hotel. From the odd angle and the

marginal quality of the picture, Court imagined the man in front of him must have set up his own mini surveillance cam high in the stairwell, and Court was now viewing a live feed. At first there was no movement, but then four men in black came into view, floating up the stairs, slowly and carefully in a tactical formation. They held their short-barreled weapons high, pointed higher in the stairwell. In under a second Gentry registered their guns, their body armor, their communications gear.

Court's eyes flashed up, peering past his gun's front sight and into the eyes of the man in the doorway. He did not speak.

Whitlock broke the stillness, quickly but softly. He was all business. "Eight in total. Four up, four down." And then he added, his tone grave, "They've got skills, dude."

"Fuck."

Russ spoke in a whisper now. "Don't worry, Violator. We'll get through this together."

FOURTEEN

Gentry scanned the face of the man in front of him. He was roughly the same age as Gentry himself, though his features appeared more chiseled and wind-worn than Court imagined his own to be. He wore a beard similar to Gentry's; his brown hair was only a shade lighter than Court's and Russ wore it a little shorter than Court wore his, but the two men appeared to be virtually the same height and build.

From the way he talked and an air about him Court picked up from years of experience, Court identified the man as a CIA asset, a tier-one spec ops operator, or some other brand of elite soldier or spook.

In short, to Gentry's way of thinking, this Russ guy was trouble.

But not as much trouble as the assholes coming up the stairs.

Court backpedaled to his pack, keeping his gun on the man in the hall. Without taking his eyes off the stranger, he slung his backpack over a shoulder. His coat was threaded through a strap on the outside, but he didn't stop to put it on. He glanced quickly outside the window overlooking the park, but again he could make out little save for the blowing snow and the darkness. He thought about his rope on the floor, considered using it to get to ground level, but if there were four men downstairs he thought it likely two of them would be at the back of the property, and he did not want to expose himself to them for the length of time it would take to climb down a rope.

No way. He was going to have to fight his way out of this with his new friend, whoever the hell he was.

"Okay," Court said. "You got a piece?"

Russ whispered, "Waistband."

"Don't reach for it," Court ordered, still weighing the dynamic situation. "Not yet. I need to think."

"Do what you want, chief. But I'd say we've got less than fifteen sec—"

The window to Gentry's left shattered. He turned to the sound and crouched at the same time, but he missed it; he did not see the small canister that penetrated the glass, banged against the far wall of the little room, and dropped, spinning to the floor in front of the bed, just behind him.

But Russ saw it. He turned his head away and shouted, "Nine-banger!" but it was too late to save Court.

It was a souped-up version of a flash-bang grenade, called a nine-banger, and in the space of three seconds nine two-hundred-decibel brain-hammering cracks battered the little room, along with nine brilliant flashes of light designed to disorient anyone in the vicinity. Court fell to his knees, dropped his pistol on the ground, and grabbed at his head. He'd shut his eyes before the first flash, but still the searing light had penetrated his eyelids and now he could barely see or hear.

Whitlock was fine, however; he had avoided the effects by turning away in the hallway. He drew his Glock from his hip and raised it at the stairwell. The first member of the Trestle team was just rounding the corner; only the suppressor of his HK was visible. Whitlock lined up his weapon and fired, striking the man between the eyes before he'd even fully turned into the hallway. He fell back, slamming into his three mates behind him, sending them all tumbling down the stairs.

Whitlock fired twice more up the hall to keep anyone in the stairwell from poking their head back out, and then he turned and grabbed Court by his black shirt, pulling him into a standing position and pushing him up against the wall. He retrieved Court's Glock from the floor and stuck it into his own belt. He then grabbed Gentry again and led him along with him as he advanced toward the stairwell, his gun out in front. He shot out the two hall lights; both bulbs exploded in showers of sparks and the hallway turned dark.

As Gentry's legs strengthened and he slowly regained his wits, Whitlock picked up the pace.

———

"Man down! Man down!" Trestle Actual shouted into his mic. He himself was on his back on the landing between the second and third floors. Trestle Three had been the first man into the hallway from the stairwell, but now he was on top of Nick; blood ran freely from his face and his goggles had a ragged hole in them, right between his eyes. Nick knew there wasn't a damn thing he could do for his man; all he *could* do was get himself and his two other teammates back in the fight.

He pushed Three to the side and started to climb back up to his feet.

Just then he saw movement at the top of the stairs. He lifted his weapon toward the movement but saw a quick series of muzzle flashes, moving left to right, as whoever was shooting crossed the stairwell in the hall.

He felt the slap of a handgun round on his Kevlar chest panel and sparks flew off his magazine stowed there. He dropped back to the floor of the landing. To his right and one step behind him, Trestle Six lurched backward with a grunt of surprise and stumbled back into the wall, ending up on the floor of the landing next to Three's body.

Trestle Actual returned fire at the movement above, but the shooter was gone.

"I've got two men down! Get me two more in here!" Nick shouted as he returned to his feet. He scrambled back up the stairs with Trestle Five, leaving Trestle Three dead and Trestle Six wounded on the landing.

———

Court felt himself being pulled along, his shirt yanked by the right arm and his weak legs shuffling as fast as possible below his body. He slammed into the wall hard, only after he hit he realized he'd been pushed there, and he saw that the man named Russ had deposited him here so he could turn and shoot at something in the hallway behind them.

Court processed the gunfire as distorted low thuds, more felt than heard, as his ears still rang from the effects of the nine-banger. His eyes were whited out in the center of his field of vision, so he had to turn his head to the side to see what the hell was happening.

With a quivering hand he reached down to his waistband to draw his gun, but it was not there.

"Hey!" he shouted at the stranger, but Russ grabbed him again, and again they started running up the hallway.

There was a T intersection in the hall, and the other man led Gentry to the right. Just as they turned the corner, jagged holes tore into the wall in the main hall, and through his ringing ears Court barely heard a gun behind them firing suppressed rounds.

Court was getting the feeling back in his body now, and his eyesight returned slowly. He arrived behind his new partner as Russ stopped at the end of the hall, then leapt up and grabbed hold of a chain attached to a door in the ceiling to the attic. He pulled down a folding staircase, then turned around and knelt in the hall, training his weapon back up the hallway.

"My gun!" Gentry shouted, louder than he had to, and Russ pulled Court's pistol from his pants and handed it over to him.

Russ fired a pair of shots up the corridor, then turned and moved up the attic stairs. Court covered him; he kept his blurred eyes locked on the corner and his shaky gun raised as Russ ascended the rickety and narrow wooden steps.

As Russ disappeared into the hole in the ceiling behind him, down at the end of the hall a man in a black helmet and goggles peered around the corner. Court aimed at the man's forehead and fired once, grazing him in the left shoulder and sending him scrambling back around to cover.

Whitlock was in the attic now, but he positioned himself over the hole. Facedown he hung out from the waist, hanging upside down from the corridor ceiling, directly above Gentry. His body faced the threat at the end of the hall, and he pointed his gun toward the T.

"Move!" he shouted, and Court turned and climbed the attic staircase now, covered by the man hanging upside down behind him.

Two men in black tactical gear shot across the hallway ahead, trying to make it to the other side of the T. Dead Eye opened up on them, his Glock snapped three times, and a round struck one of the men in the side of his head.

Court climbed up to the attic, then turned and stomped down on the rickety folding stairs, breaking one of the hinges that held it to its frame. He then stomped on the other hinge, and the staircase fell to the hallway floor. It was now useless as a way to get up into the attic from the hallway, but he knew it would not slow the attacking force for long.

"Let's go!" Russ said, and he grabbed Court by the collar again and pulled him along. While Russ reloaded his pistol they moved together through the long, narrow attic, holding their heads low as they ran to keep from bumping them on the bare support beams protruding from the sharply angled roof. Russ shouted into Gentry's ear to be heard. "This attic connects with the building next door. We can get back down to the street from there."

At this point Court realized he was just along for the ride. He stumbled across the low dark attic, following a stranger who seemed to know a surprising amount about not only the property, but the opposition, as well.

———————

Trestle Actual had taken a round through the top of his left shoulder before he'd been able to focus on the threat at the end of the hall, and the impact had spun him around and knocked him to the floor. Two more of his men came up the hall from the stairs just after he assessed his wound. They'd been at the front of the building, outside in the snowstorm, and snow now fell from their black body armor as they ran past him to take up a position on the other side of the T. Nick climbed back to his knee pads and faced the opening to the T intersection just in time to see two of his men cross the space in a sprint.

Trestle Eight took a gunshot wound to the right side of the head as he ran. His helmet jolted and blood sprayed from the left side of his forehead and splattered on the wall and he tumbled down, his forward momentum pitching him into Trestle Seven, who fell to the ground just clear of the intersection.

Trestle Actual crawled to the corner, went flat on the floor, and rolled out with his HK in front of him. Ahead in the hall he saw a middle-aged couple in pajamas stumbling out of a room and toward his position.

He aimed at them, ready to shoot them dead to get to his target, but his target was no longer in the hallway behind them.

Just behind them he heard a gunshot and saw a set of attic stairs on the floor. Dead Eye had been wrong. There *was* attic access here on the third floor. Trestle Actual doubted Court would try for the roof. The roof of the building was pitched at sixty degrees and covered in several inches of ice and wet slippery snow. There would be no way he could maintain his footing well enough to escape by running across it, and if he had rope all he could do was rappel down the side, where other members of Nick's team would be waiting for him.

Instead, Nick decided Gentry would try to make his way to an adjacent property by using the attic. There was a collection of private flats next door; Actual figured his target would try for those. Nick did not want to chase him through the attic; he knew that anyone climbing up through the hallway access would find themselves vulnerable and exposed to Gentry's weapon.

Into his headset he shouted, "Two and Four, breach the building to the east of this location, Nine Kooli Street. He'll be heading down the stairs from the attic."

"On the move!"

Two and Four were on the other side of the building in the park; they would have to make their way through the back door of the apartments. Trestle Actual himself leapt up to his feet and began running back to the stairwell, followed by Seven and Five.

FIFTEEN

Court followed Russ from the attic down a staircase and into a private flat. The occupant, a middle-aged woman, had hidden herself in her bathtub when the shooting began next door, but she did not peek out into the living room when the two came bursting into her flat from the attic.

Russ ran toward the front door of the room, but Gentry caught up with him. Shouting over the ringing in his ears, he asked, "Where are we going?"

"Staircase to street level."

"They're going to be waiting for us!"

"Unavoidable. We'll have to engage them."

Court shouted, "Let's take the roof!"

Russell shook his head. "Pitched slate, covered in snow and ice. We wouldn't make it fifty feet before we fell off."

Court looked around the apartment, still cocking his

head to see past his scorched pupils. "We need twenty feet of cording. More if we can get it quick. Lamp cables, extensions, phone wire, whatever." As he talked he yanked a banker's lamp off a desk and ripped the wire from the wall and from the lamp itself.

Whitlock started to protest, but he saw that Court seemed certain of his plan, so he grabbed a telephone and pulled the cord out of the back, then traced it back to where it attached to the wall. He removed the cord from the wall and turned his attention to a thick extension cord on the floor.

Court said, "We each get on one side of the peak of the roof. We support each other and move laterally. You get it?"

Russ got it. He nodded approvingly. "We act as each other's counterweight. Let's do it!"

In seconds they had a bundle of wires, strong enough to hold them both, some twenty feet in length. Court then ran to the window, opened it, and climbed out into the snowstorm. He held the wiring at one end, and Russ took hold at the other end. They each wrapped it around one of their wrists, and Court climbed out onto the snow-covered roof carefully. Snow and ice slid down on him as he grabbed on to the outside of the window to pull himself up, his fingers and knees stinging in the cold. He took hold of a satellite dish to get him to the peak of the roof, and behind him Russ slipped out the window and followed him up. Court slid down on the other side of the peak a few feet, and stood tentatively, leaning out, using the tension in the cord for balance. He shouted to Russ. "East or west?"

"East!" Russ shouted over the whipping wind.

Court did not respond; he only began moving eastward along the south side of the peaked roof. Russ felt the tugging, and he, on the north side of the roof, began moving along as well.

After a couple of tentative steps the two men began moving faster along opposite sides of the roof, their boots slipping on the snow and slick tile, but the cords between them gave them something to hold on to so they could remain upright while their bodies hung out away from the roof. The wires themselves dragged in the center along the peak as they moved, giving them stability. A chimney jutted from the peak, but Court and Russ closed the distance between each other by moving up, creating slack in the cords, and then together they flipped the wires up high and over the chimney. The wires dropped down on the other side and they returned the tension to the cabling to help them balance as they ran on.

Court slipped and fell to his knees suddenly and violently; he still had not completely regained his equilibrium after suffering the effects of the nine-banger. The cables lashed to his left arm kept him from sliding off the building. He quickly pushed himself back to his feet and continued on, squinting in the blowing snow.

———————

Trestle Actual had just made it into the apartment building entrance at Nine Kooli Street; Seven and Five remained directly behind him and Six was still staggering out of the hotel, wounded but alive, and heading for their van.

A door opened near the stairwell, just a few feet in front of the two Townsend operators. Trestle Actual flashed his weapon's tactical light on the movement, illuminating a man leaning out the doorway.

The man raised his hand to shield his eyes from the bright light. Nick fired at the quick movement, shooting the Estonian civilian through the chest with a three-round burst. The Estonian fell backward into his apartment, and even before he hit the floor all three Townsend men knew the victim was not their target. They heard noise inside the apartment, a woman's scream, and Five fired a burst at the noise, shutting up the wailing woman.

A voice came through their headsets. "Someone's on the roof!" It was Trestle Six, the injured man he'd sent to the van. "Moving east. I can't see shit in the storm, but he's knocking snow off the building."

"Use your damn light!" Nick shouted.

"The taclight is just reflecting off the snowfall!"

"Then fucking shoot! ID the body when he falls off the building!" Nick was already on his way back out through the lobby of the apartment building; Trestle Seven remained on his heels.

"Engaging!" Six shouted, and Actual heard the cyclic metallic thumping of a suppressed weapon outside.

Sparks exploded below and in front of Court on the slate tiles of the roof; he was under fire from a man at ground level.

Gentry looked back over his right shoulder; through the snow and ink-dark night he saw only muzzle flashes, back down in the parking lot in front of the hotel. He drew his pistol, reached, and, while running, fired twice at the flashes.

Another flicker of light from the same location told Court he'd missed. He stopped now, and with his left hand cinched to the wiring he reached back again with his right hand and fired three more carefully aimed shots.

As soon as he finished firing he felt an intense tug at his left shoulder. At first he thought he'd been hit, but as he tumbled forward onto the snow-covered roof he realized his abrupt stop had surprised Russ on the other side, and he'd obviously yanked the wires and fallen back ass first, his own shoulder no doubt wrenched by Gentry's sudden stop.

Court used the barrel of his Glock to help him back up to his feet, pushing off with it in the snow and struggling with the acute angle of the rooftop.

The flashes of gunfire from the parking lot stopped, and he felt confident he'd hit the man targeting him.

Court started to run forward again, glad to feel the tension leave his shoulder as Russ did the same on the far side of the rooftop.

This roof ended just feet from where they ran; they could barely see through the darkness and heavy snowfall, otherwise they would have had time to decide what to do. Instead the four-story drop just appeared and there was no time to stop on the icy surface; there was only time to rush forward, pick up speed, and then launch off the roof into the air.

Both men, lashed together at the wrists, kicked out over open ground; fifty feet below them was a cobblestone alley bathed in gaslights. Across the alley was a three-story wooden building; the pitched roof above it was as steep as the one they'd just leapt from.

They crashed onto the sheer three-story roof as one, Gentry on the right of the peak, Whitlock on the left. Both men splayed out flat, landing on the steeply angled surface, but again, the fact they were connected saved them and they did not slide off to the ground below.

The men were up again and moving in seconds.

———————

Trestle Actual ran along narrow Kooli Street, trying to get line of sight on the roof high above. Just behind him was Trestle Seven.

Five had headed back to the parking lot in front of the hotel to bring the van to pick up the team up the street. They all stayed in contact with Trestles Two and Four, who were now racing through the park on the opposite side of the buildings that ran along the old town wall. It was difficult for the Townsend operators to see anything high on the rooftop in the whipping blizzard, and the tactical lights hanging from the rails of their HK rifles were less than useless, as they only illuminated the whiteout conditions between themselves and any potential target.

As they neared the end of the block Trestle Seven shouted, "Got him!" and Nick looked back over his shoulder to see what his colleague was focusing on. Seven's eyes and the barrel of his MP7 pointed across the alleyway that separated the row of buildings next to them with another block of lower structures. Nick could not believe Gentry had managed to move that quickly along a sixty-degree roofline that must have been as slick as glass, but he, too, saw a figure ahead.

He and Seven both fired at the same time.

———————

Court and Russ had just dropped down off the peaked town wall and onto a roof that was not as steeply angled as the others; it had more packed snowfall frozen to it, several inches high and hanging over the street below, terminating in long icicles. When another burst of fire from the street blew out a window just below where he ran along the roof, Court looked down again and saw that two men had gained on him, and they were running in the narrow cobblestoned alleyway just below his position.

Court looked ahead through the blizzard at the next connected roof. It was less steeply angled than the others, and the snowfall here was a foot deep. He shouted over the storm, "Give me ten feet of slack!" Within a second he felt the wiring wrapped around his left hand lose tension, and he shouted, "Belay!"

Court leapt high in the air and came crashing down on the next roof on his back, and a massive block of white broke off and cascaded down the side like an avalanche. Court was held up by the cables connecting him to Russ on the other side of the apex, so he did not slide off the roof with the snow.

———————

Trestles Actual and Seven had been running below their target, and both men had just reloaded their MP7s and trained them back up above them when they heard Gentry yell something. They looked for their target in the heavy snowstorm, but instead they saw a huge foot-thick sheet of white falling from the roof, some twenty-five feet above their heads. The avalanche of packed precipitation was the size of an automobile, weighing several hundred pounds, and it dropped through the air, picking up velocity and power. Trestle Seven took the brunt of the avalanche, and Nick only caught a glimpse of the man before he was buried alive. Trestle Actual himself dove out of the way of the brunt of the mass of frozen precipitation, but his legs were momentarily buried under the pile.

———————

Russ Whitlock didn't have a clue what was going on on the other side of the building, but he had heard gunfire and Court's call for slack. He'd run up toward the crown of the roof, giving Court the freedom he'd asked for, and then he'd dropped to his knees to support him when Court called for the belay. Now Russ was back down where he'd started, racing along again as fast as possible on the slick roof. He and Gentry had to climb up to the next building, but within moments they were hustling again, still heading east, getting closer and closer to the end of the block.

While he struggled along the pitched rooftop Russ tapped his earpiece and placed a call to a number he had programmed into it.

"Yes?"

He spoke loud enough to sound agitated, but softly enough so that Gentry would not hear him through the storm. "This is Dead Eye. It's turning to shit over here!"

"Say iden, Dead Eye."

"Metronome, it's me. Trestle is getting slaughtered! You've got to pull them out of—"

"Say iden key."

"They are outside! There is a running gun battle in the streets! Pull them back!"

"If you can't establish your identity—"

"Fuck you, Parks! I'm going in!" Whitlock shouted this, and then disconnected the call.

"What?" yelled Gentry.

Russ shouted over the roof. He'd expected Gentry to hear something and was ready. "I said, the roof ends up ahead. We can jump it again!"

"Roger that!"

Another narrow small street marked the end of the block. On the far side was a lower brick storage building behind an art studio. It had a lean-to roof, a single slope that started high on Dead Eye's side of the building and ran to only ten feet above ground on Gentry's side.

Both men launched out over the cobblestones, as they had done at the last alleyway.

Russ kicked through the air, his eyes locked to a landing zone near the top of the lean-to roof, barely visible in the storm. But when he was only halfway over the alley he heard gunfire behind him. He knew there wasn't a damn thing he could do about it. He crashed onto the snow-covered roof next to Gentry, hitting awkwardly on his left side, and he grunted with the impact. Both he and Gentry skidded and rolled off the roof, creating an avalanche that cascaded to the ground with them.

Both men and hundreds of pounds of fresh snow

crashed in a heap in the forecourt of the art studio building along the little street. They fought to uncoil themselves from all the cabling, dig out of the mini avalanche, and get themselves back in the fight.

———————

"Two targets! Repeat, two targets!" Trestle Actual heard the call from Trestle Two, but he had no idea what the man on the other side of the row of buildings was talking about. Nick was behind the action, still moving up Kooli Street by himself, having left Seven under the avalanche of snow from the roof.

He stopped in the street and struggled with the boom arm of his mic, which had gotten turned around when he fell in the snow. He twisted it back around to his mouth so he could transmit. "Repeat last? Who is the second target?"

"Two men . . . uh, two people jumped to the roof on the other side of the alley. I think I hit one of them."

Actual started to move again, but headlights washed over his body from behind. He stopped, looked back over his shoulder, and saw a small police car racing up Aida Street. Its siren squawked out an angry wail and it slid to a stop just thirty feet from him.

"Fuck!" Nick dropped his HK into the snow and stood there in the middle of the street, clutching his bloody shoulder wound with his hand.

———————

As soon as Russ and Court crawled out of the snow pile, Russ shouted, "Contact rear!" Both men scrambled to their knees and trained their pistols on the alleyway. Two men in black tactical gear appeared from around the corner. Both of their weapons were trained on the roof above; they clearly did not realize their targets had fallen off the building into the forecourt.

Gentry and Whitlock opened fire together, dumping over a dozen rounds into their targets at a range of twenty feet.

The two Townsend operators fell into the snow.

"This way," Russ said, and he turned away from the dead men in the street and began moving toward a low stone passageway between the art studio and the city wall.

As Court climbed out of the snowdrift he noticed blood in the snow around him; he'd smeared it with his hand as he stood up, so the streak moved in an arc in the impression left by his glove. Quickly he turned behind him and saw more blood, drips and smears all over the snow pile.

Russ saw it, too. "You're hit," he said.

Court entered the passageway, feeling himself for holes as he went. He felt the smeared blood on his left hand, but as he ran his hands over his body he could find no other injuries.

He turned to Russ as they arrived under a streetlamp on the southern exit of the passageway. "I'm good. It must be you."

Russ slowed and performed the same blood sweep; he ran his hands over his torso, then down the front of his midsection and his upper legs, and finally back up his hips. He winced in pain. He pulled his hand off his left hip and saw his fingers red with blood, watery from the dampness in his clothing. "Son of a bitch," he said. "I'm shot." He held his hand to his hip to stanch the blood flow and called out to Gentry. "Head south. Away from the port. Find a place to go to ground and watch for me. I'll catch up in ten mikes. Stay to the east. Their police HQ is on Kolde, to the west; they will—"

Court said, "I know where the police HQ is. Where are you going?"

"Have to take care of something first." He handed Gentry a fresh magazine for his Glock, and then reloaded his own weapon.

Court reloaded his own pistol, and then said, "More important than that gunshot wound and getting away from the cops?"

"As a matter of fact, yes. Wait for me."

"Sure."

Whitlock turned and started running in the other direction, one hand holding his pistol and the other holding his hip. He had no idea if Gentry was going to do as he said, but he had no alternative.

There were still Trestle men out there, and he had to kill them all.

———

Trestle Actual stood in the middle of the cobblestoned alley with his hands in the air. The two cops stared at him through their windshield; one spoke into the radio, and the other just pointed his pistol at him through the glass.

The cops had started to exit their car as soon as they arrived, but a long salvo of gunfire a block to the east sent them back into their vehicle, content to wait on the dozens of police cars that were on the way from the station.

While Actual stood there, listening to gunfire and an increasing chorus of approaching sirens, waiting to be arrested and already imagining the uncomfortable international incident that would begin just as soon as these two bozos grew a pair of balls and climbed out of their cruiser to handcuff him, he spoke into his mic. "Two and Four, this is Actual. Tell me you got him."

No response.

"Two and Four, are you receiving?"

Nothing.

"Dammit! Kip? Dave? Talk to me, guys."

The gunfire he'd heard seconds before sounded like multiple handguns firing simultaneously. *What the hell? Two targets? His men were down?*

"Fuck this shit," he said aloud, and then his arms shot down to his sides in a blur; he drew the SIG Sauer P226 pistol from the retention holster on his right hip and dropped to one knee as he raised the gun at the cops.

The two young Tallinn municipal police saw the movement, but neither the officer with the gun in his hand nor the officer talking into the radio had any reaction that was fast enough to defend themselves.

Trestle Actual opened fire on them, spraying the two young men and their patrol car with round after round of nine-millimeter hollow points. The windshield exploded, glass turned to white dust, and blood sprayed throughout the car's interior.

The echoes of gunfire died in the alleyway, and sirens neared from the west and south.

Nick reloaded his weapon quickly and turned back in the street to catch up with Trestles Two and Four, but as he did so, he saw a man coming toward him in the darkness. He raised his pistol, but Dead Eye moved into the glow of a streetlight.

Actual lowered his pistol and shouted angrily, "I thought I told you to stay inside your damned—"

Dead Eye raised his weapon.

"The fuck is wrong with—"

Whitlock shot Nick, Trestle One, through the jaw. He fell back onto the icy street, his arms wide, his pistol tumbling from his hand.

Russ stood over him, and their eyes met through the snowfall. He shot the man again in the forehead, then knelt and retrieved the gun.

A minute later, Trestle Five climbed behind the wheel of the van in front of the hotel. He'd found Six, dead out here in the parking lot, and dragged his body into the vehicle. All around him lights were on in the buildings; a few people looked out from windows, but the majority of those in the neighborhood had the good sense to keep their heads down.

With the door still open he started the van, and then he saw a shadow to his left. He turned quickly, raising his MP7 at the threat, but almost immediately he lowered it and breathed a sigh of relief.

It was the singleton, Dead Eye. He was holding his left hip with one hand, and he held a pistol in his right.

Trestle Five said, "Get in! I can't raise anybody. The whole fucking team is down, man! We've got to—"

He stopped speaking when Dead Eye drew his pistol

up to eye level. He tried to get his own weapon up to meet the threat, but Whitlock shot him once between the eyes. Five flipped away from the side window, out of the seat, and over the center console of the van, and his foot slid from the brake. The van began rolling forward across the little parking lot through the heavy snow, and it crashed into the entrance of the hotel.

Dead Eye turned away and disappeared into the shadows.

SIXTEEN

Gentry had moved southeast away from the Old Town and into a newer district full of restaurants and office buildings that were empty at this time of morning. From all directions he heard sirens as first responders raced to the scene of the gun battle, and flashing lights beat off glass and metal surfaces. Court ducked into doorways and behind bus stops when emergency vehicles came into view, but this was slowing him down, and he searched for a faster route out of the area.

He had lied to Russ; Court had no intention of hanging out here at the edge of the kill zone where eight guys had come out of nowhere to punch his ticket, especially now that every cop in town was racing through the blizzard and into the area.

Court leaned into the blowing snow and pushed on. He

wore his black coat now and stayed in the shadows, and he concentrated on remaining low profile while putting some distance between himself and the scene.

Court thought back to everything that had happened, or at least everything that happened after his head had cleared from the effect of the nine-banger. He was pretty sure he'd dropped three or four of the opposition. The guy he'd fired at in the hallway of the hotel before running up the staircase, the dude who'd been shooting at him from the hotel parking lot, and the two guys he and Russ had shot in the alley after falling off the roof into the snowdrift. He'd also tried to bury a couple of shooters in an avalanche as he ran along the roof, but he had no idea if he'd been successful with that low-probability plan.

And he also had no clue if Russ had managed to take out any of the enemy, which meant there could easily still be four or five able-bodied assholes in the neighborhood with a mandate to kill him.

No thanks, Gentry thought to himself as he walked through the storm. *I'm not going to sit around and wait for that.*

Whoever the hell Russ was, Court knew he could take care of himself.

Except for the fact he'd gotten himself shot while saving Gentry's life.

Dammit.

Court kept walking, perhaps a little slower now, but he kept walking.

Kaubamaja Street was dark and quiet, so he turned onto it, moving through the heavy snowfall and out of the streetlamps' glow. Sirens squealed on a parallel parkway, but Gentry felt safe enough to keep walking here for the next few blocks.

He had not asked for Russ's help. He had no idea who he was or what his intentions were. For all Court knew, the man was a bounty hunter ordered to bring Court back alive, back to Madrigal or LaurentGroup or whoever the fuck was now running Sid's operation. Just because the bastard spoke English like he was American did not mean he wasn't a bad guy.

Meant nothing at all. Some of the biggest pricks Gentry knew were American.

But the guy had taken a bullet, a bullet that was meant for Court.

Court slowed down a little more.

"Dammit, Gentry," he mumbled aloud.

He had to do something for him. Something to help him out or, more precisely, something that would allow Court to walk away from this shit with a clear conscience. He could find a place to get out of the weather for a minute to warm up and, at the same time, to watch for Russ, just to make sure he was good to go.

Court found a dark alley that gave him a good line of sight of the intersection, and he stood in a doorway there, out of the wind. He shook off the snow that covered his coat and eyed the streets leading back to the Old Town. Every thirty seconds another whining flashing emergency vehicle passed, and up the hill in the district where it had all gone down it looked like a damned fireworks display. Flashing, glowing red and amber lights bounced off every reflective surface for a square mile. The lights were visible even through the blizzard, and they indicated to Court that the area was crawling with cops now, and the streets would be full of onlookers.

Court figured Russ didn't stand a chance of getting out of there unseen, especially hobbled with a gunshot wound.

He had his eyes focused on streetlights in the mid-distance, not expecting to see anyone passing, and he did not, but suddenly he saw a brief movement on the sidewalk much closer. Just fifty feet away he saw a figure in a dark coat, wearing a backpack and limping slightly. Though obviously injured, the man seemed to float easily through the urban landscape, avoiding the lights of the passing cars, just as Gentry himself had done.

The man—clearly now it was Russ—stopped in the snow, lifted his left hand to his face to check the blood, then pressed his hand again to his hip and limped on.

Shit. Court wanted to watch the man pass and disappear in the snow, but his innate sense of self-preservation was eclipsed, in this instance anyway, by his innate sense of honor, and he could not bring himself to leave the wounded American behind.

Court stepped out of the alley and whistled. In moments Russ crossed the street and joined him in the doorway.

Russ said, "I was beginning to think you hit the bricks."

"No," Court replied, wondering if he should have done just that.

"I heard shooting. You run into more assholes?"

"Yeah. Nothing left but us good guys now." Court moved Russ's hand away from his left hip and pulled a flashlight from his backpack and shined it on the area. There was a hole in Russ's jeans just below his belt on the far left side of his hip, and blood had soaked the denim all the way down to the knee.

Court said, "You aren't trailing blood, not yet, but we've got to find a place to treat that wound. We can lie low for a bit, at least until all the first responders get out of the way."

Russ just nodded, pressing down on his hip again to slow the flow of blood.

They moved down the alley and found a staircase in the darkness that led down to a basement door. Court picked the lock with help from his flashlight and a set of picks from his pack. While he did this Russ sat silently on the steps and watched.

In under a minute they were inside and found themselves in the tiny kitchen of a pub that had closed for the evening hours earlier. They made their way to the bar area, and Russ stepped behind the bar and grabbed a bottle of Redbreast Irish whiskey. He bit off the cork, spit it on the floor, and took a long swig.

Court headed to the front of the establishment, parted the vinyl curtains, and saw that the entrance to the pub was belowground, just like the rear. A tiny staircase led up to street level at the front.

He checked his watch; it was four forty-five A.M., and the sign on the window said the bar did not open until three P.M.

"We'll be fine here," he called back to Russ. "No one can see us from the street."

Court moved back to the bar, and for the first time

since the action in the Old Town he realized he was also banged up. He had his own bumps and bruises and scrapes and pulls; the adrenaline in his bloodstream and, to a lesser degree, the cold air had numbed him, but now all the jumping over alleys and falling off roofs was catching up to him. Still, Court knew from experience that most things on his body that were hurting were going to hurt even more tomorrow no matter what he did now.

Russ, on the other hand, was truly injured, and Court knew he had to treat him quickly. He flipped on a small table lamp on the bar, and, motioning to the wound, he asked, "You okay with me checking that?"

Russ took off his coat and lifted his shirt, then undid his bloody jeans and lowered them a few inches. He leaned his elbows on the bar, bracing himself for the pain that was sure to come.

Court grabbed a bottle of cheap vodka from behind the bar and unscrewed the cap. He didn't bother to tell Russ that it was going to hurt; he had no doubt the other American would know that as well as he. Instead he just poured half a bottle of the clear spirit over the bloody injury, washing away the blood and giving Gentry his first chance to assess the damage. He saw both entry and exit wounds, two inches apart just below the man's belt line on his left side. "Nice one," he said.

Russ grunted with the burn, then growled, "In what sense is it 'nice'?"

"You aren't about to die, so that's nice for you. You've got an exit wound, so it's through and through. That's good, too. You okay with me checking it for frag?"

Again, Court was certain the other man would know exactly what he meant.

Russ tensed up, holding on to the side of the table. He grunted again in anticipation of the pain. Then whispered, "Do it."

Court poured the vodka over the fingers of his right hand, then began feeling around the outside of the entry wound. He said, "No fragments. It's a little hole. Not a handgun. They were rocking MP7s, so you took a four-point-six-millimeter round. Personally, I'm not a fan of the caliber."

Russ said, "I am developing a bias against it myself."

Court snorted out a polite laugh. He kept digging, feeling into the hole now with his semisterilized fingers. Court fought a slight trembling in his hands, concentrated on his task, and hoped this stranger would not be able to pick up on the fact he was unnerved by his close brush with death.

Russ showed he had more pressing problems by grunting with pain.

Court poured more vodka on his hand, washing off the blood. "I need to see if your hip is broken. You ready for this?"

Russ did not speak; he just nodded. Sweat covered his brow.

Court's finger felt its way through the path of the bullet; he rubbed against the bone under the torn skin and muscle and felt a scored and jagged hardness, but no major fracture. "You are a lucky son of a bitch. It just grazed the bone. It will hurt for a couple of weeks, but if you don't get an infection, you'll forget it ever happened."

Court pulled his hand out of the wound, then emptied the bottle of vodka into the hole. "Jeez, man. You're a bleeder, aren't you?"

Russ bit his lip from the pain. His face was almost white, and the only thing holding him up was the bar.

Court wiped away blood with a bar towel. "We'll need a compress and some ice."

Court fashioned a bandage from a bar towel, then soaked it with more vodka to clean it and tied it tight around Russ's waist with a cotton apron. He filled a plastic bag with ice from the bar freezer and cinched this over the bar towel with another apron.

Russ then walked around the bar for a moment to test his leg and his hip. He gave Court a weak thumbs-up. "Good work."

With the ice numbing the wound area and the blood flow under control, Russ appeared stronger almost immediately. He washed the blood off his hands, drank some water from the tap, then grabbed the bottle of Redbreast and two shot glasses from behind the bar. He looked at Court. "How 'bout you let me buy you a drink?"

SEVENTEEN

The two men sat in a booth adorned with dusty vinyl cushions, staring across the table at one another and sipping in silence. The only light was from the lamp on the bar across the room, and a little residual glow from the street that filtered through the curtains.

Court had questions for the man, of course, but for now he tried to feel him out via nonverbal cues. Tried to read his face and body language to see what kind of a threat he still might be.

Court Gentry could accept that Russ had saved his life, but he was still not ready to trust him.

Under the table, Court had pulled the Glock from his jeans and placed it between his knees. His right hand rested just next to it on his thigh.

While he kept his fallback option under the table, he realized he was getting nowhere with his nonverbal evaluation above the table. Other than an occasional wince of pain when he moved, the face of the man across from him was as unreadable as Gentry imagined his own to be.

"Your hands are shaking," Russ said, and Court looked down and saw he was right. The tremor in the fingers of his right hand was slight, but obvious. He wrapped them around the shot glass, and the tremor went away.

"Just cold."

"Adrenaline," Russ corrected. "Lots of people get the shakes when they're under fire."

Gentry downed his drink. Repeated, "I'm cold."

Russ did not argue. Instead, he refilled Court's glass. "I'm sure that's all it is."

Court fought to keep his hands still while Russ eyed him from across the table. To change the subject, Court said, "One question. None of my business, but I'd like to know."

"I'm an open book."

"What are you on?"

"What am I 'on'?"

Gentry nodded. "That hole in your hip is bleeding more than it should. You seem too young and fit for blood pressure meds, and you aren't coked up, so I figure you are taking amphetamines of some form."

"Spoken like a man who knows his pharmaceuticals," Russ replied.

Court did not respond to this. He had developed an addiction to pain pills after an op a year or so earlier, but he could not imagine how this stranger across the table would know about that.

After a moment Russ answered, "Adderall. Helps with reaction time, cognitive function, mutes pain."

"Are you trying to sell it to me?"

"Just explaining why I do it."

Court said, "I'm not your mom." It was still in the dark and dusty pub for a moment. Finally he said, "I've got a lot more questions."

To this Russ nodded. "I bet your head is spinning with them."

"Who are you?"

"My name is Russell Whitlock." He looked Gentry over with a searching gaze. "Mean anything to you at all?"

Court shook his head. "Should it?"

A shrug. "Doesn't hurt my feelings."

"You called me Violator back there."

"I did."

"You are Agency?"

"Used to be." Russ sipped some more whiskey from the little glass, the movement of his shifting in the vinyl seat providing most of the noise in the room now. Russ reached out a hand. "Code name Dead Eye."

The men shook hands.

"Never heard that one either, have you?" asked Russ.

"No."

Russ smiled. "We weren't supposed to know about each other. OPSEC and PERSEC and just good manners to mind our own business."

"But you know me."

"I know everyone."

Court did not press. Instead, he said, "The team that hit us this morning. They were Agency assets?"

"No."

"Then who?"

"Townsend Government Services."

"And that is . . . *what* exactly?"

"Private contractor. Bounty hunters, basically."

"How did they find me here in Tallinn?"

"They had a UAV on station over Sid's compound. It tracked you to the *Helsinki Polaris*. Townsend assets hit the *Polaris* the night before last, but you'd already sneaked off. I was the one waiting for you to turn up here, and when you did, I tailed you to the hotel, then called in Townsend's strike team."

Court put his half-empty glass of Irish whiskey down slowly. "You?" His right hand slid to the pistol under the table between his knees, and he took it and pointed it at the man across the table.

"Yeah. I probably should have told you." He cleared his throat and looked down at his hip for a moment, then said, "I work for Townsend."

Russ heard a muted click under the oak table now. He identified the sound easily; it was the hammer of a SIG Sauer pistol being pulled back, readying the gun to fire with only slight pressure on the trigger. He said, "Let me guess. You've got *another* gun pointed at my dick."

"Tell me more about Townsend."

"Privately held. Been around forever. Ten twenty-four contract. Paid by CIA with black fund money."

"What's their mission?"

"Brother, right now, *you* are their mission."

"And they sent you to kill me?"

"They sent me to *find* you. The direct action team

was supposed to kill you. The goons who hit the hotel tonight, Trestle Team, have been in St. Petersburg for sixty days, waiting for you to stick your neck out at Sid's place. There is another team, run by a guy called Jumper. He's in Berlin. A third unit, Dagger, is back in the States. I expect they'll be cycling over here to Europe before long."

Court lowered the pistol under the table but kept his finger ready over the trigger guard. "Who's in charge?"

"The guy after you is Leland Babbitt. He's about fifty. Ex-military, Air Force, then a civilian at DIA for a while. He moved over to FBI counterintel. He got drummed out of the Hoover Building for his methods, strong-arm shit that was getting cases tossed on grounds of civil liberty abuses."

"He runs Townsend?"

"Affirmative. His number two is Jeff Parks. All-American-looking prick. He was a case officer at Langley, tossed during the harsh interrogation pogroms a few years back. The rest of Townsend is mostly ex-agency folks. Midlevel bureaucrats. Not seventh-floor material, for one reason or another.

"Townsend has been doing government-contracted dirty work since the 1800s. They were in the Indian wars, and in the Philippines when that blew up. They killed a Supreme Court nominee in the fifties. Rumor has it that James Earl Ray, the dude who shot Martin Luther King, was a Townsend asset. They whacked Olaf Palme, prime minister of Sweden, a shitload of human rights lefties in Latin America. Most anybody the administration in power didn't like but couldn't be caught targeting, Townsend got the call."

This sounded, to Court, like a load of horseshit. He'd done his own share of denied black ops. He'd never got wind of a commercial enterprise doing the same sort of thing, especially an enterprise that had been in existence over several generations. "Are you going to tell me that Lee Harvey Oswald was a Townsend man?"

Dead Eye shook his head. "Negative. Oswald was just a narcissistic prick with a bolt-action rifle and an entry-level job that gave him line-of-sight on POTUS's open-faced limo."

Court knew this to be true. He was relieved to see that Dead Eye was not too far off into fantasyland.

Russ continued. "Townsend does other stuff as well. Training and security and investigations and arrests and renditions. They work for American concerns in industry, not just the Agency or the White House. But the feds like to use them as a proxy force for untouchable ops. They worked for Noriega back when he was our guy, and they were involved with bringing him in when he wasn't our guy anymore."

Court had been around too long to be surprised by much of anything, but this was all news to him. "What else?" he asked.

"They did CIA-supported hits for Saddam Hussein in Iraq and the apartheid government in South Africa in the eighties, for Mubarak and the Croatians in the nineties. After 9/11, Townsend worked with Afghan warlords that the CIA wouldn't touch with a ten-foot pole."

"That's saying something."

Russ pressed down on his bandage with one hand and waved the other in the air. "Look, Court, you probably should spend less time worrying about Townsend's old contracts, and instead concern yourself with their present-day target."

"Me."

"Yeah."

Court said, "Okay. But before we get to me, what's *your* story?"

Russ sipped. Said, "Thirty-four years old, born and raised in Washington State. Little town outside Olympia called Sequoia Park."

Court reached across the table with his left hand and poured himself another shot. "And you like unicorns and long walks on the beach."

"Who doesn't?"

Court said, "Everything I saw you do tonight. It was like looking in a mirror."

"I'll take that as a compliment."

"I mean to say I can tell you are a solo operator. We were in the same program?"

Russ nodded. "The Autonomous Asset Development Program. I was recruited out of the Marine Corps. A two-year workup, marathons in combat boots, scuba training, flight training, sniper craft, tradecraft, Krav Maga and Brazilian Jiu-Jitsu, language immersion, alpinist work in Wyoming, desert survival and land nav in the Mojave. All the same fun and games you went through, I guess."

"I was in the Sonora."

"Mexico? Ha, you old-timers *were* hard-core."

Court did not smile.

"Anyway, I was approved for operational status, activated, and then I moved around the next several years, mostly in the Middle East and North Africa."

Court thought this over. His career with the Autonomous Asset Program had primarily taken place in the former Soviet Union, but he'd done time in the Middle East as well. More when he joined the Goon Squad. He wondered if he and Russ had run around the same AOs at the same times through the years.

"And then you left CIA?"

"Moved over to Townsend a year ago. Better pay and less bureaucracy. Really, other than the fact they target American heroes like you for termination, it's not such a bad gig."

"Why do you think I am a hero?"

"I was read in on your dossier to prep for the op. As I studied you, it felt like I was reading my own history. You spend a lot of years doing your thing for the USA, snappin' necks and cashing checks, and this is the thanks you get? The shoot-on-sight against you is bullshit. I could no more be involved in your assassination than I could in my own. We're both good guys in a bad world." He held his shot glass out for Court to clink it. "Two brothers."

Court did not reach for his glass. Instead he asked, "Did you tell this Babbitt guy about these reservations of yours concerning the shoot-on-sight?"

"*Fuck* no. They would have just fired me as unreliable, and they would have sent someone else. Court, I'm not looking for a pat on the back, but if I hadn't been the guy here in Tallinn tonight, you'd be dead."

"Thank you." Court said it flatly. He was having a hard time understanding this man's motivation. The cynic in him could not allow himself to believe Russ had gone through all this just because he thought Court was being treated unfairly.

"You're welcome," said Russ. Then, "I've got to admit, I'm surprised to see the tremor."

"The tremor?"

"In your hand. As much action as you've seen, I didn't think it would affect you like that."

"Just cold," Court said again.

"I don't get the shakes," Russ declared. "Never did really. All the shit I've been through." He held his right hand up over the table. "Nothing. The Agency had me tested. My blood pressure stays low through high-stress events; my pulse is unaffected. It gives me an advantage in combat."

"Lucky you."

"What's *your* secret? I've read over your ops. How do you survive everything that has been thrown your way?"

Court shrugged. "I don't have any superpowers like you, if that's what you're asking."

"Don't sell yourself short. I've seen the after-action report on Kiev."

"Kiev?"

"Oh, please."

Court said nothing.

"The analysts at CIA don't believe you did the Kiev op alone. I don't believe you'd work with anyone else." Russ waited for a response, but when none came he said,

"So I think you did it alone. But, I have to admit, I don't have a fucking clue how you did it."

"I didn't do it at all," Court replied.

Russ rolled his eyes. "You can tell me. Confidentially, of course. C'mon. Satisfy my curiosity to pay me back for pulling your ass out of the fire tonight."

Court just shook his head. "I wasn't involved with the Kiev thing. I'm always getting blamed for shit I didn't do."

Russ stared at Court a long time, but finally he let it go with a sigh, finished his drink and reached for the bottle of Redbreast. Court thought he was going to pour another, but he pulled the bottle to him, then grabbed the cork from the table and closed it.

"We need to scoot." Russ pulled out his phone. "If you give me your number, we can get in touch tomorrow."

"Look, I appreciate what you just did. I don't understand it, but I appreciate it. But I don't know you. Why the hell would I give you a way to trace me?"

Russ put his phone down; he did not seem surprised by Gentry's reluctance to give Russ a way to contact him. With a shrug he reached into his backpack, pulled out a scrap of paper, and handed it across the table. Court opened it and found a fourteen-digit phone number written in pencil. Below it was a website URL.

"What's this?"

"*My* phone number and a link to MobileCrypt. It's an app you load on your phone. It's how I can keep from being listened in on or traced. You can do the same thing, and you can be sure I don't know what phone you are using or where you are calling from. We'll go our separate ways right now, but call me tomorrow, as soon as you're clear of the area."

Court put the paper in his pocket. "You want to catch a movie or something?"

Russ pressed down on the bandaging covering his hip to mute the pain that grew there. "Look, here is what's going to happen. I leave here, skip town, find a secure location, and then I call in to Townsend House."

Court was surprised by this. "I am not exactly an expert on good employee/employer relations, but I think your boss is going to be pissed about you killing a bunch of your coworkers."

"I'll be fine. And in order to keep you safe from them, I've got to work within the system. They are going to be after you with a bunch of bodies and a ton of high-tech shit. You check in with me and I'll keep you informed on their hunt."

Court almost yelled his next question. "Why? Why are you making it your job to protect me?"

"Because very soon I'm going to leave Townsend. I have something on the horizon, something big, and it does not involve them. I could use your help, and it's your kind of job."

Court's eyebrows rose. "Ah. Now comes the sales pitch."

Whitlock said, "Yes. I do have a sales pitch for you. Let's work together. You and me. Fucking unstoppable."

"I retired after the Sidorenko hit." Court wanted to immediately quell Dead Eye's enthusiasm for this stupid idea.

"Bullshit. That's just nerves talking. You're a little

burned out, but you won't leave the game until you make peace with CIA or catch a round to the brain stem, which-ever comes first. No, this is in your blood, same as me.

"Let me ask you something. You ever feel like you're swimming against the tide?"

Yes, Court thought. That was exactly how he felt.

"Go on."

"You've made more enemies in the past couple of years as a freelancer than you ever did working for Lang-ley. But what you're doing is important. I know you are looking for the next righteous op. I know your objective is to do good. To fight the good fight." Russ put his hand over his heart. "That's *me*, too. I want to be a part of that."

Court remained cynical. "And we split the take? No thanks."

Russ shook his head adamantly. "Don't bullshit me, dude. You aren't in this for the money, and neither am I. We can do good, man. Twice as much as you could alone. We need to stick together."

Court rolled his eyes. "Like Batman and Robin?"

Russ snapped back angrily, "I'm not talking about some Batman and Robin shit. We operate independently, of course. I am just talking about coordination. We can watch out for each other, help each other."

Court did not respond.

Russ said, "Anyway, call me tomorrow when you're clear. We'll talk about details. You owe me that."

Court took out the paper with the phone number on it for a moment, then slid it into his fleece. "Fair enough."

Whitlock eyed Gentry's face long and hard. Looking

for any signs of deception. He smiled a little, then stuck out his hand, and Court shook it.

Both men were back out in the snow a few minutes later, separating in the dark, running away from a dawn and a manhunt that was only just beginning.

EIGHTEEN

Mossad targeting officer Ruth Ettinger turned away from the path in front of her and leaned her face close to the face of the man sitting next to her on the park bench. He moved in as well, and their lips closed to within a half-inch separation. She shut her eyes and brushed her lips against his playfully, and they kissed, lovers accustomed to each other's every move and every thought. Her tongue reached out and brushed the inside of his mouth before she pulled away an inch, slid her fingers into the hair behind his neck, and opened her eyes with a soft smile.

The man kissed her back and then smiled at her. "Ruth, my darling. Have I told you that you are getting fat?"

She smiled at this, kissed his mouth again, and spoke with his lips so close to hers he felt the warm breath of each syllable. "The new parabolic mics only have a three-band equalizer. I'm going to call technology to see if we can switch out the EQs on the new mics for the old five-channel ones. We'll get better midrange vocals at distance that way."

They kissed again. Embraced lovingly through the thickness of their down ski jackets. The man said, "Would it kill you to take a shower once in a while? You smell like a goat."

And to this she replied, "If Technology won't let us use the five-channel EQ, I'll see if there is something we can do in the software to boost midrange. That might help us during replay, but it won't do anything in real time to isolate vocals from background noise."

"I love it when you talk dirty."

Smiling the smiles of lovers who'd suddenly realized the extent of their public display of affection, they both sat back straight on the park bench, and Ruth grabbed the bag of warm honey cashews she'd bought at the Nuts4Nuts cart next to the ice-skating rink. She popped a cashew into her mouth and offered the bag to Aron, her younger lover, or at least the twenty-eight-year-old man posing as her lover for today's surveillance in Central Park.

Aron was one of three on Ruth's team; the other two, also posing as a couple, sat on the far side of the path just outside the entrance of the Central Park Zoo. Mike Dillman and Laureen Tattersal were both in their early thirties, both nice looking but not distractingly so, and they were also spending their time kissing on a bench, thirty yards up the path. Like their senior officer, Mike, Aron, and Laureen were all Israeli citizens who had emigrated from the United States, and they all looked perfectly at home here in New York City.

Directly between the two sets of fake lovers, an Arab man sat with his wife on a park bench, their baby in a stroller in front of them. The father rolled the stroller back and forth while he and his wife talked.

Laureen had a long, narrow, directional microphone that just jutted out of a small hole in the side of her over-sized purse, and with it she and Mike were able to pick up the vast majority of the conversation between the man and his wife. The audio was piped into their tiny Bluetooth earpieces; both of them spoke Arabic fluently and, in the past twenty minutes of surveillance here in the park, they had covertly listened in on a long conversation about diapers and baby shit. It was an argument hinging on how he was not pulling his share of the diaper duties and, as far as Laureen was concerned, the wife seemed to be making a lot of good points.

While they sat on the park bench Mike and Laureen enjoyed spicing up their sweet nothings, just like Aron up the path. Sometimes Laureen giggled, leaned into Mike's ear, and whispered obscenities. Mike never blushed, never reacted with surprise or distaste; instead he gave as good as he got, replying softly with his own crude comments.

In contrast to her team, Ruth was all business in times like this. She stayed in character with her body language, but her whispered voice remained on task, discussing the technical or logistical minutiae of surveillance work. She allowed her junior officers latitude to be silly, if they had nothing important to say, but she had done this long enough that she no longer felt any awkwardness in locking lips with her subordinate when in close foot follow or static watch.

Ruth and Aron scooted close together on the bench again, combating the December chill that filtered through the quilting of their heavy coats. They kissed again. "I'd rather make out with Mike," Aron said.

Ruth stopped talking about parabolic audio equipment and said, "I can arrange that next time."

Aron laughed at this.

Despite these brief moments of levity, they were hard at work now, just hours after arriving in the United States. They had been in Faro, cleaning up a few loose ends after the operation that led to the death of the two bomb-making brothers targeting Prime Minister Ehud Kalb, when Ruth received the order to fly with her team to New York City. Here in Manhattan, a thirty-five-year-old schoolteacher and father of a newborn had been under surveillance by the FBI for his recent purchase of a large quantity of ammonium nitrate, a fertilizer that also served as a key component in a potent explosive.

The FBI found the purchase curious but not strictly illegal, so they began what Ruth Ettinger considered a painfully slow and underwhelming investigation. That the professor was Palestinian and related by marriage to a midranking Hamas functionary in Gaza piqued the interest of the Mossad, and, because Prime Minister Ehud Kalb was scheduled to speak here in Manhattan at the United Nations in a few weeks, Ruth and her team rushed from Faro to Manhattan without delay to begin their own accelerated investigation.

She did not mind coming back to the States, although she knew she'd feel guilty if she didn't drop by her mom's house in Brooklyn before it was all said and done, and she really would much rather chase blood-soaked terrorists than sit at her mom's kitchen table over beef brisket or matzo ball soup.

Aron put his hand on her knee while he leaned into her face. He smiled as he spoke, but the jokes were over for now. "Initial impressions?"

Ruth smiled back and shook her head, then whispered, "This guy is not a threat."

"How can you be so sure?"

"Look at him."

Aron did so, discreetly, then looked back to his "girlfriend." "Terrorists don't take their kids to the park?"

"This is no terrorist. I can smell a terrorist."

Aron conceded this point. "I won't argue with you on that. You do seem to have a nose for the worst of them."

Ruth took his hand and held it through her mittens. "This one feels like a complete waste of time, and I fucking *hate* wasting time."

She turned her attention back to the Palestinian couple, watching them take turns rocking the stroller as their low-intensity argument continued.

Ruth was bored, but she was accustomed to the boredom. She could not help feeling that she and her team were overqualified for this assignment, but she did have to admit that her close knowledge of the area and her ability to weed out the real terrorists from the wannabes and nobodies made hers the perfect team to send. Despite the light banter of the junior officers, all four members of this team were exceedingly professional, and they took their work seriously. The psychiatrists who worked for the Mossad told Ruth she took things *too* seriously, but she found their supposedly learned opinions to be nothing more than government-funded guesswork bordering on quackery.

Ruth was fine, she'd told everyone, and she was *most* fine when she was out in the field and hard at work.

Her phone rang in her purse and she snatched it up, knowing it would be Yanis Alvey, her superior. He'd promised to call her with more information on the subject.

"Hello?"

"Ma nishma?" What's up? Yanis always broke protocol and spoke in Hebrew when he called from Tel Aviv.

She answered back in English with her native Brooklyn accent. "Hi, Jeff. How are things?"

By calling him Jeff, she was reminding him to speak English. Of course it was unlikely that any subject she might be tracking could hear the man talking to her through her telephone, but it would be easier for her to slip up and start speaking Hebrew if the other party's end of the conversation was in the foreign tongue.

Yanis answered back. "Your subject is clean. The purchase he made was benign."

"In what way?"

"He is a high school teacher, true, but he also recently became a member of an agricultural co-op in Sullivan County, Pennsylvania. His crop is beans and figs, but the co-op grows all sorts of things. They are small scale; one of the farmers purchases equipment, another seeds, another fertilizers, and it all is pooled into the resources of the co-op."

She looked around and then whispered, "And he bought the ammonium nitrate for *farming*?"

"Hard to believe. But yes."

"And the FBI didn't know this?"

"They still don't. We hacked his banking records and saw that he was reimbursed by the co-op for the same amount he spent on the fertilizer. We checked them out; they've been around for years, and they farm acreage that corresponds to the amount of ammonium nitrate they purchased. We'll keep an eye on them, but it looks kosher."

She rolled her eyes at his use of the phrase, coming from a Jew born in Rashlatz but delivered like an American.

She said, "So . . . he is about as harmless as he looks."

"It appears so," Yanis said.

"All right. We'll shut it down here."

"You sound crestfallen. Once again, Ruth, you seem disappointed that we don't have more imminent dangers against our nation's leadership."

"I like to work, Yanis."

He hesitated before saying, "It's more than that. You take too much on your shoulders."

"Since Rome, you mean."

"Since Rome."

"The increase in my operational tempo since Rome has been driven by the increasing enthusiasm of our prime minister's enemies, not by any overzealous desire on my part to atone for mistakes."

"I did not mean to suggest otherwise. And, Ruth, you *made* no mistakes."

She did not respond to this directly. "Maybe if Kalb stopped pissing people off I could sit at home and raise orchids or something."

"Well, there's not much chance of that. I'll find you some trouble to get into before long. Don't worry. I'm sure something terrible is just around the corner."

"Funny."

"Send your team back here, but you take a couple of days to see your mom."

"That's not the trouble I'm looking for. I can come back with the others."

"That's an order."

She groaned inwardly. "Okay, Yanis, but I want hazard-duty pay."

He laughed as he hung up.

It had been a wasted day. A wasted trip. Making out with Aron Hamlin wasn't the worst way to spend her time, she admitted to herself, but she was hungry for her next target, and sitting in Central Park watching a Palestinian family man who had done nothing but buy some chemicals to help his pistachios grow had done nothing to make her prime minister safer.

She decided she would call her mom, tell her she'd just gotten off the plane, and invite her to brunch the next morning. Two or three hours listening to her mom drone on always seemed to go by a little faster when the Bloody Marys flowed.

Russell Whitlock trudged through the snow along a long row of drab apartment blocks in the Estonian city of Paldiski, some thirty miles west of Tallinn on the coast of the Baltic Sea. It was midafternoon; half a foot of powdery accumulation had been dumped here in the past twenty-four hours, but the puffy gray clouds above had stopped their onslaught for the time being, and the temperature was in the low thirties, balmy for this time of year.

He stopped in front of a tiny inn; it was dirty and basic and as far off the beaten path as one could imagine, but Russ decided it would do for a night. Russ much preferred five-star accommodations, but right now he couldn't indulge himself. He needed a quiet out-of-the-way place to treat his gunshot wound, to wait for Gentry to call, and to spend a safe night.

This town was no tourist destination. It had been a closed city during the cold war, used as a massive Soviet nuclear submarine training center, a city encased in barbed wire.

Two decades later, Russ Whitlock found the city nearly as uninviting as it must have been back then.

Dead Eye sat in his hotel room as the afternoon turned to evening and the light through the window dimmed and extinguished completely. He'd found a pharmacy near the hotel, and next door a liquor store. Russ saw the placement of the two establishments as serendipity. He returned to his room, disinfected his wound and changed his bandages, and then opened a bottle of vodka and took a long swig.

He waited nearly ten hours to call in to Townsend House, but he was finally ready. He hoped all the action had been quick and confused enough to where no one on Trestle Team had reported his treachery against his employer, but the only way to find out for sure was to report in himself.

He pressed the speed-dial button on his phone that connected him to Babbitt's line at Townsend House.

After a hurried identity check, Babbitt said, "We thought you were dead."

"I made it out," Russ replied. "But all the rest are fucking toast, sir."

"What the hell happened?"

"I wish I could tell you, but I was ordered to sit in my damn hotel room while your boys hit the target. Gentry definitely fired first; I heard his G19 open up before any return fire came from the suppressed MP7s. Other than that, I can't really re-create the action to help you figure out what went wrong."

It was silent for a moment until Babbitt said, "I understand." He cleared his throat. "You called in during the attack, said you were going to engage."

"Yeah. I wish I could have done something, but I wasn't read in on the op, and it went tits up before I got involved. I tried to play catch-up, but I was too far behind Gentry. I only saw him for an instant. Unfortunately he saw me first and tagged me."

Babbitt almost shouted in astonishment. "Do you mean to say he *shot* you?"

Russ lay back on his little bed as he answered, moving gingerly to avoid putting pressure on his left hip. "Yes."

"You're injured?" Babbitt seemed to have trouble taking this in.

"I'll live. I dumped a couple of rounds his way. May even have hit him, although I don't know for sure. The point is, if you had let me do this my way from the beginning, I would have slipped a stiletto into Gentry's spine the minute he got off the boat yesterday morning, and you wouldn't have eight dead operators and an escaped target."

"Seven dead operators," Babbitt replied.

Whitlock bolted upright on the bed. "Seven?"

"One member of Trestle survived. Somehow Trestle Seven was caught in an avalanche or something, buried under snow. We are still trying to get the full story on that. He was pulled out by the locals with a broken vertebra in his neck and four broken ribs, but he's going to pull through."

Russ took a couple of slow breaths. Anger began to well up in him, stiffening his body and clenching his muscles. "That's good news, Lee."

"Well, he may wish he'd stayed under the snow. He'll be spending some time in Estonia as a guest of their penal system, even when he does get out of the hospital."

"Do you want me to do something about that?" Russ asked. The insinuation would be clear to Babbitt. Russ was asking if he should kill the survivor to keep him from talking. Russ had no idea how he'd do it, but he had his own motivation. He knew Trestle Seven might have seen him with Gentry, and he certainly did not need *that* making its way back to Townsend.

Babbitt hesitated before replying. "For now, no."

Russ pushed this new problem out of his mind. There was nothing he could do about it. He said, "This whole thing was a mess, sir. Unprofessional."

Whitlock knew Babbitt would admit no wrongdoing. He was an executive; he would remain aloof and above any repercussions of his decision making. He did exactly what Russ thought he would do. He changed the subject. "We've got to get you back to the States. You're hurt and that AO is too hot to have you running around in it after what happened this morning. Do I need to send a doctor to you to get you ready to travel?"

"I'm not coming back to the States. I'm going after Gentry."

"Negative, Russell. I can't have you getting picked up right now. Listen, we've got brand-new facial recognition suites running on our servers, taking in every camera within a hundred klicks of Tallinn. We've sent advanced microdrones to the UAV team so they can hunt him in urban environments. We'll widen the search if we don't get a ping by midnight local time there. I want you to stand down, at least for a couple of days."

Russ knew it was useless to fight. "Fine. But I want any intel you have pushed to me immediately."

"Agreed."

"And, Lee, I'll take a couple of days to stay below radar, but I'm not standing down for long. It's in your best interests to have me involved. Your UAV guys and your direct action assets don't know Gentry like I do."

"I understand. Just get somewhere safe and tend to

your injury. We'll work on locating him in the mean-time."

Russ said, "Dead Eye is out."

———————

Lee Babbitt put the phone down, leaned back in his chair, and closed his eyes. *What a fucking disaster.* Of course he was annoyed with Dead Eye for taking his time in check-ing in, but more than anything he was relieved his solo asset was still alive. And he sure as hell wasn't mad at him for what happened in Tallinn. On the contrary, as far as Babbitt was concerned, that freak Russ Whitlock was the only Townsend employee who'd done his fucking job.

He knew the next days and weeks were going to be a clusterfuck dealing with all the fallout from the Tal-linn op. CIA would step in; they would smooth things over with the Estonians, but they would not do it with-out taking a pound of flesh from Babbitt for Townsend's failure.

But he could not worry about that now. He had to find Gentry and put him in the dirt before he could con-centrate on anything else. He knew he couldn't let his injured, insubordinate, and half-crazy solo operator con-tinue the search now while all of European law enforce-ment was aware of what had happened in Tallinn.

He also knew if Townsend's signal room continued to push intel to Russ, then Russ would continue to act on that intel. Babbitt decided he would tell his people to stop sending information to the singleton's phone. If they were lucky enough to have a sighting of Gentry in the next couple days, he couldn't risk having Dead Eye rush to the scene and get himself picked up in the process.

Lee ran his fingers through his hair and rubbed his eyes. *What a fucking disaster.*

NINETEEN

Court Gentry stood outside the Tallink Ferry terminal building at five P.M. It was dark outside the huge terminal except for the lights from passing cars on the street and moored boats in the harbor, but Court didn't mind the dimness—he used it to disappear in a corner by the front wall. He had changed every scrap of his clothing, shaved off his scruffy beard, and approached the area in a cab from across town to avoid walking the streets that he and others had thoroughly shot up early that morning.

Still, he was closer to the location of the action than he would like. He'd reluctantly dumped his pistol in the bay just a half hour earlier. He knew he couldn't run the risk of being caught with the gun, but he knew he was in danger here, back in the city center. Just as he climbed out of his cab a government Lynx helicopter landed up the hill near the Old Town, no doubt delivering investigators or government officials or someone else who needed to see the site for himself or herself. Even now, some thirteen hours after the action, the crime scene would be intact, although the bodies had probably been bagged and carted off to the morgue. Court had no idea how many had died during the action, but figured it must have been at least four or five.

He checked his watch, worrying that he might have cut it too close and arrived too late for his plan. But these fears were unfounded as the first gaggle of ferry passengers poured from the front door of the terminal, having just disembarked from the incoming ferry from Stockholm.

Soon it turned into a steady stream, hundreds of people, all rolling out their luggage, moving alone or with family in tow, heading into taxis and buses or just walking off through the heavy snow on the ground into the evening.

Court waited for just the right man.

There. A young man who looked Estonian rolled a cart through the terminal door. The cart was empty, and the man also wore a large backpack.

It was common for entrepreneurial Estonians to buy items in their home country, sometimes even duty-free items in the ferry terminal itself, and then cart them to Stockholm, where the goods would sell for a higher price. This man appeared to be one of these ferry traders, and Court decided he would suit his needs perfectly.

He followed the man along the street, but only until he had broken out of the scrum of people leaving the terminal.

In the parking lot of a Statoil service station Court caught up with him and walked alongside. In Russian he said, "Pardon me, do you speak Russian?"

The man stopped. Nodded. His eyes flitted around; he was definitely on guard, but not afraid. These traders, Court knew, often bought and sold other items, things of a contraband nature, so these types were at once looking to make a score from a stranger and watchful for cops or thugs out to steal their money or beat them off their turf.

Court affected a nonthreatening voice and posture to put the man at ease. He knew his time was short, so he didn't want to hang out in this parking lot any longer than necessary. "I am a friend," Court said. "I need something, and I am willing to pay for it."

"What do you need?"

"I need a ticket to Stockholm on tonight's crossing."

The man looked at him a long time and then began walking again. He saw no money in this conversation. "So go buy one."

Court walked along with him, kicking heavy powdery snow with his shoes as he trudged. "That is the problem, of course. I have lost my passport."

The man stopped again. "Then you aren't going to Stockholm. You need a passport to buy a ticket."

"Yes, but I don't need *my* passport if *you* buy me a ticket. I will pay you two hundred euros."

The Estonian looked left and right, then back to Court. "Two hundred euros, just to walk back to the terminal and buy you a ticket."

"Yes."

"How will a ticket in my name help you?"

"They don't check passports at the turnstiles. Only at time of purchase."

The Estonian thought about this himself and nodded thoughtfully. "And there is no control in Stockholm, either."

Gentry smiled. "You see?" It was clear to Court the man did see, and he was already scheming on ways to use this idea to make money from others in the future.

Then he hesitated. "If you are caught. If you do anything to—"

"I destroy your ticket as soon as I get on board. I don't even go to the berth you reserve. Once I am on the boat, I disappear until Stockholm. If something happens to me, you are not connected."

The man thought this over, and Court knew the man was going to up his fee.

"Four hundred."

"Three hundred." Gentry pulled out the exact fare amount without showing the man any more money. "This is for the ticket; I pay your fee when you return. And we must go now, and hurry, because the ferry leaves in thirty minutes. If I am not on it, you do not get paid."

The man agreed; Court followed him back to the ferry terminal, even offering to push the man's cart, and he stood in the hall behind him as the man bought the ticket.

The building was crawling with police, and they were alert but clearly not certain who they were looking for. Surely the hotel desk clerk would have given Gentry's description to them, but Court was the Gray Man; the clerk would have forgotten more than she remembered.

The police would also be looking for Dead Eye, Court knew, and that potentially could present a problem, as he and Court were both American and similar in appearance, and Court did not know the other man's level of tradecraft. But, he decided, Dead Eye would not have been able to survive as a solo NOC for long if he walked the earth leaving a memorable impression.

The cops had their eyes open, Gentry could see this plain enough, but Court himself spotted a hundred or more brown-haired men in their thirties walking around the busy terminal, all of whom fit every bit of the description the hotel would have to give.

Back outside, Court exchanged three hundred-euro bills for the ticket to Stockholm in the name of Ardo Tubool.

The entire transaction had been done with an air of friendliness, but when the two men shook hands at the end of the deal, Gentry darkened.

"I will ask for one more thing."

"Yes?"

"Your discretion. I have friends here in Tallinn who will know if I made it safely to Stockholm, Ardo."

"So?"

"So nothing. I will not worry about you telling anyone of our transaction, and you will not worry about my friends."

Court had met hundreds of men like Ardo in his career, and he knew guys like this weren't the type to go running off to the authorities to rat out others. They had enough problems with the cops without seeking them out. But Court also knew it was likely Ardo Tubool would learn just as soon as he got back into the city that early that same morning groups of foreigners—Westerners, all would say—had shot it out with each other. If Court had not left behind a little encouragement for the man to keep his mouth shut, he might have been tempted to mention his transaction with the Russian-speaking foreigner who left on the ferry to Stockholm.

It was a calculated risk Court was taking, but he saw it as his best option to get far away quickly and efficiently.

Minutes later Court stood in line on the second floor of the ferry terminal, passed his ticket through an automated turnstile, and boarded the ship for a twelve-hour passage to Stockholm.

No one asked for his passport, no one asked to see his ticket, no one spoke to him at all.

He bought coffee and bottled water and plastic-wrapped and plastic-tasting sausages from a vending machine next to the piano bar on the boat, and he went outside on the deck. He sat down on a bench, bundled tightly in his coat and hat and scarf and gloves, and he looked out into the vast darkness of the Baltic Sea as the ship left Estonia, heading west.

———————

Russ ate a simple meal at a restaurant around the corner from the inn in Paldiski, keeping his Bluetooth set in his ear the entire time. He was anxiously awaiting Gentry's call, but it did not come during dinner, so he returned to his room, changed his bandages once again, and sat at the desk with the bottle of vodka in front of him as the hours ticked away.

Whitlock looked down to his watch again. Midnight. Gentry should have called by now, but he had not.

He realized Gentry would not be calling. Not today, anyway.

Dead Eye gritted his teeth.

He felt the anger boil in him, but he stopped himself from giving in to the rage. He knew the Gray Man would do things in his own way, on his own schedule.

Russ smiled a little at the irony of his frustration. He felt the way Lee Babbitt must have felt every time Russ himself failed to report in on schedule.

This was karma, biting him back for his own misbehavior.

Russ knew he should have expected this. In the scheme of things it was just a tiny bump in the road. He knew the Gray Man would get in touch with him. Not because he really wanted to work with him in the future. No, Whitlock had no illusions about Gentry signing on to that ridiculous idea, but rather because there was no way in hell Gentry could pass up the bait Russ had set out the night before. The offer to help him avoid the Townsend hunt.

Russ swigged vodka from the bottle, then opened the little window by the desk. An icy wind whipped into the room as he poured the remnants of the alcohol onto the parking lot below, and then he tossed the bottle into a snow-covered bush by the window.

Russ was pissed, but he would shake it off. Trusting Gentry to happily bounce along to the next stage of

Russ's scheme like a bunny rabbit hopping to a head of cabbage had been foolish of him. He saw this plain as day now. But he would not let the anger take over him.

He blew out a long, controlled exhalation. "All right, Court, you piece of shit. We'll have to do this your way, but we're damn well still gonna do it."

He stood from the table, grimacing along with the throbbing sting in his hip, grabbed his bag, and headed out the door.

There was no sense waiting around in this shit hole. He'd get on a train and head south for Vilnius, Lithuania.

Russ had a plane to catch there tomorrow, and, he decided, he might as well get moving.

TWENTY

Two black Lincoln Navigator SUVs pulled into the gates of Townsend House and negotiated the winding drive through the cherry trees up to the parking circle. Leland Babbitt and Jeff Parks stood on the expansive front porch, both men dressed in dark blue suits, their lapels and their hairstyles blowing gently in the cold morning breeze.

The SUVs parked in the parking circle in front of the main house and five dark-suited men climbed out; their jackets hung open and the wind exposed the FN P90 submachine guns hanging at their underarms. The grips of SIG pistols on their hips were even less well concealed. Four of them took up positions in the drive, and the fifth man opened the back door of the rear SUV.

Another man climbed out now. He was tall and thin and older than the others, his suit was gray, and he carried no obvious weapon. His face showed little expression as he regarded the two men at the front door, but he walked up to them, flanked by his security detail.

"Good morning, Denny," Babbitt said as he extended his hand.

Denny Carmichael, Director of National Clandestine Service for the Central Intelligence Agency, shook both men's hands without replying, and within moments the three of them, surrounded by Carmichael's security entourage, entered Townsend House's opulent ground-floor conference room. Two large Frederick Remingtons were displayed adjacent to a huge showcase of Civil War–era weaponry. Perfectly maintained Whitworth and Enfield muzzle-loaded rifles hung above Henrys and Burnsides and Spencers. All the firearms were surrounded in the glass case by edged weapons of the period, each polished to a mirror finish and appearing as sharp and as ready for action today as they had been one hundred fifty years ago when they were wielded in battle.

Coffee was poured and pastries were offered by Townsend canteen workers, but Denny Carmichael himself waved the Townsend staff out the door along with his close-protection detail.

As everyone but the executives filed out of the conference room, Babbitt and Parks sat down across from their guest. Babbitt said, "Heard your daughter is expecting. Congratulations."

To this Carmichael replied, "This morning's meeting will be brief, and it will stay on theme. What, in God's name, happened in Estonia?"

Babbitt kept his chin up and his voice strong as he spoke. "Resistance from the target. We expected him to mount a robust defense. He is, after all, the Gray Man. But our direct action team was, nevertheless, disabled. We lost a lot of good men."

Babbitt bowed his head over the shiny tabletop almost as if saying a short prayer to himself over his fallen men.

Carmichael leaned forward, speaking with unmistakable anger. "You could not have possibly been more aware of the capabilities of Courtland Gentry."

"Certainly we were aware, and we remain so. We sent in eight of our best men, and then only after real-time intelligence from the singleton operative."

"And still, Gentry wiped out the strike team."

Babbitt nodded. "Seven dead. One wounded and arrested."

"Christ," Carmichael groaned. "We didn't need *that!*"

"No," agreed Babbitt.

"And your solo asset survived?"

"My intel about what happened came directly from Dead Eye, who was ordered to stand down before the raid. He reported hearing the target fire first. We don't know if Gentry just got lucky, happened to see the strike team as they approached his location, or if he had some sort of warning or countermeasures in place that were missed by our men."

"And where is Dead Eye now?"

"He was wounded, but he is still operational."

"If he stood down before the op, how was he wounded?"

"On his own initiative he entered the engagement. He was unable to respond in time to save the direct action assets, but he caught a round from Gentry's gun in the process."

Denny sighed, strumming his fingers on the table. "And collateral damage? We are told that two policemen were killed, along with a civilian."

Jeff Parks chimed in quickly. "All at the hands of Court Gentry." He paused. Then said, "A CIA-trained asset who has gone rogue." This was clearly an attempt to deflect a touch of responsibility for the disaster back on the CIA itself.

Denny just gave Parks an *eat shit* look.

Babbitt cleared his throat. "Look, I'm not going to tell you no mistakes were made last night. We'll do an after-action hot wash with the surviving member of the direct action team as soon as we can, and we will make any improvements in our tactics and procedures that we need to make to reflect the data he can provide. But, Denny, you handed us a very difficult case here, and we *will* sort it out for you. We just hit a snag."

Carmichael looked off into space a moment. "None of this would have happened if you had warned Sidorenko about Gentry's impending attack. I am told Sid had fifty men at his dacha. With the heads-up you had that Gentry was ingressing into the AO, you could have just picked up the phone and allowed Sidorenko to prepare a defense that Gentry would have walked right into."

Babbitt shook his head. "We did not see a high probability that Sidorenko's security measures could have been employed to eliminate the target. Added to that, there was a chance that Sid or his people could have unwittingly tipped Gentry off about the advance warning, at which point he would know he was under aerial surveillance. We could *not* allow that to happen if we were going to track him in the future."

Denny's steel-gray eyes narrowed. "That's the biggest crock of shit I've ever heard, Lee. You were afraid you wouldn't get paid if Gentry died at the hands of the St. Petersburg mob."

Babbitt rolled his hands over and opened them on the table, a palms-up gesture. "It would have been nice to have had the proper assurances from you that our contract bonus conditions would have been met without physical presence of our personnel at the point of elimination."

"I can terminate your contract right now," Carmichael said angrily.

Babbitt did not blink. "You can. But you won't. We got guns in Gray Man's face; Dead Eye says he might have even wounded him. That's something CIA hasn't managed to do in five years."

"We've had eyes on him," Carmichael countered.

"You had him in Russia, and you let him go. You had him in Sudan, and he got away. You had him in Mexico, and again, he escaped."

"Just as he escaped *your* net, Lee."

"We will pick him up again. Soon. If you have a minute, we'd like to take you down to the signal room to show you some new technology we are deploying in the hunt."

Carmichael shook his head. "Every minute you spend telling me how you are going to catch and kill Court

Gentry is another minute you aren't catching and killing Court Gentry."

The CIA's top spy stood up from the table, indicating the end of the meeting.

He said, "This isn't fun anymore. Find him. Kill him." He paused. "I will approve an update to your contract to stipulate that Townsend will be rewarded for Gentry's termination."

"Regardless of the circumstances?"

"Barring undue collateral damage, yes."

"Define *undue*," Parks said with a raised eyebrow.

Carmichael looked at him with cold eyes peering out of his tanned and deeply lined face. "No."

The silence in the room lasted several seconds. Finally Babbitt walked around the table. "Excellent, Denny." The two men shook hands, but Babbitt was the only one who looked happy. "This will facilitate the hunt."

Denny started walking toward the door of the conference room. Babbitt walked along with him, and Parks trailed behind. "Lee . . . you have done good work for us in the past. We value our relationship with Townsend. It keeps my testimony to congressional hearings simple, and your people always get their man."

Lee put his hand on Denny's back as they strode up the hallway to the foyer. "We're patriots here at Townsend. We're proud to serve. You know that."

Denny did not respond to this. Instead he said, "Court Gentry is a different animal. His very existence is creating a dangerous rift in the U.S. intelligence community. When he goes away, America will benefit greatly."

"How so?" asked Babbitt. "I've read every word of his file that's not redacted, many times, and it leaves me with more questions than answers. I understand he killed other personnel on his task force. But . . ."

"His termination has been approved by the Director of National Intelligence. If that's not good enough for you, then you are in the wrong business."

Babbitt persisted. "There's something more. Something not in the file. Isn't there?"

"It's classified, Lee."

"It's *me*, Denny."

Carmichael stopped walking. They were in the center of the foyer now. Denny's security team had formed a diamond shape around him, ready to usher him outside and back into his Navigator, but Babbitt remained inside the coverage.

Denny seemed to struggle with his next comment. Finally he said, "American national security vis-à-vis a crucial ally has been severely degraded by our inability to take Court Gentry off the playing field. You and your organization are our last best hope for nothing less than the future good relations with an important partner on the world stage."

He patted Babbitt on the shoulder. "Don't fail me, Lee. You can expect more oversight on this. I will not allow another massacre like what happened last night in Tallinn."

Denny acknowledged Parks with a brisk nod, then turned and left with his security detail.

Babbitt stood there on the marble floor of the hallway,

thinking over what D/NCS Carmichael had just told him. Another country wanted Gray Man dead, so the CIA was pulling out all the stops to make it so.

What the hell?

Parks stepped up to his boss. "That went swimmingly." His sarcasm was clear.

Babbitt was still weighing over Denny's nonexplanation of the reasons behind the Gentry contract. He shook away his confusion and addressed Parks. "Additional oversight, my ass. He's not going to move us to Langley, and he's not going to send Langley personnel to us. The reason we have this job is so there are no comebacks on the Agency. Carmichael sees Townsend as his own private army. He won't fuck that up by sending over official eyes and ears. He's bluffing. We'll be fine." He held a finger up. "Correction. If we find Gentry in the next few days we'll be fine."

Jeff Parks knew this was his cue to fill Lee in on the status of the hunt.

"I've got our best hackers pulling feeds from every municipal and private security network in the area. The newest facial recog software is processing it all."

"How wide a net?"

"All of the Baltic, of course. Part of Poland. We can pull in Germany and Ukraine if we need to, but the costs will skyrocket. Also, there is a daily ferry from Tallinn to Sweden that also stops in Norway, so I've added Oslo and Stockholm to the collection haul."

"Can the software keep up with all that data?"

"It's the best there is. Better than the newest stuff they

are using at the Fort." Babbitt knew "the Fort" was Fort Meade, home of the National Security Agency.

"Good. You have the personnel you need?"

"I have everyone working on it. It's a matter of time before Gentry shows his face in front of a camera. When he does, we will be on him within a few hours."

TWENTY-ONE

When they were still in the arrivals cab stand at Beirut's Rafic Hariri International Airport, the taxi driver asked his passenger if he was absolutely certain he had the correct address. The passenger was, after all, a Westerner, and the address he gave was, after all, in the Dahiyeh, the southern suburbs of Beirut. The Dahiyeh was the tough part of town, and the particular neighborhood that was the requested destination of the brown-haired man with the eyeglasses and the sport coat was populated predominately by poor Shias; crime was rampant there and kidnappings of Westerners was certainly not unheard of. The driver pictured this fare of his paying him and then stepping out of the taxi, only to be grabbed off the street, dragged to a basement, and chained to a radiator.

Hence the cabbie's plea that the man double-check the proffered address.

But the foreigner's Gulf Arabic was surprisingly fluid and his reply was confident; he explained with a comfortable smile that he had influential friends in the government here in the capital, as well as friends in that neighborhood in particular, and he was not concerned for his safety in the least.

The taxi driver took that to mean this stranger—this Westerner—was tight with Hezbollah, and if true, that should get him out of most dangerous situations in the streets around their destination.

After all, Hezbollah was the law around here.

Russell Whitlock had not told the truth to the taxi driver. He had no associates here in the government whatsoever. He had worked in the Middle East during a large portion of his career with the CIA, and he had been in and out of Beirut enough times as a NOC operative and a member of the National Clandestine Service's Autonomous Asset Program, but he wasn't exactly drinking tea and smoking a hookah with the town council on those trips. No, here in Beirut he'd assassinated a Syrian general and a Hezbollah politician and an al Qaeda banker, but those operations did not come with the free time or the backstories to allow him to cavort with the local intelligentsia or glitterati.

So he was going to have to bullshit his way through today.

As they drove south they passed bombed-out buildings from Lebanon's most recent war with Israel, and they passed armed men in military uniforms driving motorcycles and standing on street corners eyeing every vehicle they passed. They drove by posters glorifying suicide bombers, men and, in many cases, women who had "martyred" themselves over the border in Israel. It seemed to Russ that on every block there was another picture of a bearded young man or a woman with her arms and head covered, always in front of a flag and always holding a Kalashnikov. All these young men and women were dead now, and Russ muttered "Good riddance" under his breath while he looked out the window, careful to keep his head low and his eyes unfixed on anything that looked like it might have been official military business, lest he cause his taxi to get pulled over and his papers to get scrutinized.

Finally the cab arrived at the address. Russ paid the driver and climbed out, taking his small leather tote bag with him. He stood in the street as the taxi drove off, then looked up at the building in front of him.

It was a mid-rise apartment building, maybe a dozen stories high, with antennae and satellite dishes bolted onto every horizontal or vertical surface. At street level, older boys and young men sat smoking and standing around in front of a souk that spilled out of an alley just up the sidewalk, and Russ had not even shaken his collar down and straightened out his slacks from the cab ride before a malevolent-looking group of young toughs began walking his way. He ignored them, acted oblivious to the danger, and strolled toward the sliding wire mesh gate in front of the building.

A security guard stood inside the locked gate, staring back blankly. Russ told him he had a meeting with two men inside. The guard asked which two guys he was talking about, and this was Russ Whitlock's first indication that he would have to bypass whatever flunkies were here in order to speak to someone with actual authority.

A call was made from the guard to Russ's hosts, and after a perfunctory search, he was let into the building.

A few minutes later Russ knocked on the door to an apartment on the fifth floor. Behind him stood two security men who had just searched him. They seemed competent enough with the frisk, although they let their guard down to do it. As one man stood behind him, patting down his arms, the American knew he could ram back an elbow into the guard's throat, spin him around, and stomp on the inside of his leg to break it. Then he could draw the man's pistol from his waistband as he fell and with it shoot his partner.

But none of this happened; Russ just war-gamed scenarios in his mind like this in order to stay prepared for days when such moves might be necessary.

The door opened, and Russ found himself in a room with two dark-skinned and clean-shaven men in shirtsleeves. The men shook his hand while eyeing him warily. One looked to be over fifty, and the other might have been thirty-five.

There was a poster of Ayatollah Khomeini on the wall; otherwise the apartment was all but barren. A teakettle whistled on the stove in the kitchen to Whitlock's left, but the men ignored it. They asked to see Russ's passport and his visa. He produced both from the inside breast pocket of his sport coat. His documentation was passed back and forth between the two men; it claimed his name was Michael Harkin and he was a Canadian citizen, an import/export consultant from Toronto.

They handed him back his documentation, and all three sat down on threadbare sofas. Russ smiled at them, and they smiled back, but their body language read uncertainty.

The men were with VEVAK—the Iranian Ministry of Intelligence. They did not know who Russ was, really; they'd only been ordered to meet with the Westerner by bosses who themselves did not know Russ's true identity.

Russ knew this meeting would have happened somewhere else if the men he was coming to meet had had even an inkling of what he was about to offer them. Instead, Russ had contacted a man he knew to be an Iranian intelligence officer in Iraq posing as, of all things, a travel agent. Russ gave the man the Michael Harkin backstory and told him he had information to offer Iran regarding Iranian dissidents in Montreal who were operating in a computer hacking club that had created problems for the Iranian government.

The computer hackers did exist; Russ had learned about them in an article on the Internet. When the VEVAK man in Iraq asked how this Canadian man knew his identity, Harkin demurred, said he would make everything clear in a face-to-face meeting. He offered to come to Iraq, but instead he was given a counterproposal.

When it was proposed that the persistent Westerner who knew the right people would have to journey to Beirut to meet with Iranian intelligence, Russ knew he could have balked. He could have asked for other arrangements, *safer* arrangements, to be made. Perhaps he could have gone to a third-party embassy or consulate in Denmark or Lithuania or Ukraine, maybe met agents there who would have then passed his message up the chain. Certainly, if his goal was to stay in character as Michael Harkin, there was no way in hell he would have come to Beirut.

But Russ thought a few moves ahead on the chessboard—he'd studied from a master, after all—so he agreed to the meeting. He was not Michael Harkin. In order for his "true" identity to be believed, he had to display confidence in his ability to travel anywhere in the world.

So here he was, sitting in front of Iranian intelligence in the center of the most dangerous part of Hezbollah-controlled Beirut.

With a relaxed smile on his face.

They offered him tea and he accepted; he'd spent enough time as a guest of Arabs and Persians to know how to behave.

They spoke in English. A little small talk began as he told them about his flight and the traffic from the airport; the conversation was completely driven by Russ and not the two wary men who wondered who the fuck this guy was and what the fuck this guy wanted.

Finally the older man said, "We were told by our colleagues in Tehran that a man who knew the right people and said the right things would be coming today. But we were warned that you have not given a credible reason as to why you chose to fly around the world and come here to talk to us. Something about computers, I understand?"

"I was vague, yes," Russ acknowledged.

The younger of the two men—neither had offered his name—asked, "How can we be of service to an import/export consultant from Canada?"

Russ smiled. "I am not an import/export consultant from Canada."

"Oh?" said the younger man with one raised bushy eyebrow.

"I can give you my real name."

"You are not Michael Harkin? Do you realize you could be punished for applying for a Lebanese visa under a false identity?"

Russ laughed. Sitting on the sofa with his legs crossed now, he was the epitome of self-assuredness. "Do you want my name or not?"

"If you wish."

Russ's smile faded and he leaned forward a little. "My name is Courtland Gentry."

TWENTY-TWO

The older man seemed unfazed, but the younger was not able to hide a reaction; his eyes widened just slightly, but he recovered. "Is that a name that should mean something to us?"

"If your organization is worth anything, then yes, it should mean quite a lot, in fact."

The older man was genuinely confused; the younger turned to him and spoke low and fast in Farsi. Russ did not speak the language, but it, like Arabic, was a member of the Indo-European family of languages and he recognized the sound of it.

The older man asked his colleague for clarification, then turned to the American on the tattered sofa in front of him. With feigned nonchalance he reached for his tea and took a slow sip. "We are to believe that *you* are the Gray Man?"

"That name was given to me by others. There is nothing official to it."

Both men looked incredulous, but the younger one said, "What is it that you want?"

"Your superiors at VEVAK have been pursuing a business relationship with me for some time. I wanted to discuss this with them, in person, but I did not want to just walk through the front door of an embassy. Your diplomatic buildings throughout the world are under surveillance by American intelligence, and I'd rather avoid our relationship coming to light. So I came through the back door, so to speak."

Again the two men conferred for a moment in Farsi; Russ just watched them talk. They seemed to have no idea what to do, so he decided to help them out. "Gentlemen, I suggest you contact the highest-ranking member of your service you can get on the phone, and tell him I am here and ready to do business. They will send someone, someone who will verify my identity through whatever means VEVAK has to do so, and I will wait patiently until then."

Without another word the younger of the two stood and headed out of the room, down a hall to the rear of the flat, pulling out his mobile phone as he walked. The older man sat in silence for a moment, then held up a finger to Russ, stood, and went into the hall. He left the door open as he conferred with the two security men standing there, and seconds later they entered, their jackets open and their eyes locked on the man on the couch. They took up positions near the doorway to the kitchen, some twenty feet away from where Russ sat.

Russ smiled at them and nodded, then turned to the older VEVAK officer. "I assure you, I am a friend."

"Yes. I need you to wait, please."

"Of course."

"Would you like some more tea?"

"Love some."

Russ Whitlock sat on the sofa alone for more than an hour. From the rear of the flat he heard conversation; it sounded like both VEVAK men were working telephones frantically, but neither popped his head out to let him know what was going on. The two security men in the living room were professionals; they did not even look directly at him but just stood there, doing their best to show themselves to be competent badasses who were ready for anything.

Russ passed the time brainstorming ways to kill them.

Finally there was a knock at the door. The guards looked concerned, but they did not move; it was the young intelligence officer who appeared from the back and opened it, then embraced the visitor, an attractive and well-groomed man in a blue double-breasted suit. He entered with a smile, car keys, sunglasses, and mobile phone in his hand, and he placed them on the counter by the kitchen with a delicate movement.

Russ could see instantly by the deference given to him that this man was the local power. Beirut was ground zero for Iranian intelligence outside Tehran, so Russ knew this man must be quite high on the food chain, indeed. Perhaps the local VEVAK assistant chief of station, Russ surmised, but he did not ask.

Russ stood to meet him, and they shook hands.

"My name is Ali Hussein." This name was akin to *John Smith* in Iran, and Russ figured it was phony.

They shook hands. "Court Gentry."

"That remains to be seen," Ali said with a smile, and he held Whitlock's hand for a long moment. The two men were close now, their faces a foot apart, and now Russ detected a hardness, a malevolence behind the polished veneer of nice clothes and nice manners. This man was no assistant station chief riding a desk for an intelligence agency. Instead, Russ determined very quickly that this man was Quds Force, a special unit of the Iranian Republican Guard tasked with exporting Iranian power around the world.

Ali Hussein was a dangerous hombre, indeed.

Good. *This* was the asshole Russ had come to see.

Ali and Russ sat down across from one another in the living room, and the Iranian retrieved a folded sheaf of papers from the breast pocket of his coat. "I have some information about the Gray Man. I am going to ask you some questions. Are you ready?"

"Yes."

Ali smiled. "I hope so." He looked back to the kitchen just as the young VEVAK officer stepped out with tea on a tray.

"*Mamnoon.*" *Thank you,* he said, then returned his attention to the American across from him.

He asked, "What is your CIA code name?"

Russ did not hesitate. "Violator."

"And your CIA call sign?"

Whitlock raised his eyebrows in surprise. "I am impressed with your knowledge. My former agency does not give you the respect you deserve."

"Can you answer my question?"

"My call sign with my SAD unit was Sierra Six."

"SAD?"

"Special Activities Division."

"You were a commando."

"Something like that."

Ali Hussein nodded thoughtfully before continuing with the questions.

"Your place of birth?"

"Jacksonville, Florida."

"You have a sister. What is her name?"

"I *had* a brother. His name was Chase."

Ali Hussein did not react to this. He only glanced back down to the page in front of him.

Russ was comfortable with the questions because he had read Court's dossier; he knew it backward and forward. And there was another reason for his comfort. Russ himself had leaked a tiny portion of Gentry's file to Iranian intelligence months earlier, so that his answers would coincide with their knowledge.

But the next question was not a part of the intel he had leaked.

"You completed an operation in 2004 in the Bekah Valley. A Syrian brother, a member of al Qaeda in Iraq, was kidnapped from his home by you and your colleagues, and he was rendered to a CIA prison in Morocco. What can you tell me about that operation that would prove to me that you were there?"

Russ had read about this mission in Court's dossier, but he did not know where Iran came by the information. "I apologize," Russ said. "I am, as you know, no longer a member of the Central Intelligence Agency, but I remain a patriot. I love my country, and I am not here to commit treason by giving classified information to a foreign intelligence agency."

The Quds man said, "We have ways of obtaining that information from you."

"If you do anything to mar our new friendship, then you are a fool, Ali Hussein, because what I am here to offer you today is worth one hundred times the intelligence value you could gain from learning details of a decade-old operation."

"What is it that you are offering us?"

Russ leaned back on the sofa now and crossed his legs. "I want to relieve you of your biggest problem."

Ali Hussein cocked his head. "What is our biggest problem?"

"Not what. *Who.*"

"All right . . . *who* is our big—"

The Iranian stopped in midsentence, because he had the answer to his question. "Ehud Kalb."

Russ nodded. "Your government has proposed this to me before. My former handler, Gregor Sidorenko, told me that you extended this contract to me, and only me, over a year ago. At the time I was unable to accept your offer."

CIA had been reading Sid's mail for a long time, and

through them Russ knew that Iranian cutouts had gone to Sid to extend the offer, unaware that by this time Sid and Court had become mortal enemies.

Ali looked at him, not trusting, not convinced, but intrigued. "You are saying you have reconsidered?"

"Possibly. If the terms are improved."

"The Gray Man wants to assassinate Ehud Kalb for Iran?"

Now Russ shrugged. "Not for Iran. Sorry, but that is not my objective. I will do it for twenty-five million dollars. Before you tell me you don't have this kind of money, I know you and the intelligence agencies of the wealthy Gulf States would find it worthwhile, and certainly worth . . . what? A half hour of crude production to pay to decapitate the nation of Israel."

"If we offered this to you a year ago, and I am not saying we did. But . . . how do you know we have not simply arranged for someone else to do this?"

Whitlock leaned forward quickly, shaking his finger dramatically. "You don't dare; you will give no one else the opportunity, because you know that whether they succeed or fail, it will be revealed, somehow, some way, that Iran was the one who extended the contract. Iran cannot have that happen, because Iran knows it would be attacked, sanctioned, embargoed, blockaded, and otherwise squeezed and punished for attempting to decapitate the Jewish state."

The Quds Force operator did not disagree with this, but he also looked like he was out of his depth in the conversation. Russ expected this; he knew his plan would have to be kicked upstairs several times in the Iranian government before finding someone who could extend a formal offer.

"Please wait here." Hussein stood and headed toward the back of the apartment.

"Of course," Russ said as the man disappeared.

He returned in twenty minutes. "My colleagues would like you to come to Iran to meet with them."

Russ shook his head. "Out of the question."

Hussein nodded as if he expected this answer.

"They want to know why the world's greatest assassin would come, alone, to Beirut. Why did you not have an intermediary reach out to us? That would be standard tradecraft for this type of arrangement."

"I just killed my last handler on Sunday." Hussein's eyes widened as that sank in. Russ added with a shrug, "I've decided I will make my own arrangements from now on."

After a nervous clearing of the throat, Ali said, "They are not convinced you are who you say you are."

"But?"

"But there is a way you can convince them."

Russ knew what was coming next, and he also knew it was going to be a problem.

"They want to know about Kiev."

Ali Hussein was impressed. "Exactly. If you are the Gray Man, then you know that there were Iranians present during the event in Kiev three years ago."

"Of course I know. And they were not just Iranians. They were Quds Force operatives." Russ's eyes narrowed. "Friends of yours, maybe?"

Ali Hussein just shook his head. "No."

"Well, nevertheless, I saw the Iranians."

"What else did you see?"

"You are asking me for a complete after-action report of my Kiev operation?"

"It would settle any doubts as to your identity."

"I never kiss and tell."

Hussein seemed disappointed. "Then you must allow us time to investigate you and your proposal. I can't tell some stranger that he has Iran's blessing to target the prime minister of Israel. You can see how that could ultimately be very harmful for Iran, should something go wrong."

"I can't wait for you to perform your due diligence. If I am to take this contract, I must act immediately. The prime minister will be making a trip to Brussels, London, and New York next week, and then he has no more scheduled travel for several months. The time is now."

"Then prove you were the man at the Vasylkiv Air Base the evening of April 8, two thousand—"

"I will not tell you about Kiev. But I will prove to you I am who I claim to be."

"How?"

"Go back to your telephone, have your superiors give you a name. One name of one man. Or woman, I do not care."

"*What* man? *What* woman?"

"The person your organization would most like eliminated in the next five days. Someone located in Europe, that is a requirement, simply for geographical expediency. Other than that . . . I don't care. They can be behind guarded gates, a public figure with security. It doesn't matter. I will leave Beirut this afternoon, I will find this person, and I will rid the Iranian government of this problem immediately. Who could make this promise other than the Gray Man?"

Ali Hussein did not hide his surprise at the offer. Twice he began to speak, but twice he stopped himself.

Whitlock added, "No charge. And no comebacks to you. If I succeed, you win. If I fail, you lose nothing. We are not working together."

"You are saying you will kill anyone on the continent of Europe? Within five days."

"Yes."

Hussein said nothing for several moments. He seemed, to Russ, to be a powerful man unaccustomed to the concept of running out of the room every few minutes to get approval from on high. But after a time he stood from the sofa. "I will make a call. You have not convinced me of anything, but perhaps my colleagues will entertain your request."

Whitlock smiled and gave a polite half bow, supercilious, though he doubted Hussein would pick up on it. The Iranian left the room, and Russ turned his attention back to his tea and his fantasies of killing the guards.

It was midafternoon by the time Ali returned to the apartment and extended a hand with a folded sheet of paper. In the interim the number of security around Russ Whitlock had increased threefold. Russ ignored the half-dozen men with guns exactly as he would imagine Court Gentry would ignore them, and he looked at his watch with an annoyed or bored expression every few minutes.

Russ took the folded paper, but he did not look at it.

Ali said, "There is a name for you. He is—"

Whitlock interrupted. "It doesn't matter who he is. I will take care of it, we will be in touch, and I will expect your organization to uphold its end of the bargain."

"By giving you the Kalb contract."

"Correct. Twenty-five million dollars, deposited into a numbered account at a bank in Dubai."

"I must tell you, this is truly a remarkable boast you have made."

"It is a boast, yes, but I don't see it as remarkable. It is, quite simply, what I do."

"The name on that sheet of paper is a hard target."

"Then I'd better get to work." The men shook hands, and Russ made his way through the scrum of gunmen in the room toward the door.

TWENTY-THREE

Court arrived in Stockholm on the Tallink Ferry after a twelve-hour Baltic Sea cruise that left him exhausted. There was nothing physical for him to do on the boat, but he forced himself to stay awake, to maintain constant vigilance, a tiring and stressful task for someone already tired and stressed after the actions of the past few days. But the ferry crossing was uneventful; the Estonian authorities had added security at the departure point in Tallinn but not on the ship itself, and now Court looked forward to finding a place in a massive city where he could disappear, simply go to ground and rest until it was time to move on.

He had a taxi take him to the center of town, and although he had to fight the urge to lay his head down on a snow-covered bench in a park, he forced himself to begin an SDR that lasted until the early afternoon, walking through the Olstermalm district, taking cabs and streetcars and buses, occasionally stopping in cafés for coffee and protein to stay awake.

He strolled through a department store, entering through one door and leaving through another, but while passing through he went into the housewares department and bought a high-quality paring knife with a four-inch blade and a vinyl sheath. He would rather arm himself with a Glock, but they were not exactly off-the-shelf items here in Sweden. Firearms were available for hunting, but Court wouldn't very well be able to fill out the form for the background check necessary to buy one, so he'd just have to protect himself with his brain, his body, and a kitchen utensil.

Once he felt certain he was not under surveillance he branched out, beginning his hunt for a secure-enough rooming house or other cheap place to stay.

It was nightfall before he found a suitable location on Rastatgaten, just north of the city center. He stood on the sidewalk under a window with a handwritten sign offering rooms, and he looked up and down the street, deciding the security situation here would suit his needs.

He entered a steakhouse on the ground floor of the building to inquire, and was sent back outside and up a narrow stairway adjacent to the restaurant. He stood alone in a dark hall for a while, but soon a Serbian man who spoke English came up the steps and offered him his choice of three rooms. Court looked them over and settled on a corner flat with windows that offered views up the streets in two directions. The room was tiny; the bed was just a mattress on the cold wooden floor and the kitchen consisted of a card table with a chair, a hot plate, and a teakettle. The toilet and shower were down the hall and shared with a few other rooms on the floor.

It was a dump, but it was also low profile with a fair line of sight on the street. Court was well accustomed to austere living conditions; he'd slept in shit holes on four continents, so he told the Serbian man he'd take it.

He paid in euros, which annoyed the Serb but he took them anyway, and he gave Court a key. Court immediately locked his door behind the man and lay down on the mattress fully dressed.

His body ached from head to toe, but he slept like the dead until morning.

———

The next day he walked the streets of the city, learning the area and picking up provisions. He studied the dress and the mannerisms of the locals, the accessories men carried, the way people covered themselves from the cold or the method by which women would greet one another with a kiss or men would shake hands.

Whenever Court found himself in a new environment he endeavored to know the people intimately by observation. He needed to fit in, of course, and an awareness of how a man his age should dress and act and talk would help him play his role correctly. But there was more to this exercise than that. Gentry had to be able to pick out others here who did not belong. If he saw a man wearing an odd style of coat or two women who seemed either stiffer or more familiar than normal when they met on the street,

Gentry knew those people merited a second glance. Could they be trackers sent by any one of the myriad organizations hunting him?

There was a science to his study, but it was not rocket science; it was automatic for Court now, and almost easy for him to discern those who did not fit in to the landscape. Enough years on his own in strange lands had made him a uniquely adept people watcher.

As he ventured through the districts he also noticed security cameras; he found them virtually everywhere. On street corners, in shop windows, along building exteriors, in parking lots, even mobile police camera stands.

Court countered this surveillance by moving through town with the hood of his coat up, a wool scarf wrapped over his nose and mouth, and, when the weather and lighting conditions allowed, sunglasses over his eyes. He did not know the quality or efficiency of the facial recog software used by U.S. authorities, or even if Stockholm would be a city covered with electronic surveillance by his opposition, but he planned on leaving nothing to chance. With the low temperatures his winter gear would fit in perfectly, so he decided he'd remove his scarf only when indoors, and take off his hood only when he was back in his room.

Being identified by Townsend or CIA or NSA electronic surveillance was his main concern here in Stockholm. Money, by contrast, would not be a problem, not for months anyway, as the Moscow *Bratva*'s cash would last for a long time in the manner in which Gentry was accustomed to living. But he had to exchange euros for kronor, and he did not want to enter banks or deal with aboveboard currency exchange booths, because he'd be forced to stick his face in a camera to do so.

He solved this small problem in Hortoget neighborhood, the tiny Chinatown of Stockholm. He identified several black-market moneychangers within minutes and chose one at random; he'd used men like this for years when moving about off the grid. He pulled five thousand euros from his pocket, the man charged him a usurious exchange rate for his trouble, and just like that, he was flush with local currency.

After stopping back at his flat with his groceries and other provisions, he ventured back into the cold, this time on a different mission. Again, he covered his face and head, taking a mental note of every camera he could find in his AO; he even crossed streets to avoid them, although he knew no recog algorithm on earth could identify him from the half-inch of exposed cheekbone that remained uncovered between his scarf and his sunglasses.

He found a small used electronics store on Klara Vattugrand near the train station, and he entered, passing the televisions and audio equipment at the front of the store before removing his hood and lowering his scarf, lest any distant street camera catch a fleeting image of him. There were security cameras here in the little store, of course, but Court kept his scarf over his jawline and his sunglasses on, and he identified the location of the cams immediately and did his best to avoid them.

He'd come to purchase a laptop. He planned to use the computer to research secure communications with which he could contact Russ Whitlock. Yes, Russ had passed Court a URL that he claimed would lead him to a protocol to do this, but Court wasn't going to simply follow instructions. He would look into the technology independently, find his own means of establishing secure comms, and only then would he reach out to the other former AAP asset.

Gentry had decided to contact Russ, telling himself he would take his time to do it carefully and securely, and also telling himself he was doing it only because it was prudent, from a PERSEC perspective, to do so. If the man had information about Townsend's training, tactics, and procedures, Court knew it would be in his interest to stay in touch, to bleed out as much intel as the man would give.

There might have been other reasons Court wanted to communicate with Whitlock, but he did his best to deny them. Russ had said it himself: They were the only two left, they were singletons, and they were alone out in the world. Some level of communication, if ultrasecure and based on the highest levels of encryption and not even the lowest degree of trust, might be a good thing.

The salesman in the electronics shop was young and an ethnic Indian, but he spoke English as perfectly as most Swedes. He sold Court a used MacBook Pro, a faux leather case, and an external battery.

Court paid in kronor, wrapped himself back up like a mummy, and returned outside to the cold.

He was completely unaware that a partial image of his face had been collected by a camera built into the bezel of a laptop on a display stand in the back of the store. The feed had been networked to the wireless router of the computer shop, which was protected only by off-the-shelf security encryption.

Court did not head back to his flat immediately. He spent an hour on an SDR, and while doing so he stepped into a convenience store and purchased a prepaid mobile phone.

Court liked it here in Sweden, and it was nice to move around fully cloaked. With a little luck, he thought, he might stay in Stockholm till late spring, when walking the streets with a hood over his head and a scarf across his face would no longer work. Then he would move on, smarter and slicker, and by then he just might have a plan.

His plan, he was certain, would not allow him to stop hiding, but he thought maybe, just maybe, soon he could stop running so damn much.

TWENTY-FOUR

Ruth Ettinger, senior targeting officer in the Collections Department of the Mossad, reasonably assumed her meeting this morning would take place in the unincorporated community of Langley, Virginia, at the George Bush Center for Intelligence, the headquarters of the Central Intelligence Agency. But a phone call just before eight A.M. that Thursday morning, just as she was climbing into her cab in front of her hotel in Tysons Corner, directed her instead to the Office of the Director of National Intelligence, some three and a half miles away from the CIA.

The cab dropped her at the outer gate in front of Liberty Crossing, the name given to the intelligence campus in Tysons Corner that housed both the National Counterterrorism Center and the Office of the Director of National Intelligence. Ruth's destination was Liberty Crossing

Two, or LX2, the office building that held ODNI, the bureaucracy created after 9/11 and placed in charge of all seventeen American intelligence organizations and agencies.

At the Tysons McLean Drive gate to Liberty Crossing she handed over her cell phone and her handbag to federal security officials; then she was wanded and badged, and soon she boarded a golf cart driven by an armed security officer. The golf cart dropped her at the front door of LX2 and here she was met by a woman waiting outside, bundled in her coat and stamping her feet to stay warm.

Inside Ruth passed through a metal detector and was ushered into a small conference room on the third floor of the building. She was left alone at a conference table with a coffee service and a tray of glistening Danishes for over a half hour. She ignored the pastries, sipped black coffee, and wrote notes to herself on a notepad, anxious about the meeting to come.

Finally the door opened and she found herself face-to-face with Denny Carmichael, the director of the CIA's National Clandestine Service.

He strolled in with confidence; before the door shut behind him she saw that he had an entourage of at least half a dozen men and women left behind in the hallway, and she was thankful he had chosen to meet with her alone.

This particular quick get-together had been arranged by the director of Mossad's Collections Department, Menachem Aurbach, an old friend of Carmichael's. The two men had served in the trenches of their respective agencies since Ruth was in preschool, and they shared a professional and personal respect for one another, despite the occasional rivalries between the two ostensibly friendly nations. Aurbach had called Denny at home the evening before and implored him to meet with a young targeting officer already in the States on a matter that he promised would be of mutual importance for both agencies. Menachem had also suggested Denny keep the meeting off the books, as there were matters to be discussed that he might not want jotted down for the public record.

Carmichael agreed; he and Aurbach went back over thirty years, after all, but Ruth imagined he must have been somewhat put off by the request.

"Thank you for agreeing to meet with me," Ruth said as she stood and walked around the conference table, her hand extended.

"My pleasure," he said, but no pleasure showed on his face, only a mild surprise that the woman from Mossad that he was here to meet was actually quite attractive.

Ruth noted his attraction. It neither insulted nor flattered her; she only saw it as something to file away, to use if possible and if necessary.

Denny's eyes lingered over her a little longer than necessary, and he smiled a craggy smile at her as they sat. There were so many deep-set worry lines in his face that it looked to Ruth as if his smile might cause his head to shatter. She put him in his midsixties, but he was fit and moved like a much younger man, and, it seemed to her, this was an impression of himself that he was more than happy to convey.

He said, "I'm sorry we had to change the venue on you at the last minute. Got called over here to ODNI early for a quick confab with the director."

"No problem at all, sir."

"How is Menachem?"

"He is sick and tired and disagreeable and pushy."

Carmichael chuckled, surprised by the frankness of the young woman. "Unchanged in the past thirty years. That's good, I guess."

"He sends his regards."

"He called me at home last night, asked me to make time to meet with one of his best people. He speaks very highly of you."

Ruth did not smile at the platitude. Instead she said, "I solve problems for him and make him look good."

"I see you don't lack confidence," Denny said with another surprised chuckle. He sipped water from his bottle, then smiled at Ruth once more. "I come from a different age, Ms. Ettinger, so you will have to forgive me if you find this out of line. But I just have to say it. The Mossad has always possessed the best-looking female officers."

Ettinger did not miss a beat. "And the CIA has always possessed the most impertinent executives."

Carmichael's eyebrows rose at the young woman's comment. She'd seen this before, many times. That moment when the man in front of her realizes she is not just a pretty face. He shuffled a little in his chair, and she liked this, liked making lecherous men uncomfortable with her intelligence and willingness to confront them. He laughed finally, finding her candor refreshing. "Your statement is true, but so is mine."

Ruth only smiled politely.

"Tell me about the problem that brings you here today."

She got right to it. "We have a source in Beirut. Not a joint source. One of ours exclusively."

"Any good?"

"He has been reliable in the past."

"And you want to share him with us?" He said it as a joke, and she obliged him with a smile before shaking her head. He moved on. "What is your source telling you that you, in turn, would like to tell me?"

"He is telling me—he is telling his case officer in Beirut, I should say—that Iranian agents met just yesterday with an American. A man whom they have hired to assassinate my prime minister. A contract killer who was, if rumors are to be believed, trained by your agency."

"Who is this killer?"

"The Gray Man," she said, her eyes locked on his, searching for hints of what this news meant to him.

Carmichael did not react. Instead he sat quietly for a moment before saying, "That particular nom de guerre comes up more often than you could possibly imagine, Ms. Ettinger."

"As I said, we deem our source reliable. The Iranians, from what we understand, have a file on Courtland Gentry, and they compared their knowledge of him with information he was able to provide, and they determined they were dealing with the authentic Gray Man."

"What information did he provide?"

"Our informant was peripheral to the meeting. He is passing on secondhand intelligence, admittedly, but his information in the past has been proven reliable enough to where we take this new threat very seriously, and we will be acting on it."

She read something in his eyes now, and it surprised her for two reasons. For one, she was surprised he could not keep his craggy old face impassive. He'd been a case officer himself for decades, after all; he'd surely heard many things over his career that left him startled but nevertheless required him to hide any show of alarm or excitement.

And second, his reaction seemed to be less what she expected, which was *Oh shit!* and more of what she did not expect, which was *Hell yes!* It was an open secret that the CIA was hunting their former assassin turned rogue hit man, but it did surprise her to see that Carmichael was pleased to know the man had turned up mentioned in a plot to kill the head of a friendly nation.

Denny said, "Okay. He's out there. We know that, so I'll have to entertain the possibility your man in Beirut is credible. What is it that I can do for you?"

"I would like you to provide me everything you have on the Gray Man. He is . . . *was*, your man. You have been unable, despite what I am sure are your agency's best efforts, to rein him in for a number of years. We would like to look for him ourselves. To take care of him ourselves."

"The Gray Man is our problem, Ms. Ettinger."

She shook her head. "With due respect, once he took the contract on our prime minister, he became our problem. I have hunted down many individuals in the past several years. If Menachem alluded to my abilities and competence in your conversation last night, this is exactly what he was talking about. I am certain, with your help, I will be able to track him and stop him before he is able to do any more harm."

"And by 'stop him' you mean . . . ?"

Ruth leaned forward over the table. "Kill or capture."

Denny smiled and leaned back, then scooted his chair out and crossed his legs. Ruth was offended by the gesture, but she did not let on; she surmised that the man's intentions were to insult her, and she would not play into his intentions. He said, "Ms. Ettinger, my service is not without its own resources. I'm not sure what you know about the Gray Man, but certainly your organization is dialed in enough to be aware there has been a five-year manhunt by us, not just CIA but also members of our Joint Special Operations Forces, to effect the capture of him."

"But our prime minister is now in—"

He waved his hand dismissively. "Your asset in Lebanon says your PM is under threat. I get it. But what I don't get is why Menachem Aurbach sends a young woman such as yourself to talk to me about this. I see you are all piss and vinegar and energized about your mission, but this building, the building next door, the CIA campus, hell, a dozen other buildings across D.C. are all chock-full of bright young people who have been working hard to locate and terminate this man, and yet he continues to create a swath of death and destruction around the world."

"I'll find him, Director Carmichael. I always do."

"Ms. Ettinger, you come from a small agency in a small country. You fill yourself with delusions of your importance. You aren't half as special as you think you are."

He started to stand up, to end the meeting. "I mean you no offense, of course."

Ruth stood herself, leaning over the table now with both hands gripping the edge. "Obviously, Director Carmichael, you don't know a thing about me or my capabilities. I have personally effected the arrest or elimination of thirteen direct threats on Israel's national leadership. Believe me, if you had office buildings full of people"—she lifted her hands, making sarcastic quotes with her fingers—"'just like me,' you would have already killed Gentry, ended the war on terror, and liberated both Cuba and North Korea. But you haven't, have you?"

She slowed down a little, but the intensity in her voice did not lessen.

"You don't know me, obviously, so you can't be sure if I am as capable as I claim, but I have to think if CIA doesn't know about me or my record by now, then that says more about *your* people and *their* abilities than it does about me and my abilities.

"If our prime minister is threatened by a CIA project gone haywire, a supersecret asset who went rogue to knock off some mafia dons and third-world despots but has now graduated to decapitating first-world democracies allied with the United States, then this five-year-long dull headache of yours is going to turn into an immediate bullet-to-the-brain head wound and it will come back to harm your agency in a very real and very public way.

"But starting today, your situation will improve, because I am here and I will find your little fuckup named Court Gentry, and I will call in my own set of killers,

Metsada men who make your Joint Special Operations Forces look like pimple-faced pubescent Boy Scouts, and together we will kill your man because obviously you and your people can't manage it yourselves."

She sat back down slowly and finished with, "I mean *you* no offense. Of course."

The door behind Carmichael opened slightly and a young woman leaned in, obviously checking on the noise. "Sir?"

"Out," he barked.

The woman disappeared.

Denny sat quietly for a moment. Ruth watched him carefully, trying to discern what he was thinking. She felt she could see a rekindling in his eyes of the excitement she had noticed before. Otherwise, she was about to be thrown out the door and deported back to Israel.

But his next words—"What do you want to know about him?"—told her she had won.

She softened her tone. She knew when to bludgeon, and she knew when to coax. Now was the time for the latter. "Everything you can give us would be greatly appreciated. Obviously there will be sources and methods you will want to protect, even from your friends, and I can understand that. But I'm not Menachem; I don't care about any big picture in our relationship. All I am concerned with, in any way, is finding this man and stopping him in any way I can."

Carmichael did not respond immediately, so she pressed gently. "For example, before Court Gentry became a hit man, what did he do for you?"

"He was a dynamic operations specialist."

She wrote on her pad and spoke aloud. "He was a hit man, then."

"I did not say that."

Ruth nodded, but she did not strike through her note.

Carmichael asked, "What does your service know about him already?"

"Mossad's dossier on Court Gentry's time with the CIA is thin. We don't make it a point of compiling a large amount of information about operatives at allied agencies; our enemies keep us busy enough."

Denny raised his eyebrows, giving off the message that he did not believe that for a second. The Mossad was legendary for spying on their friends as well as their enemies. Ruth knew what she was saying was not true, but she also knew she had to say it. Moreover, she knew Carmichael would know it was a lie, but she also knew he would let the comment go.

Such was the nature of relationships between friendly intelligence agencies.

She continued, "We don't have too much more on his days post-CIA, but from what we know, his assassinations have seemed to follow some sort of a moral code. He has killed for money, repeatedly, but all his targets have been personalities with large amounts of blood on their hands. When discounting all the Gray Man killings that are nothing more than rumor, we have never seen him target anyone like our prime minister in his past."

She summed up her dilemma. "We understand why the Iranians want Kalb dead, but we do not understand why the Gray Man wants Kalb dead."

Carmichael sipped water from his bottle. "He's a snake."

Ruth cocked her head. "Kalb, or Gentry?"

"Gentry. Court Gentry has built up a reputation for two things. First, that he is the best black operator in the world. That reputation is, quite possibly, valid. His performance evals in the field were stellar. But the second part of his reputation is a complete and utter fantasy. That he is some sort of Robin Hood with a sniper rifle. A virtuous paladin."

"Not true?" Ruth asked with a tone of genuine surprise.

"Forgive my language, but that is bullshit. Since he left CIA he has been a cold-blooded killer. Nothing more."

"Perhaps our intelligence is faulty. It is our understanding he is an assassin with a conscience. We know he has turned down many contracts, lucrative contracts, because of the nature of the target's history. There seems to exist some moral code involved, even if it is hard for us to discern."

Carmichael responded tersely. "Gentry has killed colleagues of mine, Ms. Ettinger. Men with families, futures. I will begin to take it very personally if you continue to talk about how he is one of the good guys."

"Of course I am not saying he is a good guy. I am only trying to understand how his sense of morality would be satisfied by killing Ehud Kalb. This information is very much pertinent to hunting him—"

Ruth stopped speaking. She understood. There was something personal going on here that she had not detected until now. "You knew him. You actually knew him personally."

He waved his hand in the air and sat back. "Not well. There are a lot of guys like him. Not like him in the sense . . . You know what I mean. A lot of tip-of-the-spear operations personnel. So, no, I did not know him well. But yes . . . I did know him."

Ruth wrote something down. "Well then. You may be the best person to ask. The legend of him is quite re-markable. They say he could pass you on the street and you would not notice him."

Now Denny smiled thinly. "Ms. Ettinger. He could pass you in your kitchen and you would not notice him."

She stopped writing. Looked up. "He's that good?"

He smiled. "Find him and you can see for yourself."

Ruth smiled back now. "If you let me see his file, I will do just that."

Denny drummed his fingers on the polished table for a moment. "There is a man I want you to meet."

"Director Carmichael, unless this man is Courtland Gentry, I am already talking to the most important person in the equation."

"That's not exactly true."

Ettinger cocked her head.

Denny said, "I'm talking about the director of the operation against Gentry."

"Very well. Is he available?"

"If I tell him he is available, then he is available."

She smiled. Fighting the urge to stand up. "Is he here at Liberty Crossing or over at Langley?"

"Neither."

"He is posted to a foreign station?"

"He's not with the agency."

Now Ruth Ettinger was utterly confused. Denny saw this and said, "We have found it prudent to bring in private sector assistance to help us with the Court Gentry situation."

"You've *outsourced* the hunt for your number one target?"

Denny nodded, picking lint off the collar of his suit. "Townsend Government Services."

"I've never heard of them."

"And I hope, when this is all over, you will forget that you ever did. They are based here in D.C. I can get you a meeting immediately with director Leland Babbitt."

Ruth was still having trouble understanding. "A private company of manhunters?"

Now the American smiled. "That's pulp fiction dramatics, Ms. Ettinger. The real world is rather more boring. Townsend is staffed with ex-military and intel folks, all cleared and vetted, all perfectly capable. They'll get him, soon enough, but I will have them read you in on status of the investigation, and I will let Babbitt know that you will be joining his hunt."

"That would be ideal, Director Carmichael. I'd like to meet this Mr. Babbitt this morning, if possible."

TWENTY-FIVE

Back when he stood in front of the Quds Force operative who passed him the assassination target in the south Beirut hotel room, Whitlock had appeared relaxed and indifferent as to his target's identity. But as soon as he returned to Rafic Hariri Airport he'd locked himself in a bathroom stall and ripped open the sealed folder, already counting down the hours remaining and hoping like hell he had some previous knowledge of the man he was being sent to kill.

Within seconds he saw the name of his target and his place of residence. The name was familiar to him, but he could not place it, and he didn't take the time to investigate immediately. Instead, he looked at the location of the target, then rushed out of the bathroom and to the counter, where he bought a first-class one-way ticket to France. Within ninety minutes he was airborne on his way to Charles de Gaulle in Paris, and three hours after this he boarded his connecting flight to the Nice Côte d'Azur airport. He arrived at his final destination before ten P.M., less than eight hours after being handed the name of the man the Iranians wanted him to kill.

The name handed over by Quds was that of an Iranian-born French citizen, Amir Zarini. He was a fifty-six-year-old filmmaker who, if the Iranians were to be believed, had blasphemed the prophet and insulted the Iranian government repeatedly during his high-profile career.

During the two flights from Beirut to Nice he re-searched his target on his laptop. Sitting in the first-class cabin Russ researched the man's history, known associ-ates, and living arrangements via open-source web searches. Zarini had made a number of successful feature films in France about the plight of women and Chris-tians under oppressive Islamic regimes. He'd been nom-inated for two Palmes d'Or, but clearly not everyone saw the art in his work. Virtually every nation besmirched by the films had made threats against Zarini, and the direc-tor was well aware he was a target of the Iranians as well as other Muslim fanatics around the world.

Russ didn't make it to many movies at all, much less mopey foreign films about women's rights in the Middle East. He considered watching one of the movies on his computer to get a better picture of his target, then tabled the idea; he didn't have time to spare, and he couldn't really care less about the subject matter.

He found an article about Zarini on the online version of *Le Monde*, and Whitlock put his command of French to good use to read it. The piece went into helpful detail about the director's living situation, even showing the interior of his seaside mansion. There was a mention in the article about two attempts on Zarini's life, and this jogged Russ's memory. He'd seen the news of an attack on a home in Nice a few months earlier, and he assumed that was where he'd first heard the name Amir Zarini.

Russ made a mental note to research the attempts on Zarini's life further, in order to find out what *not* to do.

Whitlock knew Nice well; he'd spent years of his life across the Mediterranean in North Africa and the Middle East, and this made the city a particularly attractive R & R getaway for him. As a man accustomed to the danger and intrigue of the Arab world, he'd enjoyed escaping the dust and strife and sobriety of his work there, exchanging it for the casinos and nightlife and beaches of the French Riviera. More than once Russ had left behind a spartan safe house in Alexandria or Beirut or Damascus, from where he had just spent a month or more tracking an al Qaeda operative or holding surveillance on a Muslim Brotherhood terrorist, and checked into a deluxe room at the Palais de la Méditerranée. He figured since America owed him far more than what it could ever repay him for the work he did on its behalf, he might as well enjoy himself on America's dime in his downtime.

Russ had a long list of favorite haunts here, but now he was in town under double cover, playing the role of Court Gentry masquerading as a Canadian businessman. He had to forgo his regular five-star accommodations and make other arrangements. He took a suite at

Le Grimaldi, just a few blocks from the water; ordered room service; popped an Adderall to stay awake; and worked on building his target folder of Amir Zarini.

Once Russ was firmly ensconced in his hotel room, he took a half hour to clean his painful and seeping gunshot wound. That task completed, he opened his computer back up and pulled up a secure Townsend Government Services network that gave him back-door access to a classified U.S. intelligence database. The information stored here was considered secret in nature, not the most sensitive intelligence known to the U.S. intelligence community, but certainly information he would not be able to find in open sources. He punched in Amir Zarini's name and within seconds he was reading detailed French National Police records of both assassination attempts.

The first attempt on the director's life, just under a year prior, had been executed by a group of Islamist civilians, and, it came as no surprise to Russ, it failed miserably.

Zarini was in Nice, speaking at a film symposium at the Museum of Modern Art. He had just taken the stage when three young French nationals with Moroccan backgrounds rushed onto the stage, screaming and brandishing knives. Zarini himself knocked one of his attackers to the floor, suffering a gash on his wrist in the process. The young French Arab was then tackled and disarmed by spectators who charged up from the front row.

A second would-be assassin was waylaid by a security officer employed by the museum and knocked unconscious before he made it to within ten feet of Zarini.

The third member of the group of hapless attackers, a female, carried in her hands not only a fixed-blade knife but also a large banner she apparently had planned to unfurl on the stage after the assassination. Her plan went awry when the banner became caught on a railing in the crowd as she ran forward, and she accidentally unfurled it, then tripped, her knife skittering across the floor and out of reach as she was brought down by the unarmed low-risk security officers hired for the event.

Russ laughed aloud at the dim-witted attack, but he did not laugh long. The CIA reported that Zarini's personal security was doubled as a result of the event, and the filmmaker severely curtailed his public appearances afterward.

The second attempt on Zarini's life had been as professional as the first had been amateurish. Russ read pages of material, studied diagrams, pored through witness testimony, and viewed autopsy reports of an event that took place just a few months earlier.

The perpetrators of this assassination attempt were a force of five military-aged males. From the data on the Townsend Network, Russ learned that the CIA suspected them to be members of the Quds Force, though they held Syrian and Lebanese passports.

Russ marveled at their plan's audacity. Late on a warm July evening the men hit the beach behind Zarini's walled property in a rubber landing craft, climbed a gate, and continued up the rocky beach, spreading themselves wide. One of Zarini's guard dogs was alerted to their presence and started barking. A security man on a second-floor balcony waved his flashlight over the rear of the property and immediately died in a hailstorm of bullets from three AK-74 rifles.

The Quds Force officers breached the villa, killed four security men and both guard dogs, and made their way to the director's bedroom, only to find that their target had escaped into an adjacent panic room moments before.

Russ read it again.

Panic room.

Damn. His hopes for a nighttime infiltration were dashed in an instant. Whitlock felt he could breach the property. In fact, he was certain of it. But could he make his way to Zarini, past guards, guns, and gates, past dogs and motion lights, completely undetected? Russ assumed Zarini would need no more than a few seconds to get inside a panic room, and that complicated any attack on the home exponentially.

As it had complicated the attack for the Quds officers. When the Iranians realized they had failed in their objective, all five killed themselves as a French police tactical unit entered Zarini's home. The Iranian director and his family escaped the attack without so much as a scratch.

The main takeaway from the two attacks was clear. This was going to be a tough op. Zarini made few public appearances, and he held all the advantages in his home.

So Russ had to take him on the move.

From his suite at Le Grimaldi, Russ next used the network to find the name of the private security company with the contract to protect Amir Zarini. At the opening of the business day the next morning he contacted

Sécurité Exclusive de Paris directly and spoke with a company representative in Paris. He struck up a friendly conversation with the woman, using one of his Townsend Services identities and dropping the real names of real men in the security industry in the United States and France, ex-soldiers and spooks Russ knew from his years as a NOC. Though Russ remained cagey about the specific nature of the relationships, he said enough to convince the representative he was legit, and he told her he was looking for work. She politely passed him on for an immediate phone interview with a Sécurité Exclusive executive.

He spent an hour on the phone with the company's personnel director in Paris, at first inquiring about employment, but within minutes the two men were deep in conversation about the equipment, training, and tactics used in the security field. Russ made the personnel director feel that he was the one benefiting from the conversation; Russ knew so much "inside baseball" information about the high-risk security field that the personnel director found himself asking for information about hot spots where the company might solicit work in the near future.

Ultimately the executive and Russ mutually decided the American was overqualified for the positions available at the moment, but since Russ happened to be in Nice, the exec gave Russ the names and numbers of a couple of company men working in the area.

By late afternoon Russ Whitlock sat with a Sécurité Exclusive contractor enjoying a beer at Le Pirate, a restaurant-bar in Saint-Jean-Cap-Ferrat, just a few kilometers up the coast from Zarini's multimillion-dollar mansion. The man was not on the Zarini detail himself, but he worked for another wealthy client in the same neighborhood. Soon enough the conversation turned comfortably to the attack on the director's home several months earlier. Russ was pleased to learn that his new drinking buddy had all the intimate details of the operation, as one of his close friends had died in the attack.

He was also friends with a few men on the current detail, and he told Russ that while Zarini did not make many public appearances, he made a weekly trip to a friend's villa twenty minutes away, just over the border in Monaco. The contractor revealed that the Zarini detail felt the outing was a dangerous habit, and they had warned their client of their fears, but the Iranian had dismissed them by saying the event was the one time each week when they actually had to work for their money.

Russ told his own lengthy made-up story about his issues dealing with a rich asshole client in Hong Kong and the man's penchant for routines that made for clear security violations.

The Frenchman ordered another round of drinks and began recanting war stories about his own jackass protectee, but soon enough the conversation returned to Amir Zarini and every Saturday morning at noon, when he and his detail poured into two vehicles and headed up the coast for the twenty-minute drive into Monaco.

Within minutes Whitlock had everything he needed. He learned there were four men in Zarini's mobile security detail; they were French, private contractors now but former members of RAID—Recherche Assistance Intervention

Dissuasion, a tactical unit within the French National Police service. They were armed with HK UMP-9s, submachine guns that they kept folded and stored in the vehicles, and CZ pistols chambered in the potent .40-caliber Smith and Wesson.

Additionally, Zarini traveled in an unarmored Mercedes SUV driven by an armed driver, and a second Mercedes SUV, also driven by an armed man, served as a chase car, ready to scoop Zarini up if his first vehicle became disabled.

The American remained in Le Pirate with his new friend for another round of drinks, then bid him adieu.

And just like that, within thirty hours of receiving Zarini's name in Beirut, Russ Whitlock knew his target's schedule; the disposition, tactics, and training of his security team; and the structural capabilities of his vehicles.

Next Russ drove the route from Zarini's property to Monaco. He decided a powerful explosive placed along the road and detonated as Zarini's Mercedes passed would be the easiest and smartest course of action, but he also knew this was not the MO of the Gray Man. No, Court would jeopardize his own life to eliminate the risk of collateral damage, and as stupid as Russ found that mind-set, he knew he had to make this look like a Gray Man op.

Russ went back to his suite, popped an Adderall, and drank coffee to stay awake through the night to work on his plan.

The best course of action, Russ decided after looking at the maps for hours, would be to position himself along the hillside high over the one road Zarini and his detail would have to pass, and then fire on his target's vehicle with a long-range scoped rifle. There would be no collateral damage, and he could then slip away through the trees and get out of the area quickly and cleanly, unseen by the security forces and, hopefully, witnesses.

It would be a Gray Man–like hit all around.

Satisfied he had a workable plan, Whitlock ordered a chilled '94 Dom Perignon from room service and drank it straight from the bottle when it arrived. He'd done all he could do this evening. Tomorrow he would work on obtaining the rifle he would need to make the shot. He knew who to contact, and he was near certain this next piece of the puzzle would fall nicely into place.

But as he downed the champagne, worry returned to the forefront of his mind. The one piece that was crucial, more crucial than anything else, was completely out of his hands.

He needed to hear from that bastard Court Gentry.

TWENTY-SIX

Ruth had spent nearly the entire day in conference rooms. After her morning at ODNI in McLean, she was taken by a CIA car to the Adams Morgan neighborhood of D.C., and up the long driveway to Townsend Government Services.

She was led by Jeff Parks through a building she found almost comically surreal. Seemingly every square inch of wall space was occupied by some homage to the Old West. Knowing what little she did about this company—that they were a glorified posse deputized by the CIA to bring back their man, dead or alive—she half wondered if Parks and the other men in the building wore ten-gallon hats and stirrups when they were not conducting meetings with outsiders such as herself.

Parks led her into a room and presented her with an accordion file full of papers about her target. He seemed unhappy about passing her the information, but he was clearly under orders by the CIA to do so and, like a good dog, he was doing as he was told. Still, he made her agree to certain ground rules. She promised to stay off her mobile phone and her laptop, and she was not allowed to make any written notes of the information. She agreed, Parks left her to her work, and she eagerly tore into the file.

Despite her requests to see everything the CIA could give her, she was immediately disappointed to find an incredible number of black strikethroughs on the paperwork—it appeared as if 75 percent of her target's history had been redacted.

The file began with Gentry's recruitment into the Agency, and Ruth was fascinated to learn that he had been headhunted by CIA after being convicted of a triple murder. The dossier had all the details of the crime. Gentry had been nineteen years old at the time, working as a bodyguard for a low-level drug smuggler working out of Opa-locka airport in south Florida.

From all the evidence available in the file, Gentry's employer had been targeted for assassination by a group of Colombians, but young Court came to the rescue, killing the three hit men from Cartagena. The police showed up moments later; Gentry dropped his gun and was taken into custody.

He was convicted of murder and thrown into prison, but almost immediately the CIA scooped him up and put him through a two-year program to develop him into a nonofficial cover asset.

It was clear to Ruth the program was irregular, to say

the least, because here the dossier became suspiciously vague. Mentions of the Balkans, a reference to St. Petersburg and Laos and Buenos Aires, but never an explanation of just what, exactly, the young man was doing in any of these far-flung locations.

In 2001, however, the paperwork picked back up when Gentry became a paramilitary operations officer for the CIA's Special Activities Division, assigned to capture or kill al Qaeda personalities around the globe. She read details of operations conducted by CIA Task Force Golf Sierra, renditions and hits all over the world, and though the operations were well documented, there was nothing in the files to help her build a psychological profile on her target.

He was a member of the team, call sign Sierra Six. Nothing more.

Then came details of the events that led to what the file described as the kill/capture order on Gentry.

Ruth read it twice, the first time with rapt fascination, the second time with growing skepticism.

According to the report, Gentry had been home in his apartment in Virginia Beach when the rest of his field team came over for a visit. And then, with apparently no warning, Gentry murdered the entire team.

All four men.

There was no explanation in the documentation as to why he had done this, other than a report from an agency psychologist suggesting that post-traumatic stress disorder brought on by years in the field had caused him to snap. That he had somehow misinterpreted his teammates and colleagues as a threat.

To Ettinger the explanation seemed suspiciously conve-

nient. And there was no reason whatsoever for why all the
rest of his team happened to be in his apartment. He'd invited them over to watch a football game, maybe? She
looked at the after-action report. The gunfight took place
in predawn hours. A late-night party that turned into a tier-
one shootout?

Sure, she said to herself, *that* happens.

Ruth Ettinger's bullshit detector spiked into the red.

That the fight did take place was not in question.
There were photographs of several bodies. Blood on the
walls. A smashed window. Shell casings strewn across
the floor. But Ruth was having a difficult time buying the
official version of events.

The last portion of the accordion file dossier on Gentry was perhaps the most complete and most interesting
to her. It detailed Townsend Government Services' own
hunt for the Gray Man. This hunt, if the documentation
was to be believed, had led them from Mexico to Europe,
and teams of assets were deployed even now in northern
Europe.

As soon as she finished perusing the last document,
she looked at her watch and realized three hours had
passed. She had done her best to commit pertinent information to memory and to form a mental list of questions
to have ready for her scheduled four P.M. meeting with
Leland Babbitt, director of this odd enterprise.

Babbitt entered the conference room right on time, with
Jeff Parks behind him. The director of Townsend Government Services was a big man with a thick neck and a

wide smile on his face. As he shook her hand he said, "I was told to prepare myself."

"For what, sir?"

"To keep my professional demeanor in the presence of such a striking woman."

Ruth faked a little smile and worked to keep her eyes where they were, not rolling into the back of her head.

Babbitt sat down and said, "Denny has asked us to provide any assistance we can. I am happy to have help from the legendary Mossad on this difficult project."

She doubted his sincerity but thanked him for his kind words.

He added, "I am sure you must have questions for me after looking over the dossier."

"I do. These files are heavily redacted."

He nodded somberly. "Yes, I know."

"I was told I could see the internal documents. All of them."

"The redactions are on the source docs."

She wanted to say *Bullshit*, but instead she said, "I see. You are saying Gentry was run off book."

"In the early part of his career he was part of a program that, for purposes of security, was not completely committed to paper."

Ettinger cocked her head and held it there, urging Babbitt to provide her more information. But he did not bite.

"So there is nothing else about Courtland Gentry that you can provide me?"

"It's all right in front of you. He was a solid operative

for several years, working alone. After 9/11, CIA put together strike teams in the Special Activities Division. His name came up as a suitable candidate, and he joined a task force."

Ruth picked up a page of the file and looked at it. While she scanned it again she said, "Where he was involved in targeted killings and extraordinary renditions."

"Exactly."

She lifted another series of documents and thumbed through them quickly, finally finding the ones she was looking for. "Looking over his freelance operations since his departure from CIA, this just doesn't add up." She held up the pages. "I see motive in these hits. His motive was justice. But I don't see the motive in assassinating Prime Minister Kalb."

Parks said, "According to what you told Denny, the Iranians are offering twenty-five million dollars. Money is motive, Ms. Ettinger."

She shook her head and spoke softly, almost to herself. "Not really, no. Not with Gentry." She changed gears quickly. "When and where was your most recent sighting of Gentry?"

"Tallinn, Estonia. Tuesday morning. An arrest team had him cornered there, and Gentry wiped them out."

"Killed them?"

"Most of them, yes."

"A Townsend arrest team?"

"Yes."

Ruth had read a cable about the shootout in Estonia, but Mossad had not connected it to the Gray Man. She made a mental note to dig deeper into the details with Tel Aviv.

"Your sanction includes lethal means."

"Of course. He is a dangerous man."

"I understand that. Israel has its own file on the Gray Man, of course. We have been able to attribute several high-profile extrajudicial killings around the world to him over the past four or five years, and although there is nothing in your file here about it, my organization feels confident he single-handedly pulled off the Kiev operation a few years ago. If that was, in fact, the Gray Man, he is every bit as dangerous as his reputation."

Babbitt put a hand up. "He is the best out there. But he did *not* do Kiev. It's disappointing to me that an organization as talented as the Mossad is helping to spread that urban legend."

"How can you be so sure it's not true?"

"Court works alone. What happened at the airport in Kiev could not have been perpetrated by one man, despite his skill."

Ruth leaned forward into the table. "Tell me why."

"Do you know what a 'command fire' event is, Ms. Ettinger?"

She shook her head slowly. "I confess I do not."

"It's a tactical term, used by snipers, mostly. It is the simultaneous fire of multiple weapons against multiple targets to gain a tactical advantage."

"I see."

"That night in Kiev, four targets in two different locations were shot at the beginning of the engagement, all at the same exact instant. Two of the four targets were moving. Two of the targets were killed with the same bullet. All four men were shot through the head. There is no way in hell any one sniper does that. There were three snipers, which means three spotters." He held up six fingers. "And then, after this, is when the close quarters engagement took place, so there were probably another six or eight guys. Langley figures there were twelve to fourteen operators involved in Kiev . . . not one."

Ruth made a mental note to pass this information to Mossad so they could adjust their Gentry file accordingly, and then she moved on. "One more question."

"Shoot."

"Is Courtland Gentry a villain, or is he a hero?"

Parks laughed aloud.

Babbitt said, "Why do you ask that?"

"Quite frankly, he's done some great work. Everyone he's targeted has been human debris who, to be honest, this world is better off without."

"That's your opinion," Babbitt said.

"And even in your heavily redacted—one might even say 'doctored'—file on him, I see so many vague references to operations, ops in which the CIA obviously was satisfied with the result. And then, one day, out of the blue, he throws a pizza party at his apartment and kills all his coworkers."

Babbitt responded immediately. "That is not how I read the events of the evening when he—"

Ruth interrupted him. "I am sure I have it wrong. I am sure there is more to the story." She looked both men over. "*Much* more to the story. Frankly, none of that matters to me. I only need to know where he is, and whether he poses a threat to Ehud Kalb."

Babbitt said, "You are going to have a hard time focusing on bringing him down if you hold on to the illusion that he is being treated unfairly."

"Mr. Babbitt. That is not the way my world works. My job is to stop the Gray Man before he kills my prime minister. I don't care what he is; if he is a threat to Ehud Kalb I will track him, I will find him, and I will take him down."

Parks raised a hand. "Just so we are clear, *we* will let your team tag along with us, advise us, but we will find him, and we will do the taking down. If you want in on our operation, you will heed our terms."

Ruth knew it was pointless to argue, and she also knew this was better for her organization anyway. "This is about a paycheck to you. It is about the survival of my nation to me. I'll go along with your conditions, because Gentry may very well be a threat to my prime minister. But I don't believe half of what I've read here today, and I don't believe 25 percent of what you've told me."

Babbitt ignored the accusation. He just nodded, glad the matter was settled.

Just then the door to the conference room opened and a man called Parks out of the room.

He returned a moment later. "Excuse me, Lee, can I talk to you in private for a moment?"

He started to excuse himself, but Ruth said, "I'm sorry, but if this happens to involve the Gentry operation, this would be the time to start including me in the intelligence."

Babbitt turned to Parks. Ruth saw a questioning look, something deeper there. Parks gave a slight nod.

Lee Babbitt sat back down. "Go ahead, Jeff."

Parks said, "We have a potential ID. It is *very* preliminary, probably not actionable at this stage, but it—"

"Where?" Ruth asked.

"Facial recognition software picked up data points that may or may not be—"

"*Where*, Mr. Parks?"

Parks sighed, not hiding his frustration with the woman's impatience. "Stockholm, Sweden."

Ettinger pulled her phone out and held it up. "I am calling my people." She pushed a button and slid the phone under her thick hair.

Parks warned her, "You are jumping the gun. Something this preliminary won't cause us to deploy assets. We will just tune the software, focus our attention on the cameras in the traffic areas near where the potential sighting occurred, and then, when we get—"

He stopped talking because she clearly was not listening to him.

"It's me. He's in Stockholm. I'm on the way. I'll meet you there in the morning." She hung up the phone without another word.

Babbitt just shook his head in mild surprise. He looked like he was going to say something more, but he stopped himself, then waved away the thought. "I have a technological surveillance detail in Estonia right now. If you are going to Stockholm, I'll send them over. You and your team can coordinate with them. They have some amazing new tools to help in the hunt. You just might get lucky."

Ruth stood, shook his hand. "Thank you for that."

Babbitt himself stood now. "We'd planned on taking you to dinner. There's a hell of a good Italian place around the corner."

"Thank you, but no thank you. My next meal will be in Stockholm."

"Right. Of course."

Babbitt and Parks escorted Ruth outside to a waiting taxi. As it drove off through a late afternoon rainshower, Parks turned to his director.

"Do you think Gentry is going after Ehud Kalb?"

Babbitt shook his head. "Not his MO at all. Kalb is no saint, but Court wouldn't take out a world leader unless the man was extremely dirty, and that's not Kalb."

"Mossad got bad intel?"

"Happens all the time." He then asked, "What do we know about the girl?"

Parks looked down to his tablet computer and pulled up a file. "She's American, as you probably surmised. Though she has dual citizenship now. Typical Brooklyn Jewish family. No politics, intel, or military background in her tree at all. She was an honor student throughout high school, lettered in track and field. Graduated Columbia with a psychology degree, top of her class, of course."

"Of course."

"She was in her third year of law school at NYU when

her fiancé was killed on 9/11." Parks checked his notes. "He was in international finance. Ninety-second floor of Tower Two."

Babbitt guessed the rest. "Lover boy gets killed, she shucks law school and goes into intel work for Mossad."

Parks nodded. "I understand the need to join the fight for the people who killed her lover, but why Mossad? Why not her own country?"

Babbitt shrugged. "If she had the raw materials, a good psych degree and law school, for example, and she started sniffing around at FBI or CIA, it's a good bet Mossad got wind of the fact that a Jewish girl was looking to get into the game. They might have approached her. Told her the truth."

"The truth?"

"The Mossad hits harder than CIA or FBI. They are smaller, faster, less restrained by politics." Babbitt spoke with approval. "That woman didn't give a shit about politics. She wanted to strike back."

Parks looked back down at his tablet. "And apparently, she still does. She was involved in that clusterfuck the Israelis had in Rome last year. She was the only senior officer in the collections department who was not reprimanded or shit-canned for that. She even got a letter of commendation, saying had her concerns been given the care they deserved, a tragedy could have been avoided."

Babbitt smiled. "She's a bitch, but she's a survivor. I can live with that. She certainly talks a good game. Carmichael forced her on us, but I think we can use her to find Gentry. Dead Eye is hurt, Jumper and his boys aren't surveillance experts, and the UAV team might be able to pick him up, but drones can't do what human beings with eyes and feet can do. We'll fold her and her unit into the operation."

"And when it comes time to kill Gentry?"

"We kill Gentry," Babbitt said coolly. "Mossad can take the credit. We'll take the cash."

TWENTY-SEVEN

A silver Range Rover rolled slowly up Rue Masse, a short two-lane road near the Gare du Roch train station in eastern Nice. The driver was not a local—in fact, he'd driven all day long from his home to get here—and his growing fatigue along with the moonless night made it difficult for him to see the addresses above the numerous shuttered garages lining the street on both sides of Rue Masse. Finally he pulled alongside the one open garage on the entire street, looked above the darkened entrance at the address, and realized he'd arrived at his destination.

Slowly, and with some trepidation, he pulled inside and put his vehicle in neutral. He left his headlights on; there was no lighting here in the parking garage and although he was not as wary as he normally was during a transaction such as this, there was no way in hell he was going to sit here in complete darkness.

He reached under his leather jacket and thumbed open the buttoned leather strap that held his Colt .45 pistol in its holster.

Just in case he was wrong about the identity of his customer.

His phone chirped in the cup holder on the Range Rover's center console, and the call was picked up by his vehicle's radio. He pushed a button on the steering wheel and answered. "Brecht."

The man in the Range Rover was Austrian, and it was customary to answer with his last name.

The caller spoke English; it was the same man he'd spoken to twice in the past twenty-four hours. "That's fine," the man said. "Right where you are. Get out of the vehicle."

Brecht replied. "Let me see you, please. Let me see that you are alone."

A light flicked on suddenly over the Range Rover, startling Brecht for a moment. A second later another light came on, this one at the other end of the garage, some fifty feet from where Brecht sat. A man, dressed head to toe in black and wearing a ski mask that completely obscured his face, stood by the light switch on the wall. His hands were empty; Brecht assumed he communicated through an earpiece.

The Austrian was not completely put at ease by the scene, but in his line of work he knew he must take risks, and this transaction could not very well take place if he did not do as instructed. He turned off the engine and climbed out of his truck, then walked around to the back.

The man in the ski mask approached, stepping out of

the light in the corner and into the darkness, stopping ten feet from where the Austrian stood.

"Guten Abend." Good evening, Brecht said.

"Good evening." The man spoke American English, just as he had in their phone conversations.

"Do you have the money?"

The man in the mask reached to the small of his back, pulled out an envelope, and tossed it forward; the Austrian lost it in the dark but got his hands up, fumbled with it in the air for a moment, but brought it into his chest, and then he opened the envelope.

Thirty thousand euros takes a moment to count, and Reinhold Brecht counted carefully, but from time to time his eyes flashed up to check on the man in front of him.

He was on guard, of course, but much less so than usual today. Normally he would have taken many more measures to ensure his safety; he would have employed cutouts and brought armed associates to check out the area beforehand and to stay close by, but just out of sight, in case the transaction fell through and there was trouble.

But not tonight. Tonight he was here alone, and while wary, he was reasonably comfortable with this exchange.

He looked up from the envelope full of euros and smiled. "All there, of course. I expected nothing less." He shoved the money into his jacket and walked to the back of his Range Rover.

"May I bring it out?"

"Please do," said the American.

Reinhold Brecht pulled a large black leather satchel from the backseat and placed it on the cement floor of the parking garage. He unzipped the satchel and reached inside. The American shined a small flashlight on it, and Brecht pulled out a Blaser R93 sniper rifle in five pieces. He took a moment to assemble the weapon, occasionally looking up at the masked American or back over his shoulder to the street.

Once completed, he reached into the case again and pulled out a Leupold Mark 2 scope, and he snapped it into place on the rail at the top of the rifle. He reached once more into the satchel and produced a box magazine, loaded with four rounds of .300 Winchester magnum ammunition.

He snapped the magazine into the mag well and handed the weapon up to the American.

"The zero?" the man in the ski mask asked as he took it and looked it over.

"As you requested, it is ranged for one hundred meters." Brecht looked up and winked. "It will do the job."

After a few quiet moments where the masked man examined the weapon professionally, opening the bolt and looking through the optics, he handed it back to the Austrian.

"Pack it back up."

The Austrian knelt down, did as instructed, and then stood back up.

"Fifty rounds of ammunition in the case as well. Will you require anything else, sir?"

"No. You may leave now."

"With your permission, I would like to say something first."

"Okay."

Brecht smiled a little. "I only know of one man who requests the collapsible Blaser rifle in .300 Win Mag ammunition."

The man in the ski mask did not reply to this.

Brecht added, "Two and a half years ago I procured a similar weapon for you. I did not speak with you directly. Another man ordered it, but I knew this other man worked for Sir Donald Fitzroy, your handler. I delivered the weapon to Italy. I saw soon after that a human trafficker in Greece, a man responsible for bringing many women from Europe and selling them into servitude, was killed by a single round of .300 Win Mag, right between the eyes, at a range of seven hundred meters." Brecht grinned excitedly. "My contacts in the business began whispering the name of the Gray Man."

Brecht puffed out his chest and said, "I was proud to play a small role in that operation."

Again, the man in the ski mask did not say a word, and Brecht took note of his silence.

"It is no problem." A slight touch of nerves in his voice now. "I am discreet, of course, and I would not normally mention I am aware of the identity of a customer. It's just that . . . well . . . in this business, one does not have a chance to work with people of such impeccable character.

"I am a businessman; I don't care what one does with my products. But it is nice to know today my tool is put in the hands of a good man who will use it for good. I want you to know that I remain at your service for any needs you might have in the future."

———————

Russ Whitlock fought a smile, though he doubted it would hurt his cover much to show a stupid grin to this man. Gray Man would probably eat up such platitudes.

Russ had chosen this arms trader, for three reasons. One, he was reliable enough. Russ had known of him for years. He had access to quality guns and he delivered the guns quickly.

Two, Russ had read in Gentry's dossier that he had obtained a sniper rifle from Reinhold Brecht once in the past. Brecht would, of course, remember the sale and he would, of course, know that the Gray Man had been the killer of the Greek pimp and human trafficker.

And three, despite Brecht's claim that he was discreet, he was anything but. From time to time he took money from the CIA and other Western intelligence agencies in exchange for information he picked up plying his trade. Russ knew the Austrian would not keep his damn mouth shut about supplying the Gray Man, and that was exactly what Russ was counting on. A successful execution of this phase of the operation depended on the loose lips of Reinhold Brecht.

"Thank you," Russ said. "I hope to work with you again."

"It would be an honor." And then Brecht actually bowed.

What a fucking suck-up, Russ thought. He wanted to draw his Glock and pistol-whip the motherfucker to the ground. Instead he just nodded back at the man, stood there, and waited for him to climb into his vehicle and drive away.

When the Range Rover had rolled off into the night, Russ hefted the leather satchel with the Blaser rifle, walked back to the light switch, and flicked it down, returning the entire scene to darkness.

TWENTY-EIGHT

Ruth Ettinger and her three-person team of targeting officers met at the Israeli Embassy in Stockholm, borrowed a black four-door Skoda from the Mossad motor pool, and then drove together to the Townsend safe house just set up on Sankt Ericksgaten Street. They parked their car in a snow-covered lot, slung their luggage over their shoulders, and headed up four flights of stairs.

The only two occupants of the flat were a two-man Townsend UAV team who had themselves only just arrived: a drone pilot named Carl and a sensor operator named Lucas who stopped unpacking their equipment just long enough to introduce themselves.

Ruth, Aron, Laureen, and Mike all moved into a large bedroom at the back of the flat, while the drone operators pulled mattresses off beds in another bedroom and dragged them into the living room so they could stay close to their gear at all times.

And they had a lot of gear. While the Townsend men got set up, Ruth and her team watched them install four laptops on tabletop rack mounts, attach and calibrate flight control joysticks, uncoil microphone headsets, and finally unpack three identical UAVs. They were microdrone quadcopters, an X-shaped design with a small enclosed rotary wing topping each of the four arms, and a bulb-shaped center that held the power, brains, and cameras. The three identical devices were only sixteen inches in diameter and each unit weighed less than five pounds.

Mike Dillman whistled. "We've got some cool stuff, but we don't have those."

Lucas put one of the devices on a charging station on the floor. "Cutting edge. We've played around with these back in the States, but we've never fielded this model before. No one has. It's called the Sky Shark. Got it from DARPA, the Defense Advanced Research Projects Agency, the folks that build all the latest and greatest gadgets. They gave it to us to field-test it in an urban environment."

"Sweet," said Mike.

Laureen asked, "You plan to just fly this around downtown Stockholm and hope no one will see it?"

Carl answered this. "This thing is damn near silent, but it's not invisible. We have some techniques to employ to keep it out of sight. Obviously we fly as high as we can, but this isn't a Reaper or a ScanEagle where you can cruise at eight or nine miles up. With these you have to stay within a couple hundred feet of the target in a moving surveillance, so we fly behind the target in most cases, and we can use the sun, when there is sun around here to be had, so that our target won't know he is being watched."

Lucas added, "In the dark it's better. The camera has night vision, of course." He smiled. "Nobody's going to detect this baby at night."

Ruth asked to see the video the Townsend facial recognition software had identified as Court Gentry, and Carl brought up a still photo on one of the rack-mounted laptops. He explained that the image had been taken the previous day at an electronics store a few kilometers from where they now sat. The still photo was taken from the clearest image from the quick snippet of video.

Ruth leaned close to look at it, then raised an eyebrow. Townsend analysts had provided images of Gentry to her and all her team, and she called up a picture on her smart phone. She looked over a photo of Court Gentry wearing a suit and eyeglasses, then looked up to check the video still again. "Certainly not definitive."

Carl shook his head, but said, "We put it at 60 percent prob."

"How so? The photo isn't clear and you can only see about two thirds of the face."

"True, but the camera captured the periocular region, the area around the eyes, which actually has more biometrically identifiable features than fingerprints. And from the photographs of him we have on file we have built a virtual 3-D model of his face, and the reconstructed periocular region on that is close enough to this guy here to make the 60 percent assessment."

This technology was not new to Ruth in theory—she tracked people for a living, after all—but she had never seen periocular data pulled from such a grainy, off-center image in the field.

The rest of her team looked at the photo on the laptop and compared it to the photos of Gentry on their smart phones. Aron and Mike thought they were looking at the same person, but Laureen and Ruth remained doubtful.

Ruth asked, "What's your plan to find him, if he is in fact here?"

Lucas took his cue and said, "Babbitt wants you folded into our search, so this might be a good time to show you how we do it."

Carl took one of the Sky Shark drones to the balcony and returned a moment later without it. He sat down at the flight controls while Lucas worked the laptop next to him for a moment.

"Ready."

The drone took off from the balcony, lifting a few feet into the air and then drifting sideways. It climbed again, out of sight, and then Ruth and her team moved behind the two American UAV operators to watch several live images on the laptops. One of the cameras was positioned on the drone to show a straight-ahead view; a second was the rear view. A third camera was obviously below the craft, and it could be turned and zoomed by a toggle on the sensor operator's console.

They watched the screens as the drone flew over the

buildings in the neighborhood, made a series of turns, and then descended between two buildings to hover over a pedestrian shopping street. The sensor operator picked out a young woman strolling along; she wore a fur coat and a matching mink hat, and her arms were laden with shopping bags.

While they worked, Lucas said, "As technology improves, it gets harder and harder for runners like Court Gentry to hide."

"Because of biometrics?" Ruth asked.

"Exactly. It's a biometric ID world now. Just a few years ago facial recognition software was nonexistent or unreliable. But as it improves, guys like Gentry are dinosaurs, waking up to the cold.

"The biometric database for CIA employees is quite extensive now, but Gentry was lucky to get out before most of it started being harvested. There is no soft biometric profile, which is his gait, the way he stands, stuff like that. All we have is an iris scan and fingerprints on file for him, which is useless in this situation. But the facial recog we are using should get the job done."

Carl spoke now as he flew the UAV with the joystick and toggle throttle. "From the cam image in the electronics shop we know what he is wearing: the coat, the hat, the shades. We know how tall he is and how much he weighs. All that goes into an algorithm, and the Sky Shark camera goes out and records everyone it sees moving on the street and passes the images back to these computers. The software can evaluate over two hundred individuals a minute—"

Lucas spoke up here. "When it's working right."

"Yeah," Carl allowed, "when it's working right. Ninety-nine percent of the individuals are going to get tossed out immediately. Wrong height, wrong weight, different coat, female form, whatever. But anytime the computer finds someone that needs a second look it will let the drone know, and the drone will take another shot. The second look will go back to the computer for evaluation, as well. And a third look, to narrow it down more."

"After that?" Aron asked.

"After that any image that is deemed a possible match will pop up on the screen. Those have to be weeded out manually."

Lucas said, "I do that while Carl concentrates on not slamming the Sky Shark into a wall."

Ruth said, "And if you find him? What then?"

Carl answered. "That's another cool part. If I see him in one of the images, I just tell the computer to let the drone know we have a match. At that point the Sky Shark goes from hunting mode to tracking mode. It remembers where the individual was, goes back and relocates him, and locks on like a dog on a scent."

"This is impressive," Ruth admitted. "What are the drawbacks?"

Carl had an answer ready. "The electric engines use a ton of juice. Sky Shark can loiter only about a half an hour before we have to bring it back for a recharge. It shouldn't be too much of a problem; we've got three, so we can keep circulating them."

As the Townsend UAV team began what they freely

admitted could be a lengthy hunt, Ruth sent Mike and Laureen to the electronics store where Gentry bought the computer. They would interview the salesman, branch out and check hotels nearby, and keep their eyes peeled.

Ruth called in to Yanis to let him know they were up and running here in Sweden.

"How are the Americans treating you?"

"Like we're part of the team. CIA is desperate to get this guy."

Yanis heard something in her voice. "You are, too, right?"

"So far, I'm more curious. It's obvious the Americans want us to help, but it is not obvious at all to me that Gentry has any interest in taking out the PM. I can't stop thinking about all the good this man has done, on his own initiative, while on the run."

"Good guys do bad things. No reason bad guys can't do good things once in a while, too."

"I guess so. I've got an open mind on this, but I'm not sharpening my dagger just yet."

Yanis said, "This is time critical. The likelihood of any danger to Kalb right now is only increased by the fact that he will be more vulnerable over the next two weeks during his travel. You don't have the luxury of spending too much time on building a perfect target folder. I need you to find him, identify him, and monitor the Townsend people to make sure they stay on target. If they want to send their hitters to go in and kill him, they have their reasons, and you stand back and let them do it. Whether he's a threat to Ehud Kalb will become a moot point if the Americans eliminate him."

"I understand, Yanis," she said, but still, there was reticence in her voice. "But when did we become the hunting dogs for the CIA?"

"When the fox started sniffing around our hen house, Ruth."

"Right," Ruth said.

"Get to work, but be careful. CIA conducted a teleconference briefing with us this morning about the Gentry case. He is a slick bastard, well trained to spot a tail. Find him, but stay loose."

"Thanks for the concern, Yanis, but I'll be fine."

"Of course you will."

TWENTY-NINE

Court had spent the day in his room, mostly surfing innocuous travel websites about Stockholm on his laptop. He also spent an hour and a half on a punishing series of bodyweight-only exercises. Push-ups and jackknives and handstand press-ups against the wall, enjoying the workout even less than normal because his body was still banged up after the operation in the forest near St. Petersburg and then the ambush in Tallinn two days later.

After a shower to ease his tired and sore muscles and an hour lying on the bed flipping channels on the tiny TV, he sat at the little table in the corner and ate a dinner of cold salmon out of a can and cold rice from a microwavable bag.

He drank a beer with his meal, all the while thinking he would rather be sitting in a dark, out-of-the-way bar somewhere in the neighborhood.

Not tonight—he had other plans for his evening.

When he was finished with dinner he went to the window and spent a few minutes looking through a narrow partition in the curtains, taking his time to check for cars or trucks that looked out of place and to follow passersby with his eyes, watching one person at a time as they strolled by on the sidewalk one floor below him. He scanned for faces he had seen before, though he felt confident he had made his escape from the Baltic without anyone tailing him here to Scandinavia.

After spending thirty minutes watching the flow of vehicles and pedestrians outside, he shut the curtains and sat down on his bed. After a slight hesitation he picked up his mobile phone and the scrap of paper with the phone number written on it.

He began to dial Whitlock, but he changed his mind. He had read everything he could find on the Internet about how secure the MobileCrypt application was, satisfying himself that using the app to obtain information about the Townsend men hunting for him was worth the risk, but Court was still a careful man. He put on his coat and slipped his earphones into his ears, then headed out of his flat and down to the street.

He'd make the call, just not from here.

––––––––––––

Fat snowflakes floated and swirled under a streetlamp in Tegnerlunden Park, just a few minutes west of Gentry's rented room. Court stood there under the light for a moment to read the number off the paper, holding his phone in his hand. He wore wired headphones with a built-in microphone under the hood of his coat. He dialed the number through the MobileCrypt app, but he did not press the send button. Not yet. He began walking, away from the park and toward the west, hoping that if all the information he read was somehow wrong, and it was, in fact, possible to trace the call, he would be harder to pinpoint if he was on the move.

Am I really doing this? he asked himself. Court did not seek out conversations with others; he did everything he could to avoid them. He preferred to order food from machines, buy train tickets from automated kiosks, and obtain information necessary for his missions from online searches at Internet cafés. In the past five years Court had, several times, gone weeks without talking to another human being other than an occasional two-or three-word exchange, usually in the form of a cash transaction at a market or directions for a cabdriver.

Tonight, in contrast to years of self-imposed solitude, he would actually reach out.

He told himself he had to do it but he worried, maybe, he just *wanted* to do it.

"Don't you fucking go soft, Gentry." He said it softly, admonishing himself for what he was about to do.

Despite deep reservations, he pressed the send button.

———

Russ Whitlock sat on the floor of his room at the Grimaldi. In front of him, the Blaser sniper rifle lay in pieces. He'd spent the past half hour taking it apart and putting it back together. First slowly and carefully. Then quickly, as if under stress. The next time he put it together normally but disassembled it only employing his right hand, simulating an injury to his left arm or hand. Then he tried the same trick with his left hand, which took considerable time.

Next to him on the floor, a tray of artisan cheeses and an iced open bottle of Lenoble Grand Cru Blanc du Blanc sat ignored. He wanted to put the weapon together and disassemble it a few more times before he rewarded himself with the luxurious indulgence.

He'd had a busy day, spent in intense preparation for his planned Saturday late-morning assassination of Amir Zarini. He'd taken a train to his planned area of execution and then surveyed the surroundings and the target location to determine both the ingress and egress points. He'd made it back to his hotel in the early evening, taken off all his clothes, and then removed the blood-and-pus-soaked bandages on his hip.

When he was finished undressing his wound he stood there nude in front of the full-length dressing mirror examining the holes, caked over with scabs, and the black bruising around them. His eyes lifted from the injury, taking in the rest of his body slowly and with no small amount of appreciation. He began a martial arts kata, never taking his eyes off his own face and body while he exercised. His hip burned and sweat began to flow within minutes. His face became a mask of intensity and even fury as he punched and kicked, performed throws and elbow strikes designed to break bones.

It took him several minutes to come down from the angry high of the simulated fight; his hip began bleeding freely and the pain was excruciating.

After his exercise Russ showered and changed and by

now he was famished, but he imposed more discipline on himself by ordering food and drink and then letting it sit while he worked with the rifle, steeling both his mind and his body to as much hardship as he could generate in a four-star hotel on the French Riviera.

Russ had a lot of experience with sniper rifles, but little experience with the Blaser. As a scout sniper in the Marine Corps he had been issued the M40, and he loved the weapon. For the sake of familiarity he would have preferred an M40 for this job, or its civilian equivalent, the Remington 700. But, he had to admit, Gentry had chosen well with the R93. The German rifle had a straight pull-back bolt that allowed for slightly faster follow-on shots, faster than the M40 although certainly not as fast as a semiauto rifle. Still, Russ imagined he could empty the weapon's four-round box magazine quickly and accurately at the distances he had planned, even without spending much time at the firing range with this particular weapon.

He had just begun reassembling the gun for another left-hand-only takedown when his earpiece chirped on the floor next to him. His phone was on the desk across the room, so he just put his Bluetooth set into his ear and tapped a button to answer the call.

"Go."

"Hello."

It was Gentry. Russ bolted up from the floor and pumped his fist in the air. He composed himself quickly and spoke in a relaxed tone. "I was just thinking about you."

"Sorry about not calling the other night."

"Not a problem, brother. I didn't expect you to call for a few days." It was a lie, but he wanted to seem nonchalant about the conversation.

"Why not?"

"I know you, dude. I know how you think."

"Why is it I don't know how *you* think?"

"What do you mean by that?" Russ pulled the bottle of Lenoble from the ice and took a sip. It was time to celebrate.

"I don't understand what your game is."

"No game, Court. I just want to help. Why can't you believe that?"

"I don't know."

"Well, I'll answer that question for you. You have been dicked around and lied to by everyone you ever worked with at CIA. Carmichael, Hightower, Hanley—"

"How is Hanley?"

"You mean since you shot him in Mexico City?"

"You *do* know everything."

Russ swigged champagne. This conversation was going just the way he wanted it. "Matt Hanley's okay. He's back at Langley. Getting shot by the Gray Man is a career builder, I guess."

"Speaking of gunshot wounds, how's the hip?"

"It hurts," responded Whitlock.

"Yeah, they have a tendency to do that."

Russ asked, "Any trouble getting out of Tallinn?"

"You tell me. What do your friends at Townsend say? Is there any heat on me I haven't noticed?"

Russ lied again. He'd heard nothing at all from Townsend for a couple of days, but he needed to keep his value high in Gentry's eyes. "They said they might have a target for me very soon. They did not elaborate. Wherever you are, stay there, but you might want to check back with me sooner rather than later."

After a pause Court said, "Okay. What about you? No problems with fallout from them after what happened the other day?"

"I told you, I can handle them." Russ took a long swig of champagne. "This other opportunity I told you about is coming up pretty soon. Have you thought any more about our conversation the other night?"

"About you wanting to go freelance?"

"Yeah."

"Help me understand just why you want to do that."

"I want to be my own boss."

Court chuckled. "Working freelance means you have more bosses, not fewer. I never would have had to hit that dacha west of St. Petersburg if I didn't have trouble with my employers. You can't trust anyone in this line of work."

"Thanks for the tip."

Court replied, "If you are taking career advice from me, then you are an idiot." He added, "Guys like us are better off alone."

"I disagree, Court, because there *are* no guys like us. There is only us. We're the last two. We should stick together."

"The last two?"

"Nineteen men entered the Autonomous Asset Development Program. The oldest was Joseph Pelton, at twenty-eight. The youngest was Courtland Gentry, at nineteen. I was twenty-five when I got in."

"And?"

"Four died in training."

"Can't say that surprises me. I almost died a couple times."

"Me, too. Eight died in the field working in AAP. Five more died during subsequent work, either in CIA, high-risk private sector security postings, or suicide." Russ drank from the champagne bottle. "And that, my friend, leaves Gentry and Whitlock, alone in the world."

"Shit."

"Hey, it's not so bad. If there were more of us, we'd be less valuable."

"Higher value just means a bigger target on your head."

"It means a bigger payday if you are freelance," countered Whitlock.

Court asked, "Do you ever wish, sometimes, that you could go back to the way you were before?"

Russ asked, "Before what?"

"Before we got trained? Before we were made."

Russ swigged again. "No. *Hell* no. Never."

Court said nothing.

"You do, I take it," said Whitlock.

"Just sometimes," admitted Court.

"You should appreciate what you are." He paused. "You should appreciate it a lot more than you do. You have a skill set that, arguably, only one other person on the planet has."

"You?"

"Yeah, me. Like I said the other night, I've studied your ops. Down to the letter, everything you've done, I would have done exactly the same way."

"How about that," Court muttered, a little sarcasm in his voice.

"Yep." After a slight hesitation, Russ said, "Of course, the only one that has me stumped is Kiev. I sure wish I knew how you pulled that off."

"Again with Kiev?"

Russ drank his champagne. A few days earlier he thought he would need all the details of the Kiev op to secure the Kalb contract from the Iranians. But he'd bluffed his way past this gap in his knowledge and cajoled them with the promise of the Zarini hit, and now the details of Kiev were no longer so important. Still, he *was* genuinely curious. He said, "Someday, Court, I'll get it out of you."

The line was silent for several seconds, and then Gentry said, "I've got to go."

"You have a hot date?"

"No. I need to get back to my place and set up a barricade in case you can trace this call and you plan on sending another crew of shooters my way."

"Court, use your brain. If I wanted you dead all I had to do was stay in my bunk Monday night and let the Townsend gunners kill you. You might have all sorts of good reasons to be paranoid, but in this case you aren't being logical. I'm a friend. Not an enemy. We are one, you and me. Sooner or later you are going to realize that. We would make one hell of a team."

To this Court just said, "I'll check with you tomorrow."

"I hope you do, for your sake. Townsend might have a fix on you. Help me help you."

"Tomorrow. No bullshit this time. I'll call."

The line went dead, and Russ sat on the edge of his big bed with the bottle of cold champagne in his lap. He would have liked to string Gentry along a little further, pulled him deeper into his plan, but tonight's baby step forward was much better than no step at all.

The dumb son of a bitch had made contact, and that was key. And when Court realized that no one was going to attack him after this conversation, well, Russ concluded, that poor lonely sad sack Court Gentry would probably start calling him every motherfucking night.

———————

Ruth and Aron had spent the afternoon and early evening walking the choke points of the city within a two-kilometer diameter of the electronics shop where Gentry bought his computer. At eight P.M. they grabbed carryout Indian food for themselves and the UAV team and took it back to the safe house. As the two climbed up the stairs to the fourth-floor flat, Laureen and Mike were heading down the stairs, ready for three or four hours of man-hunting in the evening snow.

In the safe house Ruth passed the food out to the three men and sat with them at the laptop control center for the UAVs. Carl was flying a Sky Shark over the Gamla Stan, the Old Town portion of Stockholm, but while he flew he was able to one-hand a few bites of naan dipped in sauce and wash it down with beer.

Lucas reported that in their seven hours of near-constant

flying, they'd had more than sixty possible sightings, each one of which had to be manually ruled in or ruled out by the UAV team by looking at images on the laptop.

Lucas and Carl had eliminated them all.

"Still," Lucas said, "it's only the first day. Parks will probably have us keep the coverage up for three or four days more unless the facial recog software they are using on all the hacked cameras around the area turns up something somewhere else."

"He's here," Ruth said. "I can smell him."

Carl and Lucas exchanged a look but did not respond.

Ruth and Aron finished their meal and headed to their room to get some sleep; they'd planned to hit the streets before first light the next morning. The Townsend UAV technicians decided to make one last slow track over a heavily trafficked pedestrian-only street before bringing their drone home for the evening.

———————

Fifteen minutes later Ruth brushed her teeth in the bathroom wearing only shorts and a tank top. She thought she heard someone calling out, so she turned off the tap.

"Aron? Did you say something?"

But it was Lucas who had shouted, and now he repeated himself, this time louder. "We got a hit!"

THIRTY

Ruth raced into the living room in her shorts and tank top; she'd taken out her contacts, so she fumbled to get her glasses on, and her bare feet slapped the wooden floor as she approached. "Are you sure?"

Lucas said, "*I'm* not, but the computer is. Well, relatively sure. We've been tracking a guy for about two minutes. He's turned back twice to look behind him, which kind of looks like tradecraft to me. More importantly, the facial recog software puts his periocular region at 73 percent chance of a match."

Ruth looked past Lucas's shoulder to the screen and saw a greenish image of dozens of pedestrians moving along in the dark in both directions through an outdoor mall. A lone individual in the crowd walked through the snow and slush wearing a hooded black three-quarter-length coat. He or she faced away from the camera. Ruth would not have known which person to focus on in the scene except the figure in the dark coat was framed by a superimposed red square.

"That's him?"

"Watch him for a second. He'll look back."

Ruth did as Lucas suggested, but while she waited for him to check his six, a thought occurred to her. She asked, "How is it that no one is noticing the UAV? You are pretty low."

Carl had been quietly piloting the Sky Shark, but he answered now, his face remaining a mask of concentration as he spoke. "It's a little trick. You fly about four stories up, moving along as close to the wall of the buildings as possible. During the day the gray and black UAV isn't silhouetted in front of the sky, it just blends in with all the concrete and glass and metal. But at night you are above the streetlights, so it's even more invisible."

Lucas swiveled his chair quickly over to another laptop on the rack, and he began feverishly manipulating the mouse and clicking keys.

"What are you doing?" Ruth asked.

"I'm setting the computer to record his gait so we can track him. The human gait is actually quite unique. Once it has a good reading of Gentry's particular walking pattern, we can find him and track him automatically when he's on foot. It's not the best biometric identifier, but if it's him, it will be a cinch to get a usable reading to narrow him down in a crowd later."

"*If* it's him," Ruth added.

Just then the figure moved out of the flow of foot traffic and closer to the building on his right. He slowed and looked into a shop window. He stopped fully now, people passed by, and he turned and looked back up the street.

On the computer in front of Ruth the image zoomed automatically on the man's face. The resolution was surprisingly good, though the face was green because of the night vision optics.

Ruth said, "It *might* be him. I still can't—"

Just then Lucas, who was in front of the other laptop, said, "Recog has bumped probability up to 90 percent."

"Well, then," said Ruth. "I guess we've got the bastard!"

Ruth and Aron quickly rushed back into the bedroom to dress for the cold. Sixty seconds later they rushed back into the living room.

"Where is he?" Ruth asked Lucas as she pulled her boots on.

"He's on . . . Shit." Lucas struggled to read the Swedish name on the moving map display on the laptop. "Drottningatten? However you pronounce it, it's about twenty minutes from here on foot. He's headed north, away from us."

"We'll take the car." She put her phone's receiver in her ear. "Call us with updates."

Ruth put her hood up on her coat and followed Aron out the door.

———

Ten minutes later Ruth parked the embassy Skoda next to Tegnerlunden Park, and she and Aron began walking briskly through the snow shower, following Lucas's instructions coming through their earpieces. They'd also called in Laureen and Mike, who would soon approach on foot from the south.

"Listen up," Lucas said over the team comms. "He's a couple minutes ahead of you on . . . Radmansgatan, if I'm saying that right."

"Understood," Ruth said. "We can track him. You make sure your drone is out of sight."

"No worries."

"I worry, Lucas. Tell your partner to keep the Sky Shark back."

After a quick pause he replied. "Lady, how 'bout you do your job and you let us do ours? He won't see the Sky Shark, but he might see you guys."

Ruth sighed, expelling a long plume of vapor from her body.

Before she could say anything else, the American sensor operator spoke again. "Bingo! He just went inside a building. Made a beeline right for it; I think he knew exactly where he was heading."

"What building?"

"Wait one." There was a pause while Lucas waited for Carl to get his drone in position to see the address and any signage. While they waited, Ruth and Aron picked up the pace even more. If he was inside now, he wouldn't see them unless they got too close to the building.

As they walked, Mike Dillman and Laureen Tattersal folded in behind them on the sidewalk. The two couples did not acknowledge each other at all. They just walked on in the same direction, some hundred feet or so apart.

"He's on the southwest corner of Radmansgatan and . . . Shit, how the fuck do you pronounce this?"

Ruth barked at him. "Sound it out, Lucas! Hurry!"

Slowly he said, "Sveavagen, or something like that. Just two blocks west of the intersection is an outdoor pedestrian space that's higher than the road below. There is a staircase with a pretty good overlook on the building the target entered. There's no cover there, but you should be able to see the entrance without having to get any closer."

Ruth and her team arrived at the overlook as he finished describing it.

"Got it," she said.

"All right. He's in the building down there on your right. Forty yards away."

"What is that place?"

Lucas typed the address into a computer, then said, "There is a steakhouse on the ground floor, but he did not go in that entrance. He took the staircase next to it up to the second floor. It's cheap rental apartments. Immigrants. Families. That's Gentry's MO. He likes staying in low-rent tenements. I'll wager that's where he's living while here in town."

Mike Dillman put his hand over his earpiece so he could not be heard by the Townsend men. "Let's call in Metsada and we can get on the next plane home before I freeze my dick off."

Aron and Laureen laughed.

Ruth looked at him with annoyance. She covered her own mic. "We don't even know what he's up to. Metsada won't be targeting anyone on this operation unless we know the man is a threat. I don't want to hear any more talk like that."

Mike said, "It was a joke, boss."

Aron looked at Ruth for a moment. "What's wrong, Ruth? Why can't we just let Townsend put him down and be done with it?"

"This one feels different. I can't put my finger on it."

Lucas transmitted over their headsets now, "We're pulling the Sky Shark back home and calling it a night. We'll get back on him in the A.M. You guys can stay out there if you want, but we're low on juice."

The four Israelis remained at the top of the staircase looking down to Radmansgatan Street for several minutes, surveilling the urban area from this high ground to find the best place to watch the building. As people passed, heading up and down the staircase next to them, the four operatives discussed softly among themselves where they would post their overnight watch on the building.

As they stood there, a family of seven passed the Mossad team, then trudged through the snow to the stairs to the second-floor property. The youngest in the family could not have been more than two years old, and she bobbed along in the line, her thick boots kicking up snow almost to her eye level.

Laureen said, "Kids. That complicates things."

Ruth nodded. "Immigrant tenements like this are usually full of children. We will need visibility inside that building. Aron, tomorrow I want you to see if they have a vacancy. We'll pull up the schematics of the building and run fiber optics through the wall into Gentry's room."

While they talked it over, Aron looked around at the raised area they were standing on. "You know, right here is the best place to watch the building tonight. You don't even need to rent an apartment in the neighborhood. It's not a perfect sight line, but it's not bad."

"No," she agreed. "Not bad at all." She looked back over her shoulder, then down again toward the street and Gentry's building.

She said, "He's made something of a mistake, tactically speaking, hasn't he?"

The question was to herself, but Aron responded.

"You mean hiding out in that tenement? With this overwatch covering the entrance just up the road?"

"Yes," she answered, even more distracted now.

Laureen offered, "He has a lot to think about, I guess. Only so many places in the area he can rent."

"But why this one? Why here?"

Mike answered. "It's convenient. Close to the tram. Close enough to the river if he wants to jump on a vessel to get out of town. Our file on him says he's used urban waterways in a pinch. Plus there are good options for food in the neighborhood."

Ruth shook her head. "That's not how this man thinks."

"Then what?" Laureen asked. "He just screwed up? Got lazy?"

Ruth shook her head again. Slowly at first, but then more emphatically. "No. No, that's not what's going on."

"What's going on, then?"

She turned away from the stairs down to the street,

away from the narrow view of the windows leading to the second-floor apartments. Her movement was slow and unconcerned, but her words to the others were severe. Demanding. "Turn around and walk with me. *Now*, dammit!"

"What's wrong with you?" Laureen asked, but she did as she was told.

"He knows where to look."

"What?"

"He saw the vulnerability this overwatch created; there is no way he would miss that. But he chose that location anyway. He did that because he knew staying there would funnel any surveillance of his safe house into that one spot. Every time he comes out of the front door of that building, he'll look right up here, first thing. All he has to do is keep his eyes on this overwatch; as soon as he sees someone here he doesn't buy, someone who doesn't fit, someone like the four of us idiots standing in the snow watching his door, for instance, he will know he's been compromised and he will disappear."

Together the four of them left the overwatch, heading in the other direction. They wandered up the street, back up a slight rise on Radmansgatan Street.

"That's fucking brilliant," Aron said. "If you're right, that is. Maybe you are giving him too—"

"I'm not giving him too much credit. He's *that* good."

"So, did he see us, then?"

Ruth shrugged as she walked, her hands jammed in her coat pocket and her head leaning forward, into the snow. She was mad at herself, but she did not want to harp on it in front of her people. "No. I don't think so. If he's got a corner window he might have line of sight on the overwatch from his flat, but it's a small chance. I think we dodged a bullet." They were clear now, so she turned to her team. "We have to be smarter with this one. Slower, more thoughtful in our actions. Lose him, short term, if you have to, but do *not* get compromised. I don't want Gentry to disappear from Stockholm and reappear at Kalb's assassination."

"What do you want us to do?"

"I want someone out here, all night. There was a bus stop up the street; it's a shitty line of sight on the entire building, but it will get us eyes on the front door, at least. Tomorrow we can look for apartment space or office space on the street to get twenty-four-hour line-of-sight coverage."

Ruth sighed, more vapor pouring from her mouth. She was confident in her abilities and those of her team, but she realized now she was up against an adversary who had been playing this game at an elite level for a long time. She could make one call to Mossad and have a dozen more surveillance technicians here in twenty-four hours, full electronic suites, vans and cams and forged credentials to get them access to anywhere they wanted to go.

But Ruth wanted to keep this investigation small. This target would spook at the first sign of trouble, and the Townsend drones seemed to be an effective technology with a low probability of compromise.

That would do for now.

And more than this, she was nowhere near ready to call in more of her countrymen, because she did not yet know she was hunting a man who posed a threat to her leadership.

All she knew for sure was the Americans sure wanted him dead.

THIRTY-ONE

Russ Whitlock had finished his bottle of champagne and his plate of cheeses, and now he stood on the fifth-floor balcony and looked out at the Friday night traffic of Nice grinding by on Boulevard Victor Hugo. A cool breeze blew through the buttons of his dress shirt and it, along with the alcohol, relaxed him into a state he had not felt in a long time.

The satisfaction that came from Gentry's call gave him even more of a sense of repose right now. When this was all over, two weeks from now at the outside, only a few would have any idea what he had done, and those few would be disinclined to celebrate his act. No, he would not be famous, and he would not be a legend.

He lamented this for a second, standing there on the balcony, but then he smiled.

All famous assassins live a life on the run, just as Court Gentry did now.

And all legends are dead, just as Court Gentry would be when this was all over.

His phone rang, and he pulled it from his pocket and looked at it in the dim light. It was Townsend House.

He placed his earpiece in his ear. "Go."

"Graveside."

It was clearly Babbitt, but Russ kept to the protocol. "Proceed with iden."

"Identity key eight, two, four, four, niner, seven, two, niner, three."

"Dead Eye here. Four, eight, one, oh, six, oh, five, two, oh."

"Iden confirmed. How are you feeling, Russell?"

"I'm recovering."

"Good. Where are you?"

Russ knew he could not reveal he was in Nice. Instead he said, "Frankfurt."

"Are you ready to get back to work?"

Not exactly. Russ turned on the balcony and began heading back into his room. He said, "Of course."

"Head to Stockholm."

Whitlock stopped suddenly. *Huh?* "Okay. Why?"

"We've identified the target. We have surveillance on him now."

Fuck! A pause. "That's good news," Russ said, although it was anything but. "Where is he?"

"He's rented a flat on Radmansgatan Street, right in the city center. Get into town and we'll lead you in, unless we don't need you there anymore by the time you make it."

"What does that mean?"

"Jumper will act at first opportunity."

"Jumper is on him now?" *Shit. Shit. Shit!*

"Negative, but they will be there within a few hours. He was ID'd by our UAV surveillance, and there is a small unit of Mossad officers keeping an overnight watch."

Veins in Whitlock's neck began to throb. "Wait. What? *Mossad*? How do you know Mossad is after the Gray Man?"

"We are liaising with a targeting team from their Collections Department."

Whitlock's jaw flexed now. He controlled his anger well enough to ask, "Why am I just now hearing about this?"

"I needed you to stand down after Tallinn. I told the signal room to cease all intel pushes to you for a few days so you didn't throw yourself back into the mix before I thought it was safe or prudent for you to do so."

Whitlock fought to keep his voice calm. "And what is Mossad's interest in Gentry?"

"They received a tip that he accepted a contract to assassinate Ehud Kalb."

Russ dropped down on the bed and put his face in his hands. The swollen and torn flesh on his left hip screamed at him for the thoughtlessness of his move, but he ignored the pain and fought to keep the tone of his voice measured. "Lee . . . I find it very hard to believe Gentry would target Israel's PM."

"We do, too. Our analysts don't see Kalb as a likely Gray Man target."

"So . . . *why* are we involving Mossad in our operation?"

"Carmichael at Langley mandated it. Between you

and me, he is punishing us for Tallinn, and just using them as oversight on our op. Making us coordinate with them, knowing they will complain directly to him if there is something in our op they don't like."

"Too many cooks, Lee."

"I hear you. I do. But my hands are tied. The four-person Mossad team is already there, already integrated with our UAV crew on site, and I'll expect you to liaise with them when you get there. I can send an aircraft to Frankfurt, but if you want to make your own arrangements, that will be fine."

Russ wasn't listening; he'd dropped back on the huge bed, and he stared at the ceiling. *The Iranians have a mole in Beirut. What did they know?*

In the long term he wanted the world to think Kalb had been killed by the Gray Man. But that was after the fact. Now it only served to turn up the heat on Gentry, to send Mossad after him just when Whitlock needed Gentry to fly under the radar.

"Russell? You there?"

Russ sat up. There was nothing he could do but continue to play his part and hope Gentry could defy the odds one more time in his career and slip the noose tightening around him. "Yes. I will make my own way to Stockholm. I will contact you when I get there."

Babbitt said, "Hurry. If Jumper has a delay, or screws up in any way, there is the possibility that Mossad will send its own people in to take care of Gentry."

"Metsada," Russ said, and his face darkened even more. He stood and began pacing back and forth in his suite.

"That's a problem," he said, more to himself than to Babbitt.

"You're damn right it's a problem! Jumper needs to act before the Israelis get even more involved. We're running out of time here. I need the target eliminated within the next twelve hours."

"Roger that." Russ ended the call, but he kept pacing for a moment.

He was angry at Gentry most of all. The supposed world's greatest operative had gone and gotten himself compromised by facial recognition, ID'd by a drone, and tailed by Mossad targeters, and within hours, he would be surrounded by a cordon of armed killers.

And Russ was fifteen hundred miles away, unable to control things. Yes, he could warn Gentry, if he called in the next few hours, but they had just spoken, so he saw no chance he would hear from him for twenty-four hours or more.

Court was on his own now, and Russ could do nothing but hope the obviously highly overrated jackass escaped on his own.

If Gentry died before Kalb died, then Whitlock's master plan would fall apart.

He screamed aloud in his hotel room. "Gentry!" And he punched a fist against the wall, bruising and scraping his knuckles.

Court opened his eyes quickly and looked left and right, searching in the darkness.

Down the hall a baby cried, but he did not think the cries had roused him.

He sat up from his mattress on the floor and rubbed his eyes. Reached for his cell phone to check the time.

Four A.M.

He put the phone back on the floor and dropped back onto his back, still staring at the ceiling.

The sounds and the smells of the tenement building were pervasive—there must have been fifty or sixty people living just on the second floor of this building—but Gentry had spent a significant percentage of his nights during the past five years in places just like this, and the rustling and crying babies and arguing in incomprehensible languages had long since ceased to bother him.

The other renters were all immigrants. Poles or Turks or people from the Balkans. Most of the rest of the single units were occupied by families; there were kids all over the place, and they'd been running up and down the halls during the early evening.

But now, other than a crying baby, it was quiet.

And the kid wasn't keeping him from sleeping. No, that was not it.

It was the phone call to Whitlock. Russ had not said anything that made him nervous or concerned about his PERSEC. No, on the contrary, the guy had made something of a case for himself by pointing out that if he wanted Court dead, Court would already be dead.

That was true, Gentry conceded as he lay there and thought about it, but it wasn't the airtight case Whitlock made it out to be. People change, as do their motivations, their desires, their orders. Court could rattle off a list of names of men he'd known who had not wanted him dead, until the day they suddenly *did* want him dead.

Court's life was funny that way.

But even though Gentry still considered Whitlock a potential threat, Whitlock himself was not Gentry's main concern. It was the technology itself. The MobileCrypt. Court did not trust technology he did not fully understand, and he was going to have to accept that technology out there was improving in many ways, and very few of these ways gave him an advantage.

Most of the advantages went to those chasing him.

Court worried he was not changing with the times. He was still walking around looking back over his shoulder and attaching strands of hair to his door frame to see if anyone had entered his room. Meanwhile, Whitlock had told Court that Townsend had compromised him with a *fucking* flying robot.

He *had* to get out of this game. The rules were changing, they were weighed more and more against him, and he saw it as inevitable someday soon he would zig when he should have zagged, and he would get his ass killed all because of some technology that he'd never even fucking heard of.

All that said, he didn't know where he would go to be any safer than he was now. He liked Stockholm so far. He liked his chances here, moving around with his face covered. He did not want to leave, to run away from unknown and possibly imagined space age forces hunting him.

Stockholm wasn't the problem.

But the phone call and vulnerability that it placed him in was the problem. He decided right then that he would not call Russ back, and he would relocate somewhere else in the city this morning.

The resolution of thought relaxed him somewhat, but still he couldn't sleep.

THIRTY-TWO

Ruth woke at four A.M. She'd slept less than four hours, a fact her body made clear to her before she'd even had time to pick up her phone to check the time.

Right now Mike would be huddling for warmth on a bench about eighty yards away from the target's location on Radmansgatan, tucked into a covered bus stop in the dark and away from any line of sight on the windows of the building. Ruth had to get up and go relieve him for three hours, and then Laureen would come and relieve her.

Ruth pushed her team hard, she knew it, but it was the only way to avoid a repeat of what had happened the previous spring in Rome.

In Rome her intelligence had been perfect; she and her team had tracked a Hezbollah gunman to a home in the Monte Sacro district of the city, and their surveillance determined that he would attempt to strike Ehud Kalb at an upcoming climate conference.

Ruth passed her information on to Metsada, along with a request for a few more days' surveillance to get better visibility inside the Monte Sacro home.

But she was vetoed, and Mossad leadership ordered an immediate raid. An internal report issued after the fact suggested that an increased Special Operations funding request in the Knesset the following week was the cynical impetus behind the order for immediate action.

Whatever the reason, Metsada hit the house, ignoring the request of the targeting officer on sight.

Five innocent people were killed. A father, a mother, and three children. The Hezbollah assassin had kidnapped them and kept them prisoner in case he needed a bargaining chip. When the commandos burst through the front door of the home, he pushed the family down a staircase; the Israelis mistook the rushing falling figures in their weapon lights as threats, and they gunned them all down before exchanging fire with and killing the Hezbollah terrorist.

Ruth was a basket case after the catastrophe. But she was almost immediately cleared of any wrongdoing, and she demanded to go back to work. Yanis had pushed back against this; he forced her to spend some time in counseling. But, damaged or not, she was damned proficient at her job, and there were many threats to Prime Minister Kalb, so she was cleared for duty within days, and she had been working twice as hard ever since.

Ruth rubbed her eyes and checked the local temperature on an app on her phone, and she rubbed them again, making sure she was seeing the screen correctly.

Out loud she groaned, "Three degrees Fahrenheit? Really?"

As she rolled out of the warm bed she heard noises in the living room of the safe house. Male voices. At first she thought it was just Carl and Lucas in conversation, which surprised her, considering the hour. But within a few seconds she was certain there were new speakers in the mix.

Next to where Ruth had been sleeping in the queen-sized bed, Laureen did not stir.

"Who the hell is that?" It was Aron asking from the bed on the far side of the room.

Ruth did not answer; she headed out of the bedroom, slipping her glasses on, and fumbled her way up the hall in the dark, toward the bright lights of the living room.

The voices were louder as she approached, and she also heard the thumping and slamming of equipment being moved around. She began to suspect she knew what was happening even before she saw it for herself.

Oh no.

Ruth walked into a room full of men, ten in all, including Lucas and Carl, who themselves had clearly only just awakened moments before.

She did not know the new guests, but Ruth didn't need thirteen years working in the intelligence field to determine she was looking at the Townsend kill team.

"Mornin'," a burly and bearded American man in a knit cap and a ski jacket said in a gravelly southern twang. He talked and moved like he was in charge of this entourage, and he crossed the room to her like he owned the place. "John Beaumont. You must be Ruth."

She shook his hand, but it was a gesture of obligation, not amicability. "Don't tell me you are planning a raid on that tenement."

"I go where they send me, ma'am. Do what they tell me. Just the same as you, I'll bet."

She shook her head violently. Ruth liked to be in control, and she felt the growing panic of losing control. "We don't know anything about the positioning of the target inside the building. What room he's in, how many others are in there. We know there are families. Kids. It's way too early for action."

"We're hitting it at oh six hundred, which is late in my book, but first light 'round here isn't till oh nine twenty-five."

Ruth's panic grew. "No! You've *got* to give us more time. At least half a day."

Beaumont pulled a tin of dip from his back pocket and began a snapping motion with his hand to tamp it down inside the can. "I don't work for you, honey, so I ain't *gotta* do shit."

"Excuse me?"

"You need to chill out. We aren't going to shoot any kids. Look, I'd like a better picture of the interior layout of that place myself, but we'll just have to adapt and overcome. We'll be going in light, civilian dress." He smiled a crooked grin. "We'll be super friendly to everybody who stays the fuck out of our way." Beaumont put a pinch of dip in his mouth and winked at her.

A couple of his men chuckled behind him. She looked

at the others and saw the weapons for the first time. Micro Uzis, a small sub gun of Israeli manufacture, and pistols that she did not recognize in holsters festooned with extra magazines. Ruth herself had been trained on weaponry, of course, but she did not carry firearms in the field, nor did she have any desire to.

"You're going in with Uzis? Yeah, *that's* friendly."

"I'm about to make breakfast," he said. "I'm thinking about an omelet. You know what they say about how to make an omelet?"

"What the hell are you talking about?" Ruth was lost.

One of his other men answered the question by raising his Uzi. "You gotta break some eggs, boss."

"That's right. Now, sweetie, we're going to do our best to avoid civilian casualties. Seriously. But we damn well *will* neutralize Court Gentry in that building at oh six hundred."

"You're a prick."

Beaumont ignored her; he'd tried his hand at international diplomacy and failed. He turned away and began helping his team with the equipment.

This felt like Rome all over again, and Ruth had to find a way to stop this. She turned to Lucas and Carl. The two men looked small and out of place in this room full of snake eaters. They did not seem happy about the new guests in their living room, but they certainly did not air any objections.

She rushed to her room and yanked her phone off the end table. Her first thought was to call Yanis in Tel Aviv, but instead she dialed Babbitt in D.C., where it was just after eight in the evening.

She started the conversation in the softest tone she could muster. "Mr. Babbitt, I am begging you to give us a few hours to continue surveillance."

"Why would we do that? Lucas says you know where he is. He says you've got an operative watching his place right now."

"Outside, yes. It would be idiotic to do surveillance inside the location now."

"No need for that. All we have to do is go in and get him."

"Kill him, you mean."

"That's up to him; however, I will say this. He murdered several of our people the other day, so I've ordered my direct action team to take no unnecessary chances."

Ruth was certain their plan was to kill Gentry, and there was no plan whatsoever to bring him in, but she did not make the accusation. Instead she pressed on with her campaign to get Townsend to wait. "At open of business today I'll send one of my guys into the building to rent a room, and with a little luck we'll have a live covert feed from in there by noon."

"I trust you've met Jumper Actual?"

"Beaumont? Yes."

"Well, he's *my* guy, and I'm sending him in there this morning. They aren't going to get video, they aren't going to rent a room. They will simply move through the property, locate the target, and neutralize him by whatever means are most expedient."

She said, "You know there are kids in there. Immigrant families, probably packed in like cordwood. There will be illegals; they'll scramble when they see white guys with guns. It could become a bloodbath if Gentry starts moving through all that!"

"We can't lose the target again. It's as simple as that." He added, "Beaumont and his team are quite good. This is how your Metsada operators do it."

"Metsada goes in only after I provide them all the information they need to do their job without collateral."

"Like in Rome, Ms. Ettinger?"

Ruth forced herself to take a deep breath. "Rome was a mistake. Honorable people can make a mistake. Metsada has honor. American SF soldiers have honor, too. I've worked with them before. But these guys of yours? Who the hell are they? They act like a posse heading out on the prairie to collect Indian scalps. You can't just run through a capital city with your guns blazing! This isn't the Wild West!"

"I beg to differ. These times are difficult. America's enemies are certainly more far-flung than they were back in the Old West and, I would argue, the threats are more pervasive and their impact more profound on my nation than anything that went down back then. But our mind-set here at Townsend is very similar to the deputized lawmen of that day and age."

It sounded to Ruth like Babbitt was reading from a bronze plaque on the wall at Townsend House. She said, "I have a feeling you don't even know what Court Gentry did to earn the shoot-on-sight. Whether you know or not, I am *certain* that you do not care."

"I have to go now, Ms. Ettinger. You and your team can feel free to stand down from this operation if you don't feel comfortable with it. We thank the Mossad for your help in this matter."

"I'm calling Carmichael. I'll put a stop to your operation right now."

"Ms. Ettinger, I seriously doubt you have the clout to get Denny on the phone, but assuming you do, I will save you some trouble and frustration. Carmichael has almost single-handedly carried the banner on the Gentry operation for the past five years. Whatever the fuck Gentry did—I am speaking about what he did previous to killing his field team—it was clearly something very personal to Denny Carmichael. If you call him right now and tell him you need Team Jumper to stand down ninety minutes before they neutralize Court Gentry, either he will laugh in your face or, and this is what worries me, he will call me and ask me to have Mr. Beaumont hog-tie you and your team so that you don't get in the way of their operation."

Ruth Ettinger fumed.

Babbitt let out a long, audible sigh that sounded to Ruth about as phony as his company's pseudo-cowboy image. He then said, "It's an ugly thing that's about to happen there, Ruth." He paused. "Let's not make it any uglier."

THIRTY-THREE

In the past thirty minutes it had become clear to Ruth Ettinger that even with all the layers she wore—every bit of her own cold-weather gear and even the extra jacket she made Laureen take off her own body and give her before Laureen climbed into the warm Skoda and returned to the safe house—the bottoms of her boots were composed of only a rubber sole and thin insoles. Even with her thick socks, the frozen ground transferred its cold into her feet and legs. After just a half hour out here in the dark, it felt like the bones in her lower legs, all the way up to her knees, were beginning to freeze solid.

She stamped her feet, sat down on the cold bench at the bus stop occasionally and lifted them off the ground, but there was really no way for her to get warm outside when it was only three degrees.

Of course things were going to heat up soon, in a

figurative sense anyway. In less than an hour a goon squad of American gunmen would roll up the street, enter the door of the apartment building eighty yards from where she now stood, move up the flight of stairs, and then train their guns on dozens of people on the second and third floor. The Americans would find their man, who was himself a very violent individual, and then it would go downhill from there.

Ruth had called Yanis Alvey to complain, of course. As she drove through the dark city in the embassy Skoda, she woke him up from a deep sleep in Tel Aviv and angrily told him she did not get into this business to help private American bounty hunters set up a half-assed and ill-conceived raid on a house full of children to kill a man who had committed many heroic acts in his career, and who she suspected was being unjustly pursued by American intelligence.

She did not mention Rome. She did not have to. Yanis knew what she was thinking.

Yanis did what he always did when Ruth got angry. He listened politely, made gentle and reasoned counterpoints, and then he asked Ruth if she wanted to drop the operation and come home.

She said no; she always said no. She also always found a way to complete her objective, and for this reason Yanis Alvey indulged his extremely hotheaded but also extremely brilliant targeting officer.

This time was different, however, in that this time he told her in no uncertain terms that Mossad leadership had ordered him to provide the Americans any assistance they required on this operation.

Ruth was incensed by this, but she did not take it out on her boss. If Yanis's hands were tied, she wouldn't waste her breath complaining to him. But she was puzzled by what he told her. Mossad leadership had always stayed out of her investigations in the past. Yes, in Rome they had pushed to have the operators move in, but that was only after Ruth and her team had been satisfied of the threat.

Why the hell were they now second-guessing her on Gentry?

Sitting in the covered bus stop, she took her eyes off the building up the street for a moment, but only a moment. She looked back up to the building and, just as she did so, the door opened and a single man walked out. A streetlight shone on the sidewalk near the door, and as he passed under it she saw the black coat with the hood, the blue jeans, and the black backpack in his hand.

It was him. He looked up and down the street, slung his pack on his shoulder, and headed off down Sveavagen toward the south in the direction of the river.

Ruth was hidden in the dark at the bus stop, but she stood now, backing deeper out of his line of sight.

He'd left the building; Jumper could take him right now on the street. And she knew that when she called they would do just that. Beaumont and his men would race up in a van and riddle Gentry with submachine gun rounds, drop him in the snow, and then race off.

She reached for her phone, ready to call Aron back at the safe house so he could let the Jumper team know that the target was on the move, but she stopped herself suddenly.

She found herself facing a dilemma the gravity of which she had never experienced. Nothing about this operation smelled right. She thought about the Gray Man, the operations he had undertaken on his own initiative. The man fading from the gas lamplight ahead of her had personally done more against America's enemies, enemies that Ruth and her nation shared with her birth nation, than anyone Ruth had ever known.

And now she found herself at the center of a frantic campaign to kill him, run by people she did not trust, people for whom, she had seen firsthand, collateral damage seemed to be of tertiary concern, well behind dropping their target and protecting their own asses.

She'd read all about the Tallinn fiasco. Two cops killed, a civilian killed. In none of the Mossad data on known Gray Man ops in the past five years had any noncombatants been wounded by the assassin.

Why this time?

She thought it was a hell of a lot more likely that the Townsend men, guys like that asshole Beaumont, had killed the cops and the bystander. Killing noncombatants was not Gentry's MO. Avoiding them was clearly not Townsend's MO.

Ruth pulled her hand away from her phone. She would not be a part of this. She had never forgiven herself for not fighting more forcefully against the attack in Rome. Even though she was cleared by Mossad leadership, she knew the truth.

Rome was her fault.

This time she would do what she had to do.

She called no one. Not the UAV team, not Beaumont, not even Aron.

No, she would find a way to get Townsend out of the picture, and then she would call in Metsada. Sure, they might still kill Gentry, but they would give her the opportunity to investigate further, not turn her operation into a precursor for a massacre.

She stood in place at the bus stop for three minutes, enough time for the Gray Man to disappear several hundred yards ahead of her. Then she hurried over to the front of the tenement building. The fresh snowfall and the virtually empty streets and sidewalks at five fifteen in the morning made tracking his footprints easy. She followed them south for ten minutes; they stayed on Sveavagen, although once they crossed to the other side of the street, and once it was clear that he tried to cover his tracks by walking along inside the tracks from a truck that she had seen passing by in the distance. But she picked the trail back up when the truck turned and the fresh prints continued on.

She could also see places where his gait changed, times when he'd slowed to look back over his shoulder, and each time she saw these she stopped herself, took her time shivering and waiting, making sure he was far enough ahead that there was no way he could be waiting for her to catch up to him.

The tracks turned and turned again on Drottningatten, the shopping street where the UAV team had first found him the previous evening. On this street several people were walking around, those unlucky ones who had to be at work by six A.M. As a result of the other pedestrians she found it harder and harder to track his prints, but she picked them up for a short time just before the end of the street, along the banks of the Norrstrom River. The footprints went onto the small bridge that crossed the river to the Gamla Stan, a tiny island in the center of the river and the location of Old Town Stockholm.

Ruth did not get on the bridge. She'd walked this area the day before and knew that the roads and passages on the island were narrow and tight. She would have no way to follow him now covertly; he could be waiting around any corner, so she backed off.

She'd lost him, and she wondered now what she had done.

Waves of self-doubt crashed on her, and twice she almost called in to Aron to tell him to get Jumper here on the double because he was getting away.

But she stayed herself.

If Gentry was leaving town he would have gone to the train station, or climbed into a cab for the airport, or headed to the docks. He'd done none of these things. He was staying in Stockholm.

She'd find him again. She had to.

She turned around and headed back to retake her watch over the tenement building, even though her target was long gone from the scene.

———

Jumper team hit the tenement at oh six hundred. Ruth had returned to the safe house to pack up with the rest of her team, and she and the three other Israelis took a break from packing to stand behind the UAV team while they piloted their drone through the predawn sky above the building on the southwest corner of Radmansgatan and Sveavagen.

Of course she knew Jumper would not find Gentry there, although her concerns remained that noncombatants could be killed or injured during the hit. Twice while the Americans were en route to the target location she spoke into the microphone on the table, reminding Beaumont and his team that they were likely to encounter central Europeans wary of police or government officials, and they might try to run or resist, even though they had no relationship with or knowledge of the target.

The first time she made the point, Beaumont responded with, "This ain't exactly my first rodeo, lady," which the Brooklyn-born Ettinger translated to mean he was aware of the potential for noncombatants in the line of fire.

The second time she reminded Beaumont and his men to keep their fingers off their triggers until they were certain they had the Gray Man in their sights, the big American responded tersely. "Lucas, I want that woman off my commo net!"

Lucas pulled the microphone away from Ruth.

And then Jumper Actual initiated the raid.

The American contractor's radio headset communications came through the speakers on the table. Ruth heard shouting men, then screaming women and children and what sounded like breaking doors or furniture.

Jumper team was not subtle in their tactics, but, Ruth

did have to admit, they were mercifully speedy. Within five minutes Beaumont barked angrily into his mic. "Negative contact! His room is empty. Looks like he cleared out."

Ruth pulled the microphone back from Lucas. "Did you ask the manager what time he left?"

"He didn't know. Either he slipped past your team or he was never here to begin with."

Lucas said, "He was there."

"He might have sneaked onto the roof," suggested Ruth. "We only had coverage from distance. Not a perfect sight line." She wondered if she'd overbaked her explanation, but she did not detect any suspicion from either those around her or the American team leader at the target location.

"Are we going to assume he's left town?" Carl asked. "I mean, why just reposition in the city when you don't know anyone has a fix on you?"

Jumper replied, "He's probably flown the coop, but we'll stay here and keep looking till Townsend House gets a hit on facial recog. They have everything covered for a couple hundred miles; he's not going to go far."

"Roger that."

"Fishing boats," Ruth said over the mic.

"What about them?"

"It's his MO. He likes to hire fishing boats to take him out to freighters. He's worked with the Russian mob to get passage on Russian-flagged haulers."

After a short hesitation Beaumont said, "Yeah. She's right. I guess we'll run down to the docks and sniff around."

She did not feel bad about sending Jumper off on the wrong scent. She hoped they searched the waterways all day long.

Ruth and her team finished packing; she told Carl and Lucas that they would be in touch, but for now the Mossad would do their own recon. She hated to lose the intel from the UAV; she wouldn't have found the Gray Man in less than a day in Stockholm without the work of Lucas and Carl and their Sky Shark. But she knew if the drone got another ping on the target they would just recall Beaumont and his cowboys, and they would be right back on the verge of another catastrophe, and Ruth did not want to be involved in that.

She decided she and her team would do it the old-fashioned way. They would head to where she last saw him, and then they would branch out and search until they found him.

She did not tell her team she had lied about seeing him leave the building earlier. She knew they would back her, but there was no need for them to be implicated if Yanis Alvey found out the truth and recalled or even fired her for her insubordination.

THIRTY-FOUR

At ten A.M. local time on Saturday morning, Russ Whitlock climbed off the train at the town of Èze-sur-Mer, hefting a large pack onto his back as he did so. He left the tiny station and began trudging up a steep road that wound its way into and through the hamlet of Èze. Behind him as he walked, the blue waters of the Mediterranean reached to the horizon line; in the near distance dozens of small pleasure craft sat still in the morning sun, from Monaco to the east to Nice to the west and beyond.

Russell Whitlock only occasionally looked back over his shoulder toward the water and the roads below him. He wasn't worried about being followed today; he was certain no one knew he was here. He also wasn't terribly concerned about witnesses to what he was about to do.

This was the low season in the south of France; there was very little foot traffic, even in the more touristy areas. He was, however, worried about cameras, and for this reason he avoided the cobblestoned main streets of Èze with their shops and hotels and restaurants, all of which would have some form of Internet-based or CCTV cameras for security purposes, and instead he worked his way around the backs of buildings, ever climbing, away from the sea and toward low scrub brush and rocky outcroppings on the hill to the west of the hamlet.

His hip hurt, of course; it nagged him with every step.

Whichever fucking Trestle operative had shot him—Russ had no idea who'd made the lucky shot—Russ knew the odds were seven in eight that the man was now dead, and he took great pleasure in that.

He neared his destination, still ascending through the trees and brush. He'd climbed the route the afternoon before, searching for just the right spot, and determining the manner in which he could avoid others while ingressing to and egressing from his sniper's hideout.

Of course, broad-daylight work like this was not his first choice, but this was the only chance to hit his target. Yes, Amir Zarini would pass by on the same road this evening on his return from Monaco, and then it would be past nightfall, but Russ would not be able to identify his vehicle in the dark, not even with the Leupold scope.

If he was to hit Zarini within his promised five-day window, he had to do it this way, and he had to do it now.

He found his spot fifty minutes after leaving the train station, and he took his time to secret himself in the low green brush. He lay in the dirt, his backpack next to him, but he did not open it yet to retrieve the rifle. He had a few minutes to kill now, and the last thing he wanted was for some hippie French hikers to happen by his hide and see him with a long black gun.

He was certain he would be seen by someone before this was all through, probably over in the medieval hamlet of Èze just a hundred meters off to his left, but that was no problem, because what would they see? A white male in his thirties, with an athletic build, brown hair, and a brown beard?

That sounded a hell of a lot like another guy to Russ, a more famous guy. And that was, of course, by design.

He pictured the action to come, and, just as when he'd planned every other part of this operation, he thought about the Gray Man. He wanted to do everything just the way Gentry would do it, if he were the man here to kill Amir Zarini.

Russ knew what that entailed. He'd read every scrap the CIA had on Gentry, and they all led inexorably to one conclusion.

Gentry would do it right.

After all, Russ thought, if you read the reports about him, Gentry was smooth. Gentry was clean. Gentry was the best.

"Well, fuck Gentry," Whitlock said aloud.

Russ could do smooth and clean as well as the Gray Man, and he knew it. He'd smoked the number two al Qaeda commander in Baghdad in 2008, and again he'd taken out his successor, this time in Peshawar, in 2011.

Both times he'd slipped into a no-go zone undetected, used an M40 rifle with a suppressor—not this foreign-made Blaser bullshit that the Gray Man fancied—and he'd made it out clean.

Yeah, Russ could do it just like Gentry.

Better, in fact, and today he would have a chance to prove it to himself. Of course, no one else would know that the Zarini hit had been the work of Russell Whitlock, and that was by design, although Russ regretted the fact. The intelligence community in the United States would chalk this op up to the Gray Man; they would scratch their heads a bit because the target would look odd compared to a normal Gray Man contract, but they would attribute it to Gentry nonetheless.

Today Russ would kill two birds with one stone. He would convince the Iranians that he was the Gray Man, and he would set the table for the world's intelligence agencies. They would see soon enough that the Gray Man was working for the Iranians.

Yes, he had promised the Iranian Quds Force man that there would be no comebacks to Iran on either this hit with Zarini or the assassination of Ehud Kalb. He'd actually said it with a straight face.

But the truth was quite different. The truth was, once Whitlock got paid for this operation, he would make sure the world knew the Gray Man had killed the PM and the Gray Man worked for Iran.

And by then, poor Court Gentry would not be in a position to defend himself.

Whitlock looked down to his watch.

It was time.

He unzipped his backpack and began assembling the Blaser R93. He put the entire weapon together in less than ninety seconds. Not his fastest time, but he was in no rush. Once he'd snapped the four-round magazine into place, he loaded a fifth round into the chamber and closed the bolt.

He did not expect to need five bullets. Just one. But it was always good to be prepared.

He took up his position behind his weapon and looked through the scope. He scanned the road far below him, the Avenue Raymond Poincaré, and found a suitable location to fire upon. He checked his range to target and saw that the distance was 335 meters. He set the elevation on his scope. He gauged the wind and determined the values to be negligible for a shot of this distance.

Now he waited, but he did not have to wait for long. Just four minutes after placing his eye behind the Leupold optic and beginning his scan for the vehicles, two Mercedes G-Class SUVs appeared on the road as they passed the train station.

They were a perfect match.

There were three people in the lead Mercedes, two in the front seats and one in the back. Through the scope Russ had difficulty identifying the man in the rear of the vehicle, and when a glint of sun off the windscreen of the lead SUV caused Russ to shut his eye into his scope for a moment, he lost another few seconds to make his identification.

As the time neared to fire, he realized he could not

positively identify Zarini in the front car. He swung his
scope quickly to the rear vehicle, scanned through the
windshield of the Mercedes, and saw two men in the
front seat and two in the back. None of the four looked
like his target; they all appeared to be bodyguards.

With his window of opportunity rapidly closing, Whitlock pushed the stock of the rifle up, pointing the muzzle
down a fraction, and centered his optics back on the lead
SUV. As the vehicle neared the point directly below his
position, he no longer had visibility of the man in the
backseat since he was sitting on the other side of the Mercedes.

He could only see the driver now, and in another few
seconds he would lose him as he passed around a bend.

Shit, Russ thought. *No way to do this clean.*

He lined up his scope, took in a breath, blew it halfway out and held it.

He fired the Blaser.

One third of a second later, the driver's-side window
of the lead Mercedes shattered; the driver's head slumped
to the side, and the vehicle veered dramatically to the
right. At speed the SUV scraped along a low retaining
wall that ran alongside the road and, with a dead driver
behind the steering wheel, it jacked back to the left, into
the opposing lane.

The SUV slammed headfirst into an oncoming Volkswagen Cabriolet; an explosion of metal and glass and
steam and spraying fluids erupted into the air, instantly
killing Amir Zarini, the two other men in the Mercedes,
and three college students inside the Volkswagen.

The rear Mercedes swerved almost sideways on the road to avoid the carnage in front of it, coming to a stop just twenty-five feet from the accident. All four occupants of the rear vehicle poured out; one of them ran to the wreckage, but the other three drew their P90 submachine guns and pointed them at the hillside, reacting to the sound of the sniper rifle.

Russ pulled the bolt back and chambered another round, and he scanned the wreckage below him, looking for any signs of life. Although the Mercedes now lay on its side along a short scatter path of wreckage, there had been no massive fireball or other event that told Whitlock, definitively, that the wreck was unsurvivable. After deciding he needed to be absolutely certain his target was dead—the Gray Man would not leave a scene with a wounded target behind him, after all—Russ fired on the Mercedes quickly. Four equidistant holes in the roof; each round would strike a different portion of the backseat and, Russ was certain now, would kill anyone left alive after the crash.

Russ also knew exactly what four more gunshots, all from the same portion of the hillside, would do to the four armed men below. All the private security officers began firing bursts from their P90s. Gunfire echoed off the hills all around Whitlock while he calmly ejected the magazine and replaced it with a fresh one. The high-pitched screams of rounds ricocheting off rock around him only encouraged him to work more quickly. He added one more bullet in the chamber to make five, and then he aimed at the first security man on the Avenue Raymond Poincaré below and shot him through the chest. The man fell back to the street; his suit coat whipped up crazily as his arms flailed, and his weapon skittered to the asphalt.

A second security officer sprayed rounds toward Whitlock's hide. The P90 was out of range at 335 yards, which meant only that accurate and effective fire was difficult, not that a round from the gun could not strike Russ dead. But Russ fired his long-range rifle and sent a big bullet into the forehead of the security officer, dropping him dead next to his colleague on the seaside roadway.

By now the last two security men had seen the futility of their predicament, and both turned and ran, leaping for the low retaining wall that ran along the road. Russ tracked the movement of one man and fired once more, striking him with a shot to the low back.

The fourth executive protection officer made it to cover and, Russ felt sure, he would keep his head down for some time to come.

Just as Russ took his eye out of the scope to begin the quick takedown of the gun, he heard shouting to his left. He looked across the hillside and saw several locals as well as a uniformed police officer, a member of the local *police municipale*, standing there, at the edge of the hamlet of Èze. The cop had some sort of pistol in his hand, and he fired it at a distance of 125 yards. He missed; dirt and dust kicked up ten feet from where Russ lay, but he quickly spun his rifle toward the cop and aimed at the top of the man's head to allow for the fact that he'd adjusted the scope for the 335-yard shot. Russ fired just as the *municipale* fired; the cop missed again, but Whitlock's .300 Winchester magnum round nailed the man between the eyes.

Russ fired one last round at the crowd of idiots standing there watching, missing the civilians by inches, and then he quickly and calmly disassembled his weapon, stuffed it in his backpack, and began running up the hill, limping through the pain in his hip.

It took him less than three minutes to make it to the Moyenne Corniche, a winding hillside road almost empty of traffic. He'd parked his BMW at a scenic lookout, and he leapt into it, throwing the rifle bag into the passenger seat, and then he sped off in a cloud of white dust, minutes before local authorities could respond en masse.

Four hours later Russ Whitlock stood in front of a full-length mirror in a three-star hotel room in Genoa, Italy. He had showered, shaved off his beard, and cut his hair short and neat. He had rebandaged the wound on his hip and then dressed in an Armani suit he'd had waiting on him here in the room.

He admired his look in the mirror, and he felt the pride in today's accomplishment wash over him. No, it had not gone according to plan; there had been some collateral damage. Killing the cop had been unavoidable and very much necessary to achieve his objective, in Whitlock's opinion, and the dead civilians in the car had just been in the wrong place at the wrong time.

He did not blame himself for any of the deaths, though

he remained objective enough to know that this assassination did not look exactly like a Gray Man assassination.

But still, he told himself, it would suffice for his purposes.

After straightening his tie once more in the mirror, he zipped closed his Italian leather roller bag and headed out the door.

He went downstairs and rolled his luggage out onto the street. A taxi driver motioned to him, but Russ waved him away. Instead, Russ took out his phone and walked up the sidewalk, away from the entrance to the hotel, so he could have some privacy.

He dialed a number using the MobileCrypt app and waited for an answer on the other end.

"Yes?" It was Ali Hussein, the Quds Force operative he'd met earlier in the week in Beirut. Whitlock recognized the voice.

"It's me. It's done."

"I know. It is all over the television. We had hoped for more . . . discretion."

"You are not implicated in what happened."

"That is not what I mean. My organization is highly uneased by today's events. We are impressed you succeeded in your mission, but the collateral damage makes us very concerned you are not the man you say you are."

Whitlock squeezed the cell phone tightly as he tensed with anger. He said, "The tactical realities of the event resulted in unanticipated loss of life."

"What does that mean?"

Angrily Russ said, "It means 'shit happens.'"

After a delay, Hussein said, "This, what transpired today, does not look like the work of the Gray Man."

Russ tried to calm himself before continuing, taking two long, silent breaths and telling himself everything was riding on his powers of persuasion. "I understand your concerns. I do. I am disappointed in some aspects of the operation. But I am who I say I am, and you only have to ask yourself who else could have executed this operation on such a tight timeline to see that I am telling the truth."

"There is only one way you can convince us."

Russ knew Hussein was referring to Kiev. He closed his eyes; he had to force himself not to throw the phone into traffic and then turn around and slam his fist into the wall of the hotel.

The Quds Force officer said, "We have statements from all the Iranians present the night in question at Vasylkiv Air Base in Kiev, Ukraine. If your description of the events of that evening coincides with what we already know, then we have a deal regarding Ehud Kalb. If you will not tell us, or if what you tell us does not agree with the witness statements, then there will be no further communications between us." The line went quiet for a moment, then Hussein said, "It is as simple as that."

Russ felt himself losing control of his emotions. The anger welled within him, pushing hot blood through his heart and his brain. There on the sidewalk Whitlock thought he might explode with the fury inside that had no way to vent from his body and into the atmosphere.

"I'll call you back," was all he could say before he hung up the phone.

Russ knew there was no way around it now. He had to somehow get Gentry to tell him about Kiev. Before he even began thinking of a way to achieve this seemingly impossible objective, his phone buzzed in his hand. He looked down at it, hoping like hell it was Gentry.

Instead, it was Townsend House. Distractedly, Whitlock answered.

"Go."

Babbitt's voice came through his phone. "It's Graveside." After the identity check, Babbitt asked, "Have you made it to Stockholm yet?"

"Yes," Russ lied.

"Jumper hit a dry hole this morning. Looks like Gentry slipped the Mossad watchers the night before."

Whitlock breathed a slow sigh of relief. Finally, some good news. Then, "No ideas where he is?"

"The UAV team is up and Jumper has split into four two-man teams. They are watching choke points."

"And Mossad?"

"They are still in the city, but operating independently of us for the time being. We expect they will bring in reinforcements from Tel Aviv." He paused. "If you were ever going to use your sixth sense about Gentry and what he's up to, this would be the time."

"Understood. I'll work on it."

He hung up the phone and stood there on the sidewalk, struggling with his own next move. He'd planned on flying from here in Genoa to London so he could start the prep for his hit on Ehud Kalb eight days from now, but he could not just assume Court would be able to avoid all the forces lining up against him in Stockholm.

And if Gentry died before Kalb died, then Whitlock knew he'd lost his lifeline.

He knew he had no choice. He had to rush to Stockholm, to help Gentry slip the noose and somehow convince him to talk about Kiev.

THIRTY-FIVE

Court chose to spend the majority of the day in his small attic room in the Gamla Stan. The accommodations were opulent compared to where he had spent the previous few evenings, as this unit had its own bathroom and shower, and even a small refrigerator. But as the day turned into night and snowfall picked up outside, Court felt like he was going a little stir-crazy. He decided he would head up the narrow street to a corner market and grab dinner, and then perhaps even venture out for a beer in a dark local bar he had noticed earlier in the day.

At 7-Eleven he bought some cheese spread and packaged toast to smear it on, along with a bottle of water. As he stood in line to pay he noticed a table in the back, upon which three computer terminals had been set up, serving as a tiny Internet café. After paying he strolled to one of the machines and sat down, and soon he was reading up on the Department of State facial recognition system, thought to be the most advanced recog software in use today. Court suspected there were technologies out there that hadn't made it to open source just yet, although whether Townsend possessed such capabilities he had no idea.

He spread cheese on his dry toast and sipped water, flipped his eyes up to the front of the market, and noticed a woman entering. He looked her over quickly and perfunctorily, and then went back to his online reading.

Thirty-three-year-old Mossad targeting officer Laureen Tattersal stepped through the doors of the 7-Eleven, brushed snow off the hood of her down coat, and pulled off her gloves. She took a few seconds to warm her face with her hands and then headed to the coffee area hunting for an espresso, desperately needing one last jolt of caffeine before checking the twenty-first potential target location, just up the street.

It was past eight P.M. now; fat snowflakes drifted around the gas lamps hanging from the colorful buildings of the Old Town. The temperature was heading back down to single digits, and the Israeli woman planned to enjoy every second of warmth she could before heading back outside.

It had been a long day for the entire team. They'd moved into a hotel in the city center, less than a half mile from the Townsend safe house and only a hundred yards or so from the bridge to the Gamla Stan, where Ruth had last tracked Gentry. They had then bundled up in their cold-weather gear and hit the area, visiting hotels, apartments, tenements, and B&Bs and even checking under bridges where the homeless lived on cardboard in dirty rags.

So far they'd found nothing, and they planned to knock off for the night in two hours and try again the following day.

Laureen dropped a sugar cube into her espresso and brought it to her lips. As she did so her eyes lifted up to the rear of the brightly lit store, and she froze, nearly scalding her mouth and tongue on the hot coffee.

Laureen looked back down as the man glanced up from the computer in front of him, and she added another sugar to her drink. Then she turned and headed to the register to pay.

It was him. The Gray Man sat at a tiny three-station Internet café set up in the back of the 7-Eleven. He wore his black knit cap just over his eyes, and a scarf hung loosely around the lower portion of his face. He'd bought a new coat since the last time she'd seen him, but still she felt certain this was her target.

She left the convenience store and, in an abundance of caution, walked a full winding, descending block, checking to make certain she was not herself being followed before she pushed the button on her earpiece and announced to her team that she had located the target.

———————

Ruth, Mike, and Aron converged on Laureen a few minutes later. They parked the embassy Skoda in an hourly-rate lot there on the Gamla Stan and sat in the sedan for a few minutes, satisfied with the location though it had no line of sight on their target at the convenience store, because Ruth did not dare risk compromise. For now they searched the Internet on their smart phones, looking for tenements or inns around the neighborhood where the Gray Man might be staying, and searching for suitable rooms for themselves to rent in the neighborhood so they could set up a base of operations close by.

Mike called out, "Castanea hostel is two minutes away from the market. It's the closest location that looks like his kind of place."

Ruth pulled it up on her phone. "Yeah. I don't see anything else around here this cheap; I think this has got to be it. We'll check it out in the morning to make sure."

Aron was researching places for the team to use to bed down for the night. "There's a place called the Gamla Stan Lodge just around the corner from us now. I can go get us a couple of rooms there."

"Do it," Ruth said.

Aron climbed out of the car and headed up the street on foot.

Ruth decided to give Yanis Alvey the news about finding Gentry, but before she could make the call there was a beep in her ear. Ruth looked down to her phone and saw that it was Yanis calling her.

"Hey," she said.

"Where are you?"

"I'm in Stockholm. We found the target. He's still here."

There was a short pause. "Are you sure?"

"Of course I'm sure. Laureen picked him up thirty minutes ago."

"But you've had no visibility on him all day, is that correct?"

"Correct. But we've got him now. We think we know where he'll stay the night, and we'll move into a place a couple blocks away."

"You lost coverage last night at . . . ten P.M.?"

Ruth was confused by the questioning. "Around that, I guess. Maybe nine thirty. Why?"

Yanis said, "Because your target went to the south of France and killed a man. If you are certain he is there now . . . You *are* certain?"

"Back up. What do you mean he killed a man in *France*?"

"Amir Zarini was murdered this morning."

"Oh shit," she said. Then quickly she added, "But not by Gentry."

"We just got off a conference call with Langley. They say all their preliminary intel indicates Amir Zarini was gunned down by none other than Court Gentry. He must have flown down from Stockholm last night. I can get you airline manifests, but for anything chartered, you're better off going yourself to the fixed-base operators at Stockholm Arlanda and talking to them directly."

"He did *not* go to Nice. That's impossible."

"Why is it impossible? You lost him for twenty-four hours. It's not only possible, it's perfect. He left Stockholm last night, did the hit this morning, and arrived back this afternoon or this evening. You guys picked him right back up. Nice work."

Ruth knew Gentry had been in Stockholm that morning; she'd seen him herself. But letting Alvey know she'd purposefully short-circuited the Townsend attack in violation of her orders would get her pulled off the case and recalled to Tel Aviv.

She said, "Send me everything you have on the Zarini assassination."

"What we have is preliminary. Hell, it was only nine hours ago. But CIA is working with French federal police and they—"

"Just send me everything. Now, please."

———————

The Mossad team moved into two rooms at the Gamla Stan Lodge, a small hotel in the Gamla Stan that looked out over a tiny cobblestone square. Across the street a bar popular with students and other patrons of the cheap hotels and hostels in the area was in full swing; young men and women moved across the snowy open space heading to and from the bar's bright entrance in a steady stream.

While Mike parked the car at a neighboring lot and Aron and Laureen unpacked, Ruth sat at a little desk and read everything Yanis had sent her about the assassination in Nice. Ruth also scanned online news reports of the hit on the websites of CNN and the BBC.

When Mike returned, they turned on the TV hoping to find more information on the attack. The lodge's satellite broadcaster received France 2, and the state-owned station showed a lengthy story on the attack, with footage from the scene. Twisted wreckage, bodies covered in yellow tarps, incongruous in front of a backdrop of azure water dotted with pleasure craft. As she watched the news, the others read the CIA info sent by Yanis. When they were finished Ruth said, "You guys have read the after-action reports from the operations Court Gentry has pulled off?"

Everyone had read the Mossad files, and Ruth had filled them in on the dossier she was allowed to see at Townsend House.

"Then you see this is bullshit. This operation in Nice does not fit the Gray Man pattern at all."

Aron disagreed. "The rifle used in the Zarini hit was a Blaser R93, a favorite of the Gray Man. A weapons smuggler in Austria identified the Gray Man as the purchaser of said rifle. Witnesses at the scene described the Gray Man. Zarini was a known target of Iran, which has also been linked to the Gray Man, just in the last week." He shrugged. "Sure, certain aspects do not fit, and I can't deny that, but most of the details do fit, and you should not deny that, either."

Ruth countered. "There are a lot of white guys with brown hair in their thirties. Anyone can use a particular weapon. But the target, the collateral damage . . . the killing of the police officer. *That* is not Gentry."

Mike said, "He got sloppy. He missed the target and hit the driver, and that caused the collision. After that his operation went tits up, and the cop had time to close in on him, so he didn't have any options. He took him out."

"Missed his target? The Gray Man doesn't miss his target!"

"Listen to yourself," Aron said. "You sound like you are infatuated by a myth."

"It's not a myth. He's that skilled. And that principled. He doesn't shoot innocent cops."

"You told us yourself that he killed his own field team."

"I told you the CIA *says* he killed his own field team."

"And you don't believe them?"

Ruth hesitated. "I think that *if* he killed those guys, he had a reason."

Aron said, "Well, the timeline doesn't rule him out of the Zarini hit. Nice is fifteen hundred miles away. Four hours flying time tops with a small corporate jet. Add an hour each way in a turbo prop. That is more than enough time for him to fly to Nice, whack Zarini, and then get back to Stockholm."

Ruth couldn't argue with this, because she did not want to reveal to her team that she'd seen Gentry that morning.

Mike Dillman had been standing by the window. He looked out, then quickly moved to the overhead light switch. He flicked it off and said, "Speak of the devil."

Ruth leaned away from her desk to take a look into the little square. Within a half second she shot back straight up, removing herself from the window. Quickly she turned off the TV with the remote, enshrouding the room in complete darkness.

"Is that him?"

"Yep," said Mike.

She looked again now and saw a lone man heading toward the lights of the little bar on the other side of the courtyard. She would be invisible up here in the dark from this distance, but still she felt his eyes on her as he glanced around.

After he entered the bar Laureen said, "I guess he doesn't want to drink alone tonight," she said.

"Sad life this guy lives," Dillman said. "No wonder jackasses like him go out to kill people. They get trained, the humanity is drained out of them, and they don't know how to do anything else."

Ruth disagreed. "If there were no humanity in the man, his career as an assassin would be very different. He would take money and kill people, no questions asked."

Aron said, with no small amount of frustration in his voice, "He's taking money to kill Ehud Kalb. Are you okay with that?"

"We don't know that." After another moment she said, "And we aren't going to find out sitting here." Ruth stood. "I am going in."

"You're joking," Laureen protested. "You can't go in there. He'll make you." And then she added, "He's a killer, unless you forgot."

"There is nothing in his file that gives me any indication he will shoot a woman in the head if she sits down in the same bar as him."

Aron was against it as well. "Way too risky. You might need to get close to him in another environment. Don't blow your cover then by your actions now." He talked to her the way she lectured her team about tradecraft and operational security, and Ruth knew he was right, but she knew something he did not. Gentry had not been involved in a massacre that day in Nice. Someone was railroading him into taking the fall for that, and Ruth wanted answers. She was willing to gamble on pushing this investigation by getting closer to her target.

To justify herself she said, "Is he in there meeting with the Iranians? How the hell are we going to know what he's up to if we don't press this?"

Aron looked at her like she was crazy. "I'm going to go out on a limb and say he's not having a powwow with the Iranians in a Swedish pub."

"I can't just follow this man around and wait for the Americans to exterminate him." She stood and turned on the light, pulled a blond wig and a wig cap out of her bag, and rushed to the mirror.

Aron stood by the door. "Can I speak with you privately, Ruth?"

Ruth pulled her brown hair back and slipped it all inside the wig cap. "Just say what you want to say, Aron."

He did so. "This is because of Rome."

Ruth shook her head angrily, her blond locks drooped into her eyes for an instant before she brushed them back. "This is because of right here, right now. If I had fought harder against the system in Rome, then five innocents would not be dead. I will *not* make that mistake again."

"But—"

Ruth cut him off. "I'm going into that bar, and I will decide how to proceed from there."

"You aren't going to bump him, are you?"

She walked over to her makeup case on the desk. "I don't know. You are welcome to come in and watch over me, but don't get in my way."

A few minutes later the three junior Mossad officers watched from the window as Ruth Ettinger crossed the square.

"This is a bad idea," Laureen said, and neither of her colleagues argued the point.

THIRTY-SIX

Ruth found the bar mostly full, but there was an open stool along the L-shaped wooden bar near the door, likely, she assumed, because every time the door opened the arctic air poured in. She stayed in her coat and took a seat next to a blond-haired couple in their twenties. Careful not to look around at first, she fiddled with her mobile phone for a moment, then shouted over loud rock music to order a Falcon Pilsner on draft.

As she looked away from the bartender she glanced the length of the room and picked Gentry out around the turn of the L-shaped bar and almost at the far end. Though they were easily twenty-five feet apart, this was the closest she had been to the Gray Man. She stole glances at him as she brought her beer to her lips. He had a bottle of beer in front of him, and his head hung over it. A black knit cap covered his head, and he wore his coat unzipped. Days of rough stubble peppered his cheeks and chin, dark brown with a few flecks of gray.

He leaned over his bottle, seeming to not notice anyone or anything around him, but Ruth realized she could not accurately gauge his level of awareness, as she only glanced at him once every minute or so.

She had no illusions that she would see her target sitting next to a known Iranian intelligence officer, receiving a suitcase full of hundred-dollar bills, but she felt like she needed to get this close to get some measure of this man. From the very beginning of this operation she'd been bothered by the official version of this man's biography, and she realized she was desperately reaching out to try to find some understanding of his motivations. Something that would either rule him in as a threat, or rule him out.

But there wasn't much going on in here. She finished her beer after ten minutes or so and ordered another, and she thought now Aron might have been correct. There might be need for surveillance tomorrow, and even though she had disguised herself with a wig and more makeup than she would normally wear, she would have to exclude herself from any close foot-follow, because she could not rule out the possibility that he might remember her from the bar.

If he was as good as his reputation, he would damn sure remember her face despite her best attempts at disguise.

She looked down, ran her finger along the rim of her beer glass, and quickly flitted her eyes up in his direction.

Gentry stared right back at her.

Ruth was burned and she knew it. She looked away quickly, not casually enough, she was certain, so she went in the opposite direction with her plan. She looked back, hoping to catch his eye again. She thought there was a chance she could make him think she was only eyeing him because she was attracted to him.

It took several seconds, but soon enough Gentry's eyes met hers again. She could tell he was fully alert now, wondering why the woman across the bar was locked onto him, but all she could do now was pass her actions off as flirtation.

She smiled at him and looked down and away. Internally her senses were on fire. She had no idea how he would react.

She glanced again toward him, and he looked away. *Shit,* she thought to herself. *He's not buying it.*

The door opened behind her, and a moment later Aron passed behind her and kept walking around the L-shaped bar to the tables along the far wall of the room. They were all packed, but he moved into a group of college students and started chatting with them like he'd known them for years.

Ruth looked up to Gentry and noticed he was still looking down. She thought, at first, that he was concentrating on the bottle in front of him. But to her surprise, he pulled out a mobile phone, dialed a number with his thumb, and placed it to his ear.

———

Russ Whitlock's plane had just landed at Stockholm Arlanda airport, and he walked with the other passengers from his flight toward the baggage carousel.

He checked his phone and saw that he had no new intel pushes from Townsend House, which he took as an indication that the noose had not yet closed around Gentry. He planned to grab his bag and then jump in a taxi for the city center, and along the way call Parks to see what was going on.

As he put his phone back in his coat it rang. The call was coming through his MobileCrypt app so he could not see the phone number. Quickly he checked the time. It was a little after nine here. Gentry had promised to call, so he hoped like hell it was him.

"Go."

Russ first heard background noise over the line. Music, perhaps, as well. Then Court Gentry spoke, softly, and with stress in his voice. "Anything new you want to tell me about?"

Yes! Russ had to stop himself from pumping a fist in the air, and he struggled to keep his reply low-key. "I wish you'd called me earlier. I got intel right after I talked to you last night. Townsend Group is in Stockholm. They thought they had you located in a tenement building, and they hit it this morning. A team with submachine guns, just like the other night in Tallinn. I don't know how you did it, but you gave them the slip."

"Who's the girl?"

"The girl?"

"C'mon, man. The girl making goo-goo eyes at me right now. Who is she?"

"I don't know. She *might* be on the surveillance detail."

Court looked up again at the attractive blonde sitting on the other side of the bar; she concentrated on her beer glass for a moment, then glanced his way. Her eyes lingered on him a moment, then they moved on. She was good, he had to admit. She seemed relaxed, just a lonely girl on holiday with a couple of beers in her.

"Any chance you can find out for sure?"

"Of course I can. Where are you?"

"In a bar in the Gamla Stan."

"Okay. Give me your cell number and I'll call you back."

Court just said, "I'll just call *you* back in five."

"It might be more than five. Dammit, Court. A private kill team has got you fixed, you are convinced there is surveillance on you right now, and you are worried that the guy who has already saved your life might trace your fucking phone number? Are you serious?"

Court conceded the point by reading the number off his cell phone.

———————

Ruth had a running count going of the number of times she and her target had locked eyes. At five, she decided she had no choice. He was suspicious, and the only way she could keep from spooking him further was to go over there and hit on him. She felt like she could get him to relax a little, to accept the fact that the girl with the elevator eyes was just lonely or horny, and no threat to him. And if she played her cards right, she told herself, she might even learn something more about the man and his intentions.

She stood from her stool, lifted her drink off the bar, and began walking over.

Out of the corner of her left eye she saw Aron sitting with the college kids; he looked up at her and squared his shoulders in her direction. Though he was professional and showed no outward alarm, she wondered if he would call out to her, and she also wondered if he would leap from his chair and tackle her before she could walk over and sit down next to the man with the blood of so many on his hands.

But he did not shout and he did not tackle her. She made the crossing over to her target without incident, and she focused on the man as she stepped up to the bar next to him.

Gentry looked down into his beer. He did not move a muscle.

"Hej," she said. It sounded like "Hey!" in English, but it was Swedish for "hello" and the only word she knew in the language.

Slowly the man's face turned to her. "Hello," he answered in English. His voice was softer than she'd imagined it to be.

"Crowded," she said. "I guess everyone wants to get out of the cold."

"I guess so."

"You're American?" she asked.

He nodded and looked back down to his beer, his shoulders and legs pointed forward, toward the bar, and not in her direction. His body language would have devastated her self-esteem if she had really been trying to chat him up.

"Me, too."

He did not look up or respond.

"I'm sorry," she said. "I just thought I could introduce myself."

"All right."

She used his response as an invitation to sit down on the stool just vacated next to him, although she was pretty sure that wasn't what he meant.

———————

In the intelligence world, a seemingly chance encounter with someone who is actually an enemy intelligence officer is referred to as a bump. If a male spy is riding the subway, the pretty girl who drops her purse next to him and then starts up a conversation as the two of them pick up the contents is probably bumping him. There is likely nothing at all random to the encounter.

Court had seen no specific tell indicating that this encounter with this woman was a bump. But Court was also a suspicious man. He would assume she was part of a surveillance team until he either confirmed it or somehow proved otherwise.

It occurred to him that the only true way he would ever be convinced she was not bumping him was if she walked away right now and he never saw her again.

He did not speak to her, so she started talking. "I'm here on vacation. Brooklyn, born and raised." She smiled.

He looked up now, but not at her; instead he looked behind the bartender in front of them, scanning the glass bottles, the reflections off the glass shelving, even the tap handles over the draft beer faucet.

"I'm Rebecca," she said, and she reached out a hand.

He took it and shook it softly; there was no eye contact along with the gesture.

His phone rang. "I'm sorry." And then, with a slight smile he said, "Work."

"Sure," she said politely, and then she swiveled in her stool, faced forward, and took a sip of her pilsner.

Court answered with a light "Hello."

"I've got answers for you."

"Okay. Shoot."

Russ said, "The short version is this: If I were you, I'd drink up."

"Go on."

Russ said, "I *will* go on. I've got all the intel you need right now, real life-and-death shit, but I want something for it."

"What's that?"

Russ said, "I want to know about Kiev."

Court sighed a little and said, "Good-bye," and he started to take his phone from his ear.

Russ shouted, "The woman is Mossad!"

Court brought the phone back quickly. His breathing quickened slightly, though he made no outward indication of alarm.

"Is that a fact?" The girl was on his right, sipping from her beer mug and looking ahead.

"Yes. There is a Mossad team liasing with Townsend. I've got all the particulars, but you have to give me what I want first. Tell me everything you did in Kiev."

"That's not really convenient for me right now."

"I understand, you are in public. Look, I know you

are a man of your word. You swear to me you will tell me about Kiev. The truth, no bullshit. You do that and I'll help you get away from the Israelis."

Court looked at the reflection of the woman in the mirror behind the bar. She glanced up at his reflection and smiled.

Mossad. Holy hell. In his five years on the run he'd purposefully steered clear of the Israelis. He had great respect for their abilities, and the fact that they were on him now made his guts churn.

Softly he spoke into his phone. "Deal."

"Listen carefully," Russ said. "I just talked to Jeff Parks at Townsend. The woman's name is Ettinger. Ruth Ettinger. She's running a four-person targeting team, and although she is working with Townsend, they are not operating together tonight. Still, if there are targeters on you, you know good and well there are going to be shooters close by."

"That's unfortunate," Court said flatly.

"You need to get out of town."

"I hear you."

Court looked back over his left shoulder; there was a hallway that led to a rear exit. It was his closest escape route, although there were easily thirty people crowding the floor between himself and the hallway.

"Not the back," said Whitlock. He couldn't see Gentry, of course, but he could guess what was going through the other singleton's head. "They'll have that covered with guns first. There will be eyes at the front, but they won't expect you to bolt into public."

Court knew Whitlock was right. He looked to the

front door now. There was also kitchen access next to the bar, and he was sure there would be an exit through there.

"Okay, man. Good to hear from you. Call me tomorrow."

Russ paused, then said, "She's right there, isn't she?"

"Uh-huh."

"Are you talking to her?"

"Pretty much."

Whitlock paused, and when he spoke again, the agitation in his voice was clear. "I need you to extricate yourself from that!"

"You and me both."

"They will kill you, man. They are going to smoke your ass as soon as they get an opportunity!"

Court just nodded with the phone to his ear. The girl next to him smiled at him again in the mirror, then took a sip of her drink.

"You with me, Court?"

"Yeah."

"Get the hell out of there and call me back. You give me Kiev, I'll link up with Townsend and feed you everything you need to shepherd you out of the trouble you are in."

"Sounds like a plan. I'll talk to you later." Court hung up the phone and slipped it back into his coat.

He spoke to the woman next to him. "Sorry about that."

"No problem." She turned to him and hesitated. Then, "What do you do that keeps you busy this late on a Saturday?"

Gentry rolled his head slowly, stretching his neck. His

eyes were not on the girl; they faced ahead, still looking at the shiny surfaces of the bar.

"I'm in waste management."

The girl's voice faltered. "Oh. Okay."

Now he stood from his bar stool, and as he did so he moved closer to her. His coat was open and it shielded his left hand, by the bar, from the crowd positioned to his right.

"And you are Mossad."

Ruth's eyebrows furrowed as she looked up at him from her seat on the bar stool. "Excuse me?"

"Why are you after me?"

"Look, buddy." She laughed angrily as she grabbed her purse and stood from her stool. "You looked lonely. I was bored so I thought I'd come score a drink off you. Whatever the hell you are talking about I—"

Court grabbed her by the arm, low and with his right hand. He yanked her closer still.

Behind them Aron leapt to his feet and began pushing through the crowd.

Court leaned into Ruth's ear and barked at her. "Wave your boy off or I will kill him!"

She felt a movement inside her coat, and then she felt her sweater rising at the waist. And then, hidden from view of everyone in the room, she felt a long blade pressing flat against her stomach.

THIRTY-SEVEN

Quickly Ruth turned away from her target and toward Aron Hamlin. She shook her head vigorously back and forth. The twenty-eight-year-old Mossad officer saw her signal and he slowed, but he kept coming. She put a hand up, palm down, raising it and lowering it.

He stopped in the middle of the room, surrounded by a crowd who paid no attention to the events going on around them.

Gentry leaned into Ruth's ear. "I want your right hand on the bar. I will keep your left wrist for now."

She did not move her right hand fast enough. The blade under her shirt moved, and the sharp edge burned her skin with a single soft stroke.

Her hand shot up to the top of the bar. It shook a little, so she gripped the lacquered edge.

Court said, "I want to talk to you, but I don't want to talk to him."

She just nodded. Looked again at Aron and motioned with her head for him to back up farther. He complied slowly.

"And I don't want to talk to the shooters outside."

"There . . . there is no one outside."

"What about the rest of your team?"

"There is no one else."

"Bullshit, lady." He pulled her closer with his right hand and, with his left hand, he touched the sharp tip of the knife against her ribs, right below her bra. She gasped and her lips quivered.

"Okay, okay. There are two more outside. But they aren't armed. I swear to God."

"And where are the Townsend guys?"

She fought to keep from succumbing to panic. Court could see something else in her eyes. She had no idea how he knew about her, about Townsend. "I kept them from you. I . . . I saw you leave the rooming house this morning. Townsend was going to fuck it up, so I didn't tell them where you went."

He removed the knife pressing against her stomach, but she assumed it remained just inches away. She did not look down.

He leaned in close again, and he spoke just loudly enough to be heard over the music and the crowd. "Why are you working with the Americans to find me?"

"Because of Ehud Kalb."

Court cocked his head. "What about him?"

She did not answer at first.

"What—about—him?"

"If you kill me you will never get out of here alive."

"If you don't answer me, neither will you."

A tear dripped down her cheek, but she kept her chin up. "Did you meet with Quds Force operatives in Beirut on Wednesday?"

"Quds? Iranian Revolutionary Guard?"

She nodded.

"Lady, I've never met with Quds Force about anything, and I haven't been to Beirut in years." He added, "Beirut is fucking dangerous."

He let go of her wrist now, reached across his body with his right hand, and hefted his beer, then took a drink. He appeared relaxed again, but she knew he was just trying to blend in with his surroundings, despite what was going on between the two of them.

She had not moved, so Gentry motioned to her drink. "Can you take a sip? Is your hand shaking?"

"I don't think so."

"Give it a try."

She reached for her beer, took a small sip and started to put it down, but then brought it back to her mouth and chugged a healthy gulp.

"Your intel is wrong," Court told her.

"I . . . I thought so, too. But our source is good."

"Apparently, your source sucks," Court said. "I am not after anyone, much less the PM of Israel. I just want to fade away." He took another sip. "Leave me alone and I will."

She hesitated. Then said, "There is—there is something else."

He did not like the sound of this, and he let her know with his tone. "What?"

"They think you were in Nice."

"Don't I wish?" he quipped, and he brought his beer bottle back to his mouth. He asked, "When?" and took a long swig.

"Today."

"*Today?*" He almost spit out his beer. "What the hell would I be doing in—"

"Assassinating Amir Zarini."

"The director? He finally got smoked?"

She nodded. "This morning. They are saying you did it."

"But you said you saw me this morning here in Stockholm."

She nodded.

"Does the Mossad think I can teleport?"

"I can't tell them I let you slip away this morning."

"So you'll stand by and watch them kill me?"

"Does this look like I'm standing by?"

"I don't know what you are doing. You sure as shit aren't here to pick me up."

She said, "I came in here because I'm trying to decide what the fuck is going on. I'm trying to find some way to exonerate you, because I know you weren't in Nice."

He started to reply to this, but then he stopped, leaned close to her ear suddenly, and grabbed her wrist again, startling her. It startled her more when he spoke in the loudest voice of the conversation. "Back him the *fuck* up!"

Ruth looked to her left. Aron had closed to within ten feet.

She waved him away angrily, and he backed off a few steps.

She had no idea how Gentry knew what was going on behind his back. She said, "He thinks you're going to hurt me."

"I won't unless I have to. To be honest, right now it's looking iffy."

"He'll stand down." She pointed at him again, then pointed back against the wall. Hamlin backed up farther with his hands up in supplication.

Still no one in the bar had noticed a thing.

She said, "Listen. I've read your file. I've seen our version, and . . . and the one from your country. Your agency file has a lot of holes in it. From the start this investigation didn't feel right. I told them Kalb wasn't a Gray Man target. They didn't believe me."

"You told who?"

"Carmichael, Babbitt, my people."

"Carmichael," he said thoughtfully. "That name seems to turn up when things get complicated." He sipped his beer. "And they still think I was in Beirut?"

"Yeah."

"And now Nice?"

"Yeah."

Court just looked off into space a moment, then shook his head. She looked him over closely. He appeared tired, drawn. Defeated. But his eyes narrowed with resolve, as if the heavy thoughts had cleared away for just a moment. "All right. You are going to get your wish tonight."

"What wish?"

"I'm going to buy you a drink." His left hand appeared with a one-hundred-kronor bill, and he laid it on the bar between her glass of beer and his bottle. "Are you carrying a weapon?" he asked.

"I have Mace."

He cocked his head. "Seriously? That's it?"

"Yes."

"If I check your purse and find a pistol I'm going to get really grouchy."

"I don't carry a gun."

His eyebrows rose, but he did not respond. Next he said, "I am going to step away from the bar, and you are going to move with me. When I get to the door to the kitchen, I am going to separate from you and slip out. If you come after me, if any of your little helpers come after me, somebody is going to get hurt." He stopped speaking, but she just looked at him in shock. "Nod your head if you believe what I am telling you."

"I believe you."

"All right, Ruth. I hope you will tell your leadership that I wasn't involved with what happened in Nice."

"They aren't listening to me. They want you off the map, Gentry, and I'm not going to be able to change that."

Court said, "Then I guess I'd better get moving." He turned toward the kitchen access, and Ruth followed along with him.

"I see any Townsend cowboys or Mossad ninjas, I'm going to know you lied to me."

"There aren't any," she said.

Without another word Court turned away, stepped

behind the bar, and moved into the kitchen. The two bartenders did not even notice him pass.

Ruth put her hands out on the bar to steady herself, and Aron came up beside her. "You okay?"

She nodded distantly. After a few more seconds to compose herself, she headed for the front door and Aron followed.

———

Moments later, the four Mossad officers were back in Ruth's room at the Gamla Stan Lodge. As Ruth took off her coat and did her best to calm her nerves with slow deep breaths, she had to endure a barrage of questions from her team that was peppered with none-too-subtle expressions of their opinions.

Laureen asked, "What the hell were you doing?"

"Having a drink with a knife held to my rib cage."

"What did he say?" Mike asked.

"He knew about us. About Townsend. He said he doesn't want to kill Kalb."

"Sounds like what someone would say if they *did* want to kill Kalb."

"Right, but it's also what someone would say if they did *not*. I believe him."

Mike said, "We can call Townsend, see if the UAV has located him."

Laureen said, "Or maybe you two can just meet for drinks again tomorrow and we can pick him up then."

Ruth wasn't in the mood for the sarcasm, or to be lectured by her team. "It didn't go down the way I planned it, no. But I believe the guy. He's not after Kalb and he wasn't in Nice. I'm not telling Townsend that there has been a sighting; they'll just kill him."

"So?" asked Mike. "What do we do?"

"I'm going to call Yanis, and probably hear more of the same from him that I just heard from you three."

THIRTY-EIGHT

Court walked quickly but calmly through Stockholm's central train station, his hood up, his knit cap low, and his scarf high. It was almost midnight; the grand waiting hall of the station had at most a hundred people milling around in an area that could easily accommodate twenty times that number. And Gentry looked at each and every person as he walked along near the wall, because each and every person was a potential threat.

He knew he was also under surveillance by security cameras now, and although he was confident he could avoid any facial recognition pings due to his obscured face, he also was pretty sure anyone looking for him by this point would know what his coat looked like and what his backpack looked like and could therefore make a pretty good guess that the man trudging alone through the station was probably the same guy they'd been chasing through Stockholm.

There wasn't a thing he could do about this; he knew he'd be seen and he knew assholes with guns would descend on the train station in minutes, but he hoped to be long gone by the time they got here.

But not on a train. Court wasn't here to get on a train.

Not right now, anyway.

No, this was a surveillance detection run, albeit an SDR with a dual purpose.

His main purpose here at the train station was to survey the building, to find the security cameras and to evaluate the police presence. He had a plan to come back, and when he did, he wanted to move through the building as if invisible.

He passed a small police station there in the building; the officers behind the glass were in deep conversation and did not look his way.

Court then focused on the security cameras, his greatest hazard here in the building. He noted their number and position high on the walls in the main hall. He knew they would be there, and he could have guessed where they would be and how to avoid them without coming here tonight, but he needed to be thorough, and he was well aware that there would be other cams placed throughout the building he would have to avoid.

He saw two ATM machines near the food court on the main floor, and both of these would have security cams that looked out to a distance five yards or so across the floor. Both machines, conveniently for Gentry's needs, were on the same side of the room. He also found a camera above a self-service food stand.

He detected twelve electric eyes in all, just here in the waiting hall, and each one, he assumed, was sending his face at this moment to a server somewhere, maybe in D.C., or Colorado or Silicon Valley, and there the bits and bytes that made up all the data points of his face would be run, automatically of course, because there were millions of faces going through the same process.

He descended an escalator and entered a brightly lit passage, and here he saw a camera high over a Burger King on his right. As he passed through a doorway leading to the unheated platform hallway, he saw another cam, but this one was down beyond the first platform, so he made a hard left and went up the stairs.

Up by the tracks he saw one camera on each platform, and he recognized the model of the unit and knew that although it contained a built-in panning motor that could be controlled by an operator, the lens itself only had a sixty-degree field of view, and he could avoid being captured by it if he moved along the left edge of the platform as he passed.

His entire survey of the central station took less than five minutes, and when he finished he walked far down a platform, past the high covered roof and into the darkness, and then he climbed down and began walking up the snow-covered tracks of a commuter line.

Twenty minutes later he'd climbed aboard a train that ran to a town twenty minutes outside Stockholm, and there he jumped a late-night bus that would take him a little farther still. As he rode he kept his face covered and his backpack on his lap, and he laid his face on it, knowing that he was as safe now as he could be.

For a few hours, anyway.

He considered staying outside the city for a day or two but quickly vetoed the idea. Even though the men and women watching for him would certainly be located in the capital, the crowds and clutter of the urban world were the safest place for Court to hide. If he wandered around a suburb or a village someplace he'd draw more attention, and if he accidentally tripped a security camera and his face brought gunmen down on the area, his escape and evasion options would be next to nil.

No, Court knew he could shoot out to the 'burbs for a few hours at most, but he had to get back into the city before he could slip away to the next big city.

Ruth Ettinger sat with her team in her hotel room, talking over their next move. She'd just gotten off the phone with her supervisor, Yanis Alvey, who was not pleased with her, to say the least. Although he neither yelled nor fumed—that was not his way—he made it clear he felt she'd shown incredibly poor judgment in engaging her target in conversation. He suggested it might be best for everyone if he replaced her and her team with a new set of targeters, but in the end he backed off.

Ruth won the argument, barely, although she made no ground in her insistence to Alvey that it was highly unlikely Gentry was involved in the Amir Zarini assassination. Not surprisingly, Gentry's own words carried little weight with him.

He ordered her, in no uncertain terms, to stay as close to Gentry as possible so that when the Mossad technical surveillance team on the way from Tel Aviv arrived in the city early the next morning, they would have a target to begin tracking.

She acknowledged her superior without her normal borderline insubordinance, because she knew Mossad surveillance was exactly what this operation needed. If she could get a fifteen-person tech survey operation in place around Gentry, they would determine quickly that he was not planning any sort of attack on anyone, much less Ehud Kalb.

Ruth sat there quietly after the phone conversation, and for a moment she considered revealing to her team that she knew, without a doubt, that their target had not shot across the continent last night to perform a massacre at lunch, then shot back up to be seen at a 7-Eleven just after dinnertime. Again she decided to keep the information to herself. If she could not tell Yanis—and she was more certain now after her most recent conversation with him that she could not tell him—then it was not fair for her to bring her three employees into her deceit.

Aron brought her out of her moment of quiet consternation. "I feel like we need to get back out in the field. At least to cover the train station in case he tries to skip town."

Ruth nodded. "I agree, but we need to keep it static. We start moving around the city in the middle of the night and I can guarantee you he will see us before we see him. Find a stationary survey location in or near the central station, someplace where we are ironclad sure we won't be compromised, and we'll start a three-hour watch rotation."

Aron had his coat zipped and his hood up within seconds. "I'll take first watch."

Mike grabbed the keys to the Skoda. "And I'll drive car pool."

———————

Court spent the early morning hours riding a bus to Jakobsberg, a town southwest of Stockholm. There was nothing in Jakobsberg for him to see or do; as soon as he arrived he would climb aboard a bus that would return him to Stockholm.

There were only a half dozen other riders, but Court was alone in the back, bundled in his coat with his backpack on his lap. His phone sat on the backpack and his headphones were in his ears; he'd sat like this for a half hour because he was having a tough time psyching himself up to contact Dead Eye.

He knew he needed to make the call. Whitlock was his one connection to intelligence on the opposition, not just of Townsend but also of the Mossad team working with them. Whatever Russell Whitlock's motives were for offering to help him, and whatever the reason behind the man's seemingly obsessive curiosity about the event in the Ukraine three years earlier, Court knew the five minutes it would take him to give up details could easily mean the difference between life and death.

He called Whitlock's number through MobileCrypt

and tucked his head deeper into the hood of his coat, all but insulating himself from the world around him.

———————

Whitlock had rented a BMW at the airport and then he took a room at the Grand Hotel in the city center. For the past two hours he'd sat waiting on the comfortable sofa in the sitting room of his junior suite. He was still dressed in his now somewhat wrinkled dark suit, his tie was loose and his collar was open. Next to him on the end table was a half-empty and tepid split of champagne from the mini bar, and a prescription bottle of Adderall. He hadn't taken any pills, but he had them staged and ready so that he could swing into action at a moment's notice.

His face wore a near catatonic expression. He was awake but despondent. Each minute Gentry didn't call was another minute nearer to the failure of this operation. Russ occupied his brain with thoughts of killing the Gray Man; he'd come up with a dozen savage schemes to do just that, all because the son of a bitch wouldn't play his role in Whitlock's escapade and make contact. He also thought of ways to kill Ali Hussein. The fucking Iranians weren't playing their role, either. As far as Whitlock was concerned, he'd pulled off the Zarini hit close enough to convince them he was the Gray Man; they were just splitting hairs with their ridiculous complaints about collateral damage. Their request for the one piece of proof that he had not been able to deliver them infuriated him and, he told himself, if this entire thing fell through, he would make his way back to Beirut and put a dagger into the eye of Ali Hussein.

After he did the same to Court Gentry.

His phone was in his pocket but his earpiece was jammed in his right ear. He'd all but forgotten it was there; so when it chirped he bolted upright. In the space of a single heartbeat Whitlock went from near hopelessness to heart-pounding anticipation.

He answered on the first ring. "That you, brother?"

"It's me."

"I heard you made it out of the bar," Russ said as he fished two Adderall out of the bottle and popped them in his mouth.

"Yes. What else do you hear? Any new intel?"

Russ downed the rest of the lukewarm champagne, swallowing the pills with it. They burned going down. "Yeah. I just got off the phone with Townsend House. Metsada is in play. They are in the city and moving into position." It wasn't true, but Whitlock needed a sense of urgency in Gentry now.

"Metsada," Court muttered. There was dread in his voice. "I was afraid of that."

"Don't worry about it. I got you out of trouble before. I'll steer you through it again."

"Okay," Court replied softly.

"That is, of course, if you are ready to talk."

A pause. "What is your interest in Kiev?"

"It's simple, brother. I know everything the CIA knows about that night. They've got police reports, ballistics reports, witness testimony, and gigs of bullshit analysis, but they don't have all the answers. It's the one operation in my career that I can't figure out, and if there is a tactical equation I am unable to solve on my own, then I don't mind someone passing me a cheat sheet. C'mon, Court. Let me in on the answer. How the fuck did you do it?"

"Tell me what you know and I'll fill in the details."

"No fucking way. I'll keep what I know close to my vest, so I can make sure you aren't bullshitting me."

Court sighed, long and slow. Russ had the distinct impression Gentry had never done this before, talking in detail about one of his operations.

"I talk, then *you* talk. You tell me where Metsada is. You tell me where Townsend is. You tell me everything you know."

"I'll do you one better. I'm here in Stockholm. I'll personally intervene to keep everybody away from you."

Court said, "I don't like that. As far as I'm concerned, you can waste every Townsend operator you see. But I don't want you touching a hair on the head of any of the Israelis. I don't need any more trouble than I already have."

"Whatever you say." Russ leaned back on the couch. "Now . . . Kiev."

Softly Court said, "Kiev." And then, "It was me."

"All alone?"

"All alone."

With a smile in his voice, Russ said, "I fucking knew it."

THIRTY-NINE

Nine Mig-25PD Foxbats, each wearing the yellow trident of the Ukrainian National Air Force, sat in a row on a parking apron at Vasylkiv Air Base, northwest of Kiev. Towable light towers next to each plane gave them a top-down glow. The evening rain had let up less than an hour earlier; now patchy fog hung between the wet fighters and the operations building of the air base, some fifty yards to the north of the apron.

A round and squat control tower rose from the building. On a catwalk around the tower, spotlights hung un-moving next to armed sentries, and inside the tower itself two men sat looking out over the air base. These were not air controllers; there were no official flight operations scheduled this evening. Instead they were the two men assigned to the missile battery attached to the roof of the tower. From the comfort of the heated and covered room they could aim, fire, and control the wire-guided 9M-133 Kornet, a Russian antitank weapon that was also effective against helicopters. Four of the Kornets were visible on rails above the tower.

Three hundred meters west of the control tower, near the front gates of the air base, a concrete barracks building was full of security troops, and this building was also topped with a Kornet missile battery. The two operators at this location were also shielded from the elements and from any attack. In their case an enclosed bunker on the roof right next to the missile launcher protected them. Only their heads were visible through the window, and if there was any sign of trouble, the men could duck down out of sight and operate their weapon in safety by using the camera in the nose cone of the missile.

In addition to the two antitank/antiair batteries, there were eight cement bunkers along the fence line of the air base, each manned with two sentries armed with rifles and rocket-propelled grenade launchers. Along with their weapons they controlled powerful searchlights, and all the bunkers were in radio contact with the guard force in the barracks, another sixty men ready to deploy against any threats to base security.

Several armed canine patrols walked the perimeter of the fence, adding an additional ring of protection to the installation.

Although no flight ops were scheduled and no air traffic controllers were present, the lights of the single runway came on just after midnight, and just a minute later, a Russian Antonov AN-74 cargo aircraft appeared above the runway, descending through the impossibly low cloud cover. The plane touched down, stopped on the runway, and, following orders given to the pilot via a text message on his cell phone, taxied toward a darkened hangar near the barracks.

Then the lights of the runway turned off as suddenly as they'd come on.

As the aircraft made its way toward the hangar, Court Gentry crawled out of a drainage ditch alongside the runway. Dressed head to toe in black and wearing a black backpack, he reached back behind him in the ditch and grabbed a second black backpack. It was a large British Army–issued Bergen, and it was slick with mud. He struggled to pull the Bergen out of the ditch and up onto the very edge of the runway, but once he made it to the cement surface, the eighty pounds of equipment inside and strapped to the pack became easier to handle. He'd lashed a skateboard to the back of the bag, after having painted the board and the wheels matte black, and this helped him push the gear along as he scooted along at the runway's edge.

After ten minutes of movement through the dark, much of it stop and start because he was trying to get his positioning as close to perfect before leaving the runway, he pulled the pack with him into the low wet grass between the runway and the parking apron where the Foxbats were lined up. It took all his might and patience to drag the gear behind him. He strained with the effort, but still he kept his eyes darting from one sentry position to the next.

After another few minutes he made his way to a nearby position in the grass, forty yards from the runway and two hundred from the taxiway and the parking apron. He lay there, prone and still for a moment, alert to any signal that his presence had been detected. When he felt confident his movements had not compromised him, he pulled binoculars from the pack on his back. With them he checked the position of the four men in the two missile battery positions carefully, and then he began backing up in the grass, pulling his huge Bergen with him.

He stopped and rechecked the Kornet locations with his binos. Satisfied he was in the right position for his work ahead, he took a moment to catch his breath.

Court was completely exposed here in the center of the air base; the nearest revetment he could use for cover if the shit hit the fan was over fifty yards away. But he felt good about his chances to remain undetected. He knew all the guards' positions and he could anticipate their movements, because he had been here on the property for more than twenty-four hours. He'd been delivered inside a base cargo truck that had returned from a local repair shop. While it was in the shop, confederates of the man who contracted Court for this operation had secreted him inside in a stash compartment behind the seats, and then they strapped his gear into the well where the spare tire would normally go.

Court had no problems getting into the base after this; he only had to wait in an impossibly cramped position in the truck for nine hours until he was certain all ground crews had left their station for the night. Then he climbed out of the truck, falling onto a motor pool parking lot with legs that felt like wet noodles. Once he had the use of his lower appendages, he unfastened his bag from the spare tire well and began his work, moving slowly, avoiding sentries and lights.

By dawn he'd made his way three hundred meters to the ditch far out across the field alongside the runway, and here he spent the daylight hours. He had a radio that picked up all the comms around the base, and he monitored the instructions given to the security forces about the meeting that would take place in the middle of the night.

He could tell from the radio traffic that the head of base protection forces, a Ukrainian Army major, thought tonight's event to be a potential security nightmare, but he also knew the men in charge didn't give a shit what the major thought. Court knew that an Air Force general who was well connected to the Ukrainian government was getting paid handsomely to provide the air base as a venue for a clandestine transaction between the Iranian Quds Force and the Russian FSB, and the major and his men would not think twice about killing a lone gunman caught on the base during the meet.

He looked back up to the missiles. They sat on their rails, pointing out over the base.

Those were his biggest threat.

Court was worried about the sentries around the airfield. He was concerned about the troops in the barracks near the gate. He was uneasy about the canine patrols on the fence line . . . but he was terrified of the Kornet missile systems on the control tower and on the roof of the barracks.

Tonight's clandestine meeting between Russians and Iranians would involve a swap of cash for nuclear secrets. The Persians had the dough and the Russkies had the smarts—hundreds of gigs of plans for maximizing the efficiency of Iran's nuclear enrichment program stored on three small hard drives; Court knew all this because he had been told by a Russian general, a man who had been cut out of the arrangement and felt swindled by the whole affair. The general had made a deal with Ukrainian mobsters to stop the meeting and to destroy the hard drives full of critical data. The general wasn't interested in protecting the world from the evils of nuclear proliferation. He just wanted to do his own deal with Iranians and trade them his own hard drives of critical data.

Not long after Court stopped moving in the wet grass, the lights of the runway came back on. This time it was a Lockheed JetStar that landed, a small business jet that could carry eight to ten passengers comfortably. The plane raced past him on his left and then slowed and stopped much farther down the runway. After a moment it began taxiing toward the hangar near the barracks.

Court knew these were the Iranian Quds Force agents, here to drop off the cash and to pick up the computer drives from the Russians. There was no reason the entire transaction needed to take more than a few minutes, so Court knew he had to prepare quickly for what he had in store.

He unzipped the massive canvas Bergen and from it he pulled three huge weapons. They were Russian Dragunov SVD semiautomatic sniper rifles. Each of the ten-pound guns had an eight-power scope and a ten-round magazine. All these sniper rifles already had a round in the chamber, as Court did not want the unmistakable noise of loading a round to carry across the large open field.

He opened the bipods under the barrels of the Dragunovs, positioned them in front of him, and then returned to his pack to retrieve a fourth long gun. This was a collapsed Kalashnikov RPKM light machine gun. It was similar to the ubiquitous AK-47, but it had a longer and heavier barrel and a seventy-five-round magazine. It wore a simple three-power scope and a carry sling.

Court assembled the RPKM and placed it in the grass five feet behind him, and then he rechecked the missile batteries and the hangar where the Iranian JetStar was rolling to a stop near the Antonov.

Satisfied he was good on time, he pulled two more items from his pack. They were RPG-32s, 72-millimeter antitank rockets. Each was housed in a yard-long firing tube, and each weighed six pounds. He opened the sights and the grips on the tubes, and then he laid them in the grass.

The last item taken from the pack was an electronic detonator, a small apparatus that looked like a cell phone, with a number of buttons and a backlit screen. He stood it up on the wet turf in front of him, and then returned his attention to the Dragunov sniper rifles.

He aimed one weapon at the man sitting in the control tower, two hundred sixty yards away, positioning the crosshairs on the only part of the target he could see from his position, the top of his helmet. The other soldier was standing behind him, but walking around the control tower, using his binos to monitor the action near the barracks.

Court let this rifle rest on its bipod and then he pulled the second rifle to him. This one he aimed at one of the Ukrainian soldiers on duty at the battery over the barracks, three hundred forty yards distant. He pulled a large beanbag from his backpack and used this to prop the buttstock of the weapon up, keeping the crosshairs on the target.

He placed the third Dragunov in the grass as close to the second as he could, and with it he aimed at the second sentry in the concrete structure on top of the barracks. This man was walking back and forth with his binoculars, just feet from his seated colleague, and although Court used another beanbag to keep his crosshairs positioned to a point near to where the man walked, he did not track his movements with the rifle.

Instead Court pulled a foot-long aluminum rod from his backpack, and he slid it through the trigger guards of the two Dragunovs positioned toward the antitank missile battery above the bunkhouse.

He blew out a long sigh.

This was going to be tough.

In all his preparation for this op he'd known the absolute most difficult aspect of the equation was the four Ukrainians who could fire wire-guided missiles from the protection of armored bunkers and then, calmly and easily, fly them across the airfield and right up his ass. The only way to prevent them from blowing him to bits, he decided, was to take all four men out while they were in the open. The problem with this plan was, of course, that once he fired his rifle at one target, the other men would only have to drop out of their chairs to be out of sight, where they could still operate their missiles with the onboard television cameras.

Even if he used a suppressed sniper rifle, the flash of

light in the center of the air base would be obvious to anyone looking in his general direction, and suppressed gunfire was not silent; it would still carry across the open ground.

He knew he would have *one* chance before the men ducked down out of his line of fire. If he didn't get them all at the same moment, the rest of the mission would be a moot point, because Court wouldn't be alive to execute it.

So he would fire on all four men simultaneously at the beginning of his attack. He'd spent hours on the geometry, using maps and photographs of the air base, and he'd picked all his equipment accordingly.

He grabbed his binoculars and checked the meeting going on at the hangar. Apparently he'd missed the exchange, because the JetStar was closing its cabin door and, less than thirty seconds later, it began rolling back toward the taxiway.

Gentry's heart pounded as time grew short. He pulled the detonator closer, just under his chin, then he took the Dragunov aimed at the control tower, and dragged it across the grass, and cradled the barrel in the crook of his right arm at his three-o'clock position. He supported the buttstock of this gun with his left biceps, and rested his left trigger finger against the trigger guard. To see through the scope he had to lean to his left and look upside down through the lens. He moved the gun slightly, then focused his attention on the other two rifles. These were in front of him, just four inches apart from one another, their triggers set to fire as one as soon as he pulled back on the aluminum rod resting against them. He looked through each scope and squeezed each beanbag a little to put the crosshairs in the right position. The seated man in the building was lined up perfectly, but the wandering guy with the binos was walking back and forth across the center of the crosshairs.

Court had spent a day in a ditch waiting patiently, but now things started moving very quickly. The JetStar taxied toward him on the runway. It would roll to the end and turn around to start its takeoff roll. The bigger Antonov had loaded up and it waited at the far end of the runway. Court looked left and right, and then back over his shoulder, making sure there were no canine patrols anywhere near him, and then he eyeballed the apron and the row of MIGs, and he saw there was no activity over there, either.

The Iranian jet was one hundred yards away and rolling up the runway on his left. Court started a silent countdown, and then began moving his head from one sniper scope to the next.

He checked the weapon aimed at the control tower. He had the seated man in his sights and the second man was behind him, walking in and out of the line of fire.

He checked the weapon pointed at the seated man at the barracks' missile battery. The crosshairs were on his forehead.

He checked the other weapon pointed at the missile battery on the roof of the barracks. The moving target walked a little to the left of the crosshairs.

Gentry adjusted the beanbag and then went back to the first scope to repeat the process.

In the space of thirty seconds he checked each rifle three times, made millimeter adjustments when necessary, and continued his countdown, but added a second running clock in his head, and then a third, as he tried to time the movements of the two moving targets.

After one more look through his scopes and a quick glance at the Iranian jet, he put his left trigger finger on the trigger of the rifle positioned at his three o'clock, then hooked a finger on to the aluminum rod controlling the triggers of the side-to-side rifles at his twelve-o'clock position.

He checked all four targets again, looking into both side-by-side scopes and then upside down through the scope on the rifle in the crook of his right arm.

He waited a moment, willing the moving men to move into his crosshairs. "Now," he said softly, and then he pulled back on the aluminum rod while, simultaneously, his left index finger pressed the trigger on the Dragunov positioned toward the control tower.

All three rifles fired at once, creating a single cacophonous report. The two guns in front of him were not supported by his shoulder, so they flew back into Court's face as the bullets and hot gasses left their barrels. The gun pointed at his three-o'clock position lurched hard into his biceps.

In the control tower the window glass shattered, the seated man flew back out of his chair, and the man on his feet just behind him dropped his binoculars and fell to the ground.

In the bunker on the roof of the barracks the seated soldier's head snapped back and he fell forward on the console in front of him. Next to him the man with the binoculars went airborne as he launched back over a desk, and he landed faceup on the cement floor.

Court did not know if he'd hit all four targets; he figured he would only know for sure if an antitank missile
arced into the air and began chasing him across the airfield. He did not wait around for this to happen though; as
soon as he fired the rifles, he reached for the detonator
and pressed a button.

On the parking apron the third MIG 25 Foxbat in the
row erupted in a ball of fire. Seconds later a secondary
explosion blew fragments of the fighter plane one hundred feet into the air.

In the motor pool parking lot the truck Gentry had
used to get into the air base exploded; a fiery cloud roared
straight up into the night sky and shrapnel shattered glass
in the base operations building.

Court did not stop to watch this handiwork. He
rose to his feet, grabbed the RPK light machine gun
off the wet turf, and brought it up to his shoulder. He
aimed at the Iranian jet taxiing up the runway, just
twenty-five yards away, and he fired three short bursts
directly through the cockpit windscreen. He slung the
big rifle over his shoulder and knelt back into the grass,
then he grabbed the first of the two antitank grenade
launchers.

Five seconds later a roar of light erupted from the
launch tube, and a glowing rocket shot low over the air
base, streaking toward the Russian AN-74. It impacted
directly with the fuselage at the wing, penetrated the
fuel tank, and the entire aircraft disintegrated in a fireball. The airfield came alive with lights and shadows as
the fireball rose over the area.

Court left the second rocket tube in the grass and

sprinted toward the JetStar, which was now motionless on the runway.

As he ran he began taking fire for the first time. He assumed some of the sentries in the outer fence positions had seen the rocket launch and were firing in the darkness at his position. He had intended for the massive explosions of the MIG and the truck and the Antonov to distract the guard force away from the center of the airfield, but the crack of supersonic rounds whizzing past told him that at least some of the sentries had not been taken in by the ruse. He was two hundred yards away from the nearest sentry, however, and the incoming fire was inaccurate and sporadic.

Searchlights began sweeping the ground all around him as he ran.

He arrived at the motionless executive jet on the runway, aimed his RPK at one of the cabin portals, and released a long burst of automatic fire, shattering the window and depressurizing the cabin. He attached a small stick-on "hinge-popper" to the cabin door, then he rolled under the aircraft to get away from the blast. As the explosive fired, ripping the door off its hinges, Court pulled a flash-bang grenade from his utility belt, and he tossed it through the now open hatch. Again he ducked down and away, and he dropped the RPK onto the runway. When the bang and the flash subsided inside the cabin, he spun back into the doorway, drawing his Glock 17 pistol and leveling it at the three terrified Iranian men inside.

A long burst of machine gun fire raked the runway, kicking sparks up just feet behind him. Court launched himself up and into the cabin of the aircraft, and shoved his pistol against the forehead of the first Iranian intelligence officer.

"Two seconds! Where are the drives?"

"What? What drives? I don't know what you—"

Court shot the man in the head, then pulled him to the open hatch and kicked him out onto the runway.

He turned to the next man. "Two seconds! Where are the—"

"They are here!" he shouted, and he pointed to a silver case on the floor by his knee.

"Open it!"

The man did as requested, and Court saw three boxy-looking hard drives.

"Both of you. Take off your jackets."

The men were wearing business suits. They pulled their coats off quickly, with no small amount of confusion. Outside sirens wailed across the airbase, and the bright searchlights locked themselves on the Iranian jet. No one had fired on it yet, but Court knew he couldn't wait around for the Ukrainians to decide if they would just blow the aircraft off the runway with an antitank missile.

With their coats off, Court was satisfied they weren't hiding any more computer drives. He ordered the men to climb out of the broken cabin door. They did as they were told, probably stunned that they were being allowed to live, and then both men raised their arms, waving at the searchlights, imploring anyone out there to hold their fire.

Court crawled to the cockpit now, pulled the dead co-pilot out of his seat, and started to climb into his place.

The windscreen was riddled with holes, but Court ignored the poor visibility, and he pushed the throttle all the way forward.

He had less than half the runway to work with, and he was taking off with the wind instead of against it, but Court had done his math, and he knew he had enough concrete ahead of him to get into the air.

As he picked up speed, he adjusted the flaps for take-off. Tracer rounds from automatic weapons began sweeping across the night sky in front of the jet, and he tried to lower his body down in the seat, but he did not have much room to work with, so instead just did his best to get his speed up as fast as possible.

A burst of gunfire hit the fuselage behind him, but he kept his focus out the broken windscreen ahead, and he pulled up on the yoke near the end of the runway.

The aircraft lifted into the air and was immediately enshrouded by the thick clouds.

As the damaged jet climbed past five hundred feet, Court left the controls, climbed out of the cockpit, and made his way over the body of the copilot and back into the cabin. The wind screamed through the open door, the black cloudy night pressed right up to the interior cabin lighting, giving Gentry the impression that he was flying inside a bowl of thick soup. He dropped to his knees, took off his backpack, and removed two items.

The first was a small parachute rig. It took up half the size of the backpack, and he was able to put it on in under twenty seconds.

The second item was smaller, just three pounds and no larger than a loaf of bread. The black box had a protective cap on one end, and he slipped his finger under the cap and flipped a switch. He placed the device next to the three hard drives on the floor of the cabin, and then, at an altitude of less than two thousand feet, Gentry rolled out of the cabin of the JetStar and into the wet black sky.

The aircraft continued ascending for another thirty seconds, and then the three pounds of Semtex plastic explosive detonated, obliterating the jet and everything inside it.

Gentry landed in an open field less than ninety seconds after bailing out of the stricken jet.

Russ Whitlock relayed the story he had just heard from Gentry, putting necessary details in the first person. On the other end of the phone, Ali Hussein did not say a single word while the American talked, but when Russ finished, ending the story in the field west of Kiev and telling Hussein that the rest of his exfiltration was none of the Iranian's business, Ali Hussein finally spoke. "Mr. Gray, I am more than satisfied now. Your version matches perfectly with the testimony of our two surviving operatives. The contract is yours. I only need to know where you would like me to deliver the payment when the contract is fulfilled."

Russ Whitlock smiled. There had been difficulties, setbacks, but his operation was finally back on track.

"I will send you the account information via text."

"Very well."

Russ said, "There is one more thing. When the contract is completed, regardless of the circumstances . . . my circumstances . . . regardless what you hear about me . . . you will pay the money."

Ali Hussein did not understand. "Please make your conditions clear, Mr. Gentry."

"Simply put, I will need to go to ground after this. You may hear that I have been killed. Of course it is possible that I won't survive my attempt on Prime Minister Kalb, but more likely what you see on the news will be well-orchestrated disinformation."

"I see."

"Your organization will be tempted to keep the money owed me." He paused a long time before saying, "That would be a mistake."

"I understand. Be assured. *Inshallah*, when you fulfill your obligations in the contract, we will fulfill ours. Whether you are around to withdraw the money from the account or not, the money will be there."

"Very good, Ali Hussein. I will text you the account number," he said, and he ended the call.

FORTY

The signal room at Townsend House operated twenty-four hours a day during hunts run on the scale of the Gentry operation. Technicians, communications specialists, analysts, information technology experts, and other staffers, all wired via secure comms to the UAV and direct action teams in the field, had been searching throughout the night, local time, for their quarry for months.

Earlier in the day an analyst monitoring gait-pattern and physical pattern-recognition software had gotten a hit from several camera feeds pulled from Stockholm's central train station. It was nothing conclusive; during the busiest parts of the day this new technology found on average one false positive a minute from cameras in the city, but the late-night walk through the station by the lone man wearing a coat and pack similar to those of their target and possessing a similar gait was enough to spin up Jumper team and call the Sky Shark from another part of the city.

By the time the UAV arrived there was no sign of the man outside the station, and Jumper was recalled to their safe house.

Jeff Parks had slept on the sofa in his office, right off the signal room, every night since Gentry had been sighted flying his microlight over the Gulf of Finland a week earlier. He'd just kicked his shoes off and put his feet up for a couple hours of shut-eye when his desk phone rang with the distinctive ring indicating an inbound encrypted satellite call.

He walked barefoot across the floor and answered with his code name. "This is Metronome."

"Dead Eye here." Parks was surprised to hear from Whitlock; he'd been trying to reach him for over twenty-four hours. Parks had not spoken to him personally since the shoot-out in Tallinn.

They went through their identity check, and then Russ told Parks he was in the city center.

"Why haven't you answered your phone?"

"I've been busy."

"Doing what?"

"Fieldwork. You know how it is, right?" Parks presumed this to be some sort of slight, insinuating that Parks himself had no field experience. The second in command of Townsend sat down at his desk and considered reciting the list of third-world postings he'd served in with CIA all over the globe, but then he decided against it. Individualist NOC operators like Dead Eye and Gray Man thought everyone who wasn't like them, meaning those who did not walk the earth with a gun and a knife and a kill mission in hand, was a lightweight. Even though Parks had been a case officer in the Directorate of Operations, that wouldn't earn him the respect of a lone-wolf kook like Russ Whitlock.

Parks let it go and just said, "What do you need?"

"Have you found Gray Man?"

"Negative. We know he's in Sweden, might still be in Stockholm, but that's it for now."

"When and where was the last sighting?"

"If you are there in Stockholm, why are you calling me? Why don't you coordinate with Jumper and the UAV team?"

"Because the last time I tried to coordinate with your team on site, they got dead, I got shot, and Gentry got away."

"I'm pushing you the safe house address. You need to go there. Jumper and his men aren't surveillance experts. They could use your help."

"Sure," Whitlock said. "I'll head over there and pull off their ball caps so they don't look like Americans. What about the Mossad?"

"Unknown. We are not in contact with the targeting team in Stockholm. Apparently the chick running the show for them didn't like the looks of Beaumont and his boys, so she broke off the relationship."

Interesting, Russ thought, but he didn't really have time to delve into the ins and outs of U.S.-Israeli intelligence coordination at the moment. He had another problem.

He could hear it in Parks's voice. A hesitation. A more

standoffish tone. It seemed as if Parks wasn't buying what Whitlock was saying, and this uneased Whitlock.

What did Townsend know?

There was only one way for Whitlock to find out.

He'd go meet with Jumper.

Just after five A.M. Whitlock knocked on the door to the Townsend safe house. A few seconds later the door opened, and he nodded to a bearded operative wearing a ball cap and a leather jacket. Russ didn't know the man's name, but he recognized him from the Jumper team.

The man just called back to the room behind him. "Beaumont? The singleton is here."

Russ did know John Beaumont, however. He stuck a hand out to the big southerner as he entered the dark living room of the large flat, and he nodded to Carl and Lucas at the UAV station at the same time.

"How's the hunting?" Whitlock asked.

Beaumont did not extend his own hand.

"Is there a problem?"

"I just got off the phone with Babbitt," the big bearded man said. The other guys in the room were mostly just tying up their bedrolls and drinking coffee. A couple of guys sat behind the UAV desk, where they had been watching Carl fly the Sky Shark, but now all eyes were turned toward the two men in the center of the room.

"Yeah? What about?"

"About Joel Lawrence."

"Who?"

Beaumont spit tobacco juice into a plastic cup he carried in his hand. "Trestle Seven."

Russ kept his face impassive, covering a slight concern about where this conversation was heading. "How's he doing?"

"He'll recover. Broken bones and shit like that. He's gonna do some time over there, but not much. CIA is greasing palms in the Estonian justice system to get him a year, tops."

"That's good."

After another spit Beaumont said, "Babbitt got one of his attorneys in to talk to Joel in Tallinn. He's in the hospital, under guard, but the lawyer was able to interview him about what happened during the Gentry dustup the other night. I gotta tell you, man. Joel is saying things that don't make a lick of sense."

Fuck, Russ thought. Quickly he did a head count in the room, in case things turned violent. There were eight Jumper men and the two UAV geeks. Russ immediately discounted Carl and Lucas, determined he was up against eight real threats, and scanned the men for weapons. They all carried pistols on their hips. He could see their Uzis lined up on cases along the wall, and other crates nearby held grenades, shotguns, and body armor that they would use for a higher-profile takedown.

Russ had weapons on him, his stiletto and his garrote. But no firearms.

Nonchalantly Russ asked, "What did he say?"

"He says you reported there was no attic access from the third floor of the hotel."

Russ nodded. "That's right."

"He says there was a pull-down staircase on the east side of the third-floor hallway."

"Must have missed it." Whitlock shrugged. "I can't fucking do everything."

"Hmm," Beaumont said, and he looked at his team. A couple of guys started moving in closer, but it was too early for Russ to determine if they were doing anything more than trying to intimidate him.

"There is something else. Joel says that when he got buried in the snow, he still had his radio in his ear. He heard Trestle Two report that he saw two targets."

"Two targets?"

Beaumont spit juice into the cup again, not taking his eyes from the smaller Whitlock as he did so.

"Yep."

Russ said, "Maybe he saw me when I engaged Gentry."

"You told Babbitt you were behind the action. How do you suppose he would have gotten the impression the two of you were together?"

Russ said, "I don't know, John. I know *I* couldn't have made that mistake, but Trestle team was a bunch of dumb fucks. Hell, I have no idea what passes for a thought in any of you snake eaters' brains."

Beaumont's low southern drawl slowed even more now. "Heard you got shot."

"Yeah."

"How's the wound?" Beaumont took a half step toward Dead Eye now.

Russ did not back away. "It's fine. Why?"

"I want to see it." There was an accusation in the tone, and Russ picked up on this.

"What the hell for?"

"C'mon, bro. You caught a love tap from the Gray Man and survived it? You should be showing that shit off every chance you get."

The men around him did not move, but Russ felt their presence close as the mood of the room darkened even more.

"Gentry was slinging a Glock 19," Beaumont said.

"So?"

"Trestle team carried MP7s. Much smaller bullet." He leaned closer still, looming over the smaller man. "Makes a noticeably smaller hole."

"Are you suggesting I was hit by friendly fire?"

Beaumont spit tobacco juice on Whitlock's boots. "I'm suggesting there wasn't anything friendly about it. I'm suggesting you and Gentry *both* engaged Trestle."

All eight Jumper men were up now. Russ saw no guns out of holsters, but he knew he was in serious trouble.

"You're fucking nuts, Beaumont."

"Let's see if I'm nuts. Show me your wound."

Russ chuckled, but it was just for show, there wasn't anything funny about any of this. He faked indignation. "You want me to drop my pants and show you my GSW? Is that what passes for fun back at Team Jumper's bunkhouse?"

Jumper Actual's eyes narrowed. "Ten seconds, Dead Eye, or my boys do it for you."

FORTY-ONE

At Townsend House the signal room evening shift had caught another ping a few minutes earlier, and this one was much more certain than the earlier hit.

An analyst buzzed Jeff Parks in his office, and he came running into the signal room moments later.

"What do you have?"

"We have a confirmed sighting of Gentry at the City Terminalin, Stockholm's main bus depot."

Parks walked to the front of the room and examined the grainy video of a man standing in the window of a ticket booth, in the process of purchasing a ticket. He wore a black knit cap and a big black coat, but no scarf. And it was clearly Gentry.

"This is real time?"

The analyst checked the time stamp on the feed with his watch. "About two minutes ago. We're monitoring conveyance points out of the city, and this just happened."

"Can we find out where he's heading?"

"We're on it."

It took a moment for a signal room hacker to pull up the data from the ticket booth and match a sale to the time stamp of the image, but as soon as he did he said, "One-way ticket to Gothenburg. Leaves in forty minutes."

Parks clapped his hands in excitement. "Get Jumper on it. I want the UAV overhead as well. Let's take Gentry as he boards his bus."

Russ knew that the entry and exit wounds in his left hip weren't anything like the size of that from a nine-millimeter round. They were much smaller; Beaumont would take one look at them and know he'd been shot by Trestle Team, and then everything around here would turn to shit. He knew he could take any three of the men in this room simultaneously; he'd undergone extensive hand-to-hand training to turn his body into an effective defensive weapon, and even though these guys would all be wearing sidearms Russ knew he could overwhelm the first wave or two with speed, surprise, and violence of action.

But he wouldn't take out all eight of them. Especially with the wound in his side still slowing him down.

When he did not move, did not unbutton his jeans, Beaumont said, "I'm going to take that as a no."

A phone rang on the UAV desk; none of the Jumper

men standing around looked at it, but Carl answered it, then quickly put it on speakerphone.

"We're all here, Metronome. Go ahead."

Parks's voice came over the small speaker. "Gentry is somewhere near the central bus depot. He bought a ticket from a counter about five minutes ago, and his bus to Gothenburg leaves in just over a half hour."

Carl said, "Roger that. I'm sending the Shark there now, but we will only have viz if he is standing around outside."

"That's fine," said Parks. "Jumper, I need you en route immediately. Get over there and smoke him out."

"What about Dead Eye? I can keep him here under guard."

Parks muffled the phone for a few seconds. When he returned he said, "Babbitt wants your entire team after Gentry. He wants you to let Whitlock go, but before you do, disarm him and lock him out of the safe house so he can't get to the weapons cache. We'll deal with him after we deal with Gentry. Make sure the UAV team is armed."

Beaumont ordered one of his men to frisk Russ, and he did so quickly but roughly, slapping his hand against the bandaged wound on Russ's hip while doing so. Russ wasn't carrying a gun, but a small knife was confiscated, and the operator stood back. "That's it, boss."

Beaumont loomed over Dead Eye a few seconds more, then said, "This ain't over, dude."

Russ stared back at him, bolstered now that the situation had changed so radically. "No shit. You owe me a pair of boots."

Beaumont gave another few seconds of stink eye to

the smaller man, then looked away from him and yelled to his men in the room.

"All right, everybody. Saddle up!"

———————

Ruth woke at five twenty-five A.M. to the buzzing of her cell phone. She quickly rolled to a sitting position and put it to her ear.

"Yeah?"

"It's Mike."

"You got him?"

"I've got *something*. Two SUVs drove past the station and parked across the street at the City Terminalin."

"The bus station?"

"That's right. And guess who popped out of the trucks?"

"The Townsend shooters?"

"Right again. Can't see any guns on them, but I don't think they're here to catch a bus to the coast."

Mike asked, "You want me to move closer? I'm at the train station with visibility of the main hall and the street outside."

"Negative. I want you to stay right there. We'll check out the bus terminal."

She hung up the phone, grabbed Laureen by the leg, and shook her. "Up! We're out of here in sixty seconds."

The younger officer, like Ruth herself, had slept in her clothes. Also like her boss, she had developed the skill of waking up quickly and moving instantly after years of surveillance work. She sat up now and shoved her feet into her boots even before she opened her eyes.

Ruth banged on the wall to the other room, and Aron

banged back. He'd managed to catch only an hour's sleep after returning from his watch at the train station, but he was moving in seconds.

The three operatives were outside in the parking lot in less than a minute.

———————

Russ Whitlock left the Townsend safe house in his rented BMW at the same time the Jumper team's van raced off toward the bus station, but although he and Jumper were after the same target, Whitlock did not follow the van.

He had a different destination in mind.

He parked his car in a lot of the main hall of the Stockholm central train station at five twenty-five.

Court had not told him how he planned on getting out of the city, but the decision to go here instead of across the street was an easy one for Whitlock to make. As soon as Parks announced that Gentry had been seen on cam purchasing a bus ticket, Whitlock ruled out a trip to the bus station. There was no way Court would have made that mistake. If he bought a bus ticket, he did it to deceive anyone watching him through security cameras.

Russ knew with certainty that Gentry would be heading out of the area some other way. The train station was close by, just to the south of the bus terminal; it was big and it possessed a cavernous underground area that made for good places to lie low and, more than for any other reason, it was where Russ himself would go if he were in Court's shoes.

He entered the main hall of the train station and then headed downstairs, his eyes open to any Mossad watchers that might be here inside the building.

———————

The Israeli embassy Skoda pulled into the parking lot on the west side of the bus terminal, and immediately the three Mossad officers climbed out and started walking between snow-covered cars toward the terminal building.

Ruth had an open channel to her team on her Bluetooth earpiece. "Mike, do you have eyes on us?"

Mike was across the street on an upper floor of the train station, looking out a massive window. "I've got you. The Townsend guys are outside, north of you, walking along the line of buses. Suggest you move into the terminal and find static survey locations."

"Roger that." Ruth looked at her watch. The bus was due to leave in less than fifteen minutes.

Even at this early hour there were quite a few people in the terminal, either purchasing tickets or waiting for their buses inside the warmth of the building instead of out in the lot. Ruth and her team split apart, moved wide along the walls, and did their best to scan everyone in the crowd as they moved.

As Ruth walked along the eastern wall she said, "This doesn't feel right. He's not going to be in here, just standing around. Laureen, you stay up here, find a window where you can keep an eye on Jumper. Aron and I will go downstairs. If he's here, he'll be someplace quiet."

The two Israelis took the stairs down to the lower level of the bus depot, and instantly Ruth felt the hairs stand up on the back of her neck. It was a large, almost cavernous hallway, nearly empty at this hour, with a coffee shop just opening for the morning directly across from the stairwell. To the right of the two Mossad officers, the hall continued the length of the terminal building and connected to a passage that ran under the street to the underground area of the train station. A few people stood in front of some automated ticket kiosks and a single employee sat in a ticket booth in the middle of the space, but farther on, the east side of the hallway was shrouded in darkness. There was apparently some sort of construction project under way down here; a large portion of the hallway was closed off. Non-employees were kept out with caution tape and plastic sheeting.

Ruth said softly to Aron, "If he's here . . . he's in there."

Aron nodded, and the two of them crossed the hallway to the coffee shop and sat down.

Court Gentry stood in the darkened construction area behind a metal scaffold stacked with wallboard, and from here he could see Ruth and her partner as they appeared from the stairwell. They were some forty yards from him now, and Ruth had removed the blond wig she'd worn the evening before. Court identified her only because he'd noticed the evening before that her black coat had a reversible gray interior, so he'd been on the lookout for women in gray coats since he'd left the bar.

He'd been standing here for a few minutes, keeping an

eye out for any surveillance. He had intentionally drawn his pursuers here to the bus station, showing his face on camera and purchasing a ticket, and he knew they would come for him, but he had no way of knowing how long it would take for their operation to identify him and move people to the location.

He was impressed; it hadn't taken much time at all. A few minutes earlier he'd been upstairs and he'd seen the group of men moving through the bus lot outside. They were about as low profile as a couple of Abrams tanks, but he could tell as soon as he began to track them that they weren't here to move quietly like mist. They were a kill team, and although he had judged their covert abilities to be pretty lousy, he did not want to wait around to evaluate their skill at killing people.

And now the Mossad woman was here. Ruth had told him the night before she was no longer working with Townsend, but the guys upstairs did not look like Mossad Special Operations, so he assumed she had lied to him and Dead Eye had told him the truth. Mossad and Townsend were, in fact, coordinating their hunt.

When Ruth and her colleague moved to the right of his field of view, Gentry knew they had gone over to the little coffee shop. This he took as bad news. Unless they just happened to be really lazy intelligence officers, the only reason they would take a break down here shortly after their arrival was that they decided this darkened, plastic-sheeting covered construction area was a potential location for their quarry to use as a hiding place. They'd be watching this area now, which meant he could not cross the hallway back to the stairs to go up.

But this was of no great concern, because Court would not be returning to the bus station. No, the southern wall of this hall had access to a tunnel that went under the street to the train station, and Court knew he could move through the construction area until he was out of sight of the coffee shop, and then head that way.

The train station had been his destination all along.

Court looked at his watch, determined his timing to be just about right, and began moving through the dark.

———————

Ruth and Aron had eyes on about 85 percent of the construction area from their chairs in the coffee shop; only the southern tip of the dark enclosed area was out of view. This portion ran all the way to the tunnel that led to the Stockholm central station across the street, so she knew her target could make his way over there without her seeing him.

It occurred to her this might have been his plan all along.

"Laureen, what's happening up there?"

"The Americans are still outside in the lot. They searched the area and then split into teams; now they are standing around in the crowd trying to blend in."

Ruth said, "They must have intel he is due to leave on a bus." She looked back down the hallway. "I don't buy it. They might have spotted him here at the terminal, but I bet he just came over here to throw us off."

Mike came over the net now. "I've got eight trains over here all leaving between now and six A.M."

Ruth said, "Okay, we need to shift part of our operation over to the train station. Mike, I want you to go downstairs, head over to the tunnel to the bus depot; he might be coming via underground. If he is, I want you ahead of him, in a static overwatch. Laureen, cross the street and take up watch in the main hall."

Ruth now turned to Aron. "I want you back upstairs, watching Beaumont to see what he and his guys do."

Ruth herself stood up and began walking alone slowly toward the tunnel to the train station, planning to fall in behind her target if, in fact, he'd gone that way.

Mike Dillman took the stairs in the main hall of the station down one level and then turned to head north, expecting to find the tunnel that led to the bus depot across the street. There was a significant crowd of early-morning travelers here, moving through the passages toward the exits to the platforms, many rushing from their commuter trains to catch their longer-haul trains for more far-flung destinations around the country and abroad.

He'd made it about fifty feet through the brightly lit area before coming across a map of the station, and here he saw he needed to descend one level farther. He went over to an employee-only access door, tried the handle, and found it unlocked. Inside was a dimly lit hall with a large service elevator. He quickly stepped inside the car and pressed the button that would take him down one floor.

The service elevator doors opened to a dimly lit area that was clearly under construction. Next to him, a Dumpster the size of a car was full of broken brick and discarded

PVC piping, and a long band of tape kept this area separate from the lighted passage directly ahead. Mike saw an older couple passing in front of him, from his left to his right, pulling rolling luggage behind them. They would be coming from the bus terminal, heading to the escalators down the passage that led up to the main hallway.

Mike decided this location was perfect for a static watch. Unless Gentry passed here with night vision goggles, or he happened to shine a light on the construction, he would have no way of seeing someone standing by the Dumpster in the dark fifty feet away.

Dillman stepped out into the dimness and looked into the light in the distance. He saw movement, a lone figure approaching, but he was still too far away to be sure if it was his target or someone else.

Mike settled into a spot between the elevator and the Dumpster, then whispered into his Bluetooth headset, "I'm static at the service elevator, just south of the passage. I have a possible sighting down here. Wait one. I'll confirm and transmit again after he passes."

"Roger that," said Ruth. "I'm two minutes from your position, coming from the downstairs passage."

Mike did not confirm Ruth's transmission. Right now he concentrated on the man approaching.

Just as he squinted his eyes for a better look, though, he sensed movement right in front of his face. Before he could get his hands up to protect himself he felt a sharp biting across his throat and an instant constriction of his airway; his hands flew to the area and tried to pull whatever had him by the neck free, but it was tight, too tight to pull it off.

His brain knew what was happening, but he did not want to believe it. Someone, it had to be Gentry, had approached from behind him in the dark and wrapped a cord around his neck.

He was being strangled by a garrote.

Mike fought with all his strength. His rubber boot heels grabbed on the polished tile flooring; he pushed back, simultaneously firing his head behind him, desperate to slam his skull into his attacker's face, but his attacker defended against the obvious tactic by keeping his head out of contact range. Dillman's earpiece flew out of his ear and clinked along the floor, disappearing in the darkness.

Mike pushed again with his legs, his hands again clawed at the thin cord over his throat, and he felt the wetness of blood. He had no sense of falling, but he felt the impact as his body hit the floor along with the man behind him. He felt his attacker dig harder with the garrote and simultaneously drive his own shoes down on the floor, pulling both himself and Mike deeper into the darkness, dragging him behind the metal Dumpster.

Mike's flailing arms weakened, and they dropped down. He felt blood all over his leather coat now, and when his hands reached out to find some loose item in the dark he could use as a weapon his hands slapped in the warm slick wetness of his own blood on the floor.

In the distance he saw the man approaching up the lighted passage coming closer; he would pass within no more than fifty feet within moments.

Mike tried to scream, to shout for help, but he had no open airway with which to do so. His legs kicked out, left and right, frantically trying to make some noise, but his attacker swung him to the right and then the left, counteracting his attempts by rolling him onto one hip or the other.

The passerby walked in front of Mike, but he was completely unaware of what was happening in the darkness of the hall by the service elevator.

Mike tried to call out again, but he could make no sound other than a single low wheeze of air, and when he did this the garrote cinched even tighter around his neck.

As his vision narrowed, as his mind dulled and hazed and as his panic-stricken heart went from a furious pounding beat to arrhythmia and then arrest, he saw now.

He did not understand, but he saw.

The man passing in front of him was Courtland Gentry.

FORTY-TWO

Russ held the garrote around the dead man's neck for longer than necessary, but he was winded, and the pain in his hip was excruciating. He dreaded rolling back up, climbing to his knees, and then standing, so he just lay there, the dead man on top of him.

This one had been a fighter. Deceptively strong.

Still, he was dead, Court had passed by without knowing what was happening in the dark, and by now he would be on the escalator back up to the platform access level.

He'd told Gentry he wouldn't lay a hand on the Mossad, but just like in Nice, Russ had decided the tactical situation required a small adjustment to his initial plans. He was out of the loop with Townsend now, he couldn't obtain any intel from them about their own actions, much less the actions of the Mossad, so Whitlock decided to improvise to help Gentry get out of the city.

With any luck Court would be on a train and out of Stockholm in minutes, free of the surveillance that had been on him here, and Russ's operation would be back on track.

Russ struggled to his feet; he slipped the bloody garrote back into his coat pocket, and then he wiped his hands on his pants.

That was when he felt the blood on his hip.

Dammit. It wasn't the dead man's blood; no, it was his own. His gunshot wound had ripped open again.

Russ was done, for now. He couldn't provide any more help for Gentry without running the risk of being compromised, stumbling along through a crowd with a growing bloodstain running down his leg.

No, he needed to get out of here now.

He limped into the service elevator and headed back upstairs.

———————

Ruth moved slowly through the brightly lit passageway; her eyes remained locked as far ahead as she could see, searching for any glimpse of her target.

Mike had not transmitted in over a minute. He'd gone silent after claiming to have eyes on a possible subject. It was common during close survey ops to interrupt transmissions for OPSEC, so Ruth thought nothing of the delay in his reply.

But as she walked down the passage, she arrived at the

point where it opened at the northern tip of the bottom level of the train station, and she still had neither seen nor heard from Dillman. Here in the station she noticed a taped-off area of construction to her right, and back there, in the dark, she saw the service elevator, but she did not see her man.

She stopped walking. "Mike?" she said softly into her earpiece. "I told you static survey only. If you are in foot-follow on the target, I need you to back off."

There was no response.

"Mike, if you can't transmit, can you at least tap your earpiece?"

She expected to hear a scratchy set of thumps indicating Dillman was tapping his Bluetooth microphone, but again, she heard nothing.

Aron had been listening in. He tried to raise his teammate. "Dillman, Ruth is trying to establish comms with you. Are you receiving?"

By now Ruth was concerned. She stepped over the caution tape and into the darkened closed-off area. "Mike, I want you to break off survey and communicate right now."

Laureen came over the net from her position upstairs. "I've got eyes on target, say again, eyes on. Gentry is at platform level; I'm watching him from the mezzanine."

"Is Mike tailing him?" Ruth asked.

"Negative. I don't see him."

Aron said, "I'm en route to the station."

Ruth arrived at the service elevator, then pushed the button to call the car, thinking perhaps she'd lost comms with her junior officer because of poor mobile coverage.

But as she waited to go up to the main hall, she looked around, saw the construction materials, saw the Dumpster along the wall, and she saw a pair of boots sticking out from behind it.

For an instant she thought it might have been a homeless person sleeping in the station. There were homeless all over Europe, after all. But something about the way the boots were positioned, facing up, made her grab her flashlight from her purse and snap it on.

She recognized the boots now. A small gasp came from her lungs and then she ran forward, moved around the Dumpster, and found Mike Dillman. Her light reflected off his open glassy eyes and the glistening blood around his neck. She dropped to the floor and began checking him.

In her earpiece she heard Laureen. "The subject is at platform twelve, say again, one two."

Aron said, "Ruth, you want me with you or on the target?"

Ruth did not respond. Tears welled in her eyes and she stifled a cry as she began checking Dillman's vital signs.

"Ruth? Respond, please."

But Ruth did not respond. She did not make a sound. She sat down on the floor slowly, avoiding a wide smear of blood next to Mike's body, and she put her face in her hands.

There was no question in her mind as to what had happened. Gentry had come across Mike and somehow killed him so he could get away clean. She did not understand it; it went counter to every piece of psychological and historical data she'd collected on her target in the past days, but there was no doubt. What other explanation could there possibly be?

She had been wrong. Gentry *was* a threat, a threat to her PM, a threat to her own personnel.

Her mind seemed to slow, to regain its ability to calculate, and she realized that she could not tell her two other team members. Not yet. They had to stay on mission, they had to track Gentry out of town; if she told them that Mike was lying here, faceup, dead next to a pile of garbage, they would lose all mission focus.

Aron called over the net. "Ruth?"

She reached into his coat and took his wallet, then pulled his phone. She found his earpiece on the floor, and she picked it up and pocketed it with the other items.

Laureen transmitted now, concern in her voice. "Ruth? Mike?"

Ruth hated herself right now; she detested whatever cold, calculating recess of her brain allowed her to fight off all emotions and to stay on mission.

Aron said, "Ruth, I'm heading downstairs. There in two minutes."

She could grieve later, yes, but she already knew she would only hate herself more later, when she reflected back on what she had done.

She fought to deliver the next transmission cleanly and without any hint as to the horror she felt right now. "Negative. Stay on the target. I'm coming up."

"What about Mike?"

She closed her eyes and tears streamed down her face. She bit her lip hard, lifted her chin, and said, "Mike's comms are down. I'm sending him back to the car to get another headset."

"Roger that," said Aron. "Heading to platform twelve."

Ruth left Mike's body behind, then began rushing to the escalator that led up to the platform level of the station.

Platform twelve was crowded with passengers due to the fact that long twelve-car international-bound trains were parked on both sides.

Ruth had just climbed the stairs to the platform when Laureen came over the net. She had been watching the target from the mezzanine above and behind Ruth's position.

"Gentry is on the train on platform twelve-A. I'm checking the board up here. It's headed to Oslo, and it is leaving immediately."

"Aron, where are you?" Ruth asked, her voice not as commanding as normal, though she hoped with the adrenaline rush of the close foot pursuit, her two junior officers would not detect anything amiss.

"I'm boarding the train now, front car," Aron said. He was fifty yards ahead of her, and she began pushing to get herself to the train before it left the station. "Are you on board?" he asked.

"Negative. Thirty seconds."

A conductor blew a whistle at the front of the train.

"You'd better hurry," Aron said.

Mercifully, a lane formed in the crowd in front of her

and she rushed forward, squinting in the vapor of a hundred mouths breathing frozen air, trying to keep her forward progress going before the doors closed and the train took off for Oslo.

Just then she saw a man wearing a dark coat and carrying a backpack climb off the second to last car of the Oslo-bound train. His hood was up and she could not see his face, but she thought it might have been Gentry. He crossed the platform quickly and stepped aboard an SJ express train facing in the other direction.

Ruth stopped in her tracks. "Is that him?" she said into her mic. "Laureen? Did he get off the train?"

"No," came the reply. And then, "I don't know, I didn't see anyone leave, but there are a dozen cars and a ton of people."

The electronic sign over the platform next to the second train said HAMBURG and the departure time was imminent. The conductor at the far end of the train blew his handheld whistle. "Shit!" Ruth said, unsure which train to climb aboard.

Ruth had no time to make a decision. The doors closed on the Oslo train and it began moving slowly away. She wasn't getting on that one. It was either stay here in Stockholm or take a chance that her target was on the Hamburg train.

She leapt aboard the last car of the SJ express train. Within seconds this train began to move as well.

She stayed where she was in the rear of the train in a first-class car, her eyes fixed on the door ahead that led to the gangway connection between the cars. If she saw any movement in the gangway she was ready to shoot up and head to the restroom in the rear of her car.

She sat quietly for a few minutes while she waited for Aron to slowly and carefully walk the length of the Oslo-bound train. While she waited, she gazed out to the blackness of the early morning, and she thought of finding Mike, stripping him of anything that could identify him or indicate what kind of work he was doing, and then leaving him there. She thought of her mission, a mission in which she had already failed by getting one of her men killed because of her assuredness that her target posed no threat.

It wasn't assuredness, she told herself now. It was incompetence.

She thought of Rome.

She'd come out of Rome smelling like a rose; the Mossad commended her actions for trying to warn operations that the surveillance wasn't complete, but she had always known she had not deserved to walk away with her career intact. She could easily think back to the times when she could have forcefully spoken up and stopped the Metsada hit that killed the innocent civilians. Not an e-mail to her superior in Tel Aviv saying she wanted more time to build the target pictures. But a full-throated protest of the impending attack. Screaming across departments and disciplines, standing in the way of the kill/capture unit, even tipping off the occupants of the house and giving them time to flee.

But she had not done any of that, for one simple reason.

She *wanted* the hit. Yes, she could prove otherwise after the fact with her e-mail, but she'd only thrown up a caution flag because she was trying to protect the Met-sada men. To make sure no one else inside was armed or a threat.

She never thought for one moment her target was anything other than guilty as sin. She wanted him dead, and she did not give a damn if his friends in the house died with him. Even though she hadn't had time to ID them, she felt sure that their association with him made them guilty as well.

She had no idea an innocent family was inside the house, but that did not exonerate her in her eyes. It was her job to know.

She'd gotten away scot-free because her e-mail had been worded vaguely enough to vindicate her. On top of this, she felt that the investigating committee in the Knesset wanted to find one shining light in the entire mess, and they latched on to the uplifting narrative of a young female officer who spoke truth to power and did her best to save lives, and help the tarnished image of her organization.

She'd always known she was one half-assed bitching e-mail away from the same fate as all the others involved in the Rome catastrophe.

And now this. *Mother of God.* Now *this*?

She put her head in her hands.

"I'm so sorry, Mike."

It took Aron fifteen minutes to slowly and carefully search the train. When he was finished he came over the net. "Ruth, I think he's with you. I can't find him on board."

Ruth stood from her seat, unsure if she should try to

find Gentry. No. She sat back down. That was too chancy. She would sit here and monitor the stops to see if he disembarked. She picked up a route brochure in the pocket of her chair and looked it over. She fought to calm her voice again. It took considerable effort to do so. "Understood. We'll hit Copenhagen at eleven ten A.M. Get on a plane; I want you guys there waiting for us when we arrive. If he gets off before Copenhagen, we'll adjust."

"Roger that," said Aron.

"Understood," said Laureen.

Several seconds later Aron said, "Mike, you hearing us?"

Aron waited patiently for a response.

Ruth sat in her seat in the rear car of the train. She had the row to herself, but directly in front of her a man sat facing her, reading a newspaper.

Ruth put her hands on her knees, felt a quiver in her body. Acid in her stomach surging up into her chest. Slight at first, but growing.

Laureen came over the net. "Something is going on here at the station. I've got sirens. An ambulance and several police cars just pulled up."

Aron called now. "Ruth. Can you raise Mike?" She heard alarm in his voice.

And then, almost suddenly, it became too much.

Ruth Ettinger lost it.

She launched out of her seat, turned to the rear of the car, and rushed through the door to the tiny gangway. She slammed the bathroom door shut and vomited into the sink.

Tears flowed along with the vomit, and her sobs continued long after.

————————

Twenty minutes later, Ruth Ettinger stood outside the bathroom in the gangway section at the back of the train, her phone to her ear, her face red from crying, and the hood on her coat up in an attempt to cover her emotions to anyone who might come back here to use the restroom.

On the other end of the line was Yanis Alvey. She had told him everything. She had told him about finding Mike, about lying to her two subordinates, but that was not all. She revealed to him that she had seen Gentry the morning before and had purposefully let him slip away from the Townsend kill team.

She put up little defense of herself. She muttered something about not wanting a massacre at the hands of Beaumont and his Jumper team, but she could have argued her point more vigorously.

Her self-loathing did not allow it. This was not going to be Rome all over. She would not snake her way out of the blame.

When she had nothing left to say, when the crying had stopped, Yanis spoke gently yet forcefully. "Ruth. It's over. You are being recalled, and you will be replaced. I will notify Metsada that their target is on the train and I will green-light a kill/capture operation."

"Yes, sir."

"I just want you to sit there until the next stop, then

get off, and we'll send someone to pick you up. I'm heading to Copenhagen, leaving within the hour. I'll meet with you there and I will put you on a flight back to Tel Aviv."

Ruth nodded at the phone. "Yes, sir. I'm sorry, sir."

"I'm sorry, too," he said. Then, "I'm sorry for Mike."

He hung up.

She took her earpiece out of her ear and slipped it in her purse, then turned off her phone and put that in as well. She headed back into the bathroom to wash her face.

Rome had clouded her judgment. Since the day the family was gunned down by the Metsada operatives in Italy, Yanis had told her he worried about her being back in the field, and she had scoffed at his concerns.

But he was right, and she was wrong. Rome had ruined her.

She was off the Gentry operation. She could accept this; she had no choice. And Yanis clearly had no choice in recalling her.

But with the realization that she was done came the knowledge that she now had no masters. No one to report to.

Nothing to lose.

Somewhere ahead of her on the train was the man who had murdered her colleague. He was still free, and whether or not Townsend killers were en route, she knew Gentry had overcome Townsend men before and escaped to kill again.

Ruth decided she would not leave the surveillance to them. The takedown? Of course, as much as she would like to wrap her own hands around his throat and choke the life from him, she knew that would not happen. When Beaumont and his men got here, she would get out of the way.

But until then, she wasn't getting off this damn train until Court Gentry did.

FORTY-THREE

Court sat in the fourth car on the train, a second-class coach only half full with passengers. He'd boarded without a ticket, but that was not uncommon in Sweden. He purchased a full-fare ticket when the conductor passed, telling the woman in German that his final destination would be Hamburg.

He had no idea if he would stay on the train all the way to its terminus; he'd feel out the situation as the day went on, but he was hoping to put as many miles as possible between Stockholm and himself.

As he sat with his head against the window and his hood up, his phone began vibrating in his backpack in the rack above his head. He stood up and dug it out, and decided to answer it in case Whitlock had intel about the hunt for him.

Court answered his phone. "Hey."

"You okay, brother?"

He spoke softly, although there was no one close by. "I saw the Mossad woman again this morning, but I think I got away from her. What do you hear from your friends?"

After a slight pause, Whitlock said, "I'm off the op."

"What does that mean?"

"It means I'm not getting intel from Townsend House at the moment."

"Well, that sucks for me, doesn't it?" Court growled. "I gave up Kiev and now you are saying you can't help me? You don't know if they are tailing me now?"

"Last I heard Jumper was looking for you at the bus terminal."

Court nodded, pleased that the ruse had drawn any surveillance from the train station, but also aware that this misdirection would have expired the moment the bus to Gothenburg left the station without Gentry on board.

Whitlock added, "The Mossad did have static coverage on the train station."

Court cocked his head. "What train station?"

"The train station where you caught the oh five fifty to Hamburg."

Fuck. Court leapt out of his seat, grabbed his bag from the rack over him, and began walking to the back of the train. If he was under threat here on board, he would rather be at one end of the train or the other so he would not have to defend in both directions.

As he began moving, Russ said, "Settle down. Nobody at Townsend knows. Only me."

"How do *you* know?"

"Because I saw you. I didn't see which train you got on, but there were only four that left around the time you left, and three went either north or west. I figure you'd want to head south; you'll want to ditch Scandinavia totally at this point with all the heat on you so you can get back on the Continent and melt away." He added, "That's what I'd do. So that's what you're doing."

Court moved through the gangway between two cars, entered a dining car, and continued on toward the rear. "Why were you at the station?"

"I told you. Townsend is suspicious of me, and they've cut me out of the op."

"So?"

"So . . . I had to find another way to help you out."

Court felt a cold unease welling up inside him. Something about the tone of the man's voice, something about the realization that Dead Eye had been watching him. Something about Court's more than intimate knowledge of the training, skills, and abilities of a man with Dead Eye's background, all led to this sense of foreboding.

He passed through the second-to-last car now and asked, "How, exactly, did you help me?"

The dread he felt in the answer manifested itself into bile burning in his stomach.

"That's irrelevant, Violator. You're clear, and that's all you need to—"

In a harsh whisper Court barked, "What the *hell* did you do?"

———————

Ruth had spent the last ten minutes in the bathroom in the back of the rear car disguising herself so she could move through the train to find Gentry. She had slipped on a short black wig and put on even more dramatic makeup than she'd been wearing the evening before when she'd been face-to-face with him at the bar. She put on tortoiseshell eyeglasses, the frames uncorrected, and they added a studious, almost mousy quality to her disguise.

She also removed her coat. She'd worn the reverse side this morning, switching it from black to gray, but she knew a man with Gentry's training would have probably noticed this feature to her coat, and he'd be on the lookout for both colors.

Finding Court on board without him seeing her would be a difficult task. Both the first- and second-class cars were divided with half the seats facing one way and the other half facing the other, with the dividing line in the center of the car. This meant each time she stepped into a new carriage there existed a fifty-fifty chance Gentry would be facing her direction, although if he were it would also mean he was at least forty feet away.

She put her hand on the door lever from the gangway to the first carriage and looked up through the glass, and there, on the far end of the car, Gentry approached, a mobile phone in his hand. He wore a black thermal undershirt and blue jeans, with his backpack slung over his shoulder and his coat lashed to it.

Ruth spun away, hoping like hell he either did not see her at all or only saw her short black hair and movement through the Plexiglas doorway.

She quickly stepped back into the bathroom, shut the door behind her, and locked it.

Just then, outside the door to the bathroom, she heard the unmistakable sound of the carriage door opening and closing. A moment later she heard the low mumbling of a male voice, and although she could not make out a word of it, she could tell Gentry was standing in the gangway, right outside her door, talking on his phone.

She fought a wave of panic. The man who had just killed Mike Dillman stood feet from her now. She did not think he knew she was in here—it seemed unlikely he would continue on with his call if he did—but she worried he would stand there for some time, see the OCCU-PIED sign on the door, and begin to wonder why the person inside did not leave.

She reached into her purse for her Mace, although she had no real belief that she could incapacitate the legendary Gray Man with an aerosol spray.

Gentry leaned against the wall in the gangway of the rear train car, keeping his eyes on the passenger carriage in front of him in case any threats approached. He kept his voice down because someone was in the bathroom next to him.

"I'm not going to ask you again. What happened in Stockholm?"

Russ had been cagey, but with a long sigh he relented.

"It was Mossad, dude. They weren't going to let you just hop on a train and roll out of there."

"And?"

"And there was one guy between you and freedom." A short pause. "I neutralized him."

"Killed him?"

"Only way, Court. I know that probably violates your weird moral code and fragile sensibilities, but he was as big a threat to you, *more* of a threat to you, in fact, than any of the Townsend guys or the Sidorenko guys *you* killed last week."

Court slammed the back of his head against the wall of the train car in frustration.

"You murdered an Israeli intelligence officer? You stupid fuck!"

"Watch your tone, Violator! I saved your life. Just like I did in Tallinn. You should be kissing my ass for all I've done for you."

Court understood now. Not everything, but enough. Russ wanted Gentry alive, because Russ *needed* Gentry alive. "This is about Kalb, isn't it?" There was no answer, and Gentry banged the back of his head against the wall again. "It's *you*. You're the one after Kalb."

After a short pause, Russ's voice darkened as he replied, "I guess you and your Jew girlfriend had quite a conversation last night."

"That was you in Nice, wasn't it? You smoked Amir Zarini."

"It wasn't me, Court. Ask around. Ask anyone." He laughed, then said, "It was *you*."

"That was your plan?"

With a little chuckle he said, "Affirmative."

"Why?"

"Think about it, genius."

Court did, and it did not take long. "You want to kill Kalb. You needed my name to get the contract. And then to survive after the fact, you need me to take the fall."

Russ said, "I thought I had myself a bulletproof plan. But it only works as long as you remain alive. Frankly, Violator, you have been the weak link in this whole thing. I guess I shouldn't have believed all the hype about you. You've got the shakes, you're talking about retirement, there are so many people following you right now it must look like you're leading a Mardi Gras parade down the motherfucking street. The Gray Man legend is a goddamned joke."

"What's keeping me from calling the CIA, or Mossad, or Townsend, and telling them about this plot of yours?"

"Go ahead. I'm still going to get to Kalb, so you won't prevent that. Sure, CIA might take me off their Christmas card list, but it's not going to help your situation with them. Mossad won't believe you; I've planted too many trackbacks to you, to where you can't just call them up and say you're an innocent bystander. And Townsend will be pissed, but they get paid to kill you, not me, so they're still coming at you with everything they have."

"Is all this just about money?"

Russ laughed out loud. "Ha! That's pretty funny, coming from the most infamous killer-for-hire on the planet. Of course it's about money."

Court did not believe him. There was something

more. There *had* to be. This guy was unstable. "How did you slip through the cracks? How did you make it through the AADP and into active duty with the agency? Did the standards drop after I went through?"

"What do you mean?"

"They had me take a bunch of tests to make sure I was mentally competent. I passed them all."

"I took the same tests."

"So how did you get recruited?"

Russ took his time responding. Court looked out the window. The morning had brightened to a gray day, revealing a frozen landscape of forest zooming by at 125 miles per hour. Finally Russ said, "In the Corps I spent two years in Iraq, had the fortune of being involved in twenty-two combat engagements. Fallujah, Sadr City. All the fun spots.

"Then it was Afghanistan. My company had more than five hundred contacts in eleven months. I was wounded twice, but I dished out a hell of a lot of death to the enemy.

"Then one day they pulled me back to J-Bad, then back to the States. They told me I was such a badass they were looking at me for SOF."

"SOF?"

"Special Operations Forces."

"I know what that means, dickhead. Didn't they give you a psych eval?"

"Yes, they did."

Court looked past the bathroom to the window on the door to the train. Snow-covered hills rolled past in a blur. "Let me guess the next part. Your psych eval was . . . questionable."

"Negative, it was not questionable in the least. As a matter of fact, it answered their questions nicely. The tests determined I was—"

"A sociopath?"

"Wrong again."

Court closed his eyes. *Jesus.* "You are a psychopath, aren't you?"

The delay in Whitlock's response told Court he'd hit the nail on the head. Finally Russ said, "I tried to argue that it was nurture, not nature. Twenty-four months in the sandbox followed by a year at a FOB in Kunar Province can skew a psych eval if it's not taking into account the realities I had to face—each and every fucking day it was kill or be killed."

"But the shrinks wouldn't listen to your explanation."

"They are paid to talk, not to listen to some jarhead just back from Asscrackistan."

"So no SOF for you."

"No SOF for me."

Court watched the frozen landscape pass by, his mind on his own past with the CIA. He knew the next chapter of Whitlock's story as if it had happened to himself. Court said, "And then the CIA dropped in. Patted you on the head and said they understood."

"Of course they did. There were still tests to take, and I took them, but for a sharp tack like me, with a little forewarning about what was expected, gaming the tests was no big deal. There were the agency shrink interviews, but there again, I was smarter than any of those fucks evaluating me. A smart enough psychopath can easily appear only sociopathic with a little effort. Then the CIA recruiters sat me down. I'm sure you got the same spiel. They said, 'We can make your life amount to something, but once you say yes, you belong to us.'"

Court remembered the moment it happened to him. He'd been pulled out of prison in Florida, facing a life sentence for shooting three Colombian enforcers. He was driven to a nice home in Kendall—a CIA safe house, he later determined—and run through days of meetings and tests. Push and pull. They made him feel like Superman, and then they made him feel like shit on their shoes. It was recruitment and assessment at the same time.

"But they let you in even though they thought you were sociopathic?"

Russ paused again before saying, "Court, I hate to break it to you . . . That was a prerequisite."

"It was a prerequisite to be nuts?" Gentry shook his head in disbelief. "When did that change?"

"It didn't."

Russ was right. Court did *not* understand.

"Are you fucking blind, Court? We were *all* picked for AADP because the shrinks determined we were the right psychological fit. Remorseless loners."

"That's . . . that's not true. I'm not a sociopath."

"You're a borderline sociopath. It's in your unredacted file. Give me your address, I'll send you a copy."

Softly Gentry said, "I'm *not*."

"That's what the Autonomous Asset Program was all

about. Taking misfits with nothing to lose, young men with the physical and psychological raw materials to make efficient killing machines, then building them and training them and programming them to follow orders, and finally sending them out into the world like goddamned robots to melt into foreign lands and do the dirty work without questioning the orders or building relationships or associations of a personal nature."

"That's not me. I'm not crazy."

Russ laughed. "Sure, Court. You are the one Tootsie Roll in the box of turds, right? How many people have you killed over the years? Think about that. Does that sound like the life of a well-adjusted individual?"

"Fuck you, Whitlock. I do what I do because I have to."

"Bullshit, Court. You could have escaped after the shoot-on-sight and disappeared anywhere in the world. You could have left the game, but you didn't want to drive a taxi or gut fish. You wanted to kill people. Just because you justify your bloodlust by only targeting bad guys is irrelevant. You do that to make yourself feel better, not because you are some kind of hero. Trust me, if you run out of bad guys, the goal posts will just move, and you'll start killing people who are more and more marginal."

Gentry wanted to write off Whitlock's assertions as nothing more than the fantasies of a maniac, but the truth was, Russ seemed like he knew what he was talking about.

Court said, "You've wanted me to stay in touch with you. Why?"

"You don't like our little chitchats?"

"You are stringing me along. Trying to get me to join you. This isn't just about framing me. You *need* me for something. For what, I don't know."

"I don't need you," Russ said, but Court could hear consternation in his voice.

Gentry said, "I'm not going to play into your plan. I am hanging up now, and I'm tossing this phone."

Quickly, Whitlock said, "No! I can still help you."

"How?"

"I'm going to blame the Kalb hit on you, but how is that really going to affect your day? One more country is after you? Big deal. Once you lose those people on you now, then you'll be fine. Go back to South America, or Southeast Asia, or try the outback. Go off grid and stay off grid. When I'm done with my op, say three or four weeks from now, I'll contact you again, and I'll give you all the information on the shoot-on-sight sanction CIA put on you five years ago. I owe you that." He laughed into the phone. "You are, after all, helping me make twenty-five mil, even if it is unwittingly."

Court shook his head. "I'm done with you."

"Court. Listen to me. You need to think very carefully—"

"You aren't controlling me, Dead Eye. I am starting to wonder if you can even control yourself."

Court disconnected the call and took the battery out of the phone. He put both pieces in his backpack and planned on destroying the phone when he got off the train and found a quiet place to do so.

He slung his backpack and coat back over his shoulder and left the rear cabin. The train would be in Copenhagen soon, and then it would cross the Baltic Sea on a ferry and roll on to Hamburg.

Court wanted to remain on board for the entire journey, but he needed to keep an eye out for any of the rapidly expanding number of threats against him.

FORTY-FOUR

Ten minutes after she left the bathroom, Ruth Ettinger found Gentry in the fourth car from the end of the train. She saw only the back of his head, but she recognized his nondescript black coat and the nondescript black backpack in the rack above him. Even though she felt like her disguise was as good as she could possibly make it, she knew she benefited from the fact that her target was seated facing away from her.

He sat alone, looking out the window at the foggy morning whipping by at high speed, and although he did not seem to be particularly on guard, she turned out of the carriage after a few seconds and returned to her seat in first class.

For the first time in her career she wished she carried a firearm. She had no doubt in her mind that if she had a gun in her purse she would pull it out right now, walk down the aisle of the train car, and empty it into the Gray Man's body as she drew level with him.

But she did not have a gun, and now she did not even have targeting responsibility for a unit of Metsada Special Operations officers. She felt helpless without the power to call in a crew of shooters, knowing that a dangerous threat sat just yards away.

A few minutes later the train made a stop in Hässleholm. As she had done at each stop, she made her way to the door at the rear of the train and leaned out, keeping her eyes up the cars in case Gentry disembarked. By now she expected him to travel all the way to Malmö at least, and perhaps even on to Copenhagen, so she was surprised when she saw him climb off the train four cars up, his coat on and his pack on his back.

She ran back to her seat, grabbed her things from the rack above it, and then followed Gentry off the train into a pelting shower of sleet.

Ruth moved behind a small group of pensioners walking along the track toward the central station, craning her head over them to keep Gentry in her sights. She lost him for a moment but picked him out as he walked up the platform toward an intercity train parked under the covered tracks closer to the station.

He climbed aboard near the front of the train, and Ruth jumped onto the last car as the conductor blew his whistle.

The intercity was bound for Helsingborg, on the southern tip of the Swedish peninsula. She found a seat near the rear. As the train left the station she asked a passing conductor for a ticket, and she paid in cash.

The train headed west, making frequent stops. At each station along the route Ruth looked out the window, but within an hour she had the sense Gentry was heading all the way to Helsingborg. It was a port city just across the Øresund Strait from Denmark. From here Ruth knew Court could take a quick ferry across the water and avoid the route from Sweden to the European mainland: a long ferry crossing over the Baltic Sea to the south, which Townsend would surely have covered.

Certain she knew where he was heading now, she pulled her phone out of her purse to call Yanis. But just as she did this she looked up and realized she was just feet away from the man who had murdered Mike Dillman hours earlier. Gentry walked up the center aisle of the train, then glanced away and continued on, out of the car and into the next.

Her heart pounded. He'd passed by without giving her a second glance, and she felt reasonably sure her own face had remained impassive during the eye contact. She did not think he'd recognized her in her heavy disguise, but she would not leave it to chance. She got out of her seat and headed for the bathroom in the opposite direction of her target.

Ruth moved all the way to the very rear of the train and then stepped into the bathroom and removed her black wig. She'd go with her natural chestnut hair now, as Gentry had already seen her as both a blonde and a brunette.

She wished she had her team with her. By any normal

standard of her tradecraft, she was burned; she would not show herself to Gentry again, even with a new disguise. But she was on her own, and she had to do her best to completely change her look.

She took off her tortoiseshell-framed glasses, pulled her hair back in a ponytail, and removed every bit of her makeup with makeup remover and a small washcloth she kept in her purse for just such emergencies. She also took off her black sweater and exchanged it for a thin but warm dark green Patagonia base layer, transforming her look from business traveler on an international-bound train into an athletic-looking young woman commuting from one town to another.

Satisfied with her new look, she put her makeup remover and her clothing back in her bag, then unlocked the door and opened it and began to step into the gangway.

Suddenly a man spun into the open space in front of her, put his hand in her face, and shoved her back inside the little bathroom. He forced his way in with her and smashed her hard against the wall, shutting the door behind him.

She tried to scream, but his hand pushed against her mouth and cut off all but a small fraction of the sound. She fell back to her left, her body half over the little sink and the back of her head pressed against the cold mirror. She heard her attacker lock the door behind him, and she fought in the confined space to get her Mace out of her purse. His free hand pulled her purse away and shoved it behind his body where she could not reach it.

She knew who he was, of course, even before her eyes could focus on his face.

It was Gentry.

He relaxed his hold over her mouth slightly, and she took advantage of this. She jutted her face forward and bit down hard on the soft space between his thumb and forefinger. Gentry stifled a scream and his free hand rose to punch her in the jaw, but he stayed himself and just yanked his hand away from her gnashing teeth.

"Stop!" he said, but she had created space now, enough to get a hand wrapped around a metal soap dispenser on the wall. She pulled it free and swung it at him, but he got his head back and out of the way just in time, and the dispenser slammed into the little window just to the left of him.

"Stop!" he said again, but now she had her right hand free and she swung at his face. Her fist half-connected with his chin, but he managed to grab both her hands and restrain them against the wall above her head. He pressed his body hard into hers, pinning her back over the sink, and he used his own forehead to hold hers immobile. "Listen to me! Just listen!"

Ruth started to scream again, but Court let go of her right arm and slammed it back over her mouth. She immediately began punching him in the side and back with her free hand, but she could not get her arm back far enough in the confined area to do any real damage. Simultaneously she tried to knee him in the groin, but he locked her legs down with his own.

As she hit him over and over he said, "Stop! Just listen to me for one fucking minute!"

She stopped throwing short left-handed punches, but her hand reached down to his waist and she felt around, clearly trying to find the knife he'd threatened her with the previous evening.

But Gentry had prepared for this by sliding the sheathed blade into his boot before confronting the Mossad woman.

Ruth gave up the fight. She dropped her arm to her side and went limp, breathing heavily from the effort of the fight.

Court himself was breathing hard from the exchange. "I know what it looks like—it looks bad. But I didn't kill your man in Stockholm. It wasn't me. There is another guy out there. He is using me. Framing me."

"Bullshit!"

"If I killed your friend, why would I deny it? Why wouldn't I just kill you now?"

Through labored breaths she said, "Because you want to convince me you are no threat, so I will go back to my leadership and tell them to stand down on the hunt."

"If you guys stay on me, then Kalb will die, because the man who killed your agent has a plan to kill Kalb. Believe me, he knows what he is doing."

Ruth did not believe. As she looked at Gentry, their eyes not six inches apart, she could see only Mike Dillman's glazed eyes, open in death.

"You killed Mike."

Court shook his head. "He was killed by a man named Russell Whitlock. He's the one you should be after." He added, "He's ex-Agency. Now he's a Townsend asset."

Ruth cocked her head. "Townsend?"

"Yes. They used him to track me, but he's gone off reservation. He's accepted a contract from the Iranians to kill your prime minister. He's planning to kill Kalb and frame me for it, but there is more to this I don't understand."

"You are lying. I don't believe you."

"You need to try. Because he is out there, and he will kill Kalb, and you are making it really fucking easy for him by concentrating your people on me."

She took a moment, still breathing hard, but thinking over what he was saying. Looking him in the eyes she saw an earnestness that she did not expect, and his tone was certainly convincing.

"How do you know all this?" she asked. "About Whitlock?"

"Because he told me." Court relaxed his grip on the woman, but not completely. "Townsend came after me in Estonia, and Russ fought alongside me. He told me he could help me get away from them, so I stayed in contact with him. I knew he had some agenda, but it wasn't until last night when you told me about Zarini and the contract on Ehud Kalb, and today when he told me he killed your man so I could get clear, that I put it together."

Ruth wanted to believe Gentry. If he was telling the truth, then it meant she had been right all along. Gentry was not the threat.

And Mike's death was not her fault.

She wanted to believe him because it helped her; she knew that. She also knew Gentry might be lying to protect himself. But this second rogue assassin story, as far-fetched as it sounded, was the only scenario that made any sense to her. He had not convinced her, not yet, but she was well on her way to believing.

"Whitlock is in Sweden?" she asked.

"I don't know where he is now. I guess he's going wherever Ehud Kalb is." Court looked at Ruth. "Where is your PM?"

With an incredulous tone she said, "I'm not going to tell you the travel plans of my prime minister."

Court rolled his eyes. "He's going to New York next week. I saw that on TV. But if Russ is going to frame me, he won't do it in New York."

Ruth understood. "Because you are a target of the U.S., and *you* can't go to New York."

"Yeah. I guess he could do it in Tel Aviv," Gentry said. He found himself using his own thought process to determine the actions of someone else. "But I'm sure he'd rather do it outside Israel, get him on some neutral ground."

Ruth spoke softly. "London."

"Kalb is going to London?"

She hesitated a moment, then said, "It's public knowledge. He'll be there the day after tomorrow."

"That's it, then," Court said. "Russ must be planning on hitting him there."

"It's a Pan-European trade conference," she said. "Dozens of world leaders will attend. Do you have any idea how tight security measures will be?"

"Trust me. Russ and I had the same training." He looked into her eyes. "I could do it. *He* could do it."

Ruth found herself believing him.

Court said, "I just did you a favor with that information. Agreed?"

"If it's true."

"It's true. You've got to get him to cancel his trip. Now, I need you to do me a favor."

"What favor?"

"Tell me who will be waiting for me in Helsingborg."

"No one. I have not called anyone."

Court looked at her a long time, evaluating her nonverbal clues to gauge the veracity of her answer.

"Good."

"But this new intel. You have to let me call this in."

"Not until I'm off this train."

"Please, there is no time to waste."

But Court held firm. "You have two days. That's plenty of time for Kalb to cancel his plans."

Ruth said nothing, although she worried she did not, in fact, have two days.

FORTY-FIVE

Russell Whitlock landed at London's Gatwick Airport shortly before two P.M. He wore business attire, traveled with only his briefcase and a small overnight tote, and looked exactly like all the other young male international business travelers in the border control line.

Normally when traveling within Europe, Russ would not have to pass through customs. Twenty-six European nations are members of the Schengen Area, a cooperation zone established by treaty that allows travelers from one member nation to travel to other area nations without undergoing border controls.

But the United Kingdom, unlike Sweden, is not a member of the Schengen Area, and for this reason Russ had to wait in an immigration line upon arrival. The process was of no concern to him; his Townsend credentials were solid, and his blue U.S. passport made the entire process little more than a formality. A U.K. Border Agency officer glanced at him, glanced at his document, and then ran it through a scanner to read the information housed on the RFID chip to verify that the man, the paperwork, and the digital information all matched. Since there was no block on Allen Morris, the credos used by Whitlock on this day, he was told to have a pleasant stay and then waved through the border control area.

Russ tried to hide his slight limp as he walked through the terminal. His hip was killing him, but he knew he could push through the pain and do his job here in London. He had forty-eight hours to get set up for the hit on Kalb. It wasn't optimal—he would prefer at least seventy-two—but he'd already done much of the prep work for the op on an earlier trip here to London.

As he neared ground transportation, his phone rang and he answered it, even though he knew it would be Townsend, and even though he anticipated trouble. He believed in his power to charm, however, almost as much as he believed in his power to kill. He had been successful at both endeavors for his entire adult life, after all, so his self-confidence was easily understood.

"This is Graveside. Iden eight, two, four, four, niner, seven, two, niner, three."

"Confirmed. This is Dead Eye, identity key four, eight, one, oh, six, oh, five, two, oh."

Babbitt asked, "Where are you, Russell?"

"Stockholm."

A pause. "What have you been doing?"

"Made contact with Jumper this morning, Parks called with intel that Gray Man was at the bus terminal there in the city center. You had me disarmed and disowned, so I went back to my hotel."

"That was six hours ago. What have you been doing since?"

Russ kept walking. "I took a nap."

After a short pause Babbitt said, "We need to talk."

Russ found a place to sit in the terminal, away from others.

Babbitt said, "Beaumont tells me he confronted you about Trestle Seven."

"You're damn right we have to talk. I'm sending you the bill for my boots. That redneck spit on them."

Babbitt took a while to respond to this. When he did, he said, "Did you see a second target in Tallinn as was reported?"

"Negative. There was a blizzard going on, so I didn't see too much until Gentry shot me."

"There have been more doubts raised about the events of that night."

"Such as?"

"You requisitioned a pistol from our weapons cache in Berlin, did you not?"

"I did. So?"

"A Glock nine-millimeter. Model 19."

"Correct."

"Historically speaking, that is the weapon Court Gentry uses."

"It's a Glock, the plastic fantastic. Everybody uses it."

"Not you, Russell. You have always requisitioned a

forty-caliber SIG. We checked your older work with CIA. Again, a SIG forty. You have to go back ten years to see any record of you preferencing the nine-millimeter round, but even then, you carried the SIG Sauer. Never a Glock."

"You've lost me, Lee. Do you want to transfer me to Geraldina in the requisition and outfitting department? Did I fill out the wrong form or something?"

"There are suspicions by Jumper Actual, and by Jeff Parks, that you wanted to carry a gun identical to the target in Tallinn because you wanted to engage Trestle team in a clandestine fashion. To make it look like it was Gentry firing on the team when, in fact, *you* were shooting at the team."

Russ sighed, long and audibly. "For what possible reason?"

"We don't know. I would like you to help clear the air. We are recalling you effective immediately. Come home; we'll sit down in the conference room and do a long hot wash regarding the events in Estonia."

"But what about Gentry?"

"We don't need you on Gentry any longer. We'll have him in our pocket soon. We received a call from the supervisor of the Mossad targeting officer on the case. The Mossad woman is on a train with eyes on Gentry right now."

Russ squeezed the sides of the chair. *Fuck!* He fought to keep his voice calm. "Why did the Mossad call you?"

"Gentry killed a targeting officer this morning. It's personal now with the Mossad. Mr. Alvey, the Mossad executive, wanted to let me know so we could pull our team out to avoid any . . . blue-on-blue mishaps."

"But you aren't going to pull Jumper back, are you?"

"Of course not," Babbitt said, matter-of-factly. "Anyway,

none of this concerns you. Just get home; we'll straighten everything out. We'll get your wound looked at by our docs, too."

Russ was still thinking about Gentry or, more precisely, he was thinking about his operation and Gentry's continued potential to compromise it.

Babbitt took his silence for something else. "Look, Russ. We are very close to securing a contract with CIA to target a general in South America who's pissing off the White House. I want to use you for this, so I need you cleared and in top form."

Russ stood up; he needed to catch a flight immediately and did not have time to sit around and chat. "I'm on the way. Dead Eye, out." He disconnected the call and all but race-walked to the closest departures board in the terminal. He scanned the list of flights and found what he was looking for.

Twenty-five minutes later he stood in line at the gate preparing to board a flight.

Not to D.C. Russ wouldn't be going back to Townsend House.

No, he was going to Brussels, and he had to get there quickly.

Russ realized there was nothing more he could do to protect Gentry. It was likely the Mossad or Jumper would get him, sooner rather than later, and Russ couldn't stop them, or even slow them down. The only way he could potentially salvage his operation was to speed up the hit on Kalb, to kill him before Mossad killed Gentry, so Gentry would still take the fall for the hit.

Kalb was due in Brussels at noon the next day, less than twenty-four hours from now. Each year on the date, Russ knew, Kalb traveled to Belgium to pay his respects at the grave of Piet De Schepper, a Belgian doctor who had, at great personal risk, saved the lives of hundreds of Belgian Jews by secreting them from the Nazis.

Two of the Jews had been Kalb's mother and father.

Each and every year since De Schepper's death from natural causes in 1999, Kalb had made the pilgrimage to his grave at the Dieweg Cemetery in the southern Brussels neighborhood of Uccle. The trip was unannounced because Kalb's security detail had a serious problem with their PM going to the same exposed, outdoor location at the same time each and every year.

But the CIA knew about the PM's movements; it was coded confidential, which was not terribly secure, as it was not terribly interesting to the United States. Whitlock had easy access to the information through the Townsend secure network, and he'd learned of the annual pilgrimage in his research on Kalb.

Russ had originally ruled out hitting Kalb in Belgium because the Gray Man would be more likely to choose London. Kalb doubted Gentry had access to the secret travel plans of the Israeli leader, after all. Still, Russ needed to call an audible now and change locations. He hoped the superhero legend of the Gray Man would make it easy for the world to believe he knew of Kalb's annual pilgrimage.

Whitlock had confidence in his own skill to do a rush-job assassination. Just as he had in the United Kingdom,

Russ had access to a Townsend weapons cache in Brussels. If he could do the job before Gentry was killed by the Israelis or Townsend, then he could get away scot-free.

Obviously there were potential problems with this plan. If Gentry died first, or if there was surveillance on the Gray Man at the time of the Kalb hit tomorrow, then Whitlock would have a hard time convincing anyone that the Gray Man was the killer. But Russ knew Gentry was on his way to the continent of Europe; if Court could somehow just make it over the Baltic Sea and into Germany, then he'd be only a few hours away from the location of the assassination, and Russ hoped the clearly exaggerated reputation of the Gray Man would sell his superpower ability to kill the PM on a secret visit.

Whitlock was rooting for Gentry's miserable life to continue for just one more night.

A half hour later, Dead Eye boarded a British Airways flight to Brussels, still cursing Court Gentry under his breath for making every last thing so damn more complicated than it needed to be.

———————

Court and Ruth arrived in the southern Sweden city of Helsingborg during a light snow shower. They climbed out of the train together and headed into the station, Court's eyes darting around in all directions, on alert to pick up any surveillance or pre-aggression indicators in those around him. He was armed with only a four-inch paring knife, which would be a lousy defense against a half-dozen guys with submachine guns, although Court would not go down without a fight.

Once inside the station, Ruth said, "Can I call my boss?"

"Be my guest. I'm leaving now." He started to walk away.

She called to him. "Wait. This Whitlock man is a current Townsend employee, right?"

"Yes."

She hesitated for a moment. Then she said, "Ehud Kalb is stopping off somewhere else before London."

"Where?"

"It's classified."

Court shrugged. "Fine with me. It's not my problem."

"Brussels," she said, softly, not entirely comfortable passing this information on to Gentry. "It wasn't announced, but if Whitlock is working for a U.S. intelligence contractor, he might have access to that information."

Court said, "You can be sure that if CIA knows about the trip, then Whitlock knows about the trip. When does Kalb get to Brussels?"

"Tomorrow. Lunchtime. He'll leave the city around three P.M."

Court again considered what he would do in Whitlock's shoes. "That's a tight timeline. If Russ knows about Brussels, and if he has a weapon staged there already. Maybe." He shrugged. "Get Kalb to cancel."

She shook her head. "He doesn't cancel Brussels. He goes every year. It's a personal pilgrimage. His security detail has begged him to stop the trips, but he overrules them."

Court rolled his eyes. "Then you've got yourself a problem."

"Will you help us? You can contact Dead Eye; you can tell him we know he's going to Brussels. Tell him Metsada will be there and he won't have a chance in hell at pulling it off."

Court thought it over. With MobileCrypt he could do this with no exposure to himself.

"I'll contact him. Call me in an hour and I'll tell you what he said." He reached into his backpack and pulled out his phone and the phone's battery. It took him a moment to fire it up, but when he did, he read the phone number off the screen to her. She put it in her own phone, although she wasn't sure what his plan was at first.

"That's it? You're giving me your phone number? How do I know you'll do it? How do I know you will answer when I call?"

"You don't," he said, and then he turned away, disappearing in the flotsam and jetsam of the station crowd.

———————

Ruth found a quiet place in a shopping mall near the station, and she dialed Yanis Alvey. He answered on the first ring, near breathless, though Ruth could not tell if it was from anger or worry.

"Where are you?" he asked.

"Don't play games, Yanis. You have the ability to track me through my phone. I also have Mike's phone, so you have two means to do it."

He asked, "What are you doing in Helsingborg? You were supposed to get off the train as soon as it stopped this afternoon, not switch trains and head for the border."

She hesitated to answer, but she knew she could not lie to Yanis. The only way to convince him of the truth was to be perfectly transparent. She told him about her conversation with Gentry, about a second CIA asset gone rogue named Russell Whitlock, code-named Dead Eye, and his plot to frame Gentry in the death of Ehud Kalb. She explained that Dead Eye worked for Townsend, and both she and Gentry felt it was likely he would attempt to kill Kalb in Brussels.

"Where is Gentry now?"

Now she lied. "He got on a train. I did not see which one."

"Don't move from your location. I will come pick you up myself."

"What about what I just told you? You need to be on your way to Brussels. I can take care of myself."

"Ruth . . ." Yanis spoke in a fatherly tone. "You've lost a man today. You are coming in. We'll take care of any threats against the PM."

"So you don't believe me, is that it?"

"I don't believe *him*. Of course not. But I will check it out. It's an easy call to Townsend to confirm if they have this"—he was obviously reading the name he just wrote down—"Whitlock fellow working for them. If they do, I'll dig around some more."

"Yanis. You know me. You know I don't get played by the opposition."

"I *do* know you, Ruth. You are one of the best and brightest. But I also know what losing a man in the field is like. You are flailing now, flailing about for any lifeline, any proof that you are not responsible for Mike's death."

"That is not—"

"If you had done your job in Stockholm yesterday, Court Gentry, a man wanted by CIA, FBI, Interpol, French DGSE, the Mexican Federal Police, the Russian FSB, and God only knows who else, would have been taken off the chessboard, and Mike would not have been standing alone in the dark bowels of the train station this morning with a wire around his throat. You can rationalize the rantings of a wanted murderer into some sort of exoneration of your actions, but right now I don't care about that. I only care about pulling you out of the field. The surviving members of your team are halfway back to Tel Aviv already. Stay where you are and I will come pick you up."

It was clear to her she would be pulled out of action, and Mossad would do nothing at all about the real threat to Ehud Kalb.

———

As she sat there in the shopping mall, she decided she would take one more proactive step before standing down. She called Leland Babbitt at Townsend Government Services. Babbitt took the call immediately and immediately asked where she was calling from.

She suspected he knew she was following Gentry, but she did not admit to it. Instead of answering the question, she said, "Mr. Babbitt, I've determined the threat against Ehud Kalb to be real, but Court Gentry is not the would-be assassin."

"Explain."

"There is another man out there. He took the contract from the Iranians by claiming to be the Gray Man. He killed the film director in Nice, I think, to establish his bona fides."

"Wow. That's a hell of a story. Who is this guy?"

"His name is Russell Whitlock."

Leland Babbitt did not respond.

Ruth said, coolly, "I gather he is an employee of yours."

"Where did you come by this information?"

"From Court Gentry himself."

There was a long pause with a few stumbling starts, until finally Babbitt seemed to take control of his words. "You met with the Gray Man and he told you another operator was the real problem." Clearly he was shocked by the news she'd just delivered, and although he was trying to show that he was not buying it for a second, he was obviously on shaky ground.

Ruth said, "Gentry was not in Nice. That is certain."

"Certain how?"

"I saw him in Stockholm the morning of the Nice assassination."

"You saw Gentry yesterday morning?"

"Correct."

"When you were liaising with Jumper? That information would have been useful."

"You are missing the point. Your employee is the real threat, not Court Gentry."

Babbitt did not respond.

"Are you there?"

It took her almost a minute to realize that Babbitt had hung up on her.

FORTY-SIX

For the second time today Russ Whitlock stood in a border patrol checkpoint with his Townsend-issued passport in hand. Brussels, Belgium, was a member of the Shengen Area, but since the United Kingdom was not, he had to shuffle through the line and get his passport glanced at and scanned by a border officer who would certainly be targeting a much different demographic than the thirty-four-year-old American businessman.

Virtually all the passengers on his BA flight had been British citizens, and the control process seemed to be moving along quickly and smoothly. Russ made his way to the booth and handed his passport over with a tired smile, the polite boredom of a jet-setting businessman who crossed immigration lines with such mind-numbing regularity that he could do no more than affect this gentle pleasantry.

Russ had done this a thousand times before. His papers were so good and his training so complete that he let his mind wander, thinking about taking a long hot shower in the hotel, spending some time cleaning up his excruciating hip wound, and then ordering a four-course room service meal along with a bottle of champagne.

The Belgian policeman looked at the passport and ran it through a scanner. He compared the face on the photograph with Russ's face, and Russ smiled at him once again.

The policeman looked down at his screen and then did a quick double take. He slowly held up a finger, asking Russ to wait just a moment.

Then he reached for the phone on his desk, and Russ's dreams of showers and champagne evaporated in an instant.

Two plainclothesmen appeared at Whitlock's shoulder just seconds later. They were young and fit, and they wore zip-up hoodies and blue jeans. Each man also wore an earpiece in his right ear. Instantly Russ pegged them as cops. "Mr. Morris," one said in a Flemish accent, "would you please come with us for one moment?"

"Why?" Russ asked, concerned, but still very much in his cover. He was, ostensibly, a businessman from Ohio, and an Ohio businessman would be naturally bemused at being taken out of the immigration line by two men in civilian clothing.

"Just come along, and we'll straighten it out."

Whitlock walked along with his briefcase in his hand. Neither of the two men touched him, but they moved close enough to him to where it was clear they were ready if he decided to try something stupid.

Two uniformed policemen stood in the hallway with radios in their hands. One of the men asked for Whitlock's briefcase, and he handed it over. The five of them then continued farther up the hallway.

As they walked up the hallway it hit Whitlock like a battering ram.

Babbitt. He almost said it aloud. Lee Babbitt had done this. He'd flagged Whitlock's passport.

That son of a bitch. The rage inside him was so complete that his hands balled into fists, his jaw clenched, and he had to fight the urge to kill the four men around him. He thought about bashing all four men's heads in, taking a pistol from one of them, and shooting his way out of the airport.

But he just kept walking, kept affecting the mannerisms of a confused and offended business traveler.

They took him into a holding room, patted him down, and relieved him of his phone and wallet and other personal items. One man told him there was a small issue with his passport. The door clicked closed and he sat in a plastic chair at a little desk, and as angry as he was, he remained in character because a camera high in the corner watched his every move.

Court had spent most of the past half hour since leaving Ruth trying to get in touch with Russ Whitlock. For some reason the man who had been doing his best to communicate with Court for the past week had suddenly found something better to do than answer a phone call from him.

Court did not leave a message; instead he threw his phone back in his pack and began an SDR near the banks of the Øresund Strait. He was reasonably certain no one was on his tail, but he was less certain how he would be getting out of this town.

He'd decided against going back to the train station. For all he knew Ruth was still there, and for all he knew Mossad operatives had descended on her. He considered jumping on a bus, but he'd seen more police at the terminal than he felt like dealing with.

So he'd come here, to the marina. He was looking for a boat he could rent to take him across the strait into Denmark. Once he made it across the water, he'd have easy access to the European mainland via a bridge west of Copenhagen.

But so far he'd not found a boat with a crew. Everyone seemed to be either out on the water or at home, sheltered from the frigid air.

As he watched the marina from across the street, his phone buzzed in his backpack. He put in his wired earphones and kept walking, continuing on his SDR, while he answered. "Yeah?"

"It's Ruth."

"I didn't expect to hear from you so soon."

"I want to talk to you again. In person."

"Why?"

"Name a place. I'll be there. You can watch me to make sure I haven't been followed."

Court sighed. His first thought was to tell her thanks but no thanks, but he agreed to her request. She was clearly in a desperate situation, and any help he could give the Mossad right now could have the dual benefit to him of both getting them off his ass and getting them to target Whitlock.

———————

They met minutes later in a snow-covered park next to the town library. Court had his eyes peeled for threats, but the only people he saw were standing around a pickup hockey game a hundred yards away, along with a few kids walking home from school along the sidewalk by the road.

Ruth asked, "Did you talk to Whitlock?"

"He didn't answer."

"Shit. Will you keep trying?"

"Yes."

"I spoke with my boss," she said.

"And?"

"He doesn't believe a word you are saying."

"Figured as much. I can't help you with that." Court said, "I suggest you try to get the Iranians to cancel the contract publicly. You can tell them you know they are involved, scare them away with the threat of war if it is successful."

Ruth smiled at Court's naïveté. "We've done that already. We approached Iran directly and told them we know they contracted the Gray Man to kill Kalb. We told them their plan to kill our PM with no comebacks to them has failed, and we will bomb them into the Stone Age if a hair on his head is disturbed."

Court said the next line with a tone that made clear he was being sarcastic. "So, that's that, then."

"Not exactly. The Iranians gave us the song and dance we expected. They have no idea what we're talking about and this is a misinformation campaign by us that we plan to use to justify war."

"And?"

"And, we at Mossad have come to the conclusion that they will honor the contract. When Kalb is killed they will say they had nothing to do with it. They will blame us. They will blame the USA. The assassin, after all, is American. This is the perfect Zionist plot. It will be believed in 100 percent of the Middle East, 80 percent of Europe, and 50 percent of the U.S. Shit," Ruth said, "many in Israel will have suspicions about Mossad; it would not stretch the credulity of some on the left to think this was a Mossad operation to kill Kalb and set off a war to benefit the military-industrial complex or something ridiculous like that."

"You could still bomb them into the Stone Age," Court said.

"If they kill Kalb we will do just that, I'm sure. But that's not my focus. My focus is on making sure Kalb doesn't get killed."

Court said, "My focus is making sure *I* don't get killed. So I'll be off now." He offered his hand.

She did not reach for it. "I need you to stay in this. You and I are the only chance the PM has at survival."

"You told me you've been recalled to Tel Aviv."

"I'm not going to Tel Aviv. I'm going to Brussels. I want you to go with me. If we stop Whitlock, it will clear your name. That must have *some* value to you."

"Not much. I've been blamed for so much shit I

didn't do, getting one more dead guy pinned on me doesn't faze me in the least."

She shook her head. "I don't believe that for a second. You don't want Metsada after you if you can avoid it."

"Why would they come after me? You are going to tell them Whitlock killed your man, he killed Zarini, and he's targeting Kalb. You have to tell them this to get them to act against Whitlock before it's too late."

"I can pin Mike's death on you."

Court looked at her. "You'd do that?"

Ruth said, "I will if I have to. I need your help. I am prepared to do whatever I have to do to get it."

Court stared her down. Angry at her for using him, but not surprised. He said, "That was the stick. From my experience, normally there is a carrot thrown in, as well."

She nodded. "If you help us, I can pull out all the stops. You will earn the respect of my organization, and we will leverage this to influence CIA. Maybe we can have them—"

Gentry lunged at her. She recoiled with the rapid movement.

"Don't!" he shouted. "Don't say it! I don't want to hear how you can make all my problems go away if I just play ball. I've heard that bullshit for years by those who either were double-crossing me at the time or else turned their back on me later."

She held a hand up. "I'm sorry. You're right. I can't do a damn thing about your situation with CIA." She reached out, putting her hand on his shoulder now. "But, Court, from your file, I know you have spent the past five years making nothing but enemies. In the next twenty-four hours you could make yourself a valuable friend. You do this for Israel, and it *will* be noticed. It *will* be appreciated."

"What do you want me to do?"

"In my work as a targeting officer for Mossad, my action arm has always been Metsada. I find and fix, and they finish. I don't have them now."

"But you have me."

She smiled. "I hope so."

That was it, then. She had him, and she knew it. If there was any chance at all he could rid himself and the Israelis of Russell Whitlock, he had to try.

"All right. I'll help you."

"Thank you."

Court said, "The first thing we need to do is get out of here before your people come. You are going to have to do things my way. I need you to dump your phones or any other means Mossad has to track you."

"Right." She reached into her coat and took out her phone and disabled it, then reached into her purse and took out Mike Dillman's phone and took it apart as well. She said, "I'm usually the one hoping the person I'm tracking doesn't take countermeasures. First time I've been on the run myself."

"Takes some getting used to," Court acknowledged.

"What next?"

Court said, "We find a boat."

Court walked down the length of the dock at the marina, focusing his attention on a thirty-five-foot yacht that bobbed in its slip. Ruth lagged behind him, but she made no attempt to hide herself. The boat itself was no better or worse than any of the other hundred-plus watercraft here, but this particular vessel was the only one that had anyone visible topside, and it was obviously about to set sail, so Gentry made a beeline to it before he lost his chance.

He called out to the man on board. "Nice yacht. Do you speak English?"

"Yes." He smiled. "It's been up here for repairs, and I'm taking her back to Copenhagen."

"What's that, about an hour?"

"That's right. A little less."

Court said, "Are you the captain?"

The man climbed down the boarding ramp. "Yes. May I help you?" He showed no hint of suspicion in his words or actions.

"How would you like to make one thousand euros?"

That got his attention. He smiled, bemused. "To do *what*?"

"We need to go to Germany. Now. If you take me over the Baltic and drop us off, you can get this back to Copenhagen just a few hours late."

"I'm sorry, I'm not a water taxi."

"Two thousand euros."

He seemed to think about it a moment, then repeated himself. "I'm not a water taxi. Are you in some trouble?"

"Not at all," Court said, keeping a straight face. "My friend hates to fly, and we've got the money."

The captain wasn't buying it. "There's a Scandlines ferry that makes the crossing. It's twenty-five euros each. Not two thousand."

Court adopted an embarrassed posture. "I've been banned for life on the ferry. Got a little drunk after a stag party. You know how it is."

The man looked at Gentry a long time. He clearly did not know how it was. Still, he named his price to play along. "Three thousand."

"If I give you three thousand, you wouldn't be a water taxi. You would be a water limo." Court nodded. "We leave right now."

"You are welcome aboard," said the captain, and Court waved Ruth over.

FORTY-SEVEN

The door to Whitlock's holding cell opened, rousing him from his fantasies of killing Leland Babbitt. His watch had not been taken from him, so he glanced down and saw that it was just after six P.M.

He'd been stuck here for more than three hours.

A police officer led him up a hallway and into a small room that looked more or less identical to the one he'd just left, with one major exception. A man in a blue pinstripe suit sat at a little table with a manila folder in front of him and a briefcase at his feet.

Russ did not recognize the man but instantly sized him up as coming from the U.S. embassy.

Russ slumped down in front of him, making no attempt to hide his pissed-off look. He had no need to remain in character for this guy; he'd just be wasting both of their evenings. Instead he waited for the Belgian policeman to leave and close the door, and then he waited for the other man to speak.

"I'm with the embassy," he said, and he left it there.

No shit, Russ thought, but he did not say it. He just sat there, sullen, waiting for more.

The man in the pinstripe suit added, "You sure as hell pissed somebody off. You were traveling with a set of credos that should have been clean. But they were flagged stateside." The man chuckled. "Can't say I've ever seen Langley reel in one of their own like that."

Whitlock thought about breaking the man's windpipe with an open hand to the throat, but it would only make him feel better for a few minutes, and it would do nothing to improve his situation, so he fought the urge.

"Anyway, you also seem to have some powerful friends."

Russ sat up straighter in his chair now.

The embassy man reached across the table and handed Whitlock the manila folder. He poured out the contents and looked them over. It was a new passport, a Michigan driver's license, and several credit cards.

Russ cocked his head. "You aren't here to take me back?" He knew better than to say anything more, but still, the man held his hand up to stop him.

"I'm a delivery boy. That's all you need to know."

Russ nodded. "So am I free to go?"

The American from the embassy stood up. "You can pick up your belongings, minus your passport, at the window outside. The Belgians will have a form for you to sign, basically saying you were treated with kindness and respect. Sign it"—the man reached out and took the passport back, just for a quick look—"sign it *David Barnes*." He handed over the passport again. "Don't know who you are or what you're up to, but I'll just play my part." He smiled. "Have a pleasant vacation, Mr. Barnes."

Russ returned the smile and stood. He wasn't sure what had just happened, but he was damn glad to be back in business.

———————

Lee Babbitt had spent a frustrating morning in the signal room at Townsend House. When his assets in place in Stockholm missed their target, Beaumont and his men searched fruitlessly for a few hours, until a surprise call from Yanis Alvey in Tel Aviv revealed to Babbitt that Gentry was on a train to Copenhagen, and a plan had been put in place by Israeli Special Operations to take him down when he got there.

Lee had rushed his Jumper team to intercept the train during its stop in Malmö, but when they boarded they discovered that Gentry and the Israeli woman had apparently disembarked at an earlier station.

An hour later, Babbitt received a call from Ruth Ettinger herself. She told him about Gentry's claim that Dead Eye was planning to assassinate the Israeli prime minister on behalf of Iran. Babbitt did not know if this was true, but the fact that Gentry knew of Russ Whitlock at all was suspicious enough for Babbitt to have Parks find out if Whitlock had boarded the flight to the United States as agreed. When he checked all the cover credos available to Whitlock he learned he was, instead, on his way to Brussels.

This, needless to say, set off alarm bells at Townsend House.

Babbitt immediately ordered the passport flagged and Whitlock detained. He had enough to worry about with the hunt for Gentry to also have to stop one of his own employees from assassinating Ehud fucking Kalb.

As Babbitt conferred with one of his analysts, his secretary paged him over the PA and asked him to hurry back to his office. When he arrived, he found he had a call holding from Denny Carmichael.

Babbitt groaned, but he grabbed the phone and spoke in an upbeat manner. "Hi, Denny."

Carmichael was characteristically terse and to the point. "I just had Dead Eye released from custody at the airport in Brussels."

Babbitt had to control himself not to shout. "Why on earth did you do that?"

"Because Court Gentry is loose in the wind. Because the only way we can pick Gentry back up again is through Dead Eye. According to Yanis Alvey at Mossad, Gentry is traveling with Ruth Ettinger, and it appears they are pursuing Whitlock on their own."

"Denny, can't you see what's happening? Whitlock has been using us. He's planning on killing the prime minister of Israel! He's protected Gentry so he can be around to take the fall for the hit!"

"I know this, and I feel certain we can avoid that. I want you to find Dead Eye in Brussels, put surveillance on him, and watch him until Gentry turns up."

Babbitt could not believe what he was hearing. "You want to use the prime minister of Israel as bait?"

"No, I do not. I want to use a rogue, off-reservation, ex-agency asset as bait to catch an even worse rogue, off-reservation, ex-agency asset. You have sanction to eliminate Whitlock as well as Gentry, but your primary target remains Gentry. We don't lay a finger on Dead Eye until Gray Man is dead."

Babbitt leaned forward on his desk and ran his hand over his face. "*Christ*, Denny." Even for an operations veteran like Lee Babbitt, this was a deep and murky bit of intrigue.

Denny picked up on the reticence. "Settle down. Desperate measures for desperate times. We clean up both messes at once. Got it? We will wrap this up before the PM is in any danger."

"You keep saying *we*. Are you sending CIA assets?"

"Good lord, no! Of course not. This is too sensitive to directly involve the CIA."

Babbitt thought that was pretty rich, as it came from one of the heads of the CIA.

Carmichael added, "I want you to go personally to Brussels. Take every available direct action asset you have, get over there, and find Dead Eye. He'll lead you to Gentry."

"What about the Mossad?"

"I spoke with Menachem Aurbach, head of their op wing, and I convinced him that his woman, Ms. Ettinger, is wrong about Gentry. I explained to him that Russell Whitlock is, in fact, one of Gentry's aliases. They think their young officer, a woman who was deeply damaged by the Israeli debacle in Rome last year, simply went off the rails after the death of her man in Stockholm. She is being duped by Gentry, allowing herself to be so because of confirmation bias. Quite simply, she wants to believe she was right about him all along."

Babbitt replied, "What you are asking us to do . . . There are a lot of dangers brought on by the narrow time frame, the large size of the operation, the—"

Carmichael seemed ready for the pushback. "Lee. Your cost-plus billing will not be audited."

Babbitt's eyebrows rose. He was being offered a blank check.

Slowly, and with some internal reservations, he said, "We'll be on our way within the hour."

"Good. I thank you, and our nation thanks you."

"Denny. We will do the job. As quickly and cleanly as we possibly can. But I don't believe any more."

Carmichael's tone turned guarded. "Don't believe what?"

"I don't believe killing Court Gentry has anything to do with America."

After a long pause Carmichael said, "Just kill him. Kill him and Townsend Government Services will avoid the fate suffered by so many defense and intelligence contractors during this time of harsh budget cuts."

A threat, Lee thought, but did not say. *How fucking typical.* He pushed his anger aside and said, "All right, Denny. I'll saddle up my boys and head out. I'll call you from Brussels."

———

John Beaumont, the Townsend operator also known as Jumper Actual, had spread his team of eight operators all over the ferry docks at the port in Travemünde, Germany, waiting for the seven P.M. ferry to arrive from Denmark. He had no specific intelligence indicating Gentry would be on board, but he and his team had arrived on the five P.M. ferry, and they had searched the vessel from top to bottom and turned up nothing.

It had been a frustrating day for the Jumper team. They began the morning by striking out at the bus terminal, and then they caught the bad news from Washington a few hours later that their target had fled the city. Their rushed helo flight to Malmö had been a waste of time as well, as they'd boarded the train from Stockholm to Copenhagen only to find it, just like the bus terminal, to be a dry hole.

They'd remained in the station in Copenhagen for a few hours, climbing on and off as many passing trains as they could for quick and perfunctory searches, but someone had called the local cops, asking them to come find out what the hell the tough-looking American guys were up to, so the Townsend men then boarded an express train to Hamburg. The train rolled aboard a massive Scandlines ferry for the forty-five-minute crossing of the Baltic, and then it docked here in the small seaside town of Travemünde.

Travemünde was an extremely popular beach resort in the summer months, but now it was a gray, frozen still life, virtually deserted of people other than those heading north to Copenhagen or farther up into Scandinavia on the ferries, or those who worked the fishing boats at the marina or the restaurants along the promenade.

Beaumont had received a call from Babbitt an hour earlier stating that he and Parks and the Dagger team at

Townsend House were now on their way to Brussels. Jumper would link up with them when they arrived in the morning, but before heading south, Beaumont decided he'd set his men up for an in extremis operation here to watch those departing the next ferry coming in.

Upon arrival here in Travemünde he sent some men to rent a couple of vans, and after they returned, Carl and Lucas, the UAV team, set up a drone ground control station in the back of one of them. They launched a Sky Shark drone from the terminal parking lot and now it loitered over the area, monitoring the boats as they docked in the marina while waiting for the ferry's arrival.

As the ferry came into dock, Carl piloted the UAV to the south over the marina to check a yacht that he'd noticed moving toward a little slip. He zoomed in on two passengers leaving the boat and walking along the dock. Almost immediately a red square appeared around one of the distant moving figures, indicating a possible gait pattern match with the target.

Lucas lunged for the radio on the floor of the van. "Sensor operator to Jumper Actual. We've got a possible sighting, polling 55 percent. We're moving in to get visual now and will advise."

Beaumont was a half mile away, standing in a nearly full parking lot near the ferry dock. In his low southern drawl Beaumont replied, "The hell you talking about? The ferry hasn't even started offloading yet."

"He wasn't on the ferry. Two pax disembarked a yacht. One male, one female. They are now walking along the promenade north of your pos, over."

Beaumont immediately said, "I'm sending two on foot to check it out. Vector them in to the subjects."

"Roger that."

Beaumont radioed Jumpers Seven and Eight, who were just a few hundred yards south of the marina, and he sent them toward the promenade.

Court Gentry and Ruth Ettinger shivered in a freezing wind rolling in from the Baltic Sea as they walked along the Travemünde promenade. Court could imagine this path full of summer vacationers when the weather was some sixty degrees warmer, but now only a very few hearty souls were out. He asked a man struggling to stay on top of his bicycle in the snow for directions to the train station, and the man pointed up the road, explaining in German that the *Bahnhof* was less than a kilometer away.

Court and Ruth walked in silence, each alone with their thoughts, Ruth only now thinking about the repercussions she would face for going offline from Alvey, and Court thinking about Dead Eye and his revelation that Court had been selected for admittance to the CIA's Autonomous Asset Development Program for reasons other than his reflexes and intelligence.

Neither felt much like talking now.

As Gentry and the Israeli American woman trudged up a hill past a cluster of small fish restaurants and coffee shops, he noticed two men skulking up a darkened alleyway from the southern portion of the docks. A minute later he used the reflection in a hotel window to confirm that the men had fallen in behind him and Ruth, some forty or fifty yards back.

Court spoke softly. "Those your guys?"

"Who?"

"We've picked up a tail."

She knew better than to turn around to look. "Are you sure? I didn't see anyone."

"You follow people. I *get* followed. I'm kind of an expert on the subject. I need you to tell me if they are Mossad or not."

They kept walking. They could see the *Bahnhof* now, just ahead on their right.

"To do that I'm going to have to look back," Ruth said.

"No. Wait till we turn to go up the steps to the station and then glance to the right, but do it quickly and make it natural. They are forty yards back. If we speed up a little we can time the turn to catch the two guys in the streetlight we're under now."

"You've got this down to a science, don't you?"

"Stick with me," he quipped. "I'll teach you how the other half lives."

They picked up the pace and then turned at the entrance to the *Bahnhof*. Court did not look to his right, but Ruth glanced that way. She said nothing until they were well inside the station.

"Shit. They are Townsend men. Part of the direct action team that was in Stockholm. And I'm pretty sure they just made me."

There were no trains at the platform now, but a light crowd of people stood around in the cold waiting on the seven-ten to Hamburg. Court took Ruth by the hand and led her quickly through the passengers. She marveled at the way he slipped between people effortlessly, remained in low light, and kept his head down as he walked. He even made it look natural as he bypassed security cameras positioned above a kiosk in the center of the room.

They exited the building on the far side, then crossed the tracks away from the lights of the station, entering first a small copse of trees and then a residential neighborhood. They walked briskly down a lighted street and then cut through two backyards, exiting onto a small cul-de-sac.

Ruth had no idea where they were going, and she doubted Gentry did either, but she had read enough of the unredacted portions of his file to know this was a man who knew how to slip away from danger.

Although this was clearly a valuable skill for a man like Gentry to possess, she could not help but find it sad to imagine him spending his life skulking alone through strangers' backyards like a low-end cat burglar or picking his way through wooded areas in pitch-black darkness, trying to stay ahead of hunters on his tail, as if he were a fox being chased by hounds on his scent.

Ruth much preferred the role of hound herself.

"Okay," Court said as they left the cul-de-sac and began walking up a street lined with zero-lot homes. "I think we've lost them for now."

Something occurred to Ruth and she immediately looked up. "They have a drone." The sky was black and the streetlights made it hard to see anything above them.

Court looked up himself. "I don't see anything."

"You won't see it. It's small, and nearly silent."

"How small?"

"I'd say no bigger than a pizza box."

Court sighed frozen vapor. "Now I'm being chased by a pizza." He thought it over for a moment, then passed a house with a Volkswagen GTI in the driveway and, next to it, a small two-wheel trailer with a covered motorcycle lashed to it.

He stopped.

"What?" Ruth asked.

Court headed up the little drive, tore off the tarp, and unlashed the motorcycle. It was a Kymco Pulsar 125, a nice enough low-end bike.

In seconds he was wheeling it quietly down the residential street, with Ruth following along. He said, "If there is a drone, we can't hide from it. All we can do is put as much space as possible between ourselves and the men with the guns, so the drone can't lead them to us. Make sense?"

She was confused. "But you don't have a key for the bike."

Court dropped the kickstand and knelt in the street. "Oh, please." In the low light from the streetlamp above he felt along the ignition wires, following them to the engine, where they terminated in a plastic coupler. He popped off the coupler, exposing three loose wires, then twisted two of the three together and let the third hang free.

He reached up and started the bike's electronic ignition.

The entire process took less than thirty seconds.

Court climbed onto the bike and Ruth climbed on behind him. He looked back to see if she was ready, and he noticed long shadows moving in his direction. He focused up the street and saw the two men who had tailed them to the station. They were still fifty yards back, but now they were running in Court's direction.

"Hold on!" Court shouted, and he revved the engine. They fishtailed on the icy street as they took off.

FORTY-EIGHT

"Sensor operator to Jumper Actual. Subjects heading east on the Morreder Strasse."

"Vector me to them!" Jumper shouted. He sat in the front passenger seat of the lead van while Jumper Two drove. Behind them, Jumpers Five and Six sat in the back. The other van held the UAV team and Jumpers Three and Four, but it was well behind the chase now as it stopped to pick up Seven and Eight.

From the back of the rear van, Carl and Lucas kept the drone after the target two hundred feet above. With the visual coverage they were able to keep everyone informed on the target's movements.

"Right turn," Lucas called over the radio. He was able to see both the motorcycle and the lead van, just a kilometer behind its target.

"Roger that," said Beaumont. "Can the UAV keep up with the bike?"

"Negative. We can stay on him for a few miles, at most. We'll lose him after that."

"Keep up with him as long as you can," Beaumont ordered.

"Roger that. He just turned left on Wedenberg Strasse. You'll hit the intersection in sixty seconds."

"Where's he going?"

Lucas looked at his other laptop. On it, a moving map display showed him the area in wider relief. He said, "I think he's just running. As long as he keeps heading north, his options will diminish. He's going to get pinned in by the sea to the east, and the west is just farmland." He laughed in surprise into the mic as he looked over the map. "There's not much up there at all. I think he fucked up."

Court was starting to think he might have fucked up. He knew Townsend was in hot pursuit; he'd seen a white van racing out of Travemünde behind him a few minutes ago. He'd opted to head north, to race along the coast, but as he left the town he saw the terrain turn to open farmland, with no place to hide.

The Baltic Sea was on his right, and to his left he saw nothing but low fields and the occasional little village. He wasn't sure where he was going, and without even a handgun he had no prayer of fighting back. He was in escape-and-evade mode now, and this was complicated greatly by the possibility that a UAV was somewhere overhead tracking his every move.

Just then a small aircraft passed him low on the left heading south, its lights illuminating light snowfall in front of it as it ascended.

There was an airport just up ahead; he assumed it would be a tiny little landing strip, as the largest sizable town in the area, Lubeck, was well to the south of his location.

He tried to force the throttle open further to get a few more horsepower from the little bike.

———

Five minutes later he pulled hard to the left and raced up a gravel road, stopping the bike just outside the open gates of Sierksdorf Airport, a tiny grass runway field with a single hangar and a terminal building no larger than a fast-food restaurant. He and Ruth left the bike behind and began running through the snow in the dark toward the lights of the terminal.

"We're going to fly out of here?" she asked as they ran.

"Yep."

"You're a pilot?"

Court gave a little shrug before answering. "Sure."

"I read your file."

"Who the hell hasn't?"

She had no idea what that meant, but she didn't ask. Instead she said, "Your file didn't say you were a pilot."

"Maybe you got the abridged version."

She did not press further.

They bypassed the terminal and the lights illuminating the asphalt parking lot in front of it and headed past them, over to the hangar. The parking lot extended here, but there were no lights on in or around the hangar.

Three small single-engine planes were positioned tightly in the dark and unoccupied hangar. Court recognized them as two Cessna 152s and a Piper Cherokee.

"Can you hot-wire a plane?" Ruth asked.

Court poked his head into the Cessnas one at a time, and then he checked the Piper. "I don't have to. This one has keys." He pulled off his backpack and threw it inside.

It was a four-seater single-engine aircraft that looked like it had been kept up nicely and recently flown. He checked it for fuel and oil, and then they pushed it out of the hangar and into the pitch-black night, moving as slowly as possible because the nosewheel made a loud and somewhat distressing squeak when they tried to rush the process.

"When was the last time you flew one of these?" she asked as he walked around it, feeling the control surfaces because he could barely see anything.

"When you say 'one of these,' do you mean this model, or any airplane?"

"Just answer the question in a way that will make me feel better."

Court did not answer at first. Finally he said, "I've flown a plane before."

"Oh, God," Ruth muttered.

———

The first Jumper van drove slowly with its lights off as it passed through the gates of the airport and onto the airstrip; a straight and level snow-covered lane was cut out of the middle of a grassy and rocky field.

Beaumont turned to Jumper Two behind the wheel. "Park it in the middle of the runway so they can't steal a plane and take off. We'll approach the hangar on foot." He pressed his radio's call button. "Jumper Three, how far are you from the airport?"

"We're turning onto the gravel road right now. Say two minutes."

"Roger that. Close the gate behind you, then park behind us on the strip."

"Wilco."

Beaumont leapt from the van. From under his coat he pulled his Micro Uzi, and the two men who exited the rear of the vehicle did the same.

He looked back to Jumper Two. "If you see an aircraft trying to take off, bail out of the van and shoot it. We'll fan out and approach the hangar across the field, but we'll wait on the other van before we hit it."

———————

Court walked around the Cherokee in the dark, feeling the control surfaces because he could barely see them. After satisfying himself the airframe was in good condition, he climbed into the door on the right side of the plane and then moved over to the pilot's seat.

Ruth climbed in behind him. "How much longer?"

"I'll preflight for five minutes or so and then . . ."

"What?"

He saw a van rolling onto the runway in the distance;

in front of it, another van sat motionless. "On second thought, let's get the fuck out of here."

He turned over the engine. It coughed but started almost immediately.

Ruth saw the two vehicles in the darkness now. "They're blocking the runway! How are we going to—"

Court pushed the throttle forward, and the little plane began to surge forward.

"Where are you going?"

He rolled out of the darkness in front of the hangar and along the parking lot in front of the terminal. The runway was on his right, and across it he saw men running in his direction.

Court eased off the throttle, then looked back over his shoulder. He spun the plane around in a tight turn here at the edge of the parking lot and held down the toe brakes as hard as he could. He then pushed the throttle all the way forward to the firewall.

The engine roared and the aircraft's brakes strained against the power.

"What are you doing?"

"You probably don't want to know."

"You are going to take off on the taxiway?"

"This isn't really a taxiway. It's more like a parking lot."

They saw a flicker of gunfire from near the rear van, though they could not hear the shooting over the roar of the Cherokee's engine.

Ruth clenched every muscle in her body, realizing they had no choice but to try to get into the air.

The plastic window next to Ruth tore open as a burst

of submachine gun rounds ripped through it. She screamed in shock; Court grabbed her by her head and pulled her down sideways with his right hand, crumpling her over the flap lever between the seats, because the yoke between her knees precluded her from ducking forward.

He kept his left hand on his yoke, doing his best to ignore the gunfire that kicked up snow and sparks on the pavement in front of him.

Court released the brake and the tiny aircraft jolted forward. A hundred yards directly in front of them was the eight-foot fence at the far side of the hangar parking lot.

As they bounced forward into the darkness he said, "Stay down till we're in the air. As soon as we're up, I'm going to need to pull that flap lever under you."

"Aren't you supposed to extend the flaps for takeoff?"

"They cause drag. Right now we need speed."

"Don't they help with lift?"

Court conceded the point. "Yeah."

Ruth looked up to him. "We need lift, right?"

"We're going to drop on the other side of the fence. Hopefully I can level it out about five feet off the ground, extend the flaps, pick up speed, and get us the fuck out of here."

"Oh my God," she exclaimed.

"C'mon!" Court shouted at the plane, urging it to pick up speed.

Bullets raked the back of the plane's fuselage now.

Court glanced at his airspeed indicator, but only for a moment. It was irrelevant how fast he was going. He'd gun it as far as possible and then pull up. If he had the speed, they would fly; if he did not, they wouldn't be able to stop before slamming into the fence, and they would not get a second chance. "C'mon!" he shouted again.

More submachine gun rounds traced by both sides of the cockpit.

Court screamed, "Now! Sit up!"

He pulled back on the controls, nearly jerking them back into his lap. The plane lurched back, its nosewheel popped up, and Ruth screamed at the thumping noise this made. As the plane rose quickly, Court reached between the seats and pulled back on the flap lever, yanking it up toward his armpit with all his might.

The Cherokee leveled off directly above the fence and seemed to stall right there, not thirty feet above the ground. More tracer fire shot by, arcing into the night. Court shoved the controls to the firewall and the nose tipped forward; Ruth screamed as the seat belt pulled against her body tightly and, like a roller coaster, they dropped down toward the snow-covered field.

Court tried to level the nose, desperate to return the quickly accelerating plane back to level flight before they augured into the snowy field. "Go! Go! Go!"

Even over the whine of the engine Court heard frantic automatic weapons fire below him on his left.

Ruth's stomach had felt like it was in her throat, but now it seemed to shove down into her bowels, and she waited for the inevitable crash.

As the wings reached an altitude of less than fifteen feet, the ground effect began aiding him in his task; the dropping plane started to fly, and Court pulled the yoke back, tensing his body for impact but praying he could keep the plane in the air.

They leveled off when the wheels were less than three feet from the ground. The propeller kicked fresh snow-fall around the Cherokee in a violent swirl; Court struggled to see and to keep his wings level while another nine-millimeter round popped the fuselage behind Gentry and more rounds streaked by the windscreen.

But they were flying now, they hadn't slammed into the terrain, and now Court knew he just had to get the fuck out of the kill zone as fast as possible.

The little plane shot over the gravel road at a height of ten feet; Court banked to the west and climbed, flying at one hundred knots now and accelerating. He pulled a sweat-covered hand off the yoke and flipped on all the cabin lights, scanning the instruments to check for any obvious damage from the gunfire.

While doing this he said, "Are you hit?"

Ruth replied slowly, "I don't think so. No."

"You're sure?"

"I'm sure," she said in a laugh as relief washed over her. She looked around her; out the broken window to her right the Baltic Sea was a vast blackness with only a few pinpricks of light. Ships in the distance.

They banked to port as they climbed, and as they did this Court finished his scan of all the dials in the cockpit, finding no evidence that the little plane had taken hits to its fuel lines or other critical points.

"Are we okay?" she asked him.

"Seem to be."

"Where are we going, exactly?" she asked.

"I don't know," he admitted as they climbed and banked. "Let me think a minute."

———

John Beaumont spit in the snow in front of him. He'd emptied his Uzi at the departing aircraft, but the little nine-millimeter submachine gun was hardly a suitable surface-to-air weapon.

His men converged on him quickly in the parking lot, and the vans raced forward from the runway to pick the men up.

"Where do you think he's heading?" It was Jumper Five asking.

"Haven't you read that motherfucker's file? Look at a map. He's going to Hamburg. We need ourselves a helo."

"Why is he going to Hamburg?"

"It's close and it's congested and he can hop a train or a bus there. He can't fly all the way to Brussels. He's going to have to land it within a half hour or he'll have the entire Luftwaffe tailing him."

Beaumont nodded to himself. "We'll kill his ass in Hamburg."

FORTY-NINE

Court and Ruth flew south over the German state of Schleswig-Holstein, keeping their altitude below one thousand feet and ignoring the radio, but eyeing the sky in front of them, nervously scanning for any aircraft in their way.

Ruth had taped over the bullet holes in the window with a roll of duct tape she found in the cabin, but she had not spoken since shortly after takeoff. The terror of the last few minutes had taken a toll. In all her ops in the Mossad Collections Department she'd never herself been this close to danger, from both the armed men on her tail and the unconventional aviation tactics of her pilot.

The events also caused her to second-guess her decision to push forward and hunt Whitlock without backing from Tel Aviv. Lashing her wagon to a wanted man like Gentry and pursuing a dangerous individual like Whitlock, all without support from the Mossad, had been an impulsive decision, perhaps brought on by her need to rectify a situation that seemed to be spiraling out of control as long as she was playing by the rules.

She shook herself back into the here and now and steeled herself to see this through. She was convinced the prime minister would not survive if she stayed within the lines drawn by her organization.

"Have you figured out where we are going?" As she asked the question she realized how helpless she was in this situation. As a predator, she was in her element, but as prey, she was leaving everything up to Gentry, the expert.

"Hamburg," he said confidently, "or at least most of the way there."

"Why?"

"Right now I'm only certain of one thing. I'm going to need a gun in Brussels."

"And you can get one in Hamburg?"

"Used to be able to. Hope I still can."

"How soon till they come after us?"

"Townsend? Shit, they'll probably beat us there. Nothing we can do about it. They can get a helo and fly right into the city. We'll have to take a less efficient approach."

Court added, "But Townsend isn't our problem right now. It's the Germans. They will get air after us quickly, probably police choppers, which we can outrun, but the German Luftwaffe will scramble something before long. I want us to be on the ground long before there is a major response."

" 'On the ground' sounds a little vague."

"We're going to have to land on a stretch of road or a

field somewhere. It would be nice to find something with lights. This part of Germany is flat, so we don't have to worry about the terrain too much, as long as I can see it."

"Please stop making it so obvious you are an inexperienced pilot."

Court laughed at that but then quickly refocused. He said, "We'll split up in Hamburg. You'll go directly to Brussels. I'll acquire a weapon and meet you there by morning. When I get there I'll contact Dead Eye and see if I can pinpoint his location."

"Dead Eye?"

"Yeah. That's Whitlock's agency code name."

"Will you really come to Brussels?"

He nodded. "I'll come."

Ruth stared at him, his impassive face glowing red from the cabin lights. She asked, "Why are you doing this?"

"Have you forgotten? You said you would frame me if I didn't."

She shook her head. "I know I threatened to sic Metsada on you, but I don't believe that is the only reason. You could run from this and disappear. Like you always do."

Court hesitated, glanced at her. She was surprised to see a sudden vulnerability in his regular stoic expression. "Yesterday Dead Eye said some things. Things about where he and I came from. Things I hope aren't true, but things, I suspect, are true."

"What things?"

The drone of the Cherokee's engine filled the cabin with a low persistent hum.

"I guess in the back of my mind I always knew I was damaged goods."

"What does that mean?"

"Never mind. I need to see this thing with Whitlock and Kalb all the way to the end to prove to myself he was wrong about me. There's right and there's wrong. Sometimes I teeter on the edge, like I could fall off in either direction. So I fight it. I fight against falling off on the wrong side, by doing right whenever I can. It doesn't make me pure. It just . . . it's just better than the alternative."

Ruth said, "What you do. What they made you. This does not have to be what you are."

Court smiled a little. "That sounds all well and good, but the truth is, you don't want me to stop. You want me to go after Russ Whitlock, and you want me to kill him."

She sighed wearily. "I do. I am using you just like they used you." She looked out the window. "I guess I'm no better."

Court said, "Why don't we worry about the next twenty-four hours for now, and then deal with whatever comes after, after?"

"Deal."

They landed fifteen minutes later on a road in the middle of a lighted golf course near the village of Jersbek. Court and Ruth pushed the airplane off the road and down into a gully and began walking through the little town. By ten P.M. they were on a bus that would take them into the huge metropolis of Hamburg.

A black Sikorsky S-92 helicopter raced two hundred feet above the Elbe River, its four rotors beating the icy air for both lift and velocity.

The aircraft had been cleared to overfly the Hamburg industrial districts of Hafen City and Kleiner Gasbrook at low altitude; below the helo's belly were several square miles of fat warehouses and spindly train tracks, open container lots butted up against a webbed network of harbor channels where massive cargo ships occupied seemingly every nook and cranny of the narrow waterways.

The pilot ignored the landscape below and concentrated on flying just above tall Portainer cranes loading and unloading the freighters, and he kept his eyes on the city lights on the north side of the harbor. He'd reported to air traffic control that he did not yet have a destination determined, but he presumed he would be heading somewhere near the *Hauptbahnhof,* the main train station.

Inside the Sikorsky, fifteen Israelis sat bathed in green interior cabin lights. Most of them were male and although they wore civilian attire, the XM35 rifles hanging from slings outside their coats gave away the fact that they were no regular members of the population.

They were Metsada, Mossad Special Operations.

For now there was nothing for the assault team to do but enjoy the ride. They sat alone with their thoughts; some looked out the window at the lights of the city below, and others fiddled idly with their gear.

In the rear of the cabin two female targeting officers sat together looking over a laptop, reading data from Mossad case officers already in the city and coordinating data flows with computer hackers back in Tel Aviv who had broken into Hamburg's network of municipal traffic cameras. So far they were having no luck identifying their target, but the operation was only a few minutes old.

And next to the two women was one additional male. Yanis Alvey was the oldest on board, at fifty, but he'd spent decades serving as one of the men with a rifle around his neck and a mandate to kill Israel's enemies. Now he was management, not labor, a liaison between the Collections Department and Special Operations, a job that gave him command authority over the targeters and command-and-execute authority over the spec ops boys.

Alvey carried a weapon himself, a CZ pistol in a shoulder holster under his coat, but at this stage of his career it was really more of an affectation. He was no longer a triggerman, but carrying the semiauto served to remind both himself and his team that he would always remain an operator at heart. He also wore a simple Kevlar vest under his shirt, same as his Metsada men, although Alvey's days of shooting and scooting through dangerous environs were well past him.

One of the female targeters had been in comms with an informant in the local police. She nodded into her phone and turned to Alvey.

"The plane was found alongside a golf course just northeast of the city. Shall I tell the pilot to proceed there?"

"Negative," Alvey said. "They will be long gone from the aircraft by now. We'll stay aloft over the city till we get a hit on the traffic cameras or a police report."

Yanis Alvey had begun to accept the troubling fact that Ruth Ettinger was now working with the Gray Man. He had begun to suspect it after she reported in to him this afternoon from Helsingborg. She fully believed in Gentry's innocence, and Ruth wasn't one to follow the official line if it diverged from her beliefs, but still it was a shock to Alvey that she had become so irrational after Dillman's death.

Her collaboration with Gentry had been made clear to him when Babbitt called him an hour earlier and reported them fleeing Travemünde together. Yanis caught himself wishing, for everyone's sake, that there was some evidence that Gentry was holding Ettinger against her will, but that was just fantasy. This was no kidnapping; on the contrary, as well as Yanis knew Ruth, he halfway suspected she would be leading Gentry around by the nose at this stage of the game.

He blamed himself for not forcing her away from fieldwork after Rome.

Now Tel Aviv was ordering Yanis to kill Gentry and to bring Ruth back. They wanted Gentry dead because they bought the CIA's assertion that Gentry was in play and about to assassinate Ehud Kalb. The reasons for bringing Ruth home had nothing to do with altruism. The graybeards at Mossad were concerned about word spreading that a decorated Mossad officer was working with the Gray Man to conspire in the assassination of the prime minister.

That just would not do.

It was insanity, of course, and Alvey knew it, but he'd been unable to persuade his superiors that their officer in the field had not gone completely off the rails. He had, of course, conveyed Ruth's warnings about Whitlock to Tel Aviv, but Tel Aviv was in bed with Langley on this, and Langley had a quick counter to every one of Ruth's allegations. The Mossad believed the CIA, not their officer in the field, and this put Alvey here, now, over Hamburg with a mandate to kill the Gray Man.

This directive was his actual primary mission, but it was not his greatest personal concern. Even though Tel Aviv did not care about Ruth, Yanis did, and he would do everything he could to extract her from the danger of this situation with all the resources at his disposal.

He knew her career was over now, but tonight he would do everything in his power to save her life. He doubted the Townsend men would check their fire if they had Gentry in view, and Ruth Ettinger could well become collateral damage.

He had to find Gentry before Townsend did. Alvey saw himself as Ruth's only chance.

———————

Court and Ruth climbed out of the bus at the Hamburger Strasse *U-bahn* station and immediately descended into the underground tunnels toward the trains. From here Ruth would head to the *Hauptbahnhof* and catch a train to Brussels, and Court would descend deeper into Hamburg's dirty underbelly to go hunting for a weapon.

They shook hands, told each other they would meet again in a few hours, and then separated in the busy subway station.

Minutes later Ruth walked through the *Hauptbahnhof* with her head low and covered by a hood. She climbed aboard a train to Paris via Brussels. She bought a couchette in a sleeper car, and as soon as they left the station she crawled into her couchette and lay on her back, and she fell asleep within minutes, haunted with dreams of what lay ahead in Brussels.

———————————

The Mossad Sikorsky S-92 had been circling the city of Hamburg for nearly half an hour, trying to get some actionable intelligence as to the location of Gentry. Yanis Alvey left much of the communications with local assets up to his targeting officers, while he looked out the window and thought of Ruth.

He snapped out of his repose when he felt the helicopter climbing. He put on a headset and switched to the cockpit channel on the intercom. "Pilot, why are we ascending?"

"We've been ordered to flight level two thousand by air traffic control. There is another helicopter circling the city, and they have been given the lower clearance."

Alvey looked out the window on his right, then crossed the cabin to look out the left. There, a thousand feet below and a mile to the west of where the S-92 now circled, a blue Eurocopter EC175 moved in a wide arc over the St. Pauli district.

"Pilot, can you hear the transmissions of the other helo?"

"Yes, sir."

"Who are they? What are they doing?"

"They are American; they say they are a film crew and will be doing some low-level work for the next hour."

Alvey turned to the two female targeters sitting with him. In a grave tone he said, "Townsend is here."

Quickly he dialed a number stored in his satellite

phone. In moments it was answered on the other end, but the reception was poor and crackling.

"This is Babbitt."

"Mr. Babbitt, Yanis Alvey here."

"How can I help you, Mr. Alvey?"

"You have an operation over central Hamburg."

"I am not at liberty to—"

"That wasn't a question, Mr. Babbitt. I want you to know that we are here, as well. I have a team of direct action assets and, as far as we are concerned, *you* are encroaching on *our* AO."

Babbitt replied, "My boys have the situation in hand, Alvey. You need to stand back and let them do their jobs."

Alvey said, "I want to remind you that we have a valuable and irreplaceable officer who may very well be in close proximity to your target."

Babbitt chuckled. "A nice way of saying your woman has been flipped by a mass murderer and now they are working together."

"She may be wrong about Gentry, I do not know. But I doubt very much she is wrong about Townsend Government Services. It was her assessment that your outfit is an unscrupulous band of out-of-control cutthroats."

Babbitt did not seem offended by the remark. He just replied calmly, "Do I need to remind you we have the full backing and sanction of the Central Intelligence Agency?"

"No, you don't need to remind me of that." The line was quiet for a moment as the ambiguity as to what Alvey meant by the statement hung in the air.

Babbitt said, "We don't want Ettinger. We want Gentry.

Right now we have technical surveillance over several known associates of his in the city. It is just a matter of time before we find him. If Ettinger is with him, we will use our utmost care to keep her safe." He paused. "Our two organizations should be able to avoid one another on this operation."

Yanis Alvey said, "If Ruth is hurt I will hold you personally responsible."

"Mr. Alvey, I am on an aircraft over the Atlantic right now. You have more control over that situation than I do. Keep your people away from my people, and you can avoid a disaster." He paused a beat. "Like the one you suffered in Rome last year."

Alvey disconnected the call and looked back out the window.

FIFTY

A few hundred yards east of the Hamburg *Hauptbahnhof* in the district of St. George, Court Gentry walked alone through darkness, shifting to stay out of the glow of streetlights and shop windows as he did so. He passed a phalanx of hookers on a street corner, working outside even on this evening with temperatures in the low twenties, and he negotiated his way around drug dealers who stood like traffic cones in his path trying to get him to buy hash or pills or needles filled with heroin.

Court had worked in Hamburg a few years earlier on a solo op. At the time his handler, Sir Donald Fitzroy, had equipped him with a long-range rifle to assassinate a wealthy Serbian businessman working here who, in a past life, had been a war criminal in Bosnia. But when the weather forecast changed for the date of the hit, Court realized the conditions would be too foggy to see his target through a scope at five hundred yards. So he changed his operation midstream and decided to do the job up close and personal, and to do this he needed a handgun. He spent two full days in the seedy bars and back alleys of Hamburg's St. George district, knowing the area to be rife with foreign gangs with access to weapons.

He finally made a connection with a middle-aged Turk named Ozgur who sold him a Walther P99 handgun. It was an excellent weapon, exactly what he needed for the op, and it came in handy when he killed the Serb with a bullet through the back of the head in the portico of his luxury condo.

Now Court hoped like hell Ozgur was still around and ready to make a quick and easy few thousand euros before bedtime.

He found the decrepit building and walked past the elevators to a poorly lit stairwell in the back that smelled like someone regularly used it as a latrine. He climbed up the metal staircase to the fifth floor of the seven-story building, and then made his way down a long narrow hallway.

When he had been here a few years earlier, Ozgur had kept a lookout in the hallway, just a Turkish boy with a cell phone, but now the hall was empty other than bags of trash and cheap bicycles.

Court found the apartment and knocked on the door.

He heard shuffling inside, and he expected a long battery of suspicious questioning through the door.

But instead it opened quickly.

Ozgur stood there in a white tank top; he held a baby in his arm and a phone to his ear. His eyes widened a little when he saw Court, and then he said something in Turkish into the phone that did not sound alarmed or threatened.

Court imagined it was something along the lines of *I'll call you back.*

"Guten Abend," he said after he hung up the phone. He bounced the baby on his forearm, a little boy with a shock of black hair, and Court immediately realized that the child's eyes were much more curious about Court than were Ozgur's.

"Do you remember me?" Court asked in German.

"Aber sicher. Was wollen Sie?" *Of course. What do you want?*

"If you remember me, then you *know* what I want."

A woman appeared behind Ozgur. She was obviously not Turkish; her hair was dirty blond and her eyes were blue. Court took her as a Pole, as Polish immigrants were common in Germany. Ozgur handed the baby off to the woman; she took the boy and gave Court an unwelcoming look.

Ozgur stepped outside into the hall and shut the door behind him.

He switched to English. "A gun? Are you serious? I don't deal in weapons anymore."

Court wasn't in the mood to be jacked around by someone trying to make a few extra euros by hyping up the scarcity of his product.

"I've got money, Ozgur. What I don't have is time. Name your price, but do it now."

"It's not a game, man. I don't have no gun. I sell you something else, maybe? A cell phone?"

"Look. I've come a long way, and I've had a rough day. I know you are the man around here who can get me what I need."

Far off in the distance Court registered the thumping beat of a helicopter, but it did not seem out of the ordinary in the center of Germany's second-largest city.

———

One of the Metsada operators called Yanis Alvey over to his seat on the port side of the Sikorsky and pointed out the window next to him.

In the distance Alvey watched the Townsend Eurocopter descend to just above the train tracks a quarter mile from the *Hauptbahnhof.*

"Somebody get me some binos!"

A pair of binoculars was put in his hands seconds later. He looked through them in time to see two men fast-roping from the chopper down to the tracks, twenty feet below. Soon they were running up an embankment, and seconds later they disappeared into the tight streets of the St. George neighborhood.

The Eurocopter climbed back up into the sky, then headed over St. George and began circling around an apartment building.

Alvey watched through the binos and spoke into his microphone. "They're going to fast-rope onto a building over there. Those first two were a ground-floor blocking force." He looked at the men around him. "They've found Gentry." He hurried up to the cockpit. "Pilot? How close can you get to that neighborhood without alerting that helo?"

The pilot immediately began descending and closing on the area. "Several blocks to the north there is a park by the Kennedy bridge over Lake Aussenalster. I can come in low over the water when he banks to the south. I'll land right next to the bridge, and you can all go on foot."

"Do it. We're all going to disembark, but I'm going on alone."

"What are you doing?" One of the targeting officers was listening in on the transmission from the rear of the cabin.

"I can't risk having a dozen men enter that building without knowing what the hell is going on. Especially with the Townsend gunmen hitting it at the same time. I'll go in alone, stay low profile and assess the situation. I'll call in the team once I have Ettinger."

After another minute of prodding, Court still had gotten nowhere with Ozgur, but he wasn't ready to give up. "If you direct me to someone who can get me what I need, I'll happily pay you a finder's fee."

Ozgur said, "You don't listen, man. I'm out of that. I went to prison, got out, and just want to live a normal life. Not have to deal with crazy bastards like you showing up at my door, scaring my kid and my wife. I want no part in you anymore. Just leave—"

The Turk stopped talking and looked up. The thumping of the helicopter outside the building increased.

Court could tell it was hovering just above the roof. "Is that normal?" he asked.

Ozgur looked back at the man in the dark hallway. "You see? You just bring trouble! I don't want no trouble!"

Court grabbed Ozgur by the collar of his shirt and shoved him up against the wall. "I need a *fucking* gun!"

"I don't have no gun! None! Zero! Let go of me and get out of here, you crazy American fuck!"

Gentry slammed the Turk once more against the wall in frustration, turned, and sprinted toward the stairwell.

―――――――

The Sikorsky landed next to light eleven P.M. bridge traffic, and the twelve-man team climbed off, along with Yanis Alvey. The Metsada operators wore their handguns only, as their rifles would not go unnoticed in the thick urban neighborhood. As the helo turned and skimmed the water of the lake, departing to the north, Alvey instructed the younger men to disperse themselves quietly throughout the St. George neighborhood around the target building, and to keep comms open between themselves. Alvey had his mobile phone and would contact the Metsada assault team leaders if he had a target for them.

―――――――

Gentry made it down two flights of stairs before he heard a noise far below him at the ground floor. Men had entered the stairwell; he thought he heard at least two, but he could not be certain, because above him now he heard more men, coming into the stairwell from the seventh floor.

Court left the stairs on the third floor, opening the

door to find the space totally involved with construction. It was dark, a warren of half-formed rooms and open ceilings exposing metal girders and insulation. Building material and equipment were positioned all around.

The door behind him shut with a loud click.

Court stopped and looked around. There were good places to hide, but Court knew time was against him. He had to get out of the building before his opposition had a chance to seal off the exits and begin a comprehensive search.

He moved forward, into the dark, wishing like hell he had a fucking gun.

———————

Yanis Alvey headed south through St. George. For the first minute or two he received a few open stares from passersby and shopkeepers who'd seen him climb out of a huge helicopter, a novel enough occurrence around here, but soon he was blocks away and he'd melted into the foot traffic in the seedy district. Drug dealers openly offered to sell him their wares, prostitutes bundled against the cold stood in stoops and called out to him as he passed, and Middle Eastern thugs eyed him as a potential mugging victim as he made his way confidently and unafraid, causing them to look elsewhere for easy prey.

His thoughts were focused on Ruth Ettinger. He had no idea if she was here or not, but he was operating under that assumption. Clearly Townsend suspected Gentry was here, and Yanis worried that Ruth would not extricate herself safely from an altercation between a crew of gunmen and the most infamous freelance assassin on the planet. He was not sure he would be able to rectify the situation with merely his presence, but coming alone had been an easy decision for him.

He was certain he did not want to add one more ingredient to the dangerous concoction by calling in a dozen more gunmen just yet.

Jumpers Seven and Eight had been set as a blocking force on the ground floor of the building, and originally they had planned to stay in the lobby, but the noise of the door clicking shut came from the stairwell near the lobby, and this sent them in search of their target. After peering into the first-and second-floor hallways and finding them to be quiet, they entered the third floor of the apartment building and found it to be an unlit construction area.

"Jumper Seven to Jumper Actual."

"Go."

"We're going to clear the third floor. It's open construction. No locked doors. We'll keep the stairwell under observation."

"Roger that. Seventh floor is clear and the helo is watching street level. I'll send two more your way via the southeast stairwell."

Seven turned back to Eight and whispered, "I don't think he had time to get too deep back there. Cover me from here, but keep a lookout on the stairs in case he's not here."

Eight nodded, and Seven shined his light on the end of his pistol and began searching the area.

He saw a complicated framework of metal beams, plumbing pipes, and heating ducts. The entire floor was a large skeleton, free of wallboard and full of dark recesses. He sniffed the air for a hint of another human's presence, but his nostrils only filled with the scent of plaster and dust. He moved slowly in a firing stance, listening closely for noise, but heard nothing but the sound of his own heart.

Eight called over the interteam radio. "I can't see you. Come on back and wait for the rest of the team."

Seven did not reply; he just moved deeper into the darkness. He stepped quickly around a pallet of building materials, shining his light on the empty space behind. *Where the fuck is he?* He jacked his pistol away from the floor and back up the hallway. He took one more step forward and concentrated his attention on the far reaches of his light, an unfinished flat at the end of the hall.

With neither sound nor warning a black form swept in front of his face. Close, not two feet from the tip of his nose. His pupils all but spun to change focus from lighted distance to darkened closeness, but before he could identify what had fallen from the ceiling he felt an impact on his hands. He lost his grip on the pistol as something slammed against his wrists. The dark figure had swept through the air from above, swinging from his left to his right. The pistol flew across the room and out of sight, the tactical light going dark as his forefinger came off the pressure switch.

The dark movement whipped back in front of his eyes again, this time from right to left. He heard a *whoosh* and felt another impact, just a soft tugging below his chin.

He lurched back, away from the moving shadow, and reached up to put his hand to his throat.

Jumper Seven felt the spray of his own blood before his fingertips were within a foot of his neck. The figure appeared again, and he saw it was a man, hanging upside down by the knees from a crossbeam. He righted himself nimbly and silently, and he dropped to the ground.

Seven wanted to call out to Eight behind him, but he could not make a sound. He took one more step back, away from the target, but slipped in his blood and fell on his back. Then the target disappeared in the dark. Seven looked to the ceiling and tried to understand what was happening to him; soon he realized he had not taken a breath in several seconds, tried to, and choked on a mouthful of blood.

His brain did not want to accept the fact that the Gray Man had just slit his throat and walked away.

————————

After five minutes walking through the darkened streets, Yanis Alvey made his way to the downstairs entrance to the Bremer Haus Apartments. He found the door open, and it led into a dark and dirty ground-floor lobby that smelled like rotten food. To Alvey the feel of the place was more Tunisian ghetto than German, and he suspected the majority of the inhabitants of the building were indeed Middle Eastern or North African. For a Jew, especially a Jew who worked for Mossad, it was not a terribly inviting atmosphere.

He bypassed the bank of dodgy-looking elevators and found a stairwell on the southeastern corner of the building. Once inside, he looked up. Each landing had a small bare bulb high on the wall above it, but the stairs themselves were unlit. The stairs were also metal, so Alvey slipped off his shoes and carried them in his hands so as not to make noise as he began ascending. He kept his pistol in his shoulder holster, as he knew there was a good chance he would run into Townsend men or civilians, and he needed to remain low profile.

"Jumper Eight to Jumper Seven? How copy?"

Eight stood in the stairwell with his boot propping open the door and his tactical light under the barrel of his gun illuminating the area in front of him.

He took his support hand off his pistol to switch his radio to broadcast to all elements, but as he looked down to find the right channel he heard a noise directly ahead. He looked up just in time to see a figure appear from the dark just to the right of his flashlight's beam. He jerked his weapon toward the threat but staggered back, dropped his gun to the metal landing, and brought his hands to his neck.

A knife had embedded in his throat. He tried to scream, but quickly his scream was squelched by a hand over his mouth.

The Gray Man held the man down and he drew the knife from him, and then buried the blade once again in the side of Jumper Eight's neck, silencing him completely and permanently.

Court hefted the man's SIG Sauer pistol from the metal landing, slipped it into his waistband, and then dragged the body back into the construction area, hiding it perfunctorily. He returned to the stairwell and listened for any noise. He heard a door open high above him, and men began descending; he kicked off his boots quickly, picked them up, and began running down the stairs as fast as he could, certain all remaining threats were above him.

———

Alvey climbed up the stairs in his stocking feet, ascending slowly, listening for any sound of activity on the floors as he passed them.

The lightbulb above the second-floor stairwell exit was burned out and the landing was dark. Alvey paused at the door, listened to it, and decided there was no team of Townsend men running around in the hallway on the other side.

He turned away and began climbing again, but a man spun around the landing between floors two and three, taking the stairs down three at a time, and the two men collided violently in the low light.

Both men slammed into the wall of the stairwell and tumbled down half a flight of stairs before crashing down on the second-floor landing.

———

Court landed on his side and rolled onto his back. As he did so he scanned the hands of the man in the dark with him, trying to determine in a fraction of a second whether he was a threat or just some poor schlub on his way up the stairs after a long day at work. He saw empty hands, which relieved him, but as soon as the other man pushed himself back up to a seated position across from him, Court saw his right hand move under his jacket.

Court checked the man's eyes; they were locked on his own and widening with excitement.

Court's right hand instinctively shot to his waist.

"No!" he shouted, but he saw the matte black butt of a pistol coming from under the jacket. Court drew the gun he'd just taken from the dead Townsend man from his waistband and angled the barrel up toward the threat, taking no time to raise the weapon to eye level or extend it toward his target.

The man in the suit swung his black pistol out toward Court as he himself began to shout.

Court fired twice from the hip, no hesitation between shots, and a pair of quick crashing reports echoed in the stairwell. Both nine-millimeter rounds hit their target, and the other man slammed against the wall and dropped to his back on the landing.

Court kept his gun on his target while he rose to his feet. He crossed the landing, kicked the pistol away from the wounded man's outstretched hand, and then trained his weapon high up the stairs, searching for any other threats.

The men who had been in the stairwell above him had apparently left the stairwell to check another floor.

Court holstered the SIG Sauer pistol, pulled a flashlight from his pack, and shined it on the man.

"You don't look like Townsend. *Christ.* You're Mossad, aren't you?"

The man just blinked; he did not answer.

Court knelt down and opened the man's coat and then ripped open his shirt and found a Kevlar vest. One of the rounds had hit him in the chest, and the vest caught it perfectly.

The second round struck below the ballistic protection, however, in the lower abdomen. Blood flowed with the rising and falling of the wounded man's breath.

Court shined his light on the man's face and asked again, "Mossad?"

This time the man nodded. His face was covered with sweat, his skin tone was ashen, and his pupils were unfixed.

"Oh shit," Court said softly.

He pulled on the wounded man's down coat and the man fought weakly, not sure what was happening. Court got it off in seconds, however, and he wrapped it into a tight ball and pushed it into the wound. He placed the man's hands over the ersatz bandaging. "Press down. I'm going to check your back for an exit wound."

Court rolled him on his side; the wounded man groaned in agony. Court felt around at his low back at first, then expanded his search, feeling the shirt for any sign of blood or torn fabric.

"Okay, no exit," Court said. "If your men get you into surgery fast, they just might be able to save your life. If they spend the rest of the night chasing me around"—Court shrugged—"then you're pretty much fucked."

Court stood back up. The ashen-faced Israeli just stared up at him.

Court saw the astonishment in his face.

This was the remorseless assassin known as the Gray Man?

Court heard shouting coming from the third floor now. Obviously the Townsend men had found their dead colleagues. Court drew his gun again and held it at his side. He looked back down to the injured man and said softly, "You should have listened to Ruth. You are making a mistake. You are chasing the wrong man." He shrugged. "If it were me, I wouldn't want to die in the middle of a mistake like that."

Without another word he picked up his boots from the landing, then turned and descended the staircase, his pistol in front of him scanning for threats.

Yanis Alvey kept the pressure on his stomach up with one hand while reaching into his pants pocket with the other. He pulled out his phone, pushed a button with a bloody thumb, and brought it to his ear.

Weakly he said, "It's Alvey. I'm hit. I'm in the stairwell." He took a slow breath. "Approach with caution."

He dropped his phone so he could use both hands now to keep the rest of his blood inside him.

FIFTY-ONE

Russ Whitlock spent the night at an abandoned Townsend safe house in an old apartment building on Rue Kelle in the southern Brussels neighborhood of Saint Pieter Woluwe. Townsend had leases on dozens of locations in the area, and he knew they would not be able to check them all in the short time he would be here, so he was unconcerned about the potential for compromise. He awoke early, ate breakfast at a nearby patisserie, and then returned to his flat to redress his wounded hip.

He stood in front of the bathroom mirror and winced as he took off yesterday's bandages. They were yellow with pus and black with blood; his injury had become infected and swollen from a week of lackadaisical treatment and constant travel and movement. As he cleaned and bandaged it again, he told himself that after today he could take as much time as he needed to take it easy and let it heal.

He returned to his bedroom and pulled a black trunk out of the closet, laid it on the floor, and opened it.

Inside was an Accuracy International L115A3 rifle in caliber .338. He'd retrieved the weapon the evening before from a locked trailer on a farm owned by Townsend just outside the city. This safe house was abandoned at the moment, but Russ knew a stockpile of weapons was cached there, so he dropped by, picked the lock of a storage trailer, and removed a rifle and a Glock 19 pistol, along with ammunition for both weapons.

Now he slipped the sniper rifle into a bag used to hold cross-country skis, and he tossed several loaded magazines in with it. He would not look in the least bit out of place heading to his destination with his rifle in the backseat of his rented BMW 5 Series, seeing how the suburbs of Brussels were thick with snow-covered tracks perfect for an afternoon of cross-country skiing.

———————

The Townsend Government Services Gulfstream touched down at Brussels National Airport at five A.M. A dozen men climbed off the aircraft and into a heavy predawn snow shower. Lee Babbitt and Jeff Parks, along with the ten men of Team Dagger and another two-man UAV team, quickly climbed out of the weather and into two minivans and a Mercedes, and they headed east through a moonless predawn.

By six thirty A.M. they had set up their base of operations at the farmhouse in the town of Overijse, and here they linked up with the six surviving members of Team Jumper. Beaumont and his men looked tired and worn after losing two operators in Hamburg and then driving through the night, but Babbitt assigned two of the Dagger men to Jumper so Beaumont's team would be at full strength.

Babbitt and Parks checked in with the Townsend House signal room, and Lucas and Carl worked with the second UAV team to set up two mobile ground control stations in the back of the minivans. At the same time, the direct action operators went through the weapons cache located in a horse trailer next to the barn outside. They distributed pistols and submachine guns to the Dagger men and inventoried their other options.

And in minutes they realized they had a problem.

Beaumont called Babbitt and Parks outside, and the men stood in the snow by the horse trailer. "We're missing a sniper rifle," Beaumont said.

"*Missing?*"

"Yep. An AI .338. And a Glock 19. Ammo for both."

"Dead Eye," Parks said.

Beaumont spit tobacco juice into the snow. "That crazy son of a bitch is gunning for the damn PM of Israel."

Babbitt shook his head. "We're going to get out there and end this."

He called everyone in to the kitchen of the farmhouse. "I want Dagger near the Dieweg Cemetery. Kalb won't be there till one P.M., but if that's where Whitlock plans on hitting Kalb I want you guys in the area, determining the possible locations he could take the shot from. Figure out the best options and then go to ground. Make yourselves invisible."

Dagger quickly began gearing up.

Babbitt now looked at Beaumont and his team. "You will stay with me. We're going to support the UAV teams. They are going to have to go mobile to cover the city, and if they get a ping on the Gray Man, then we want to be mobile and after him instantly."

Babbitt turned to the two UAV teams, who had just returned from setting up the UAV ground control station in the van. "I want full-time drone coverage today. I want Joe and Keith searching for Whitlock, and I want Lucas and Carl searching for the Gray Man."

Lucas half raised a hand. "What about Ettinger?"

"What about her?"

"If she's with Gentry, maybe we can find her quicker than we can find him."

"How so?"

"When we were in Stockholm I had the computer record Ettinger's gait pattern so we could find her in a crowd." Anxiously he said, "I wasn't running surveillance on her. I did it just so I could keep tabs on her to make it easier to vector her in to any Gentry sightings."

Beaumont said, "You mean to tell me you can track the Mossad chick, same as you can Gentry?"

"Yeah, even better really because, unlike Gentry, she doesn't know we're using the UAVs to hunt for her."

Babbitt nodded and spoke like the idea had been his all along. "Yes. Find me Ettinger. I can use her."

Whitlock drove south out of the city center, through the morning rush hour; his rented silver 5 Series blended nicely into the traffic in the upscale neighborhoods.

As he drove his cell phone buzzed in the center console cup holder, and he slipped the earpiece into place. "Go."

"Hello, asshole." It was Court Gentry, and Whitlock found this as fortuitous as he found it surprising. He'd lost comms with the Gray Man the day before, and he wasn't even certain he'd survived the night.

Russ smiled. "Nice to know you are still alive."

"The day is young."

"True."

Court said, "Bad news. Your little plan is dead in the water."

"Why is that?"

"Because you need me to make it work. You want to kill Kalb, then kill me at the scene so I can take the fall."

Russ said, "In a perfect world that would have been ideal. I wanted you to follow me along on the Kalb hit. I knew you would never agree to the killing of the Israeli PM. You like to pretend your version of unsanctioned mass murder is cloaked in some sort of righteous and universal order, and Kalb wouldn't fit the bill. So I was going to tell you I was after another target in London. There are a multitude of despots and shitheads attending that conference that I could have chosen from. I hoped to have you close by when it came time for the op, at which point I knew you would figure out I was gunning for Kalb, and you would try to stop me, but I also knew I could put you in the dirt. So Kalb would be dead, you would be dead, and what would I be? I would be the sanctioned American operative who had been hunting the Gray Man, and I would be standing there over your bullet-riddled body as Mossad surrounded me, and I would have tears in my eyes as I confessed I got there just an instant too late to save Kalb, and we would all cry together and they would thank me for doing my best and for killing the vicious assassin of their great leader."

Court said, "But your plan went tits up when Ruth Ettinger told Mossad all about you. They might not believe you are the man after Kalb now, but when you turn up at the scene of his murder they are going to realize Ruth had been right all along. Your little fantasy is never going to happen."

"It was too much to hope for," Russ admitted. "But I'll still do the hit. I'll still get paid." And then he paused. "And you'll still get killed."

"Hate to break it to you, but I'm clear. I'm gone."

"I don't believe that. You are here. I can feel your presence." Whitlock thought it over, gazing now at a forested hill in the foggy morning distance, his destination. "This was inevitable. You and me, Court. Two locomotives, opposite directions, same track."

"I want you to stop this. Just walk away from Kalb."

Russ's only response was laughter.

Court said, "You say this is inevitable. But it's not inevitable. You control this situation."

"That's right," Russ said ominously. "I do. You are

the one who isn't in control. You can't run away, you have to come after me, just like I planned. Good-bye, Court. I'll see you next when I kill you."

Whitlock hung up the phone with a smile on his face. He heard it in Gentry's voice. The Gray Man was committed to the cause, and he would play his part to the very end.

———————

Fifteen minutes later Whitlock parked his car on Verre-winkelstraat, pulled the ski bag out of the backseat, and began walking up the street. In moments he'd entered a forested stretch of private property midway up a steep hillside, and he trudged across frozen ground under a canopy of bare trees. Crows flew above him as he ventured deeper into the woods, heading west now, and after a hundred yards he took a narrow path that passed on a hill above a frozen pond full of trash runoff from the neighborhood higher on the hill behind him. He continued for a minute more, and then he ended up at the tree line, overlooking the expansive backyard of a farmhouse. Beyond the yard the landscape dropped off down the hill into a shallow valley, at the bottom of which were train tracks and then a residential neighborhood. Beyond this was another hill, sparsely populated by the residential Brussels neighborhood of Uccle, and then, some twelve hundred yards distant, near the crest of this hill, the ancient Dieweg Cemetery lay, in perfect view of Russ's position here at the edge of the trees.

A small greenhouse sat in the backyard of the farmhouse at the edge of the trees, and Russ entered the tiny building and stowed the ski bag containing his Accuracy International rifle.

Twenty minutes later he was back in his BMW and heading north, toward the city.

The midmorning sun shone bright on the blanket of snow that covered Brussels. Ruth stepped out of a small side entrance to the Gare du Nord with her oversized sunglasses protecting her from the glare, and a new hat on her head further shielded her eyes from the sun.

As soon as she'd arrived at the station she stepped into a boutique and bought new clothes from head to toe, and then made a beeline to a bathroom where she began working on her disguise. She put her blond wig on, fixed her makeup, and changed into her new clothes. She wore her hair down, bangs low just over her eyes, and a pair of chic eyeglasses completed the look.

When she left the station she was certain she had not been followed, and she was equally certain she was completely unrecognizable.

She caught a taxi to La Maison Degande, an exclusive men's suit maker on Avenue Louise, and here she crossed the street to a café and ordered coffee and a croissant. She sat in the window and kept her eyes on the street while she ate her breakfast.

Ehud Kalb usually dropped in to Degande for fittings when he was in Brussels. This was known to Mossad, but she did not know if it was known to CIA. If it was, she thought it possible Whitlock would use this known point of access as the location for his assassination attempt.

That said, Ruth knew Dieweg cemetery was the more likely place for the hit. It was the most open and therefore the most vulnerable site, and while Kalb did not always go to Degande, his entire reason for coming to Brussels was to go to the cemetery to pay his respects at the grave of Piet De Schepper.

Still, while she waited for Gentry to make it into the city to become her own personal action arm, she knew she needed to keep an eye out for the other American assassin.

FIFTY-TWO

After a half hour in the café with sightings of neither Whitlock nor Kalb, Ruth decided to walk Avenue Louise to increase her coverage area around the suit maker. She'd made it only a few blocks when a black Mercedes-Benz four-door pulled up to the curb in front of her.

The door opened, and Lee Babbitt climbed out alone.

Ruth stopped in her tracks, turned in the opposite direction, and began casually walking away. She heard the car drive off, and then, from behind, she heard, "Ms. Ettinger. I'm alone. I just want to talk. I've sent the rest of my men away."

She turned back to him, and he put up his hands in apology. "I tried to call you, but apparently you misplaced your phone."

"How did you know I was here?"

"One of my guys saw you in the café in front of Degande."

Ruth did not believe him. She knew her disguise was complete, and she was an expert at covert surveillance. She'd seen no one suspicious in the area, certainly not one of the Townsend cowboys she'd run into in Sweden and Germany.

But she did not let on that she found his explanation for her compromise suspect. Instead she said, "So, Mr. Babbitt. Why are you here? Are you here to help me stop your employee from killing my prime minister, or are you here to kill an innocent man?"

"I won't get into Gentry's guilt or innocence. Your bias is stronger than my need or my will to convince you, but I do think we can work together."

"In what way?"

"You want Dead Eye, we want Gentry."

"Do you believe Dead Eye has gone rogue?"

"I feel certain he has," he said, adopting a grave tone that she really did not trust. "We tracked him here last night but he . . . he got away. I think he is the real threat to your PM. I see that now. Our mutual friends in Langley, Virginia, are, unfortunately, not convinced. I am afraid their threat matrix only has room for one rogue ex-singleton operator. Occam's razor, Ms. Ettinger. The simple solution is usually the correct one."

"They need to expand their horizons."

Babbitt shifted from one foot to the other in the cold. "As for Gentry. I realize you feel like he is being treated unjustly." Babbitt paused. "The question you have to ask yourself is this. Is Gentry's life worth more than that of your prime minister?"

Ruth said, "Go on."

"I can lead you to Russell Whitlock. Today, before Ehud Kalb arrives."

"And the price for this prize, I assume, is me leading you to Court Gentry."

"That's right."

"You are playing a very dangerous game, Mr. Babbitt. If I tell Tel Aviv you are using the leader of our nation as a bargaining chip—"

"I have more contact with Tel Aviv than you do. They aren't listening to you right now, and that surely won't change before something very bad happens to your PM. I am just suggesting you tell Gentry where Whitlock is. He will go there, and we will stand back and let nature take its course."

She looked away. Thinking over what was being offered.

Babbitt said, "I know the trouble you are in. You could go to prison."

"I don't care about that. I only care about saving Kalb."

"That is my objective, as well." He smiled a little. "My *secondary* objective, admittedly. But still, I want to avoid any harm to your PM. He is a good man."

Ruth hesitated a moment longer, then she nodded slowly. "I can deliver Gentry to you."

"Call him now. You can use my phone."

"He doesn't trust phones. I have to meet with him, face-to-face."

"Where and when?"

"I tell you that and my leverage is gone, Mr. Babbitt."

"Then what do you suggest?"

She gave Babbitt the number to the phone she'd pur-chased the previous day in Sweden, and she promised to call him by noon.

Babbitt said, "I will warn you now, my dear. If you attempt any sort of a double cross, we won't be able to save your PM from Russ Whitlock. He was trained in the same program that created Gentry, you know. They are two very dangerous individuals."

"I will call you. You need to be ready to produce Whitlock when I do."

"That's not going to be a problem," he said.

Ruth left Babbitt there on the street corner, waiting for his Mercedes to come pick him up. She continued up the Avenue Louise on foot.

———

Ruth walked a couple of blocks and then placed a call to Court Gentry through her wireless headset.

After a moment she heard his voice. "Yeah?"

"Are you in town?"

"Pulling into the station right now."

"Listen very carefully. Townsend is here. And they have their drones in the sky."

"I'm low pro. I should be able to—"

"Court, they have a recording of your walking pat-tern. The drone can pick you out of a crowd of hundreds, thousands even. If you are near a train station you can bet they will be covering that. You don't stand a chance."

"Are you sure about this?"

Ruth kept walking up the street. "I'm sure. They are

following me right now. The only way they could have done this is with my gait. Trust me."

While Court talked to Ruth through his headset he looked out the front of the Gare du Midi train station in the Brussels city center. He thought about all the clear sky above him, and the prospect that a nearly invisible drone could be programmed to pick him out of a crowd and send killers to his position.

He quickly came up with an idea. "Okay. Thanks for the intel, I've got it covered." He changed the subject. "What did Babbitt say?"

"They know you and I are working together. He wants me to trade you for Whitlock. He wants me to send you to a location where Whitlock will be, and then, I assume, he and his men will sweep in and kill you both."

"Why are you telling me this?"

"Because it's a trap."

Court snorted. "Of course it's a trap. That's pretty much the definition of the word *trap*."

"No, I mean *we* can use it to trap *them*."

"How so?"

Ruth said, "Get a set of binoculars, good ones, and call me back. The UAVs they are using are new, and they only have enough electricity to run for a half hour, and their range is just a few miles. I'll let them follow me to some remote place outside the city center where they'll have to get in a vehicle to stay up with me. You get in a building and get eyes on the UAV, then follow it back to its base when it goes back to recharge."

Court nodded. "Where I will find the Townsend guys."

"Exactly. They can lead you to Whitlock."

"I like it," Court admitted. "You're pretty sneaky."

"I am indeed," Ruth admitted.

Court descended to the parking garage below the Gare du Midi and walked the length of vehicles until he found a motorcycle he liked. It was a BMW R1200 all-terrain bike, and he picked the lock with his picks, and then he hot-wired it just as he had the bike in northern Germany the evening before. He paid the parking fare and drove out of the lot, heading north, out of the city center, with his head fully covered.

He drove until he found a sporting goods store in a suburb some ten kilometers from town. Here he bought a high-end pair of Nikon binoculars and a two-piece leather motorcycle suit and a helmet, both black. He also purchased a new backpack, a different size and style from his existing bag, and he transferred his clothes, his money, his gear, and his trauma kit into it.

He called Ruth back to find her position, then climbed back on his stolen bike and began racing through the streets of Brussels.

Ruth headed out of town on the streetcar, hoping like hell the Townsend Sky Shark that she was certain was following her would be able to keep up. She climbed out at multiple stops and then boarded other trains, each time waiting at the stop and looking around, trying to make it appear like she was on a standard SDR and unaware of any eyes in the sky. In truth she was giving the UAV mobile team all the time they would need to find her, and to switch out drones as one ran low on power.

She purposefully did not look for the drone. The last thing she needed was to tip her hand, to let Townsend know she was onto them.

When Court called her back they both looked at satellite maps on their mobile phones and decided on a location that would suit their needs.

Ruth entered a freestanding department store in Etterbeek a few minutes later, a five-story structure surrounded on all sides by smaller buildings. She rushed through the store to the escalators, then ascended to the third floor. Here she raced through the linens department, then through the furniture department, and made her way to the windows.

Quickly but carefully she picked her way closer to get a view of the street, shielding herself with furniture and shoppers in case the Townsend UAV happened to be looking in the window even now.

Lucas and Carl had told her in Stockholm that in crowded daytime situations they normally operated their drone close to the walls of buildings, doing their best to make it blend in to the urban landscape. As Ruth arrived at the window she began checking the buildings across the street, but she saw nothing with her naked eyes.

She called Court and spoke to him through her headset. "I'm in position. Where are you?"

"Street level, about three blocks east of you. I'm scanning the area with my binos, but I can't see anything."

"Keep looking, it's got to be here somewhere. He should be about three stories up."

"Nothing," Court repeated.

Just then something occurred to her. "Court, look straight above my pos."

"Above the department store?"

"Yes."

"You said it would be moving alongside the building."

"Think about it—they will need to cover all the exits in case I slip out the back. They can't do that unless it's directly above."

"Okay," Court said, and he began scanning the blue sky, looking left and right above the department store. "Still nothing."

"Keep looking."

Just then, almost exactly where he'd focused his attention above the department store, he saw a small black object moving across the sky. It was easily three hundred feet in the air, and it was little more than a speck from Court's position several blocks away. He never would have noticed if it had remained stationary.

"Got it," he said. "It's leaving."

It flew closer to Court, and a second craft slipped silently into a hovering position near the first.

"Wait," he said. "A second drone just appeared from the southeast. They must have their mobile truck parked somewhere in that direction."

Ruth said, "Start heading that way. I'll keep moving closer and we can find it."

Court climbed onto his BMW bike and headed off after the drone. He'd hoped to discover a van with the

UAV team parked just around the corner, but instead he followed the black speck for a half mile and then he lost it, finding himself out of Etterbeek and closer to the southeastern edge of town. He pulled into a grocery store parking lot, hid himself with his bike under cover of a covered parking lot, and then directed Ruth to a bus stop just a hundred yards from his position.

Ruth arrived on a bus minutes later, and Court scanned the skies for the UAV. He found it this time only fifty feet in the air; it hovered confidently a block from the bus stop.

Court checked his watch a few minutes later and, like clockwork, at the half-hour mark the drones switched out again. The first UAV peeled off, again flying toward the southeast, and Court entered traffic behind it.

Soon he found himself on the A4 highway doing his best to keep his eyes on a tiny speck of black a hundred yards off his right shoulder and slightly ahead of him. Twice he almost wrecked the bike as he struggled to keep the object in sight and negotiate traffic, and all the while he was on guard, ready for the UAV to land next to a car or a truck somewhere along the roadside.

Instead the UAV left the path of the highway and entered a little village. He saw it descending between two hills, and then it was gone.

"Ruth. I lost it."

"Shit."

"We're going to have to wait another half hour."

"Dammit! That takes us past noon. That's not enough time to get to the cemetery if this doesn't work."

Court yelled back at her. "I'm close! Next time the

UAV leaves this village and the other comes back, I'll be right on top of the ground control station."

He raced into the village of Overijse, found high ground in a copse of trees just to the east of town, and then parked his bike. They were running out of time, but for now there was nothing he could do but wait.

FIFTY-THREE

Ruth took a bus that led her in the same general direction as the UAV, but she climbed out after only two stops, not wanting to reveal that she knew which village Townsend was operating from. She stood along the side of the road, killing time until the next UAV changeover.

Her phone chirped in her ear. "Yes?"

"It's Babbitt. Why haven't you called?"

She knew he was watching her, or at least he was being informed of her odd movements. She said, "I'm in contact with Gentry; he's leading me around to make sure I'm not being followed."

"It's almost noon; he better hurry it up or Kalb is a dead man."

"I know. It won't be long. Do you have Dead Eye?"

"When you have Gentry in pocket, call me back. We

know where Whitlock is, and I will tell you where to send Gentry."

"Very good," she said, and she disconnected the call.

But it was not "very good." She knew Babbitt was stringing her along. There would be no meeting between Gentry and Whitlock at the end of this trip. No, as soon as the Townsend UAV tracked her to Gentry, the Townsend men would pounce.

She climbed on the next bus heading in the opposite direction from Court. It was time to lead Jumper Team away from him.

───────────

Russ Whitlock had spent the morning preparing his escape from Brussels after his act. He staged an automobile north of town and reserved a hotel room in Amsterdam for that evening. From there he would play it by ear. He knew with certainty that his new documents received from the CIA the previous evening would be less than worthless; he would have to go to ground here in the EU and find some forged credos. This would take time and money, but Russ was comforted by the fact that, after one P.M. this afternoon, he would have a great deal of both.

He positioned himself in his rented ground-floor flat in the Brussels neighborhood of Saint Pieter Woluwe. He knew the area because the flat was in a building that also contained a Townsend safe house, a top-floor unit that Russ had used once in the past. He steered clear of the safe house unit because he thought it might have been bugged, and he knew Townsend might have been targeting him at this point along with Gentry.

He wanted to take an Adderall to amp up his reaction times and awareness, but he knew he'd have to make a plus one-thousand-yard shot, which would be impossible with the amped-up heart rate and blood pressure the drug would cause.

But this was of no great concern, because Russ knew his almost euphoric mood would take the place of the psychostimulant. He felt amazing about today, about his plan, his future.

It was just before noon now. He had fifteen minutes to kill before returning to his hide east of Dieweg Cemetery. He decided he would quickly clean and rebandage his weeping hip wound.

As he stood to head to the bathroom, his earpiece chirped.

"Go."

"It's Babbitt."

Russ chuckled. "What? No identity check?"

"You are no longer an employee of Townsend Government Services. There is nothing official to this call." He paused. "We're just two guys, having a man-to-man chat."

Russ's ebullient mood continued. He joked, "You can't fire me, because I quit."

Babbitt wasn't laughing. "I'm here in Brussels."

Russ shrugged to himself in the quiet flat. "*You?* Out here in the field? Don't tell me you brought Parks along with you?"

"Jeff is here, yes."

"Oh no." Russ's tone was sarcastic. "The sheriff and his deputy have come to bring me in."

Lee said, "If it were up to me I would do just that.

But Denny Carmichael is ordering us to continue on with the Gentry mission."

"Good ol' Denny. He is an old single-minded, grudge-holding motherfucker, isn't he?"

Babbitt cleared his throat. "I have been in contact with the woman from Mossad. She is here in Brussels and working with Gentry. They are trying to track you down."

"They won't find me."

"She wants to exchange Gentry for you."

Whitlock whistled. "Poor Court. He never met a friend who didn't stab him in the back."

"True."

"Well, I'm not turning myself over to Mossad, and I'm not turning myself over to you."

"Of course you aren't."

"Then what is it you want from me, Babbitt?"

"I want your trust."

Russ cocked his head. Where was this going? "What do you mean?"

"I want you to just listen to what I have to say without reacting." Before Russ responded, Babbitt said, "I thought it was likely you would use one of our mothballed safe houses as your base of operations, so I sent a UAV to check out all the locations you knew about. You were seen on Rue Kelle, and now John Beaumont and his team are right outside your door. Myself as well. We want to come in and talk. We have no mandate or sanction to do anything to you, we just need you to help us get Gentry."

Russ leapt to his feet and reached for the Glock pistol

on his hip, just as the living room door flew open and three men entered with their guns high. Russ dove out of the room and rushed toward the back of the property but here three more armed Townsend operatives entered through the back door and rushed toward him with their sub guns held high. He looked down and saw dancing laser dots moving around his chest as a half-dozen laser targeting systems attached to short-barreled submachine guns found their target.

Whitlock raised his hands in surrender. Beaumont stormed up the narrow hallway, then quickly brought his right knee up, hard, slamming it into the ragged infected gunshot wound on Whitlock's left hip.

Russ fell to the floor.

———————

Minutes later Dead Eye's hands had been zip-tied behind his back, and he sat on the couch in the living room. Two Townsend men were tasked with keeping their Uzis pointed at his head, and the rest of the Townsend men moved around the property, mostly helping the UAV team move their ground control station from the van outside to a long table next to a bay window in the front of the living room. As the two UAV operators, a pilot named Joe and a sensor operator named Keith, set up their gear, they glanced his way. Russ smiled at the two young men. Matter-of-factly he said, "I'm going to kill you both."

They looked to Beaumont with panic-stricken looks.

Beaumont said, "Don't listen to him, boys. He's just

a little grumpy. When we busted through that door he lost twenty-five million bucks."

Babbitt and Parks entered the living room and sat down in wingback chairs across from Russ. Beaumont remained across the room, leaning against the wall with his Uzi slung across his chest.

Leland Babbitt addressed Whitlock. "Here's how it's going to play out. The Israeli woman will make contact with Gentry and then she will call me. I will have her send Gentry here. When he arrives, we kill him, and then we sit here until Kalb leaves the city.

"Then we release you, and everyone goes their separate ways."

Whitlock wasn't buying it. "You are as full of shit as ever. Once Gentry is dead, no one at CIA will have incentive to keep me alive. You are going to kill me." He motioned to Beaumont with his forehead. "Scratch that. You will have one of your apes do it for you."

Parks and Beaumont exchanged a grin.

"Not true," said Babbitt, but he did not try terribly hard to keep up the ruse.

Whitlock leaned back on the couch. His face revealed a man defeated, but behind his back, he'd torn part of the zipper from one of the sofa cushions. His fingertips bled from the difficult task, but now he'd run the zipper through the flexi-cuffs, and he used his fingers to work it slowly back and forth, only a quarter of an inch movement for each stroke, like a tiny dull wire saw.

He'd done this before, and he knew he'd cut through the bindings in about two minutes. At that point he knew he could make it over the coffee table and onto Babbitt in less than a second.

Sure, the Jumper men would kill him, but he weighed this against the satisfaction of digging his hands into the throat of Lee Babbitt, and he was having trouble talking himself out of a course of action that would turn him into a bullet-ridden carcass on the floor.

But another thought entered his mind. He kept sawing behind his back, revealing nothing of the pain in his shredded fingertips or the soreness in the muscles of his wrists and forearms. He looked to Babbitt. "Your drone found me, but it didn't find Gentry? Is that curious to you?"

Keith said, "Not really. He could be inside some location where we don't have coverage."

"Or he could be running countermeasures to defend against UAV tracking."

Parks smiled. "I doubt that."

"He's working with Ettinger, right? Do you know where she is?"

"She's running all over the city right now. We are tracking her in case she tries to trick us."

Russ laughed. "She's already tricking you. She's leading you on a wild-goose chase. She knows about the UAV coverage, which means Gentry knows about the coverage. Right now Gentry is with her, watching from a distance, trying to track the UAV back to its home base."

Parks said, "You just sit there and shut the fuck up, Whitlock. You are done."

But Babbitt turned to him. "Why do you say that, Russell?"

"That's what I would do, so that's what he's doing."

Babbitt thought it over. He turned to Parks. "That would explain why she went almost all the way toward the farmhouse, and then started moving in the other direction."

Whitlock said, "There is a solution, of course."

"I'm listening."

"Court is loyal as a puppy. Just grab the Mossad girl, bring her here, a place where you control the territory, and have her call Gentry. He will come running to save her."

Babbitt looked to Beaumont. Babbitt was an executive; he did not like having his labor, especially his ex-employee, giving him ideas, but he clearly thought it to be a good idea. "Pick up Ettinger. Bring her here. We'll do this the old-fashioned way."

"You got it, boss."

"And tell Dagger Team to double-time it to the farmhouse to pick up Lucas and Carl. Tell them to watch their asses. Gentry is out there somewhere."

––––––––––

Court sat on his BMW bike in a lot by a flower shop, shivering in the cold as he scanned the rooftops of the little village in the valley below him. By his watch exactly half an hour had passed since he'd lost sight of the last drone. If the Townsend UAV team stayed on the same schedule, within moments he would see—"

There. A small black speck rose from a cluster of homes on the eastern edge of the village. Court could not tell which property it had taken off from, but he had it narrowed down to one particular street, with no more than four or five farmhouses on it. He fired up the bike and raced down toward the neighborhood.

He parked at the top of the street; now he was positioned between two recycling bins, and he took off his helmet to try to listen for any buzzing overhead. He fought the urge to look down at his watch. He knew the clock was ticking on this op, but he also knew that glancing away from the sky for even a few seconds could cause him to miss the returning UAV.

It took less than five minutes for the returning drone to arrive back in Overijse. As it passed over the village it came closer and closer to Gentry, then slowed and settled down behind a farmhouse not fifty yards from where he had positioned himself.

There was no mistaking it now. He knew the location of the Townsend UAV team.

Court began walking his bike to the farmhouse, not running the engine so he could remain perfectly silent. As he did so he called Ruth.

The phone rang, but there was no answer.

What the hell?

Carl and Lucas were almost done for the day, and they could not be happier. They had been working nearly nonstop for days, and they, as well as their equipment, had been pushed to the breaking point.

Twenty minutes earlier they had watched the Sky Shark feed on their monitors as their target, Ruth Ettinger, stepped off a bus in the Brussels neighborhood of Sterrebeek. As soon as the bus rolled away from the stop, a white van pulled up and members of the Townsend Jumper team leapt out, handguns drawn, and they forced Ettinger into the back.

The UAV team did not understand why the Mossad woman had been snatched, but they were not analysts or operators, they were techs, so they pushed their concerns out of their minds and went about their work. Parks had instructed them to break down their operation as fast as possible, because men from Team Dagger would be swinging by the farmhouse in minutes to pick them up.

As soon as the Sky Shark landed in the backyard, Lucas finished the powering-down process on his laptop and headed out back to retrieve it.

As he opened the door a man dressed head to toe in a black leather motorcycle outfit appeared in front of him. Before he could react the biker punched him in the jaw, knocking him back onto the tile floor of the living room of the farmhouse.

Carl saw the man in black enter over Lucas's sprawled body. He leapt to his feet and reached across the table for an Uzi submachine gun lying next to one of the computers.

Court calmly drew his SIG and shot the UAV pilot in the ass. Carl fell to the floor, writhing in pain. Court now grabbed Lucas by his hair and dragged him back to the table in front of the ground control station. Once he was in his seat it was Carl's turn. Court forced him back onto his chair and onto his wounded ass.

Court looked both men over quickly. "I have a personal rule that I don't kill nerds unless I really have to. I don't like it." He slid his gun into his waistband. "Don't make me. You boys are going to show me how all this groovy shit works, okay?"

"Yes, sir," Lucas said, and Carl nodded.

"Good. I want you to fly this drone to wherever Dead Eye is. Right the fuck now."

Lucas said, "We . . . we don't know where he is."

Court looked at Carl. "You'll bleed to death within the hour. You aren't getting a hospital till I get what I want, so you better hop to it."

Carl composed himself quickly and began preparing the system for immediate takeoff. "I . . . I might be able to find him."

Gentry said, "I have faith in you."

––––––––––––

Ruth was brought to the Rue Kelle safe house at twelve P.M. She had been treated professionally by the Jumper men, although they'd taken her phone and her Mace and they searched her thoroughly in the van on the way.

She'd protested angrily and demanded to speak to Babbitt, but then sat quietly for the rest of the drive.

She passed through the door and into the great room at the front of the flat, and was led by the arm toward Parks and Babbitt, who sat on wingback chairs facing away from her. Two Jumper cowboys stood next to the sofa, blocking her view of a man seated there facing the Townsend execs, so it was not until she was just feet away that she found herself face-to-face with the seated man. He was fit and rugged looking, but not particularly tall or overly muscular. His hands were behind his back.

She looked him over even closer now. His eyes looked exactly like Court's. They were mature and searching; they flitted around the room at first, but when they locked on hers she knew the brain behind them was reading every aspect of her person, taking in all the data and measuring her as a threat.

"You're Whitlock," she said.

"You're Ettinger," he replied, and he started to stand, but one of the Jumper men pushed the barrel of his gun into the side of his head.

He sat back down and the guard pulled his weapon back.

"Excuse me if I don't get up," Russ said.

Ruth turned to Babbitt now. "You *are* aware you just kidnapped a Mossad officer, are you not?"

Lee shook his head and leaned back in his chair, crossing his legs. "We did nothing of the sort. Time was growing short while we watched you wander the city. You had no intention of bringing Gentry here for a trade. I realize that. So we just invited you back here to speed up the process."

Ruth said nothing.

"But now we have Dead Eye and, most awkwardly, but perhaps also more importantly, we have you. You will call Gentry, give him this address—33 Rue Kelle—and then we will wait for him to come save you and kill Dead Eye."

Russ stood up from the couch again. "I think we can all come to an—"

The other Jumper man guarding him shoved his gun barrel against the side of Whitlock's head, and Russ sat back down, his hands still tight behind his back. He leaned back on the sofa, facing Babbitt and Parks, who were seated in front of him, and Ettinger, who stood next to Beaumont and the two Townsend execs.

Just then Parks took a call from Dagger Team. He put it over the speaker on the table holding the UAV gear.

Dagger Actual said, "We're two minutes from the safe house. The UAV team there isn't answering the radios."

"Roger that, Al," said Parks, and then he looked to Babbitt. "If Gray Man found the UAV station at the Overijse farmhouse, then we can end this right now."

From his seat on the sofa Russ Whitlock said, "I think it is a very safe bet Court did, in fact, find the UAV station."

Babbitt asked, "What makes you say that?"

"*That* makes me say that." Whitlock nodded toward the large bay windows across the room. Ruth, Babbitt, Parks, and Beaumont all turned to it.

A Sky Shark drone hovered at eye level, just a foot from the window. Its camera was trained through the glass at everyone in the room.

"Jesus!" Parks lurched back in surprise as if Gentry himself stood there, on the other side of the glass.

Whitlock laughed from his position on the sofa. "Calm down, Parks. It's not weaponized. He's not going to launch a Hellfire."

But even Babbitt was shaken up by the realization

that Gentry was watching his every move from a distance of no more than ten feet. "Everyone remain calm," he said. The phone on his belt rang and he jumped slightly.

From his position on the sofa, Russ Whitlock seemed to retain the most control of anyone in the room. He said, "Answer your phone, Lee. Say hi to Court, and wave for the camera."

FIFTY-FOUR

Before Babbitt answered he glanced to Parks. Softly he said, "Have Dagger hit the location the second they get there."

"Yes sir," he said, and he stepped out of the living room.

Babbitt answered his phone. "Who is this?"

After a short pause he heard, "You know who this is."

"Gentry?"

Court all but growled. "Babbitt."

"What happened to my UAV team?"

"I persuaded them to work for me."

Babbitt cleared his throat nervously, and he struggled to force an air of authority in his voice. "Yes. Well, as . . . as you can plainly see, we have Dead Eye here."

"I see that. I want to see every son of a bitch in that

room with a gun on Dead Eye. He can disarm those two idiots standing next to him in under a second."

But Babbitt was not going to let Gentry order his men around. He told the six other Jumper men in the room to stay where they were.

Next he glanced to his left, beyond the view of the camera looking in the window. Parks was there, and the younger man held up a single finger. *Ten seconds*, he mouthed.

Lee looked back to the drone's camera. "Now, Court. You have all the advantages here. What can we do to rectify this situation?"

"You let Ruth go, and I come in."

"We are taking good care of Ms. Ettinger." He glanced to his left at Parks, who stood out of view in the dining room. Parks held a phone to his ear, and his other hand up with five fingers extended, then four, then three, then two.

Babbitt smiled into the drone camera now, but he did not reply.

Parks shouted, "Executing now!"

Ruth pushed away from Beaumont and ran toward the bay window. "Run!"

———————

At the Townsend safe house in Overijse, the eight-man Dagger team breached at four different entry points, using explosives on the front and back doors and smashing through floor-to-ceiling windows in the front living room and a smaller window in an upstairs bedroom.

The four two-man teams raced quickly through the

property, working their way from all compass points toward the UAV table in the center.

"Clear!" came the call from the front-door entry team.

"Clear!" The upstairs team found the second floor to be a dry hole, as well.

The living room team cleared the kitchen and the living room. "Clear."

And the back-door team moved to the table on which the laptops and flight control equipment for the UAVs had been positioned.

There was blood on the floor, but the table was empty. The gear was gone.

"Clear," Dagger Actual reported. "Negative target."

Court Gentry sat in the back seat of a minivan with his pistol pointed at the back of Lucas's head. The sensor operator drove the vehicle toward the Rue Kelle safe house while Carl operated the drone with one hand and held his other hand tight on his right butt cheek, having to lie on his side in the back of the van to avoid putting too much painful pressure on the gunshot wound.

Court looked at the laptop and the surprisingly clear picture of the living room of the safe house on Rue Kelle. His headset in his ear afforded him fair audio coverage of the room via Babbitt's mobile phone.

Babbitt had been looking off to the side for the last thirty seconds or so, suddenly uninterested in his conversation with Court. Court assumed this was because a takedown of the farmhouse had just begun, and soon enough the men hitting the property would realize their target had gone mobile with the UAV team.

Ten minutes earlier Court had ordered the drone operators to load up the van. They took their laptops and piled into the vehicle. Court was about to climb in with them, but as he crossed the driveway he noticed all the footprints in the snow leading to a horse trailer next to a barn. He brought the two men out with him as he shot the lock off the trailer, and inside he found a huge weapons cache.

Court pilfered several items from the cache. A Glock 19 pistol and several magazines, a sawed-off twelve-gauge shotgun and a box of shells, a pair of hand grenades, and a Kevlar vest.

He threw them into the back of the van and then he, Lucas, and Carl left the property, with Lucas behind the wheel and under Gentry's gun. Seconds behind them, the half-charged UAV in the backyard launched and began racing toward the Rue Kelle safe house.

Now Court saw the confusion and dejection in the face of Babbitt as it became clear that the Townsend shooters had found nothing at the safe house. At the same time he saw enormous relief in the eyes of Ruth Ettinger. Beaumont had pulled her back near the wingback chairs, and just past her, sitting on the couch between the two armed guards, Dead Eye himself looked at first relieved, and then immediately lost in thought.

Slowly Babbitt brought the phone back to his ear.

"Well, well, well, Mr. Gentry. Once again, you remain one step ahead."

"Put me on speaker. I want to talk to Dead Eye. If I

can get him to stand down for today, and you release Ruth Ettinger, I will come in to you."

Babbitt turned the phone to its speaker setting, but he said, "Court, nothing has changed; you must come here."

Ruth said, "Do not come here, Court. Let them sit and stew. They have Whitlock; he can't get to Kalb as long as he's right here."

"I understand," he said.

Whitlock sat on the sofa, his hands behind him. He said, "Lee, why are you talking to him? I don't have time for this shit."

Babbitt looked away from the hovering drone camera and back to his prisoner. "You don't still seriously think you are going to walk out of here and kill Ehud Kalb?"

"Of course I do."

Beaumont turned away from Ruth and shouted at the much smaller man on the couch, "You're a crazy fuck, aren't you? The only way you're leaving here is in a body bag!"

Russ ignored Beaumont, continuing to address Babbitt. "Lee, your plan is not working. You want Court to come rescue Ettinger. But I know something you don't."

Babbitt cocked his head to the side. "And what is that?"

"Court does rescue. He's proven himself to be good at it. But there is something Court does even better. Even faster, even more assuredly."

"What?"

He looked into the camera outside the window, and he gave it a wink. With a smile he said, "He does revenge." Dead Eye started to stand for the third time, and again the man on his right pressed the gun barrel of his Uzi to the side of his head, but this time Whitlock leapt to his feet and, in a blindingly quick move, his hands fired out from behind his back; he snatched the barrel with his right hand and pivoted the short butt stock with his left hand, facing the weapon's business end away from him and toward Ruth and Babbitt. He yanked the Uzi now and the Jumper man was pulled off balance by the gun's sling around his neck.

Before anyone in the room could react, Whitlock had his finger on the trigger, and he fired a long fully automatic burst. Smoke and fire and noise filled the living room, ejected cartridges arced away from the gun and bounced off the walls. He then spun to his left, pulling the Jumper operator in front of him and, at the same time, aiming the barrel at the face of the guard on his left. He pulled the trigger again and the man's face exploded in a burst of dark red, blasting brain matter on the ceiling as the body fell onto the white sofa.

A Jumper man across the room got his gun up and fired, but Russ shifted to the right and squatted down, putting as much of his body as he could behind the falling Jumper operative caught in the Uzi's sling, and the rounds hit the guard's back, killing him instantly.

Babbitt crouched low, covering his head in a primal reaction to get out of the line of fire. Whitlock used the quick release on the Uzi's sling to remove it from the neck of the dead man, all the while shifting fast and hard and low to his right across the room. He put himself between the other Jumper men and Lee Babbitt, and then he launched out of his crouch and grabbed Babbitt, putting him in a headlock. The hot tip of the Uzi burned into Lee's sweaty corpulent neck, and Russ shouted at the men in the room in front of him.

"Get back! Get back!"

Russ dragged Babbitt back into the corner of the room with him, making sure that no one could get behind him.

Beaumont and his operatives held their weapons on Whitlock, but they could not engage with the director of their organization in the line of fire.

Leland Babbitt slowly opened his eyes, struggled weakly against the man holding him by the throat, and took in the scene in front of him. On the far side of the room, slightly hazy through the faint gun smoke hanging in the air, at the entrance to the dining room and the front door, Jeff Parks, John Beaumont, and five more Jumper operatives all stood with pistols or submachine guns pointing in his direction.

In front of them, two Jumper men lay dead; one face-down in the wreckage of the shattered glass coffee table, and the other nearly decapitated on the white sofa.

Both of Babbitt's UAV operators were also dead, slumped over their smashed laptops on the table next to the bay window. Blood dripped off their equipment and glistened in the glow from the electronics.

Babbitt looked down to his feet slowly.

There, on the hardwood floor, Ruth Ettinger lay on her back, two bullet holes in the center of her chest.

Her brown eyes were open in death.

Babbitt's voice cracked. "Oh fuck." His body shook.

"Oh fuck!" He shouted it now. "Oh fuck! You killed a Mossad officer!"

Behind him, Russell Whitlock looked on the scene before him with wild, intense eyes. He jacked his head to his right, toward the lens of the camera hanging below the drone hovering outside the window. "You understand, Court. She was the loose end. She had to go."

In the back of the van less than four miles to the east of the Rue Kelle safe house, Court Gentry hung his head in his hands, the side of the SIG Sauer pistol pressed against his forehead.

Tears tried to form in his eyes; but he pressed them tighter to fight them off. "Ruth," he whispered to himself.

After a moment he had a distinct sensation that Carl was reaching for something in the back of the van, and Court realized there was no time to grieve for Ruth. He was only partially aware of Carl's actions at first, but when he heard something dragging slowly across the floor, he recognized it as the sawed-off shotgun he'd picked up at the Townsend cache at the Overijse farmhouse.

Without opening his eyes Gentry said, "Carl, do you want to die? Because I really feel like killing somebody right now."

The wounded drone operator let go of the shotgun and lifted his hands in the air.

Now Court tapped Lucas on the back of his head with the barrel of his pistol. "Pull over."

Lucas pulled to the side of the road. When the mini-

van stopped, Court ordered Lucas to put it in park. Still
nearly overcome by Ruth's death, Court fought to keep
his head clear and on mission.

"I want to see the inside of your pockets." Both men
emptied the pockets of their coats and pants, tossing mobile phones, keys, wallets, and other small items on the
floorboard of the van. When they were finished, Court
had them climb out of the vehicle and stand by the side
of the road. Court climbed behind the wheel and began
programming the address he'd read on the door of the
safe house into the GPS unit fastened to the windshield.
As he did this he addressed Lucas, who stood outside the
open passenger door. "You need to get your buddy to a
hospital a lot more than you need to link up with Babbitt.
Are you following me?"

"Yes, sir. Thank you. I want you to know there was
nothing personal in any of this. We were just doing our—"

Court sped off in the van, pulling the door shut with
his actions and leaving the two Americans alone on an
empty street.

In the backyard of the Rue Kelle safe house, Whitlock
walked Babbitt backward through fresh snow, the barrel
of the Uzi still pressed to the man's neck and the six
surviving Jumper men still in slow pursuit, their guns
high as they trudged through the snow.

Jeff Parks moved along with the operators; he had his
small silver automatic pistol leveled in Whitlock's direction. Upon noticing this, Babbitt yelled for his number
two to be careful where he pointed his damn gun.

As he pulled his former employer through the snow, Whitlock spoke softly into Babbitt's ear. "Let me explain how this is going to play out. You are going to send your men out front to the cars, and they are going to load up, because Gentry will be here in a few, and he will be in a very foul mood."

"What about you?"

"I'd love to stick around, but I have made other plans."

"You're going to kill Kalb?"

"Nah. I'm on the next train out of town. Gentry's right. I'm burned."

Babbitt knew he was lying, but he felt it prudent to refrain from leveling any accusations at the man with an automatic gun held to his neck.

Russ said, "Gentry's coming here, right now, so you'd better run. Live to fight another day and all that shit. If you send your guys after me at the cemetery you won't have the forces you need to engage him."

Babbitt nodded a little, and he shivered in the cold.

"Send Beaumont and the other knuckle-draggers to the cars. Do it now."

Babbitt shouted. "Everybody go. Get in the cars. We're getting out of here."

Beaumont said, "I'm not leaving you back here with his crazy ass!"

"That's a goddamned order!"

The backyard cleared out moments later, and Whitlock let Babbitt out of the headlock.

He faced him with the little submachine gun held up at eye level. "This is a good plan, Lee. Smarter than any shit you or Parks could have come up with."

Babbitt only nodded, his eyes locked on the gun. "Yes. Yes, it was."

"You will tell Mossad it was Gentry who killed the girl, not me. Then they won't hunt me down after this is over, and I won't come back to D.C. and kill you and your entire family."

"*Jesus*, Russell."

"You scratch my back, I don't scratch your eyes out. Deal?"

Babbitt nodded. "I'll do as you say. I swear."

"Good. Now, you and your goons just have to kill Gentry for me, and I'll be back on track."

Again Babbitt nodded nervously. "We will do just that."

Whitlock backed through a grove of bushes, into a neighboring backyard.

Leland Babbitt dropped to his knees in the deep snow, his suit pants doing nothing to protect his legs from the bitter cold.

FIFTY-FIVE

Five minutes after Whitlock left Babbitt in the snow, the Townsend men left the safe house in a three-vehicle convoy. An Audi led the way with two Jumper men. Behind it was the black Mercedes E-Class, with Beaumont in the front passenger seat and Jumper Two behind the wheel, along with Parks and Babbitt in the back. And a Ford Galaxy minivan brought up the rear with two more Jumper operatives. All vehicles were in radio contact with one another.

Beaumont had a map in his lap, and he directed the lead car to a lot near a traffic circle a few blocks east of the safe house on Rue Kelle. He addressed Babbitt while looking over the map. "We know Whitlock took a sniper rifle from the cache, so we need to patrol high ground near the Dieweg Cemetery. Someplace out of range of the Israelis protecting Kalb, but still in range for the rifle. Gentry will have figured that out already, so that's where we'll find him. Dagger will meet us there and we'll split up and begin the hunt."

Beaumont conferred with Babbitt for another minute, and they found a location on the map on the other side of a small valley from the cemetery. He radioed the lead car and directed him to the location.

"ETA ten minutes," Jumper Four said from the passenger seat of the lead vehicle.

Once they had a destination, the eight men in the three vehicles rode in silence. As the motorcade passed the Eglise St. Piere, the front car slowed to make a ninety-degree left turn on a small one-lane street, Petite Rue du Eglise. This brought its speed down to nearly a complete stop, but as soon as it turned the driver began accelerating.

The front passenger of the Audi noticed him first. A lone man running up the narrow street in his direction, just a few car lengths ahead. For an instant he thought the man was just an afternoon jogger, but he was head to toe in black, and wearing a ski mask, and he wasn't jogging; he was sprinting. There was nothing leisurely about his mannerisms.

The driver leaned forward to the windshield. "What the—"

The masked runner reached behind his back now and brought out a short-barreled sawed-off shotgun. Before either Townsend man in the Audi could speak, the runner leveled the shotgun and it boomed on the narrow street, the windshield of the Audi exploded, and the driver's head disappeared in an explosion of red.

The man next to him was coated from the waist up in

blood and tissue, and he screamed as the masked man continued sprinting right at him. The masked man leapt onto the hood of the moving Audi, slamming his foot onto the roof with his next sprinted step, making a sound like a gunshot inside the vehicle's interior.

––––––––––––

None of the four men in the Mercedes had seen the shooter in front of the Audi, but they certainly heard the shotgun blast. Beaumont began drawing his handgun almost immediately, but the strange sight ahead slowed him. A masked man appeared above the lead car, leaping up and off the roof, windmilling his arms and legs for height and distance. He rose ten feet above the street; Beaumont saw the sawed-off twelve-gauge in his right hand as he seemed to hang there in midair, kicking and swinging his arms.

The driver of the Mercedes stomped on his brakes and frantically reached for the gearshift lever on the console next to him.

The attacker dropped through the cold air, toward the hood of the big black luxury car.

In the backseat Babbitt shouted, "It's him!"

––––––––––––

Court crashed onto the roof of the Mercedes and then hit the windshield, directly in front of the driver. He flipped himself up to his knees and leveled the short-barreled Remington, and then the car lurched into reverse.

Court flew onto his back with the momentum of the

Mercedes but as he did so he fired through the windshield at a distance of three feet, beheading the driver of this vehicle as he had the one in the lead car.

He tumbled off the front of the hood and onto the icy street below, losing his grip on the shotgun as he fell.

———————

Jumper Five sat behind the wheel of the Ford Galaxy minivan. He slammed on the brakes when the Mercedes lurched back in his direction.

After the second shotgun blast he could no longer see the man on the hood of the vehicle in front of him. The Mercedes kept rolling back to him, and he presumed the driver was dead and the car was unable to evacuate the area.

"Bail out!" he ordered, and he opened his car door, leapt out onto the ice, and drew his SIG pistol. He began running laterally across the tiny street, trying to find cover for himself in a shallow doorway in the middle of a long brick wall.

As he moved he scanned the snow-covered street near the Mercedes, his gun at eye level.

The black figure rolled out into the street, just in front of the rearward-moving Mercedes, his arms outstretched over his head and a pistol held in a combat grip.

Jumper Five tried to get his gun down and aimed in on the threat, but Gentry fired his pistol twice, striking the Townsend man twenty-five feet from him twice in his Kevlar vest. He fell to the ground but made it into the doorway. As soon as he tucked himself behind the cover he checked his vest and saw that he was not wounded, then he waited to hear Gentry engage other targets before exposing himself again.

––––––––––

Court scanned the street in front of him while lying on his chest on the icy cobblestones, but when he did not immediately see more Townsend men in his line of fire, he took one hand off his firing grip and reached down to a pouch on his chest. He yanked out a fragmentation grenade, pulled the pin, and then side-armed the baseball-sized explosive under the Mercedes. It skidded out the other side and slid up the street, stopping under the parked Ford Galaxy.

Court did not wait for the explosion; he scrambled on the ice, crawling, slipping and sliding in the other direction, back toward the Audi, which was still rolling down the street, with a dead man behind the wheel.

Boom!

The grenade detonated under the Galaxy, erupting the gas tank and turning the vehicle into a massive fireball. The passenger of the van had sought shelter behind it, ducking behind the right front fender.

He was killed instantly in the explosion.

––––––––––

Beaumont thought he'd been shot at first, but he quickly realized it was Jumper Two's blood that had covered the entire front seat of the Mercedes, filling his eyes and temporarily blinding him. His second-in-command was slumped next to him, behind the wheel, unrecognizable as a human being with the loss of his face and the top of his skull.

Beaumont wiped blood from his eyes with the arm of his coat as gunfire cracked in the street just outside his vehicle. Behind him, both Babbitt and Parks screamed in terror.

Twenty feet behind them, the Ford Galaxy exploded in a fireball.

Beaumont bailed out of his passenger-side door and fell into the street, crawling away from the Mercedes as it rolled backward slowly toward the burning wreckage. He ended up in the snow on the sidewalk; here he drew his pistol and began whipping it around looking for a target.

Twenty yards in front of him the Audi came to a stop in the entryway of a narrow apartment building. Jumper Eight was still alive, only now climbing out of the wreckage with his pistol in his hand but down to his side as he staggered in a daze.

Beaumont spun around quickly, looking up the street in the other direction. Just ten yards from him, the Galaxy was engulfed in rolling black smoke in the middle of the narrow street. A burning body lay next to the open passenger-side door.

But where was the fucking Gray Man?

Beaumont rose from the snow into a crouch, used the back of his left arm again to wipe blood from his eyes, then spun toward movement to his left. Babbitt opened the door to the back of the Mercedes and fell out. Crawling on his hands and knees onto the sidewalk, he rose and crab-walked over to Beaumont, keeping his head low. Jeff Parks crawled out just behind him, his silver automatic pistol waving in the air as he stumbled out of the car.

Gunfire on Beaumont's right turned his attention in that direction. Jumper Eight fired at someone on the far side of the Mercedes; Beaumont could not see what he was shooting at, but he kept his head down and moved toward the rear of the vehicle to approach from the opposite direction. Return gunfire snapped, round after round in rapid-fire succession, and Beaumont saw his subordinate spasm as a bloom of red blossomed from his coat, and then he flew back onto the trunk of the Audi as he was hit again in the lower torso.

Beaumont stayed low, knowing now Gentry was on the opposite side of the Mercedes, either flat in the street or, like himself, down in a crouch. Babbitt and Parks passed on Beaumont's left, but he ignored them, focusing all his attention on moving quickly around the car to get in behind his target.

———

Court dropped the man up by the Audi with five rounds from the Glock 19, then turned back to the minivan just as the man who'd found cover in the doorway spun out into the street and fired at him. The round slammed into Gentry's Kevlar vest, just below the collarbone, and it knocked him back onto his heels, but not all the way down to the ice.

Court returned fire, hitting the Townsend man in the pelvis and spinning him. He dropped his pistol and fell awkwardly on his knees and elbows. He reached out for his gun on the ice and Court shot him again, this time through the top of his head.

The Townsend man dropped face-first onto the cobblestones; blood poured into the street.

Now Gentry heard movement back in the opposite direction; he spun to it and aimed at two men in wool coats running away along the sidewalk. He fired a single round, shooting the second man in the back. The man toppled forward and a silver automatic pistol skittered on the ice; his body knocked the first man down as he landed on him. As Court put the first man in his sights he sensed new movement, close on his right, behind the black Mercedes. He whipped his pistol to this threat and saw a big bearded man aiming a handgun at him.

Court squeezed the trigger of his Glock and fired a single round. At the same instant his arm kicked up in the air and his pistol twirled out of his hand. It felt like he'd been hit in the forearm with a baseball bat. He saw blood splatter up into his face and felt himself spinning and then slipping and then falling down onto the street, and he knew he'd been shot even before he landed face-first on the icy cobblestones.

He lay there for a moment, shaking his head, trying to get back in the fight. He saw the road around him smeared with his own blood, steam pouring into the air. Along with it gray down feathers from where the bullet tore through his coat drifted about him like gentle snowfall.

Gentry's arm was broken midway between his wrist and his elbow; it tingled and ached and burned and throbbed all at once. He pushed pain and shock from his mind, fighting to turn himself back around toward the threat, the big bearded shooter by the wrecked-out Mercedes. He saw his pistol on the cobblestones first; he dove for his gun with his left hand, but before he reached it he saw that the bearded man was down as well. He thrashed on his back, clutching his thigh, as arterial spray launched five feet into the air.

Court continued crawling toward his Glock pistol, his right arm hanging down and useless, and he looked back over his shoulder toward the man who was running away. It was Babbitt; he could see it now even at thirty yards. The director of Townsend neared the corner at the end of the street, but in his haste he slid on the ice there and fell down, then struggled to climb back up to his feet.

Court still didn't have the pistol in hand yet. He turned from Babbitt, concentrated on it again, and reached out with his left hand.

But just as he put a fingertip on the Glock's grip, new gunfire echoed on the narrow street.

Two policemen were in front of the Eglise St. Piere at the top of the street and they fired on him, their pistols cracking.

Court took his hand from the gun, turned, and rose to his feet. He began running down the street in the opposite direction of the cops, doing his best to use the burning Galaxy and the Mercedes for cover as he did so. He clutched his wounded arm as he ran.

The gunfire stopped; he heard shouts behind him as the cops yelled at him to stop, but he kept running. He turned the corner where he'd lost Babbitt and found no one there. He looked in all directions, then screamed in frustration at losing the head of Townsend. He ran to where he'd parked the van, climbed inside, and struggled to reach the keys on the right side of the steering column with his left hand.

In seconds he was moving, the van skidding on the hard-packed snow in the middle of the street as it raced off to the south.

Behind him seven men lay dead or wounded in the street.

———————

Lee Babbitt had crashed through a small fence and hidden behind a child's playhouse in the backyard of a private home. Here he lay huddled in the snow, his hands shaking too hard to pull his phone out to call for help.

FIFTY-SIX

Gentry drove through the afternoon traffic in southern Brussels, leaving the sound of sirens behind him. He knew that although the shootout he'd survived minutes before would be the most dramatic and shocking event to hit this city in years, it would not immediately be linked in any way to the secret visit by the Israeli prime minister in Uccle, more than ten miles away from the gun battle.

Kalb would arrive as Russ expected him to, which was good news for Court.

Court no longer gave a damn whether or not Ehud Kalb lived or died. He was operating out of simple vengeance, pursuing Whitlock not because he threatened a world leader and not because he threatened Gentry himself, but because he'd ended the life of a woman Court both liked and respected. A woman who was doing her best for what she believed.

Russ Whitlock was right—Court would seek revenge.

It occurred to him that he might be able to save the prime minister by driving his van directly to the cemetery and creating such havoc that the PM's security would hustle their protectee away, but he knew the Israelis would just shoot him dead, and he'd have no way to be certain Kalb would not go ahead with his graveside visit after the fact.

And again, this wasn't about Ehud Kalb.

This was about Ruth.

His arm throbbed and the blood ran freely down his hand. He had a trauma kit in his backpack in the backseat, but he did not take the time to deal with his injury yet.

At twelve forty he neared the neighborhood of Uccle, and he immediately saw the most obvious location for a sniper to hide himself. The steeple of the Eglise St. Job was commanding over the cemetery on the hill in the distance, and just a few hundred yards away from the cemetery. It was an obvious location for Whitlock to use.

But it was too obvious. The Israelis would have that covered, no question, and there was no question but that Whitlock would know this himself.

Way off to the east in the hazy afternoon, far beyond the steeple of the Eglise St. Job, Court saw a forested hillside covered in snow. It was the highest ground in the area, but it was also another five to seven hundred yards from the church, making it a good ten to twelve hundred yards to the cemetery.

Could Whitlock make the shot?

Court thought about it for only a moment.

I could do it. He could do it.

He parked at a pharmacy on Sint-Jobsesteenweg, climbed out, and fought the urge to rush inside for medical supplies. He had no time, and he couldn't let anyone see him in this condition, because they would almost certainly call the cops.

He found a tiny one-lane road that led up the hill toward the woods and he began climbing quickly, clutching his wounded right arm with his left hand, stanching the flow of blood and preventing the broken bones from moving as he walked. The little road turned into a footpath, still rising up the hill, and the homes on either side gave way to forest. The fresh snow covered the trees and blanketed the ground.

Court passed a stack of loose branches of all sizes, piled there along the path after being cleared from the forest, and stopped, then pulled his trauma kit from his backpack. He searched a moment to find a reasonably straight branch about a half inch in diameter, and he cleaned off leaves and shoots with his free hand and teeth, then broke the stick in half. Next he struggled to take off his leather motorcycle jacket and unstrapped the Kevlar vest that had saved his life, revealing a white long-sleeved thermal undershirt beneath it. Even though the entire lower half of the right arm of the shirt was bloodred, he felt he would blend into the winterscape much better with the white top, although his pants and boots were black.

He dropped to his knees in the snow now, placed his broken arm on the ground, and put a piece of the stick on either side of it. For the first time he looked over the injury. It hurt like a bitch, but he was somewhat relieved to discover only one of the bones had snapped from the impact of the bullet. He fought through the pain, wrapped his arm and the two sticks tightly with a compression bandage from his trauma kit. He couldn't avoid scooping up a healthy amount of bloody snow inside as well.

He cinched the splint tight enough to make him cry out in the quiet forest and tied it off. He stood back up with difficulty. Even in the frozen air, sweat dripped from his forehead. He left his backpack and his coat and his bulletproof vest and his blood there in the snow, and he started climbing deeper up the forested hill.

He had no weapon, only one good arm, and he knew the pain would slow him down. But he had to push on. He had no choice.

He had no time.

———————

Russ Whitlock lay in his hide in the tiny greenhouse on the hill, his rifle in front of him. Though the week-old gunshot wound on his hip burned like fire after the action on Rue Kelle and the walk through the woods to his hide, he felt good, certain he would be able to achieve his objective today.

He checked his watch and saw that his target was due to arrive any moment.

After peering through the scope for a few seconds, he took a moment to relax himself, and to think of how things stood.

By killing the Ettinger woman, Russ knew Gentry would likely still take the fall for the Kalb hit because Babbitt would not reveal to the Israelis that one of his employees assassinated their prime minister. If the Townsend operators finished Gentry here in Brussels today, Russ felt confident he wouldn't have to worry about the Mossad hunting him for the rest of his life.

CIA would issue a shoot-on-sight sanction against him, just as they had done to Gentry, and that sucked, but it almost felt inevitable to Russ that he would pick up the mantle for Gentry; Russ would be the new singleton on the run, the new freelance killer for hire.

The new Gray Man.

Russ marveled at the irony. *He* would be the Gray Man.

He shook the thought out of his mind, and refocused his attention on his mission. He clicked the windage knob on his Leupold scope to account for a five-mile-per-hour full-value southerly breeze at a range of seven tenths of a mile. He centered his reticule on the iron gate at the entrance to the Dieweg Cemetery in the distance, and then he shifted his aim to an Israeli security officer standing to the side.

He'd like to shoot the man right now. He had no quarrel with the Israeli, but Russ truly enjoyed killing at distance. Striking a man dead with complete impunity. That he had no reason to kill the man meant nothing to Whitlock. What that sentimental fool Court Gentry called collateral damage, Russ knew to be simply natural selection. The survival of the fittest. The culling of the herd of irrelevant people populating the earth.

Still, he fought the urge to shoot the security man through the forehead. He'd get his chance to kill in moments, and that shot would reward him with much more than the burst of pride he got when he ended a life.

It would reward him with twenty-five million dollars.

He whispered to himself, his words so soft they made no frozen vapor between his eye and his rifle scope.

"Come on, Kalb. Let's dance."

―――――――――

A small murder of crows flitted between the high branches of the bare trees around Gentry, their angry accusing calls piercing the air, adding even more ominousness to the low dappled light of the gray woods.

Court climbed on, off the path and through dense forest now, certain he was closing in on danger but uncertain what he would do when he found it. He thought of Ruth and told himself that if he stood for anything at all, he stood for someone who had sacrificed everything to stop a psychopathic killer.

Maybe Court was crazy himself. Maybe the CIA had determined him to be unfeeling and uncaring and remorseless. But what was this emotion in him now if not empathy and compassion?

He also felt the bitter anger, felt it compel him forward, but he would not let the bitter anger control him.

No, he would slow himself, use his training and his cunning.

He would not, however, use his right arm. His hand was swollen and barely functional, and the arm itself quivered and throbbed inside the broken-branch splint.

He came to a clearing, and from it he could see the cemetery on a distant hill to the west. He looked around, tried to determine where a sniper would position himself, and realized the best place would be in the woods on the far side of the clearing.

Court pushed himself back into the trees and moved to his left, finally following fresh footsteps that crossed in the clearing far back in the hilly pasture, fifty yards or more below the crest of the hill on the far side of the cemetery, and surely behind any sniper overwatch. From here he made his way over a waist-high barbed-wire fence and into the trees again.

The crows of the forest cried, their movement above him in the bare branches constant, as if they were shadowing his progression in the forest. An audience to the impending show.

He was close now, he had to be. Another thirty yards and he would be at the front edge of the forest, the perfect location for a sniper to secret himself, giving him both a clear view of his target on the far hillside and cover from the woodline.

He followed the footsteps past a little ditch on his left that wound away to the south, and then, also on his left, a frozen pond lay at the bottom of a steep drop-off.

He followed a narrow walking path on a hill over the pond; with the frozen ground and the six inches of fresh snowfall his footfalls were soft and quiet, but he knew he had to leave the path to close on his target. He moved as slowly as he could, only once looking at his watch and finding he had run out of time, but unwilling to rush forward now, so close to his destination.

He had gone only a few yards off the path when he placed his right foot down on a large felled tree hidden under the snowfall. It felt sturdy, so he stepped up on it, then reached his right foot out to find another solid step.

Below his foot he felt a tree branch that jutted from

frozen mud, and he decided it was large enough to take his weight. He stepped down on it, swung his other leg over.

The branch cracked, the sound shockingly loud in the still forest.

Shit. The noise was enough to send the crows above flying from their branches.

FIFTY-SEVEN

Whitlock watched the motorcade pull up to the entrance to the cemetery, and he pushed the pain in his hip from his mind, knowing he would need a soft heartbeat and a relaxed pulse to make the twelve-hundred-yard cold bore shot.

As the first members of the entourage appeared at the entry gate on the far hill, Russ heard the unmistakable crack of a tree branch twenty-five yards behind him.

His eyes narrowed.

And then they shut. He lowered his forehead to the buttstock of the rifle and rested it there.

Just like that, he knew his plan had failed. Gentry was here. Townsend had not managed to finish him.

In the back of his mind Whitlock knew this had been inevitable from the beginning.

Two locomotives on the same track.

But wait. He lifted his forehead off the butt of his rifle. If Russ could dispatch Gentry quickly and quietly, and he could make it back here to his gun in time, he still could salvage this. The thought of a twelve-hundred-yard sniper shot with a heart rate amped up from close-quarters battle seemed improbable, but Russ knew if he slung enough bullets down there at the cemetery, shot anything in the area he could get his sights on, then he might still pull this off.

It would be ugly, but if he got the job done he would still get paid.

First things first, Russ thought, and he rose silently to his feet, wincing with the pain in his hip.

———————

Court arrived at the northwestern edge of the forest, and he saw a two-story house fifty yards to his left. The large backyard of the property ended near him, and a small greenhouse was positioned near the tree line. Court looked out past the yard and realized the greenhouse had a perfect line of sight on the cemetery.

This would be Dead Eye's sniper's nest.

To reach the greenhouse from behind Court made his way across a tree limb, then turned onto the path, over the frozen pond, careful to avoid making noise or slipping in the snow and falling down the hill.

He lowered to a crouch for the last twenty-five feet to the greenhouse, moved past a large oak tree on his right, then quickly glanced down to his left, wary of the drop-off to the frozen pond, forty or fifty feet down the hill.

Just as he cleared the oak tree he heard a whipping

sound close behind him; his reflexes kicked in and he threw his left hand up instinctively.

A cord grabbed his hand, yanking it against his face and throat, and the cord pulled him back into the trees on his right.

It was a garrote, he knew instantly, and it bit into his neck on the right and squeezed his hand against his neck on his left. His broken right arm flailed around in its splint, trying to make contact with the man behind him, but he could not effectively defend against his attacker with it.

Whitlock pulled Gentry down on top of him; they were almost prone, but the thick brush by the oak tree kept them off the forest floor.

Russ pulled and pulled and pulled, frustrated by Gentry's hand caught in his garrote, but he did not let up for an instant.

Court kicked his legs and fought to get his pinched hand out of the constriction. The hand was keeping him from choking to death, but without it he couldn't put up any fight whatsoever, so he knew he had to free it somehow. He slammed his head back, trying to hit Russ in the face, but Russ was ready for that, and he moved his head out of the way.

Court uttered a guttural scream as the panic in him grew. He swung his torso left and right, desperate to break his hand free of the thin but strong cord.

Court swung his broken right arm up to his face and got his mouth on the end of the Ace bandage around the splint. As Whitlock began shaking him left and right, doing his best to prevent his victim from mounting any kind of a defense, Court pulled the splint apart with his teeth. The two broken branches spilled out, and he managed to wrap his weak right hand around one of them.

Knowing well his maneuver would cause excruciating pain, Court threw his broken arm up over his head, and the sharp broken edge of the stick came back into Whitlock's face, jabbing him on the cheek and narrowly missing his eye.

Russ loosened his grip on the garrote for just an instant as he shifted to get away from the attack to his face, and that was all the time Court needed to free his left hand.

Once his hand was out he grabbed the broken branch out of his right hand. He felt the garrote tighten anew around his throat, and his airway was completely cut off. His eyes bulged in their sockets and his face reddened.

With his left hand, Gentry took the stick and reached back to Whitlock's waist, dug under the other man's coat and belt, found the bandaging over his gunshot wound, and pried it off. As Russ began screaming in agony Court jabbed the stick into the infected hole, turning and digging down through tender muscle.

Whitlock let go of the garrote and thrashed away, grabbing at his side and swinging a punch at Gentry at the same time.

Court rolled in the opposite direction, tumbled down into the bushes clutching his throat and sucking in a chestful of icy air.

Both men took a moment to tend to their injuries in the middle of the mortal combat. But in seconds Russ was up to his knees and climbing to his feet above Gentry. He reached into the small of his back and pulled out his Glock 19 pistol.

Court launched out of the snowy bushes, lowered his left shoulder, and slammed into Whitlock's midsection at speed. The gun flipped through the air and both men went down the embankment, rolling and sliding and banging off trees as they picked up speed.

Court fell out of control, but he did his best to hold his broken arm as he went down. Russ tumbled wildly, banging his wounded hip against the hard earth and un-yielding tree branches on the hill.

Both men rolled out of control, taking brush and snow and pieces of stone with them in an avalanche. Russ reached out and grabbed a bare bush growing out of the embankment to arrest his fall, but the bush only ripped out of the frozen ground and tumbled on with him.

Court and Russ spun through the air and then, al-most simultaneously, they hit the frozen pond. Their bodies slid out onto the ice ten, fifteen, twenty-five feet, the momentum of the downhill roll meeting the lack of friction on the ice and propelling them out a third of the way to the opposite end of the pond. They finally stopped sliding. Court was facedown and Russ was on his side, but when Russ tried to push himself up to look for the Glock, he was rewarded with a loud echoing crack. The combined force of the men's bodies caused the icy surface of the pond to give way, and the two wounded Americans disappeared below the surface.

———

As he did each and every year, the prime minister of Is-rael finished his moment at the graveside of Piet De Schepper with a knelt prayer. He rose to his feet, brushed snow from the lower part of his coat, and put his hand on a neo-Gothic column next to the burial site.

"Until next year, my friend."

He turned and began heading back up the pathway to the exit of the cemetery. As he walked he remarked to the principal agent on his close protection detail, "I can't say I am too crazy about all the damn snow, but I do so love the tranquillity here."

"Yes sir," the security agent said. "It's certainly peaceful, isn't it?"

———————

Court Gentry clawed at the eyes of the man on top of him at the bottom of the icy pond.

Under the ice they fought, their bodies spinning and their legs kicking through thick mud and trash. Neither man knew if the other had a weapon, so both fought and scrambled to keep one another's hands under control. This was harder for Gentry, whose right arm was all but useless.

The water was so dank and dirty, and the ice covering the surface was so thick, that visibility at the bottom was virtually zero. The men clutched one another, arms and legs wrapping around their torsos, using their elbows and foreheads as weapons when hand and leg movement was restricted.

The cold was one continuous, mind-numbing assault to their central nervous systems that penetrated both men's brains like they were being electrocuted.

Court broke free of Russ for an instant and pushed off the mud, trying to get above the waterline to fill his lungs. This part of the pond was only seven feet deep, so it was not far to travel, but instead of surfacing into the air, he only slammed his head against a ceiling of thick ice covering the pond.

Russ grabbed him by the waist and pulled him deeper again.

Court's extremities were quickly going numb as his blood retreated to keep his core warm. His fine motor skills were depleting quickly with the lack of feeling and mobility, and his gross motor skills were dulling, as well.

But Russ was in the same predicament. He'd gone from trying to choke Court's throat with his hands to just putting him in a headlock, hoping to drown him before he drowned himself.

The two assassins had been under the water, fighting for their lives and expending precious oxygen, for nearly a minute now. The burning in the lungs of both men became too much, and they both tried to leave the battle to find air. Together they found the opening in the ice, pushed heavy broken chunks out of the way with their heads and arms, and filled their lungs with wheezing inhalations.

As Court sucked in frozen air he punched out at Whitlock with his left hand, hitting him square in the jaw. Russ felt no pain thanks to the near-complete numbness, but the punch spun his head around.

Now Court climbed on Russ's back and pushed him back under the water, but before Russ went below the surface, he caught a quick glimpse of the Glock pistol lying on its side on the ice in the center of the frozen pond.

Russ reached up and pulled Court under the water

with him; he heard the man scream in agony as he did this, and he twisted the wounded appendage to exact maximum pain. He got above him in the water and began kicking, first at his injured right arm, and then at every portion of his body, pushing Gentry deeper by stomping on him. He took advantage of his superior position even more by using his boots to step on Gentry's head and using his hands to boost himself out of the frigid water.

Russ climbed up on the ice, splashing water in all directions, then fell on his side next to the hole. His body convulsed with the cold, but he fought it, jacking his head left and right, looking for the pistol he'd seen a moment earlier.

There it was—twenty-five feet away, near the center of the pond.

He flattened his body to distribute his weight evenly, and he crept for it as fast as he could. As he moved he looked back at the jagged hole and realized Gentry had not yet surfaced. He'd been down for a long time, and Russ hoped he'd stay down.

But Russ knew Court was a fighter, so he concentrated on making his way across the slick surface to the gun.

Firing the Glock would ruin any slim chance Russ retained to get a shot off at Kalb, but his only sentient thought was on survival.

As Whitlock crawled forward, slower now because the ice below his body was thinning and he did not want to crash back into the water, he realized that, even if he didn't have to shoot Gentry, his core temperature was far too low for him to have any chance at steadying the rifle for a long-range shot. His hit on Kalb was ruined, and he screamed in anger.

Another look behind him confirmed that Gentry was still submerged. Either he'd been unable to find the broken section of ice and was drowning while desperately feeling around above him, or else his body had gotten caught up in the weeds and trash and mud at the bottom of the pond.

Either way, Court Gentry was a dead man.

Russ was less than ten feet away from the Glock now. The ice was at its thinnest point here in the middle of the pond, but it had not cracked due to his slow and careful movement and the wide and evenly distributed pressure of his body.

His hip hurt, even through the numbing effect of the ice water and frigid air, and his body was racked with exhaustion as well as the obvious onset of hypothermia. He reached a hand out to pull himself farther, and saw his fingers were blue gray and quivering.

One more look behind. He saw the trail he had created moving from the hole, a trail of blood and water left behind by his waterlogged clothing and bloody face and hip.

The big broken slabs of ice had resettled over the hole nearer to the bank, and it looked as if the hole was already refreezing, sealing the Gray Man below the surface.

Russ doubted he would need the pistol now, but he kept moving for it, knowing the gun would come in handy when he broke into the house up the hill to get warm.

Just then, directly below the surface of the pond and directly below his face as he crept along the surface, Russ saw a hand appear, pressed flat against the ice.

Court was trying to break out.

"Jesus Christ, Court! Just fucking die!"

The hand drifted down and away, then disappeared in the darkness of the dirty water.

Russ pushed on, moving closer still to the pistol, five feet away from his fingertips, and he rose slowly to his knees to reach for it.

The crows in the trees above him cried out in an angry chorus.

Russ stopped suddenly, froze as he saw the ice in front of him shatter, exploding upward as if a bomb had detonated below it.

Water sprayed from the new hole next to the black pistol, and from the water Gentry appeared, his face nearly as gray as the landscape around him but his eyes wide with fury and determination. He slammed his hand down on the gun and raised it at Russ in one sweeping motion.

"No!"

At a distance of less than ten feet the Gray Man shot Dead Eye in the chest, center mass, knocking him flat on his back. His legs caught under his body awkwardly, his arms flailed out wide as he fell back, and his head slammed the ice, cracking it in all directions.

With the report of the gunshot the murder of crows in the still-bare tree limbs above scattered into flight, drifting off to the east in the gray afternoon.

———————

Court grunted and screamed with the pain and the effort of pulling himself out of the jagged hole in the center of the pond. He pulled with his left arm and kicked a leg out up and onto the ice, and this helped him get the leverage he needed. He looked down at the pistol and saw that it had jammed after he fired it, no doubt because of his weak grip. He lay on his stomach, crept with his weak legs and his left arm, pulling and pushing his numb body away from the hole.

He made it to Whitlock and then stopped, laid his face down on the ice. Even though Court's blood vessels were constricted by the cold, blood dripped from the gunshot wound on his arm and fresh cuts on his face and neck, and this blood moved across the cracked ice around him, forming lines of red in the fissures and creeping away from him, as if his very life were leaving him.

His lungs heaved, pushing moisture-laden warm air into the frigid atmosphere and it froze, fogging his field of view. Through it he looked at Dead Eye, saw the man's thick blood pouring from his body from his chest wound, contrasting with the white ice as it moved along the same fissure lines on the pond's frozen surface where Court's blood traveled.

Whitlock wheezed softly, and then his eyes rolled back and his lids lowered halfway. He froze in position like this, his mouth slightly open, his face still pointing straight up at the sky.

Gentry rolled onto his back now, grunting with pain and exhaustion, then heaved the Glock through the air with his shaking arm and watched it splash into the hole in the center of the pond.

Court knew he would die from exposure in moments if he did not get heat. He pushed himself on his back all the way to the edge of the pond with his waterlogged boots. His teeth chattered and he could barely see through the thick clouds of vapor that came out of him with every heavy, labored breath.

He used the bare branches of a bush to hoist himself up to his feet and then he began climbing up the hill, slowly and awkwardly, using tree limbs and brush to pull himself along when his legs would not move properly.

His right arm hung to the side, his white thermal shirt began to freeze on his body, and small icicles formed on the tip of his nose and his earlobes as he struggled to kick one foot, and then the other, through the forest, heading for the house. His teeth chattered violently and his knees wobbled.

He walked for minutes; the entire time he tried to get his frozen shirt off his body, but he could not manage it with only one good arm, on the end of which was a swollen hand that had spasmed into a claw.

Court never gave up trying, but he also never managed to even get one arm out of the thermal.

He passed an old car on blocks in the backyard of the home, then made his way up a stone walkway toward the back door, almost falling twice along the way, struggling mightily to keep his balance.

Gentry's body had been wholly ravaged by the cold, but his mind retained the ability to recognize that falling down in the snow here, on the open ground and with nothing to help him back up, would almost certainly be a death sentence.

But he did not fall; he made it to the back steps of the home and pulled himself up the railing.

With a hand convulsing wildly from the shakes, he tried to turn the door handle, but he could not grip it.

He fell against the door, pushed his numb arm down against the latch, and found it locked.

Court slid all the way to the doorstep now.

"Help." The word came out cracked and soft and nearly inaudible. He used the back of his head to knock at the door, feeling no sensation whatsoever by the action.

"Help." Softer now, almost a surrender to the futility of his situation. He banged his head against the door once more.

The door opened, and Court fell inside on his back. He looked up; his view was upside down.

Standing above him was an old man, and next to him a little boy, probably no older than five or six.

Court said, "Help."

Both the man and the boy looked him over with fascination and no small amount of terror.

Court's mind drifted; he started to fall asleep.

The last thing he felt before he slipped into unconsciousness was the thickest, warmest wool blanket he had ever felt in his life being placed over his body.

EPILOGUE

Twelve hours after shooting Russ Whitlock dead on a frozen pond in the Brussels neighborhood of Uccle, Court Gentry arrived in Amsterdam in his third hitched ride of the day.

He wore fresh blue jeans and a new black thermal he'd bought at a shop a few miles from Brussels. Also there he'd found a pharmacy and he'd patched and stabilized his arm with gauze and Ace bandages and splinted it with four pieces of broken curtain rod he'd pulled from a garbage can behind an apartment complex.

He'd done a good job with his injury, all things considered, though it hurt like hell and he knew he'd need a real doctor to work on it sooner rather than later.

But not tonight. He had shit to do. Although it was one A.M. now, he needed to perform a proper SDR and then wander around until he could find a place to sleep here in Amsterdam.

He had no trouble staying awake. Court knew from experience that the gunshot wound to his arm was going to make sleep difficult for weeks if not months.

He'd just been let out of the car, a few miles south of the city center, when his mobile phone buzzed in his backpack.

This surprised him; he'd given the number to two people, and he was quite sure they were both dead. But he would answer it anyway; he'd grown confident in the power of MobileCrypt over the past few days.

He fished the phone out and sat down in an alcove alongside an office building, lit only by a soft yellow halogen bulb.

"Yeah?"

It was a shockingly soft male voice on the line, thickly accented but understandable, even over the satellite connection. "I found this number saved on Ruth Ettinger's mobile phone. Judging from the time stamps, I am reasonably certain I am now speaking to Courtland Gentry."

"Sorry, pal. Wrong num—"

"Please! For Ruth. Just a very brief moment of your time."

Court hesitated. Then asked, "What do you want?"

"We did not believe her. About you. We had information that we determined more credible than your denials. We were wrong. *I* was wrong. She . . . Ruth . . . was right."

Court flexed his jaw muscles. "Doesn't do her much good now, does it?"

"No. It does not."

The man was Israeli, Court could easily tell from the accent, and he seemed truly pained by what had happened.

"Who are you?"

After a weak cough the man said, "You and I met last night, actually. In Hamburg."

"You're the guy from the stairwell."

"Yes."

"Are you going to make it?"

"You saved my life." He coughed again. "And now . . . Mr. Gentry, I have the reports from Brussels. Obviously you killed the assassin near the cemetery. The man targeting Prime Minister Kalb."

Court did not respond to this.

"My organization is thankful. We want to show our thanks."

Court sighed, leaned back against a window of the office building, and blew out icy steam visible under the halogen lamp. He said, "Why don't you do what organizations do? Commission a plaque with Ruth's name on it, and stick it on a wall."

"I'll see to that, of course. But we want to do something for *you*."

Court thought about it a moment. "Commission a plaque with *my* name on it, and stick it up your ass. Good-bye."

"Wait!"

"What?"

"We can do better than that. We can do *much* better."

"What are you talking about?"

After a pause the weak voice said, "Wherever you are

right now, you might want to be somewhere else. We can help with this."

"How?"

A raspy cough delayed the answer. Finally, "We are Mossad. We can make it happen."

———————

It was an early spring in Washington, D.C.; the sun was bright over the Capitol building and the morning joggers circled the National Mall, taking advantage of the beautiful weather.

On a bench in the trees in the Smithsonian Butterfly Habitat path, a thick middle-aged man sat alone wearing a black raincoat; anyone passing by who paid any attention to him would find he seemed uncomfortable and agitated.

He checked the time on his phone for the second time in three minutes, and then he kneaded his thighs for a minute more.

Finally he pushed a few buttons on his phone and held it to his ear.

The call was answered after several rings, and Leland Babbitt looked up and down the path before speaking quickly and quietly, spending no time on pleasantries. "It's a quarter after eight, Denny. You were supposed to be here a half hour ago."

Denny Carmichael replied. "I didn't agree to come at all. I just said I'd think about it."

"Oh, come on, Denny. We *need* a face-to-face."

"No, we don't. You and I won't be doing any face-to-face meetings anytime soon. I don't want you at Langley, of course, and I sure as hell don't want to set foot at Townsend in light of all the exposure you've had in the past two weeks."

Babbitt's voice rose and fell with desperation. "I get that. That's why I proposed off site. A neutral location. You and me. We can put this to bed and move forward."

Carmichael said, "Lee. Let's give it the time it needs to die down."

Babbitt gritted his teeth. His fleshy jowls rolled with the movement. "You aren't going to leave me to swing in the wind on this."

"That's exactly what I'm doing! *Your* man killed a Mossad officer. You don't think there will be repercussions for that?"

"He wasn't *my* man, Denny! He was *your* man! *You* made him! *You* fucked him up! *You* fucked all those boys up. Now Dead Eye has caused a conflagration with the Israelis and Gray Man is still out there, somewhere. You can blame Townsend all you want for Brussels, but the fact remains both the bad actors of that operation were rogue CIA assets. That's not Townsend's fault."

Carmichael's gravelly voice was low and fast. "Keep your mouth shut, swing in the wind for a few months, and you might still have a prayer of getting some sort of contract work from us in the future. But you breathe a goddamned word of any aspect of the events in Brussels, events I'm prepared to deny under oath, and you will never find work again. Public *or* private sector."

"You pulled our access to classified data. How the fuck are we supposed to stay in business?"

"I have no doubt that Townsend will be able to find lucrative security contracts in the commercial sector."

"We're American patriots! We're not *fucking* mall cops!"

Carmichael did not respond.

After a moment to calm himself, Babbitt said, "You aren't the only game in town, you know."

"Was that some sort of a threat?"

"It is what it is."

Carmichael growled, "Fuck you, Babbitt."

"No, Denny, fuck *you*. As a matter of fact, I think I'll do just that right now."

Lee Babbitt hung up the phone, stood up from the bench, and reached back like he was going to throw the phone into the trees. But he stopped himself, slipped it back in his pocket, and began walking up the path toward the National Mall.

He never looked back as he marched angrily through the joggers and commuters, but had he done so he never would have seen the man following him, because the man following him had the skills to blend into his environment.

Babbitt walked up the steps to the Capitol, disappearing after a minute in the shadows under the East Portico, where he entered a doorway.

Far behind him, secreted in the shadows of a cherry tree not yet in full bloom, the follower turned to his right and crossed the Mall, heading south.

As he walked he took his hand off the small Ruger pistol he carried in the left-hand pocket of his jacket, and he used the same hand to pull his baseball cap down lower over his eyes. His right hand remained in his pants pocket, which kept his arm from swinging while he walked.

Court Gentry headed back to his car, parked just two blocks south of the Mall in an underground garage near L'Enfant Plaza. Today had been a bit of a waste; he'd come for answers he did not get from a target who did not show, but nevertheless, it felt good to be operational again after his lengthy period of recovery.

He stopped at a hot dog cart, bought a bottled water, and drank a few sips while he stood there, allowing himself one last glance at the Capitol building. Despite the emotions welling inside him, it would not do to stop and stare. He was in cover, and his cover wasn't some wide-eyed foreign tourist.

Unlike many of his operations, in this rare case his cover identity matched his true identity. He was American. He'd been gone for a while, but he was still American, and now he was home.

TURN THE PAGE FOR

AN EXCITING PREVIEW OF

BACK BLAST

THE NEXT BOOK IN THE GRAY MAN SERIES

AVAILABLE IN PAPERBACK FROM BERKLEY

A dimly lit street in the center of Washington Highlands was a hell of a place for a nighttime stroll.

The Highlands were in the southeastern corner of the District, over the Anacostia River in Ward Eight. Full of high-rise government housing, low-income apartment complexes, and derelict single-family homes on tiny lots strewn with garbage, Ward Eight had been the second most dangerous ward in the District behind Ward Seven, but it had recently retaken the lead thanks to a triple murder in the last week of the reporting period.

But despite the late hour and the area's infamous reputation, a lone pedestrian ambled calmly through the misty evening, heading north on Atlantic Street SE as if he didn't have a care in the world. He walked along a broken sidewalk, catching the glow of most all of the streetlamps that had not been shot out or burned out and left black by a city that didn't give a damn about its poorest residents. He wore blue jeans and a wrinkled blue blazer, his dark brown hair was tousled and damp, and a clean-shaven face revealed him as white, which, around here, at this time of night, meant he was probably up to no good.

It was ten P.M., and the neighborhood appeared devoid of any life other than the solo pedestrian. But while the street itself was barren, several sets of eyes tracked the man's movements. Astonished senior citizens looked out from behind their barred apartment windows. A single mother up with a sick kid watched through the bolted Plexiglas door of her duplex unit with a wince of regret, knowing good and well the damn fool in the street was going to get rolled at best and murdered at worst. And a teen with a cell phone on a darkened stoop of an apartment building watched the man carefully, reporting what he saw to an acquaintance at the other end of the connection with hopes of collecting a finder's fee if his friend showed up with a crew and beat every last item of value off of the hapless outsider.

But the teen and his friend were out of luck, because another group of predators were closer, and they also had their eyes on this target of opportunity.

Three dark silhouettes watched the white man from where they stood in a driveway, in front of a fifty-five-gallon drum filled with burning trash.

Marvin was the oldest of the three, and at thirty-one he had eleven priors, most for B&E or armed robbery. Only two arrests had really stuck, the first one earning him eleven months, twenty-nine days in a city lockup.

And then, on the inside, Marvin had bought himself a full dime at Hagerstown for manslaughter.

He did six years before being released on good behavior—a relative term in prison—and now he was back on the streets.

And he wasn't looking for work. He was looking for a score.

In this pursuit he had taken on the two young men with him. Darius and James were both sixteen, and they looked up to the older Marvin since he'd done time and he'd killed a man, and because of this they would follow him anywhere. For Marvin's part, he liked running a crew of kids because they could take chances; any convictions they earned would likely be expunged on their eighteenth birthdays.

Marvin carried a handgun in his waistband under his baggy boxers. It was a rusty Lorcin Arms L380, a piece of junk, even compared to the other pot-metal pistols ubiquitous on the low end of crime here in the "gun-free zone" of D.C. He'd never shot the weapon, it was for show, really, which meant he kept the grip of the gun on display, sticking out from below his faux leather jacket, but only when the cops weren't around. If he saw a patrol car a couple of shakes would drop the little automatic down the inside of his warm-up pants and out onto the ground. He could then kick it away or under something, or else he could just fucking run.

Marvin had been running from trouble since long before the two boys standing with him were born.

The two kids had thin switchblades they'd shoplifted from a head shop in Hyattsville. The knives were comically cheap novelty items, but the boys didn't know any better and they thought themselves impossibly badass for carrying them inside their jackets.

Darius and James fingered their knives under their clothes as they watched the white man disappear in the mist, just past an overgrown hedge strewn with blown trash. As one they turned to each other, smiling in surprise at this evening's outrageous fortune. The pedestrian seemed oblivious to the fact he'd just walked past the three men standing by the fire, which made them think the fool was drunk, high, or perhaps a combination of both. Even though they rarely saw whites walking around this section of Washington Highlands at night, men and women of all races certainly drove into this neighborhood to buy drugs all the time, *especially* at night, and the two boys couldn't imagine any reason for this fool's presence other than a buy.

That meant he either had cash or drugs, and it didn't matter which, because around here, drugs *were* cash.

Darius and James looked back over the flames coming out of the oil drum, towards their leader.

Marvin nodded back to his crew, giving them the prompting they needed. All three left the warmth of the drum and headed down the driveway to the sidewalk, following the white man with their hands hovering inches from the weapons they kept tucked inside their clothes.

At the same instant three hunters were stalking their prey on 8th Street SE, a twenty-four-million-dollar Eurocopter streaked high over D.C., flying from Maryland in the northeast and heading toward Virginia in the southwest. The men on board discussed the chances someone below them was lining up the advanced optical sights of a man-portable surface-to-air missile on the tail rotor behind them, or perhaps tracking the nose of the helo with the iron sights of a rocket-propelled grenade launcher. On-board countermeasures were ready, the pilot made defensive maneuvers, and all eyes were focused outside the helo and down at street level, scanning for the bright flare of a missile launch.

But there was no flare and there was no launch, because although the man they feared was, in fact, somewhere below them, he had no SAM, nor did he have an RPG.

He didn't even have a pistol or, for that matter, any cash.

Court Gentry walked alone through D.C.'s most dangerous district, as aware of the footsteps closing on him as he was of the throbbing in his right forearm and the maddening itch under the plaster cast that went from his elbow to his wrist.

He knew three men were following him—a definite leader and two subordinates, much younger and completely subservient to their boss. Gentry determined all this from a quarter-second half glance as he passed them on the driveway, as well as from the sounds of their footfalls. The man in the middle was more sure, the men on either side uneasy, slowing from time to time, then rushing to catch back up to the one in charge.

Court knew something about the psychology of crime. These street thugs weren't looking for a fight; they were looking for a victim. The strength of the attackers' resolve would be reflected in how quickly they acted. If they messed around and followed him for blocks, then they would probably never go through with it. On the other hand, if they challenged him right now, that meant their confidence was high and they wouldn't be expecting any resistance, and this would indicate to Gentry they were probably armed and they'd done this sort of thing before.

Just then, still half a block from the next intersection, the man in the middle of the three called out.

"Yo! You know what this is. You don't gotta get hurt."

Court was pleased this guy was getting right to it. After all, he didn't have all night. He stopped, but he did not turn around. He just stood there, facing away. The three men behind came closer.

"Turn around, motherfucker. Do it slow."

Court took a few calming breaths, but he did not turn.

"Yo, bitch! I'm talkin' to you!"

Now Court slowly pivoted to face the threat.

The three attackers stood only six feet away on the sidewalk. Court scanned their eyes. It was always the same in a threat situation. Determine the will, and determine the skill. He pegged the leader as cocky, amped up from excitement, but not from concern. The other two tried to show confidence, but their furtive eyes sold them out.

All three clutched weapons. The leader had a small gunmetal blue pistol and the two men with him—actually now to Court they appeared to be teenagers—each held up a knife.

Court spoke calmly. "Evenin', gents."

The leader cocked his head in surprise. After a second, the thin black man said, "I want that wallet. And that phone." He looked around on the street, then asked, "Where your car at?"

Court ignored the man's voice and focused on the pistol in his hand. "What do you have there?"

"It's a gun, motherfucker!"

"Right. What kind of gun?"

"The kinda gun that's gonna pop a cap in your ass if you don't pull out that wallet and drop it off, real nice and slow."

The man raised the pistol to eye level, in Court's face now. Even though the light was bad, Court was able to identify the weapon quickly here, just three feet from the tip of his nose.

He sighed. Disappointed. "An L380? What the hell am I supposed to do with that piece of shit?"

The armed man stiffened his gun arm, then smiled. "Oh, I got it. You tryin' to die tonight."

Court looked around at the two others. "Any chance you kids are strapped?" The boys glanced at their boss, confused. After a second they held their knives up higher. "I didn't think so." Court looked up into the wet sky with a half smile. "Just my luck."